W9-BWY-663

THE
Orphan Keeper

ALSO BY
CAMRON WRIGHT

The Rent Collector

Letters for Emily

THE

The Orphan Keeper

CAMRON WRIGHT

WITH DAVE PLILER

Page vi © Taj Rowland.
Page 420, top photo © Linda Rowland.
Page 421, top photo © Linda Rowland.
Page 422, top photo © Linda Rowland. Bottom photos © Camron Wright.
Page 423, top left photo © Camron Wright. Top right photo © Taj Rowland. Bottom photo © Christopher Raj.
Page 424, both photos © Taj Rowland.
Page 425, top photo © Taj Rowland. Bottom photo © Camron Wright.

Cover title font: PrioriSer © Emigre Font Software.

Visit us at ShadowMountain.com

Library of Congress Cataloging-in-Publication Data

Names: Wright, Camron Steve, author. | Pliler, David, author.
Title: The orphan keeper : a novel, based on a true story / Camron Wright with Dave Pliler.
Description: Salt Lake City, Utah : Shadow Mountain, [2016] | ©2016
Identifiers: LCCN 2016008709 | ISBN 9781629722245 (hardbound : alk. paper)
Subjects: LCSH: Kidnapping victims—Fiction. | East Indian Americans—Fiction. | LCGFT: Novels.
Classification: LCC PS3623.R53 O77 2016 | DDC 813/.6—dc23
LC record available at http://lccn.loc.gov/2016008709

Printed in the United States of America
Publishers Printing, Salt Lake City, UT

10 9 8 7 6 5 4 3 2 1

To the lost child in all of us, searching for home.

"The Lord is thy keeper:
the Lord is thy shade upon thy right hand."

—Psalm 121:5

Erode, India, 1978. Chellamuthu (age seven)
is seated on the front row, far right, beside his brother.

PROLOGUE

The car jerks to a stop in front of my home, and two men climb out. One lugs a briefcase, the other a camcorder. When they reach my door, I'm already gripping the knob, waiting for the bell, wondering if I'm ready. Muffled sounds worm their way through the carved maple, but I catch only pieces. It's enough to know my visitors are discussing the words etched into a granite stone marker that sits near their feet, a request I make of every guest:

Before entering, please remove your shoes.

It's a habit learned from my wife, a custom in India—but there's more to it. If my journey has taught me anything, it's that home and family are sacred, to be revered.

The doorbell chimes. A measured breath skates across my lips and drops away as a sigh. *Am I ready?* Of course not, but I pull at the door anyway.

"Gentlemen, welcome."

The two men are standing in their stocking feet, holding out their shoes like baby kittens. The men grin, nod, and accept my invitation to step inside. They lay their shoes on the entry rug, and then we walk toward the living room. Their eyes dart, catching everything. They are already making mental notes, questions forming in their eyes.

"Taj, you have a stunning home!" the man closer to me says. He's someone I met previously through an acquaintance.

"What home wouldn't be," his friend observes, "adorned with so many elephants?"

I shrug. He's right. I have etchings and oils, photographs and figurines, rugs and runners—even the china standing at attention in our hand-carved hutch boasts a circle of tusks around its edges. My most impressive piece, however, has to be the splendid bronze sculpture in the center of my living room—eight noble elephants circling a helpless calf, protecting it from an attacking Bengal tiger.

My guests pause before moving to a gold-framed map hung on the far wall. It whispers to the less informed that these are Indian elephants watching over my home, not the African variety.

I nod at two chairs opposite the couch, but before my guests sit, their attention turns to a picture of my family on the table—me, my wife, our two daughters, the oldest finally a teenager.

I'm at ease in the photo: full faced, dark bristly hair, dentist-white teeth, though one tooth in front drops slightly lower than the one beside it.

"Terrific family—and you look very . . ." He picks his words carefully. " . . . *athletic.*"

"My wife would say *stout,*" I joke, "but I'm not about to argue."

As I find a place on the couch, I can feel anxious sweat already staining circles into the underarms of my blue cotton shirt.

They sit across from me. "Did you grow up in Mapleton?"

It's a fair question, considering my skin is a near perfect match to my brown leather sofa. Add that to the fact that I've chosen to surround myself with the finest décor of India, and it would be reasonable for a stranger to assume that I'd carry the British-laced accent of a man from Mumbai, New Delhi, or Bangalore. But I have no accent at all. I'm as American as they are—as every neighbor on my street.

"I've lived near the Rocky Mountains since I came as a small child," I say. "We love it here."

"Good to know," the taller one replies, and then curiosity gathers in his brow. "Taj, when you called, you said you'd never told your story in public. That's pretty remarkable, because it's a story that's . . . well, extraordinary."

I wipe at the edges of my mouth. It gives me time to collect the right words. I need to be precise; these men are writers. "True, true. Very few people know the details of my life, except my wife, Priya, a sibling or two, and my children."

His colleague fastens the camcorder atop an aluminum tripod. He fidgets, focuses, and pushes Record. "Okay, we're ready," he announces to the room.

I twist so my eyes meet the impatient camera now staring back. The man behind it shrugs, as if the first question is obvious. "Why have you kept your story a secret?"

A simple question. A difficult answer. When I hesitate, he prods. "Are you ready to tell your story because it might inspire others?"

"NO!"

It's an answer that spills out before I can stop it. I take a breath. *How do I explain?*

"You're both writers," I say. "You take ideas and words and confusing bits of life and weave them together into a captivating story—one that you hope not only entertains but somehow makes sense of the world. Is that right?"

The man holding his laptop closes the lid. His friend sets down his notepad and pen. A glance crosses between them.

"Well, isn't it?" I ask again, my tone more edgy than I intend.

"That's the goal," the writer by the camera admits.

I lean closer.

"This will appear selfish, and I don't mean to sound that way." I lick my lips and lower my chin. "I'm ready to tell my story, not just because it might help others—which I hope it will—but because it's time I try to make sense of my past. I hope that by finally talking about all of this, by pulling it out and casting a little light on it . . . my desire is to somehow . . . well, I guess I want to . . ."

"What is it?"

"I'm hoping to forgive God."

The ticking of the mantel clock is the only sound in the room.

I straighten, look again at the camera. "Is that thing on?"

"It is."

"Good. Let's begin."

CHAPTER 1

Erode, India, 1978

The city of Erode was like a thousand others that dotted the vast landscape of India. How could it not be, with over half a billion people who called the country home? Erode had hotels and hostels, factories and farms, cement homes and mud huts, hope and despair—and a mischievous boy of almost eight named Chellamuthu.

Like so many other poor children in India, the boy wore disheveled hair, warm eyes, and a naïve grin. At his age, running around the city without shoes and shirt was still a choice and not an embarrassment. Despite his family's poverty, he was generally content—except for that constant, itchy feeling of hunger. He would never get used to that.

"Are you ready?" Chellamuthu whispered, crouching like a hungry tiger beside the park fence.

His timid cousin Krishna paced the dirt behind him, head bobbing, fingers twitching. "If the guard catches you, he'll beat you like a sewer rat!"

"Not if I'm a *fast* sewer rat."

Badri Park in Erode, a short six blocks from Chellamuthu's home, had been finished a year earlier, and to the children living in its shadow, it was a mystical dream come true, as if they'd awakened to discover that the Taj Mahal had been built next door.

The day the park opened, before they started to charge admission, Chellamuthu overheard a man say that the design was patterned after children's playgrounds in *America.* If that was true, Chellamuthu was ready to stow away that very day.

At the center of the park was a tall double slide that rolled out from a covered platform like twin metal tongues. While their shiny surfaces could scald a child's skin, the thrill of plummeting down a slick piece of baking metal on one's backside was worth the risk of burns. To the east of the slide, secluded by a planted row of trees, stood three sets of spindly swings with spidery red legs cemented securely into the ground. Their soft rubber seats dangled enticingly on steel chains, and though they were at first perplexing to Chellamuthu and his friends, the boys quickly learned, by watching children of the wealthy, the proper way to pump their legs to send the swings higher.

To the west of the slide was Chellamuthu's favorite ride: a round, spinning dish with attached bars, all hovering over a soft bed of sand. It was called a Merry-Go-Round, and it was brilliant! Children would gather around it in a circle and push like a stampeding ring of mules, causing the metal platter to spin so furiously that anyone attempting to hang on would be spit into the sand like bad tobacco.

Dreams on a disk. *Exhilarating!*

There was more—each piece with a name as thrilling as the ride itself: Teeter-Totter, Monkey Bars, Jungle Gym.

Oh, what a wonderful place this America must be!

The first several weeks the park was open, admission was free for everyone—until they finished the brick and metal fence that surrounded it. The grizzled guard who began demanding rupees at the entrance explained curtly that the fence was there to keep the children inside safe. However, his words, delivered with grunting disdain, made it clear they were now charging a "small" fee solely to keep the poor and undesirables out.

But scarcity often breeds ingenuity.

A single child could easily distract the guard at the gate while on the opposite side of the park a multitude of children poured over the fence like roaches. Of course, they would often be discovered, chased, and tossed outside to the cement like rubbish. But even that was exciting, making any day at Badri Park for a poor boy in India a *good day.*

"Are you ready, Krishna?"

Chellamuthu waited for his cousin to divert the guard. But this time it wasn't so he could break into the park to play. No, today he was here on official business.

A group of older boys from Kannaian Street had befriended Chellamuthu in town and then stopped him a week later at the bridge at Barrage Road when he was driving the landowner's cattle across to feed. They had noticed that although Chellamuthu was athletic for his age, he was built with skinny arms. Even though he didn't yet know the boys' names, they had offered him three rupees to sneak into the park and see if his hand would fit through the opening of the box where the guard dropped the entrance fees.

They said it wasn't stealing, insisting that he take nothing from inside.

"Just see if you can push your hands through the hole and then tell us how deep you can reach," they said. "You know, to measure the depth of the box. We have a bet about how many rupees can fit into a box that size."

What could be wrong with that?

Nothing, except his mother's words had camped in his head, and Chellamuthu couldn't convince them to leave: "Be honest, good son, be kind. You must, if you ever hope to see the end of your suffering and attain *moksha*."

Moksha, a state of liberation where one could finally be free from the struggles of life and the cycle of reincarnation. He was sick of the grubby word.

But if there was a battle in his head as to what he should do, his resistance was so quickly pummeled that it never stood a chance. Now, as he crouched outside the park, the older boys had come into sight, and he was already supposed to be inside. He shoved Krishna toward the guard and then scurried to the opposite fence.

The job would be quick. He would never get caught. He'd earn an easy three rupees.

What could possibly go wrong?

The family home was fashioned out of poles, mud, and mountains of woolly mammoth-type thatch that smothered the roof and walls—standard construction for the Indian poor. But it wasn't a lonely structure. It stood as one of eighteen similar huts, looking like a lost herd of hairy animals who had lined up in two scattered rows to rest for the night.

At the head of their ranks, indeed, towering over them, was the only hairless building of the bunch: a modern, two-story cement home with an ornate teak door, edged on three sides by a halo of sculpted brass, standing proudly atop a rise of peppered granite steps. The structure was imperial white with a hint of rose, more stately than proud, standing in stark contrast to the humble huts it watched over.

It was the home of Mrs. Papathi Iyer, the landowner.

She was a woman in her mid-forties, with flowing black hair, flawless teeth, and a squeaky voice. Every high-pitched sound spilling from her mouth was bursting with excitement and wonder.

In place of the customary crimson dot that most Hindu women placed on their forehead, Papathi wore a delicate ruby jewel. But it wasn't her hair or her jewel or her voice that Chellamuthu found so pleasing; it was her kindness. In spite of her privileged upbringing, or perhaps because of it, she was caring to all of the children, no matter their situation or caste.

She had a husband, but he was seen only on rare occasions. He ran a business in Bangalore and was content to let his wife manage matters in Erode. Though she could have directed their affairs from the upstairs, looking out over her tenants in the dirt below, she preferred to sit by the front door where she could fish for children who might wander close.

"Chellamuthu! Come here, little one!" she called out, waving him over with eager arms.

"Yes, ma'am?"

"I want you to listen to the sounds around you and tell me what you hear."

The boy glanced behind him to see if any of his friends or cousins were watching. He didn't want them to make fun of him later. A kid had to be careful. Then again, she would often pay him and his older brother a handful of rupees to drive her cattle from the nearby corral to the banana groves across the bridge to feed. Did he really care what anyone else might think?

"Buses. I can hear buses," he answered. That wasn't surprising. The parcel of ground sat northwest of the city center, pushing up against development on one side and the Kaveri River on the other.

"What else?" she asked.

All right, so it wasn't the sound of buses.

He turned his head and closed his eyes to focus more intently. "I can hear your cattle grunting."

"Anything else?"

He tried again. "I hear Banerjee chopping coconuts with his machete."

"Good, good. How do you know it's Banerjee?" she asked.

"He's *always* the one chopping coconuts."

Chellamuthu was right. Banerjee was a wrinkled old North Indian man with few teeth, a stout right arm, and two missing fingers on his left hand. He would start early every morning, cutting open coconut husks, harvesting the meat, then stacking the discarded shells into a clumsy wooden cart.

"What does it sound like?" she asked, with her grinning lips and soprano voice.

Chellamuthu imitated what he heard. *"Whack, whack, whack . . . whack, whack, whack."*

"Do you know *why* he is always chopping coconuts?"

Chellamuthu shrugged. "He sells them, I guess."

She shook her head. "No. Banerjee is helping his son, who makes coconut oil from the meat, rope from the outer husk, and charcoal from the shells. The neighbors complain that Banerjee chops for too long and too loud, that all they hear is his incessant chopping." Her excited words practically skipped out from behind her teeth. "In truth, he is serving family. What you hear, Chellamuthu—the hacking of his machete against the coconut husk—is the sound of *dharma.* He is performing his duty because his *dharma* is to serve, and that makes it . . . beautiful. Do you understand?"

He didn't understand at all but nodded anyway.

"Good," she said. "Seek *dharma*, child. Find out how you fit in, who you are. Remember that everything around you has a purpose. Even you, child."

She leaned close, her piercing stare poking him like a boney finger, as if she could see into his head and know that he'd been getting into trouble with the older boys at the park.

When he didn't blink, she touched him on the shoulder and then steered him toward the river. "Now go, boy! Perform *dharma* and take my cattle to feed, okay?"

Chellamuthu forced his lips into a smile. "Yes, ma'am."

When he was out of sight of the woman, he closed his eyes and listened again.

Whack, whack, whack . . . whack, whack, whack.

The sounds from the machete seemed to pause, watch, and then fade.

Whack, whack, whack . . . whack, whack, whack.

Chellamuthu frowned. No matter how hard he listened for *dharma,* it appeared that the neighbors were right. The only echo circling overhead was the thumping of a determined three-fingered man chopping at the stubborn shells of never-ending coconuts.

Chellamuthu waited beside the Erode Station Bus Terminal. It was a fitting name. The place hadn't seen improvements since the British had built it in the early 1940s. It was all original: a dusty parking lot, a tiny building, feeble blue walls, homely gray floors. A lone arched entry opened to swallow hot and weary travelers who needed a ticket, a toilet, or an easy spot to sit. At one time it might have been stylish. Today it was disparaged, barely noticed, as unwitting throngs moved past.

But Chellamuthu had noticed.

He let his gaze skip off the dirt to rest beside the building where a few new vendors had set up shop. His recent exploits in the park had started him thinking about a lot of things, in particular about the fruit keeper.

He was an older man with dark skin, heavy hair, and lips that turned up naturally to offer all a perpetual smile—a true salesman. The man glanced back at Chellamuthu, staring for a split second at his scraggy, shirtless body. Had he noticed how the boy's lanky skin was doing a poor job of hiding visible ribs? Perhaps, but his answer to the boy's silent plea hung like a cardboard sign from his nose: *I'd like to help, but if I gave away free fruit to every ravenous gutter child, I'd be begging beside you by tomorrow.*

No problem. Chellamuthu wasn't actually concerned with the man. He wanted his box: a large, rectangular thing made of solid wood with a slatted front designed to fold down and display its contents to hungry travelers. At night the hinged face was locked tight with the goods caged inside, then it was all chained to a post so the keeper wouldn't have to haul the easily bruised fruit back and forth from home.

Chellamuthu glared toward the stubborn sun, as if it was clinging to the horizon on purpose, curious to see what the boy was up to.

"Poda Mayiru!"

Chellamuthu wasn't certain what the swear word meant, but he enjoyed how it tasted in his mouth, the way it slithered across his tongue and then spit into the dirt with such little effort. He would thank the older boys later, his new friends, for teaching it to him.

When the fruit keeper finally hurried past toward a waiting bus, Chellamuthu smiled.

It was time.

He scanned for the policeman who normally patrolled the area . . .

gone. He glanced at the tobacco seller who worked beside the fruit keeper . . . *back turned.* Nobody was watching.

The voice of conscience screaming in the boy's head should have been enough to convince him to give up, go home, and take his silly notion of fruit thievery with him. Instead, he approached the fruit seller's box, crouched down, and peered through the wooden slats at the jailed fruit locked inside.

It was a moment of speechless joy—there were jackfruits, mangos, water apples, palm fruit, all waiting, even pleading for freedom, asking the famished boy to help himself. He could almost hear them fighting one with another: *Eat me first, boy! No, eat me!*

Though the fruit keeper had protected his prized goods with slats and a sturdy lock, starving children come with scrawny arms. Chellamuthu pushed his hand through the narrow gap and thrust it deep into the box. His skin scraped against the wood, needling his arm with splinters. He didn't stop. He grabbed hold of the largest mango and instinctively tried to set it free. It stopped cold at the boards. The mango—like the rest of the fruit in the box—would not fit between the narrow openings.

Chellamuthu remembered watching men catch monkeys out in the villages. The process was simple. They would use a stick or a pipe to burrow a small hole into the side of a hill, about a foot deep, and then scoop out a hollow opening inside. They would then place a handful of peanuts or melon seeds in the hole and wait. Once a monkey smelled the bait, it would reach into the opening, clutch the prize—its hand then too big to pull out through the hole—and refuse to let go.

But Chellamuthu was no monkey. The boy had a plan. His hands might be skinny, but they were also strong. He gripped the helpless mango and squeezed until it shuddered and then burst. After he'd crushed it into pieces inside the box, he slipped the dripping chunks out through the front openings. To a starving boy, smashed mango is every bit as tasty as firm mango.

He'd brought a small cloth sack in which to carry away his pummeled loot, but he couldn't resist popping the first pieces into his mouth. As the sweet syrup danced on his lips, he was certain that, for just a moment, he had attained *moksha.*

Amidst his rapture, he heard footsteps.

Once, while picking cotton, Chellamuthu's father had pointed out an Indian eagle, the country's largest flying predator with a wingspan nearly the length of a man. His father had said that the first hint for a rodent that they were about to be eaten was a shadow that would cover them a split second before they were snatched.

Chellamuthu tried to turn his head as a shadow shrouded the box, but before he could coil sideways, fingers drove so deeply into his neck that he wondered if his bones might break. He squirmed in the talons of his predator, hoping to catch a glimpse. If it was the fruit seller, he'd likely cuff the boy several times and yell obscenities but ultimately send him on his way. If it was a policeman, it would be much worse. The older boys had told him stories of being beaten by the police, often severely, and they had scars to prove it.

As he was jerked to his feet and shaken, Chellamuthu twisted just enough to view the demon that clenched him tight. The angry beast roared. Fear flooded his heart like the Kaveri River. The abductor who was now dragging him forcefully away from the terminal and into the darkness of the night was swifter than an Indian eagle, angrier than the fruit seller, and meaner than the policeman.

It was Arayi Gounder, his mother.

"That's not yours to take!" she yelled.

He knew better than to talk back. He knew better than to say anything.

Without another word, Arayi towed him behind her, like tugging a stubborn goat to the butcher—past the entrance and the waiting passengers, beyond the buses and the loitering autorick drivers.

Had this been his father, a token blow or two to the back of Chellamuthu's head would have been delivered, and all would have been forgotten. The man might even have congratulated the boy for his ingenuity. But not his mother. Her fury would soon turn to hurt, hurt would become regret, regret would settle into worry, and then both of their lives would be miserable for days.

The police were never around when you needed them.

As the pair moved along in the dark toward the street that led them home, Chellamuthu heard the most distressing sound of all.

His mother was crying.

Kuppuswami Gounder, Chellamuthu's father, was a man of few words, a hasty hand, and strong drink—often in reverse order. Perhaps the man's weakness for anything fermented was cultural. After all, he was born a Gounder, the caste that bears his name, a sub-layer in the social strata of India that could aspire to little more than pulling peanuts or picking cotton.

"Life could be worse," his arranged-marriage wife, Arayi, would remind him. "You could have been born as one of the Untouchables, those of the lowest caste, or even as one with no caste at all."

"True," he'd reply, "but if life could be worse, didn't that mean it could also be better?"

As it was, he settled for odd jobs, harvesting occasional crops, living a life that was destined never to rise above the menial. He was proof that the muzzling of motivation only makes for mediocrity, that every man needs a purpose.

What man in his shoes wouldn't drink?

But there *were* men who didn't drink—many of them. So if it wasn't cultural, then perhaps Kuppuswami drank because of peer pressure. He had numerous friends and acquaintances who drank, claiming that there was nothing in the sacred Hindu *Vedas* that specifically prohibited the practice, especially if done in *moderation.*

Moderation could be a confounding concept.

Perhaps his problems were hereditary. The man's father drank and would then come home at night and beat his wife. The man's grandfather drank and would then come home and beat *his* wife. Back and back the drinking and wife-beating went, rustling through the leaves of the family tree for as long as anyone could remember. For all Kuppuswami knew, drinking was a natural, perhaps even expected, part of his existence. He was doing nothing more than proudly carrying on the family tradition.

But he wasn't proud. He was ashamed. And traditions can have consequences.

When he woke up in the morning, guilt was always grinning at him from the shadows, pointing, jeering, laughing—and he couldn't scare it away.

To drown the shame, to help him get through another day living with the fact that he was poor and unimportant, that he'd never accomplished a thing in his miserable little life, he'd devised a simple and yet reliable solution.

He drank.

"You're quiet, Arayi. What's wrong?"

The troubled mother let her sister's question drift past. Her thoughts were so entangled that the best she could offer in return were raised shoulders and a stone smile.

Jaya nodded. "Don't worry. We'll have plenty of time for talk."

The woman was right. Their six-kilometer trek from the outskirts of Erode to the fabric dyeing factory near Soolai was the shortest part of their day. For the next ten hours, the two would stand across from one another, dipping and stirring skeins of silk into sweltering copper kettles full of bubbling color.

At the factory, Arayi scooped the measured powder into the simmering water while Jaya whisked. The morning's batch was scarlet.

There had been a time when all the dyes were natural, extracted from plants or animals. The deep reds came from the root of the madder plant that was native to the country's hilly districts. Indigo, or blue dye, was extracted from the leaves of the indigenous indigo bush. Rich yellows were obtained by boiling the dry green rinds of the pomegranate fruit.

In today's world, synthetic equivalents were available for virtually every color and hue. The traditional process was changing, and Arayi didn't like it one bit. She coaxed the fire with a stick to keep the liquid hot while Jaya coaxed her sister's gloom.

"You'll feel better if you just tell me what's bothering you," she said.

With a teeming sigh that nearly spilled over into the liquid, Arayi relented. "I caught Chellamuthu stealing fruit from the vendor's cart at the terminal."

Jaya shrugged with her eyes. "Well, you must admit, the boy has always been resourceful." She tossed Arayi a smile to confirm she only meant to brighten the mood.

Arayi returned a frown. "What shall I do?"

Jaya squinted toward heaven. "A mother's curse . . . We are only as happy as our saddest child."

"I have taught him better."

"Don't fret, sister. It's not the first time a hungry boy in India has taken food. It won't be the last."

Jaya wasn't helping. Arayi's chin lifted, pulling the pitch of her voice. "Jaya, he's my son! And it's more than just fruit stealing. He's been running off at night, getting into trouble with older boys. Last week, I caught him going through the garbage at the Royal India, scavenging for scraps. What am I supposed to do?" Desperation swirled with the steam. "I curse our long hours!"

"What other choice do we have?"

Jaya was right. The poor and starving had none. Extra work from the women had been required now for weeks. The owner insisted. It wasn't just the colors and compounds of fabric dyeing that were being improved but the process. Several factories around Soolai had installed fabric dyeing machines. Technology was replacing tradition and a way of life that had kept families employed for generations. The smaller factories, like the one where the sisters worked, claimed to remain true to ancient dyeing methods proven for a thousand years—hollow, meaningless words that meant management didn't have the money to modernize. The business was clinging by its fingernails to antiquated methods that would eventually cause its death. The dyeing company was, in fact, . . . dying.

"How are your other children coping?" Jaya asked, a question that caused Arayi to groan.

"When he's not working with his uncle, Selvaraj has been watching Manju. I ask you, is it right that a child of ten is forced to watch a baby sister of two while their mother is constantly gone?"

As Jaya listened, realization crowded close. "This conversation isn't really about Chellamuthu *or* your other children, is it?"

"Of course it is. What do you mean?"

"I think we're talking about you."

Arayi's face gathered in protest. "The stench of the dye has gone to your head!"

Jaya laid a hand on her sister's shoulder. "Arayi, the only pain worse for a mother than the ache of her child is self-inflicted guilt. You are allowing it to rob your peace, and you should stop. That's all I'm saying."

Silence nodded.

A moment passed before Jaya spoke. Her voice brimmed with confidence. "We will stop at the temple on the way home. You can offer a prayer to Lakshmi that your fortune and well-being may improve."

Jaya reached across and touched her sister's hand. "You will see, big sister. Amazing things are about to happen in your life—I feel it!"

CHAPTER 2

"Jump, *kudhi,* jump!" The scattered brood of boys egged the younger Chellamuthu forward, daring him to leap from the rocks to the water below, to prove yet again that he was man enough to become one of them.

His new gang of unruly friends now stood half a dozen meters away, and Chellamuthu was thankful for the distance. Any nearer, and they'd see the terror bleeding from his eyes.

"We don't have all day! Jump!"

The Kaveri River lured boys like candy. It was almost as seductive as Badri Park but more convenient for Chellamuthu because it was closer.

The river circled around Erode the way a friend might wrap his arm around your shoulders and squeeze tight. It was always waiting, ever enticing, constantly begging for a companion to come out and play.

Beneath the searing afternoon sun, the boys buzzed like flies—and they were equally irritating.

"Come on, *porampokku,* jump!"

"Don't be a girl, *mundam!*"

While their choice of slurs changed more often than the dirt beneath their fingernails, their resolve remained as constant as . . . the dirt beneath their fingernails. The most vocal of the group was their self-appointed leader, Harisha, a name that fittingly meant *Lord of monkeys.* He was a boy with steely eyes, stained teeth, and a clenched heart—the type of person you'd never want to meet on a dark street, a boy who carried the familiar scent of struggle.

Harisha moved three steps closer to Chellamuthu, who was still planted at the rock's edge. Harisha's eyes narrowed the way a leopard squints just before snatching the life from its prey.

"What are you waiting for?" he taunted.

Harisha was at least five years older than Chellamuthu and more than twice his size, making the need for his show of dominance puzzling.

Chellamuthu held out his hand toward Harisha in a gesture that he hoped said, *I'm going to jump. Just give me a second to fix this knot in my shorts.* The only knot, however, was the one in Chellamuthu's stomach, and it was now reaching up into his throat to choke him.

Perhaps he shouldn't have lied to his mother, telling her he was going to wash the landowner's cattle. But he had little choice. When the older boys from Kannaian Street had dared him to tag along to the cliffs, an area of the river where many boys were forbidden to swim, he couldn't say no. It was like receiving an invitation from the Indian Prime Minister for tea.

The group had been splashing along the south bank all morning, staying away from the far shore where the river bends, the banks tighten, and the waters surge. They'd been chucking rocks and flinging mud and calling each other disgusting names that would have brought a certain beating if any of their parents had heard. Yes, life had been marvelous, and he'd even forgotten about his empty stomach until King Harisha had singled out the new boy for a dare.

Growing bored now, Harisha bent down and picked up a rock. His throw was perfect, striking Chellamuthu in the chest. But it was when the other boys laughed and started looking for their own rocks that Chellamuthu knew stalling time was over.

Without further hesitation, he ran back a dozen steps, turned to face the cliff, then sprinted like a madman toward the edge.

Logic pleaded for his legs to stop. Desire for acceptance demanded they keep moving. However, for boys like Chellamuthu, the blanket of belonging can silently smother common sense.

Eyes watched.

Hands waved.

Voices screamed.

It was at the cliff's very edge, just as Chellamuthu's knees were bending to propel his leap out into space, that the words the boys were yelling finally lined up in his brain.

"SNAKES! STOP! THERE ARE SNAKES!"

Too late!

Even though Chellamuthu's legs jolted to a halt, his body didn't. Instead of leaping gracefully into the air in a measured jump, his arms flailed, his frame contorted, and his heart tumbled.

Like most children in India, Chellamuthu was taught early about snakes—specifically, the poisonous five: the cobra, the krait, the Russell's viper, the saw-scaled viper, and the pit viper. The problem was especially acute in his home state of Tamil Nadu, one of the country's worst affected areas. If he were to be bitten and not reach the hospital within minutes, he'd never see his family again.

Chellamuthu smacked the dark water of the Kaveri with a thud that sounded like an angry hand slapping the back of a stubborn cow. Even hitting the water sideways, he was still plunged a good body's length beneath the surface. His skin stung from the blow, and for a second he was certain he was being eaten alive by a den of vicious vipers that had been waiting in the water.

As the sting dispersed, both relief and alarm flowed in to take its place—including thoughts of Niranjan, his friend who been bitten by a snake while the boys were picking peanuts near Pungampatti. There were adults nearby, and both boys instantly began to scream, but screams don't dissuade snake venom. Within minutes Niranjan's leg had doubled in size and despite his uncle's best effort to treat the wound, it wouldn't stop bleeding. Niranjan began vomiting, struggling for breath, and before anyone could get him strapped onto a motorcycle and headed to the hospital for life-saving antivenin, his eyes rolled back into his swollen head, and he died.

Chellamuthu was below the surface now, holding his breath, flapping his arms and looking up, his vision too blurred to see.

If there *were* snakes, if this wasn't a terrible joke being played by Harisha and the older boys, the serpents would be just above him. He was a strong swimmer, having lived near the Kaveri since birth. He could attempt a retreat by swimming away beneath the surface, but it might not be *away* at all. He might do nothing more than swim right into the snakes when finally coming up for air.

If only I were a fish.

It was a childish thought, and as burning lungs and exhausted arms reminded him that wishing moments are wasted moments, Chellamuthu broke the water's surface and sucked in a precious breath.

"SNAKES! SWIM!"

The boys were still screaming from above, still pointing toward the water—and then Chellamuthu saw the dark whipping movement of the creature barely two meters away. He couldn't tell its variety, as he'd never had the privilege of studying snakes from quite this angle before, but it looked like a krait cobra—the largest one he had ever seen.

Most alarmingly, it lay between him and the shore.

Most parents wouldn't allow their boys to swim in this particular spot on the river, not because of snakes but because of the dangerous current along the opposite shore, a surging swell that had occasionally carried children through the narrow and rocky rapids downstream.

Chellamuthu had no choice.

Legs kicked. Arms thrashed. Eyes locked on the opposite bank. Chellamuthu swam with all his strength away from the danger of the serpent and into the peril of the current. It was as if the river was politely asking, *How would you prefer to die today, boy?*

The answer was easy—until the current grabbed hold.

He'd hoped to be able to swim parallel to the shore, using the swifter water to create distance between him and the snake, and then break free when he was out of danger.

It was a nice theory.

The water mauled Chellamuthu, and with every kick he was pulled closer to the jagged teeth of the beckoning narrows. If it drew him in, the force would dash him repeatedly against the rocks and ferociously beat him to death.

The cobra's bite would have been more merciful.

Why had he come here this morning?

"*Bhagavan!* God, save me!" The words choked in his throat. "Next time I promise to stay home and wash the cattle!"

But before Bhagavan could answer, someone gripped Chellamuthu's arm. It was Harisha, the gang leader, a boy not only twice Chellamuthu's size but twice as strong. It didn't take long for the larger boy to pull Chellamuthu back to the safety of the shore.

As the two rested, neither spoke—at least not in words. Harisha's glare poked at Chellamuthu's skinny, breathless body, forcing him to turn away. The older boy had just saved his life, but instead of gloating in glory, his stare was cold and demanding. His lips didn't move, so he must not have actually spoken. But to Chellamuthu, Harisha's message was abundantly clear: *Time to pay up.*

The boys who'd been hollering from atop the cliff now circled, bunching around their illustrious leader like zealous soldiers awaiting orders. Even the river seemed to turn its inquiring head to listen.

"Dry off," Harisha finally said, tapping Chellamuthu on the shoulder with his gaze. "We're gonna go to the park now, so you can steal us all some rupees."

That night Chellamuthu lay on the floor of his family's hut in a puddle of thoughts, fingering a few of his freshly pilfered bills. Somehow the landowner's words wormed into his head through the dark, as if she could see the grimy money clutched inside his pocket.

Seek dharma, she had said. *Find your purpose.*

Thankfully he'd hidden most of the loot beneath a rock outside before his parents came home.

What else had she said? Ah, yes. Listen to the sounds that surround you.

His eyes closed and ears opened as he studied the night-time noises slinking in through the thatch: a distant late-night celebration, probably a wedding; a child's cries from a hut toward the river; the rumble of a distant truck making its deliveries. Outside sounds mixed with those from inside: his mother's weary snores, his restless baby sister—and curry. Always curry.

He couldn't actually *hear* the curry, but its scent was so intertwined with the noises in his life that the two were difficult to pull apart.

The family's daily meal was always simple—even sparse—but curry often made an appearance. Curry rice, curry beans, curry coconut, curry squash. Curry wet, curry dry. Curry this, curry that. His mother's own recipe was his favorite: a blend of cumin, garlic, peppers, ginger, tamarind, coriander, chili, cinnamon, fennel, cardamom, curry leaves, and several mysterious ingredients she refused to share.

Spicy. Pungent. Persistent.

That's not to say she curried everything. An occasional dish went bare. But the aroma always stuck to his skin, loitering like poor, hungry children hoping for more. Chellamuthu smelled his fingers in the dark. Knowing they were filthy, he fought the urge to lick them.

Then another nighttime sound barged into the hut, scattering the boy's curry visions across the dusty floor. It was a sound he recognized instantly and all too well, like a mother picking out her child's cries in a crowd. There was grunting, coughing, swaying—and sorrow.

Kuppuswami was coming home.

Chellamuthu rolled from the dirt and slipped out into the moonlight. He wasn't running away from the sound, he was running toward it. If he did nothing, their hut would soon fill with ugly sounds: arguments, shouts, blows, whimpers and tears.

He was tired of the tears.

As he raced toward the approaching figure who was staggering along the path, the boy was reaching to the ground to gather something in his hands.

He was picking up tangerine-sized rocks.

It was true that Kuppuswami had been drinking but not for his usual reasons—many of which escaped him now anyway. He'd stayed late in town, sitting at the corner gulping larger than normal swallows of *toddy,* a cheap palm wine, because of what he needed to do when he arrived home.

Tonight he would be teaching his son Chellamuthu a lesson.

Kuppuswami had been hard on the boy in the past. Everyone knew that, could see it for themselves, but few understood why. If people gossiped that it was because the man was lazy, that the boy's father drank too much, there would be a good deal of truth wrapped up in the words. If they claimed, however, that Kuppuswami was hard on his son because he didn't care, well, they'd be dead wrong.

Was Kuppuswami a drunkard? Absolutely—and when he drank, he provided little reason for his family to be proud. But until his heart stopped beating and his body was placed upon a pyre and purified to ash by Lord Agni, the god of fire, he was still the boy's father and was, on occasion, going to act like it—even if it meant making painful decisions.

Chellamuthu had been sneaking away, getting into trouble, ignoring his parents. It was more than youthful disobedience, it was willful defiance—and for Kuppuswami, it was all too . . . what was the word he was searching for? . . . familiar. If he didn't put a stop to his son's behavior now, if he let the seeds of rebellion germinate and grow, then in the end, as near as the man could determine, it was likely the boy would turn out to be . . . well, just like his father.

Kuppuswami couldn't let that happen.

The question that had been eating at the man for days was what to do. He could lecture Chellamuthu, but the boy had already been lectured. He could slap him with a blow to the back of his head, but the previous head-slappings hadn't changed a thing. No, what Chellamuthu needed was a reminder that was more . . . permanent.

As he neared home, Kuppuswami's feet dragged like anchors across the ground, scraping lonely tracks in the dirt. His head was purposely foggy—a good thing, even necessary. When he rounded the street that led to the waiting row of huts, he noticed someone standing in the dark.

Chellamuthu.

"Boy, come here!" His words wallowed in the dust with him.

"You're drunk. Go away!" Chellamuthu hollered back, and then he responded with more than just his command. He pulled back and hurled his largest rock.

Though he was skinny, the boy was athletic. The stone nailed Kuppuswami firm in the gut, dropping him to the dirt.

"It's not liquor," he called out as he stood back up. "It's medicine!" And then the combination of his joke and the image of his young son throwing rocks at him, as if the boy was heaving stones at a wild dog, caused the man to laugh.

Kuppuswami's sudden merriment didn't stop Chellamuthu. A second rock pelted the man, this one assaulting him in the shoulder. He twisted sideways but only for a moment.

"We have to talk!" he called out, luring the boy toward him, followed by more stumbled steps.

He watched Chellamuthu reach toward the ground for something else. Since the rocks were obviously not working, the boy had grabbed a broken whiskey bottle that seemed anxious to get involved. Chellamuthu pitched it with such strength and form that rather than outrage, Kuppuswami could only feel . . . pride. His boy would be a good cricket player one day, for certain.

But then Kuppuswami touched his leg. Warm. Slippery. Red. The man was bleeding. His son's aim had hit the mark. Kuppuswami had been cut just below the knee, and yet he felt no pain. The toddy was doing a fine job!

Though Kuppuswami was drunk, he hadn't lost all reason. His wound, the length of a finger, was spitting out blood like a tiny fountain. At this time of night there would be no doctor, no stitches—not that they had the money for that anyway. It was like the time Chellamuthu had smashed his fingers in the grain mill and the bleeding wouldn't stop. To cauterize the wound, an uncle placed the boy's fingers in the fire. It was that or risk the child bleeding to death.

Chellamuthu's scars remained.

Tonight, Kuppuswami would do the same. He limped to the hut's north side, to the stall where their cooking stove sat. Thankfully the coals were still glowing. A metal poker used to stir the fire was there, still hot. Kuppuswami poked at the red coals while pressing his free hand against the wound.

"Come here, boy, and help me," he called out.

Chellamuthu inched forward.

"You have to sit on my foot and hold my leg in place so I can stop the bleeding!" His tone was firm, delivered with fiery, liquored breath.

The boy hesitated, then agreed. When Chellamuthu was in place, Kuppuswami pulled the poker from the coals.

"Ready?" he asked.

Chellamuthu nodded.

Kuppuswami lowered the scorching tip—but instead of cauterizing his own open wound, he pressed it hard to the top of Chellamuthu's right foot.

Flesh seared, smoke rose. The boy screamed out in pain.

Chellamuthu kicked his foot away as he tried to wriggle free, but Kuppuswami had grabbed the boy's arm. The man had come home drunk tonight with a purpose, and he wasn't about to let his wound deter him.

Kuppuswami leaned close to make sure the boy was listening. "You keep running off, getting into trouble. It ends NOW!"

Arayi called out from inside the hut with muffled and confused words. "Who's there? Kuppuswami? Chellamuthu?"

Kuppuswami didn't wait for his wife to come outside.

"You remember!" he growled to Chellamuthu, and then he swung the tip of the poker around until it dropped on top of Chellamuthu's other foot.

More smoke, more burning skin, more pain, more cries. The boy's blistering screams mixed with the night's muggy air. Neighbors could be heard stirring in their huts.

It was enough. The deed was done.

Kuppuswami released his son's arm and let him limp to his mother, who was now hurrying from the hut.

The man's head was spinning, and he knew from experience it wouldn't be long before he passed out. He would have to hurry. When he touched the poker to his still-bleeding wound, even the alcohol couldn't hold his tongue. His words were slurred and unintelligible.

No one cared. They were meant only for himself.

"Don't turn out like me!"

CHAPTER 3

Chellamuthu pulled his knees to his chest and tried to get comfortable, but the scabs on his feet itched and ached. He didn't care. He was lucky his parents had let him come at all.

His family watched the wedding from the *mandapam,* the traditional four-post bridal canopy that had been set up outside on a grassy piece of land near Bhavani Road. His mother held his baby sister on one side, and his father and brother stood on the other. The sun had been kind all day, never getting too hot as it watched from behind thin, late afternoon clouds.

It was an average-sized wedding, as Hindu weddings go, with several hundred friends and relatives attending. Chellamuthu watched with the crowd as his older cousin circled the sacred fire with his bride, once for each of the seven marriage vows they were reciting.

"Together, we will acquire energy to share responsibilities of our married life."

Arayi had explained it all to Chellamuthu a few minutes earlier, before the ceremony began. "Remember, my son, the holy fire is a protector. It is a mediator between us and God and will act as an eternal witness to your cousin's marriage."

Chellamuthu nudged his mother, pointed at his cousin. "What's his name again?"

With his father's eight siblings and his mother's seven, it was a full-time job keeping his cousins, aunts, and uncles straight. If he included nieces, nephews, great aunts, great uncles, and second cousins—many who lived away from the city—it could give a kid a serious headache.

His mother didn't answer. When he elbowed her a second time, she shushed him. "Listen to what they are saying! We talked about this—it's the most important part!"

He hadn't come for the sacred fire.

"Together we will fill our hearts with strength and courage to accomplish all the needs of our life."

As was the custom, Chellamuthu and his family had walked from the groom's home in a formal procession with many of his relatives. While grooms often rode a horse, the young man's uncle had made arrangements with a man at the river to bring a small elephant.

When the procession arrived, the groom was greeted by the bride's younger sister who presented him with water, meant to both quench his thirst and ward off evil spirits. He, in turn, broke a clay pot to symbolize his strength and virility, and then coconuts were exchanged by the families as a token of the marriage contract.

There had been so much ceremony since the first day of the celebration that it was getting muddled. There was the *Yoktra Dharana,* the tying of a grass rope around the bride to ask the gods for strength and protection; the *Mangalasuta Dharana,* the knotting of the bride's sacred necklace with three knots to symbolize the aspects of commitment—*manasa, vachaa,* and *karmana*—believing it, saying it, executing it; and the *Talambralu,* the bride and groom showering each other with rice, saffron, and turmeric, to show their desire for happiness, enjoyment, and contentment. And that was just a portion. There had been prayers and rituals, ceremonies and celebrations, songs and laughter, dancing and games, and of course, food and drink.

To think he'd nearly missed it. Kuppuswami almost didn't let Chellamuthu attend, but his feet had scabbed over nicely, as had the cut on his father's leg. When Chellamuthu pointed out how similar their wounds looked, Kuppuswami's chest puffed out, and he relented. A scar for a scar seemed only fair. Like father, like son.

"Together we will prosper and share our worldly goods and will work for the prosperity of our family."

Ironically, Chellamuthu wasn't mad at his father. He had been warned by his parents to quit running off, to stay out of trouble, and it was a common practice for parents to scar the feet of disobedient children as a reminder for them to choose a more enlightened path.

It had throbbed at the time, and Chellamuthu had cried most of the night. But in the days that followed, several cousins and countless neighbor boys had stopped over to ask if they could see his feet. In the end, the attention made him feel . . . *important.*

One day, perhaps, he'd even thank his father. One day.

"Together we will cherish each other in happiness and in sorrow."

Chellamuthu scooted sideways. He was wearing pants for the first time in months—long-legged pants with pockets and a buttoned shirt, which now seemed to smirk at his discomfort. For a boy who owned only a pair of shorts—and wore them every day without a shirt—the acquisition was at least memorable. All part of the wedding experience.

His mother, Arayi, dyed fabric. His brother, Selvaraj, bleached cotton. Three aunts and two uncles worked at the weaving mills, and a good half-dozen relatives sewed in factories. Laboring with cloth was their background, their upbringing, their livelihood, their caste. There were so many family members working in cloth, it seemed ironic that his family had so little of it.

When it came time for a wedding, however, what the modest in India lacked in prosperity they made up for in pageantry, proving that even the poor have pride. Women strutted in sumptuous saris. Men mingled in magnificent vaeshtis. Chellamuthu admired fashions that were so alive, it was as if they'd brought along their wearers solely for the convenience of dancing around to display themselves. Saffron swirled with scarlet while canary cuddled with coral. There was so much pomp and glamour swaggering about that the president of India himself might have been attending.

"Together we will raise strong and virtuous children."

While Chellamuthu found weddings to be wonderful, they were also perplexing. Their family had little money. Most of their relatives were poor. The family of his cousin marrying today, for example, barely survived. Yet when a wedding occurred, no one went hungry—from the first day of celebrations to the last. There was always plenty to eat. It was a puzzle that Chellamuthu could never fit together. If there was scarcely enough to eat every other day, where did all the food at weddings come from?

Weddings seemed to make families, including his own, mysteriously but temporarily rich. The solution to poverty and stress in their lives seemed obvious. Chellamuthu had plenty of cousins, who also had cousins. To never want for food, they could simply plan a family wedding for every week of the year!

"Together we will fill our hearts with great joy, peace, happiness and spiritual values."

At weddings there was splendor, but it was always packaged with generosity. Once the formal ceremony was over, the newly married couple would be swarmed with relatives passing them money as a gift of kindness and well wishing. At weddings of the wealthy, the amount was substantial. At weddings of the poor—which included most of Chellamuthu's relations—it was modest. Every rupee, however, was given in love.

Children without money, like Chellamuthu, were not expected to give. Only Chellamuthu *did* have money, a large roll of it that he'd taken from the guard's box at the park and then hidden beside the hut. It was the main reason he'd wanted so badly to come to the wedding—besides the food.

If he told his parents about the money, that he'd stolen it from the park, he'd get worse than scars. If he spent it at the market, they would definitely hear about it. Being rich at nearly eight, it turned out, wasn't as rewarding as he'd expected.

His plan was simple. He had stuffed the money into his pants pockets, which were now slightly bulging, and brought it undiscovered—a feat that would have been impossible had he worn his old shorts. Surrounded by well-wishers, he would sneak behind his cousin and slip the wads of cash into his unknowing pockets.

Later, when the couple counted their rupees, it would be the best surprise of their wedding—and nobody would know who gave it.

Now, if he could only remember his cousin's name.

"Together we will remain lifelong partners in the matrimony."

It was a good plan—as most plans are before one carries them out.

Once the last of the vows were spoken, the bride and groom raced to sit down, a tradition that is said to show which of the two will take charge of the marriage.

As friends and family, including Chellamuthu, moved toward the couple, Arayi spoke up.

"Chellamuthu, don't go anywhere. I talked with the photographer, and he's agreed to take a picture of our family. We're going to stand over by those trees."

The family dutifully followed Arayi—everyone but Chellamuthu. When the boy didn't move, Arayi raised her voice.

"Son! Now! And take your hands out of your pockets. It looks nicer."

Chellamuthu was halfway to the trees, lagging behind the rest of his family, pondering what to do, when he bolted.

He hollered back to his mother as he ran. "I'll be right there. There's one quick thing I have to do first!"

CHAPTER 4

Chellamuthu's baby sister, Manju, began to fuss just after the family finished their meal. By the time the sun settled below the skyline, shooing away any lingering strands of light, the girl's tears rolled down her face like rain. Hers wasn't the common cry of hunger but the piercing sobs of a panicked child in pain.

Something was terribly wrong.

Arayi did her best to comfort the tiny two-year-old, but halfway through the night, Manju started vomiting. Unfortunately, in a muggy one-room hut without electricity, when one family member gets sick, the suffering splashes generously around.

Kuppuswami fumbled in the dark, trying to help, but there was little he could do. Near dawn, the stench persuaded him to seek refuge outside. Selvaraj, thankfully, had stayed with an uncle, as the two were getting an early start on a large bleaching contract. Chellamuthu hadn't slept well—troubled by dreams of drowning—but had eventually found refuge against the hut's opposite wall where he'd largely been spared the night's foul effects.

Arayi wasn't so lucky—but what mother is when her child is ill?

By the time the sun found enough courage to return, the inside of the hut was a churned mess.

Chellamuthu sat up, rubbed his eyes, covered his mouth, and looked for his mother. She was in the corner cradling Manju, who had finally drifted off to sleep. In addition to the vomiting, the baby had had bouts of diarrhea, diarrhea mixed with blood.

Arayi's forehead was raked with wrinkles.

"Son, I need your help," she whispered. "Do you remember the plant with the broad leaves and the long purple flowers that I showed you down by the river?"

Chellamuthu was still sleepy, slow to answer.

"Please, son!" Arayi pleaded. "Are you listening?"

"Yes."

"Do you remember the plant?"

"Yes."

"I need you to hurry to the river and bring me back a large bunch of leaves and also some of the root. Can you do that?"

"Uh-huh."

"Do it now. Go!"

It didn't take long for Chellamuthu to reach the river, and as he trekked along the bank, the coursing water seemed to run along with him, as if surprised to see a child so early. As best as Chellamuthu could remember, his mother had pointed out the plant at the river's edge, near the sandbar where the water was shallow.

Sure enough, it was waiting right there, growing in bunches with hairy stems, toothed leaves, and a strong, lemony scent that confirmed this was the desired plant. Now that he'd found it, collecting leaves and stems was the easy part; it was digging out the roots that would take more effort, especially since he had no shovel. With a stick, clutched fingers and resolve, it took almost an hour before the roots finally came free. To make his load easier to carry, he rolled the leaves, stems and roots into a loose bundle and bound them with a piece of vine.

He had climbed back up the trail only a few paces when thundering steps and breathy grunts caused him to turn. A wall of bushes near the path in front of him bent and parted.

Elephants!

Although wild elephants were known to drink and play in certain parts of the river, the two approaching now, a cow and her young calf, walked in front of a stout, ugly little man, the same man who'd brought the smaller elephant to the wedding procession. He was guiding the elephants with taps from a long pole and looked to be taking them to the river to drink. As he came close, he barked Chellamuthu aside.

"Move away! Make room!"

Behind him several meters trailed a pack of excited boys. One of them called to him.

"Chellamuthu? What are you doing here?"

It was a boy Chellamuthu knew from the temple where his family often worshiped. He didn't wait for Chellamuthu to answer. "These are my uncle's elephants. After he washes them in the river, he's going to give us rides. You want one?"

Could it be true? Free elephant rides!

When Chellamuthu glanced at the man, he confirmed the offer with a laugh and a nod.

The bundle of plants Chellamuthu carried now seemed heavier, so after he had followed the boys for a few steps, he set the roll down by the river and stopped to watch.

His sister had been asleep in the hut when he left. Surely a couple of minutes to ride an elephant wouldn't hurt anything. Hopefully he could go first, take one quick turn, and then run right home with his bundle. No one would ever know.

It was more than an hour later when Kuppuswami pushed past the plants that lined the path to the river. Chellamuthu noticed him first, as the man broke into the opening and gazed toward the trainer leading the larger elephant. It took only a second for Kuppuswami to lock his sights onto his guilty son, who was edging closer to his herd of friends, hoping for their protection.

Kuppuswami approached briskly—which meant he wasn't drunk—causing Chellamuthu to stiffen, too frightened to flee. There was only one question: would his father start with a fist or with violent words?

He did neither.

Instead, he glared at the boy, letting each second sear him with disgust—two, three, four, five. No yelling. No slapping. No violence.

When he finally spoke, it was toward his feet. "No more!"

Kuppuswami reached next for the bundle of restless leaves and gathered them tightly beneath an arm. Before Chellamuthu could exhale, his father turned his back and strode off toward home. He stopped at the path's edge to glance back again at his son, forcing Chellamuthu's shame-filled eyes to the dirt.

With impeccable timing, the boy atop the elephant called down. "Would you like one more ride before you go?"

By the time Chellamuthu marshaled the nerve to look up, his father had vanished into the trees.

"WHAT WERE YOU THINKING?" Arayi shouted, her two fingers aiming down at Chellamuthu's nose as if she were holding a stick. He'd never seen her so furious, so resolute.

He let his frown droop, his arms fold, his repentant head bow. He practically pleaded with his eyes to moisten.

She wasn't buying. No applause today.

"You had no right! She's your sister! SHE'S BEEN SICK!"

Kuppuswami watched from the shadow of a nearby palm. Normally, it would be his turn to step forward, to take over, to beat the boy just to feel that he was doing his part as a parent.

Today he calmly cradled a cup of toddy.

"Son," Arayi continued, "I depended on you!"

Chellamuthu wiped away his frown and spun to face his father. They exchanged glances.

Hurry and beat me, the boy's eyes begged. *Let's get this over with!*

Kuppuswami didn't move. Perhaps the shade was too inviting. Perhaps he was enjoying the show. Perhaps, for now, he was content to let Arayi swing the fervid words.

The man took another gulp of toddy.

Arayi brushed back her hair, as if getting ready to start again, when Mrs. Iyer, the landowner, touched her arm.

"I'm sorry to intrude," she said.

Chellamuthu could have hugged the dear woman.

"I wanted to let you know that I have extra wood. It's stacked on the far side of my house. You are welcome to take some, if you'd like. Let your neighbors know."

"Thank you!" Arayi replied, her shoulders sagging. It was hard to effectively switch from reprimand to gratitude.

"Is Manju doing better?" Mrs. Iyer wondered.

"Yes. It's kind of you to ask."

Before she turned to head home, the woman glanced to Chellamuthu. Like Arayi, she raised her finger.

"*Dharma,* child. Remember *dharma.*"

Kuppuswami edged from the shadow. He'd finished his palm toddy. He stopped beside the landowner, speaking loudly enough for everyone to hear. His voice was coarse and biting.

"He'll *never* learn—not *dharma,* not anything."

CHAPTER 5

"Wait here. I won't be long."

Before Kuppuswami disappeared into the building, he pointed to a patch of cement outside where he expected his son to stand and wait. Chellamuthu obliged. He had never noticed the bland two-story government building sitting patiently across the street from Badri Park.

His father had told him their plan was to meet the boy's uncle, though Chellamuthu wasn't certain which one, and the three of them would catch a bus to Surampatti where they had a job harvesting turmeric.

Chellamuthu leaned his back against the warm brick, away from people passing on the street, to better watch the park. He loved the place and couldn't wait to spend time there, in spite of having to sneak over the fence. However, he'd not been back since he'd taken the money. Was it fear of being caught? Or was it the echo of the landowner's voice constantly squeaking about *dharma?*

While it had been exciting after the theft to hold so many rupees in his hand and know that they were all his, it also made him uneasy to hold so many rupees in his hand and know that they weren't his at all.

Deceit always charges a price, his mother often said, and in his case, the price was contentment. Ruffled peace.

Another familiar voice pierced the din. "Hey, *koodhi!*"

Harisha, the gang leader, propped himself against the wall beside Chellamuthu. They hadn't seen each other since . . . well, since *that* day. He fingered a ripe, golden mango that he gripped with one hand while peeling it with a knife in his other. Carefully, he pulled off narrow strips of skin one by one and sucked them clean before tossing them to the sidewalk.

Chellamuthu's eyes tracked the mango like a cat stalking a wounded bird.

"You want one?" Harisha asked, seemingly surprised at Chellamuthu's interest. "We've got more." He was about to hand over the mango he was peeling, but it dropped from his hand to the ground directly at the boy's feet. Chellamuthu would have retrieved it instantly, as he'd certainly eaten dirtier fruit, but before he could stoop over, Harisha kicked the soiled mango out into the street.

"We have a whole table full of them."

It was only when he'd said *we,* with a sidewise bob of his head, that Chellamuthu noticed an older teenage boy standing like a shadow farther down the wall.

Harisha seemed friendlier than he had been at the river, but his cohort looked bothered that they'd even taken the time to stop. He was much older than Harisha, perhaps even whiskered, though it might have just been dirt smudged across his lower lip and chin.

"Let's go. We have things to do," he said to Harisha, the way a boss might speak to his workers when break is over.

"Yeah, okay," Harisha replied with a shrug, glancing over at Chellamuthu as if to ask, *Mango, then, or not?*

Harisha had no more mangoes but motioned toward his friend as they walked away.

"His father owns the fruit stand down the block, and the old man's not there now."

Praise Shiva!

"Hold up!" Chellamuthu called out, glancing back to the doors of the waiting building. He'd be quick. He'd even get a mango for his father.

Harisha and his friend turned and waited for Chellamuthu to catch up. They stopped in front of a battered, ten-seat passenger van, the kind that might offer low-budget tours.

"The mangos are in the van," the older teen said, motioning Chellamuthu closer.

Before Chellamuthu could reason through what was happening, he felt Harisha grip his arm. It was like the day he'd saved Chellamuthu from the current, only today his fingers clutched tighter.

"Quick, quick, quick," Harisha stuttered, and as if the van could understand his words, the door slid obediently open.

It was a passenger van with bucket seats in front and three bench seats in the rear, and as Chellamuthu was pushed inside, he noticed an older man sitting nervously behind the wheel.

From the back another man sat up.

It was then Chellamuthu saw a young boy, perhaps three or four years old, hunched down in the seat directly behind him. The boy had a scratched face and a dirty nose and as their eyes met, the dread in his stare conveyed a single message . . .

RUN!

Chellamuthu twisted, trying to struggle and scream, but before he could do either, he was knocked so hard to the side of his head that he crashed to the floor.

Time slowed. His vision blurred.

He sucked in air, bringing the smell of sweat, bile, and peril.

"Go, go, go!" He heard Harisha yell from the sidewalk, and as the van pulled out into traffic, the door slammed closed.

Chellamuthu's head throbbed. His stomach stiffened. His fingers shook.

His mother had often told him to be cautious, that thousands of children vanished in India every year without a trace. Naturally, Chellamuthu had paid no heed. For a child, apprehension is no match for curiosity. Chellamuthu had known of children who had disappeared, but it was never anyone close—no siblings, cousins, friends, or neighbors. He accepted the stories of the missing as true but imagined they had merely gone to visit relatives in the villages and would soon return.

As he lay now on the putrid van floor, trying to catch his breath, reality constricted in his chest, choking him.

Chellamuthu was being kidnapped, and his father would never know what happened.

When Kuppuswami exited the building, he looked to the spot where Chellamuthu was told to wait. Not seeing him, he scanned the street.

No boy.

Next he walked to the park fence and called out. "Chellamuthu?"

No answer.

One more glance over the street.

Nothing.

Normally Kuppuswami would have cursed his son for disobeying, before continuing on his way alone, with a promise to later teach the boy a lesson. This morning, though, Kuppuswami retraced his steps to the building. He waited, watching the countless faces of people passing on the street. He held the papers he'd retrieved from the building and now seemed frustrated as to what to do with them.

"Chellamuthu?" he called out again.

There was no sign of the boy.

His gaze dropped to the ground.

Nothing. Nothing but mango peelings.

It was perhaps ten minutes before Chellamuthu tried to sit up. The instant he did, the man in back raised his voice like a sword. It was gravelly, halting, and cold. "You scream, boy, I swear I'll cut you with my knife, and you'll bleed till you die."

Chellamuthu touched the side of his head where he'd been hit—no blood yet.

While common sense admonished him not to look back at the man, the blow to his head had jarred his judgment. His glance lasted for less than a second, but that was long enough to let fear bare its fangs and growl.

His captor's face was pocked, scarred, and hollow, reminding Chellamuthu of the teenagers who lived together near the train tracks—boys too damaged to attempt anything more than stealing money and sniffing paint thinner. Though new faces occasionally joined their ranks, just as many of them would be found dead along the tracks, keeping their numbers mostly constant.

They were dangerous boys with nothing more in life to lose.

He had once seen one of their dead bodies up close, the day that Selvaraj walked with him to their uncle's mill on Roja Garden Road. "You were dead the day you got here," Selvaraj had muttered to the corpse, a comment Chellamuthu hadn't understood—until now.

Chellamuthu turned sideways to check the small boy behind him. His eyes were closed, perhaps in sleep, or more likely pretending it was all a terrible dream, a horror that would somehow float away. The floor in front of the boy was empty, and it was only then that Chellamuthu realized Harisha and the older teen were nowhere to be found. They hadn't climbed in with him.

"We are almost there," the driver called out to the pock-faced man in back, as casually as if the van was dropping its customers at a local restaurant. The van slowed and then steered off the main road to park beside an abandoned sugar factory.

They waited in the stuffy vehicle for several minutes before an old Jeep, a Wagoneer with four doors, pulled up a few meters away. It had dark windows all around.

"Out!" the man in the back snarled. "And if you try to run, I'll . . ." There was no need for him to finish. The knife he flashed completed his words.

Chellamuthu had heard of boys being sold into the sex trade, and while he wasn't certain exactly what that meant, he knew one thing for sure—unlike boys who ran off to visit family in the villages, boys sold into that kind of thing never came home.

He'd also been told about children who, once kidnapped, were physically maimed and then forced to plead for money on the streets. A ruthless man could make a good living with enough disfigured children begging under his control. Either way, Chellamuthu would come out with ugly scars.

He whispered to the other child as they shuffled toward the waiting Jeep. "Can you run?" The boy twitched but didn't turn.

Their transfer to the new vehicle was orderly. The man with the knife kept it covered by his shirt, and as the exchange took place, neither Chellamuthu nor the younger child decided to risk it.

The boys couldn't hear everything that was being said, but as money changed hands, Chellamuthu heard enough.

"The older boy is thirty rupees. The younger one, fifty."

Though the Jeep was smaller than the van, it carried more people: two adults, both middle-aged, and babies.

"Sit beside me in front," the new driver said to Chellamuthu. "I'll need your help." It was a tone a father might use with a son: stern, nonthreatening. Both he and the woman in back seemed equally relieved when the man with the knife drove away.

On the bench seat, between Chellamuthu and the door, lay a bundled baby. The man continued calmly. "If the baby cries, I need you to hold him and settle him down. Can you do that?"

Chellamuthu nodded and then glanced to the back. The younger boy—still not speaking—clung to one door while the woman leaned against the other. She rocked another baby in her arms, beside yet a third sitting like a loose loaf of bread in the center, as if there had been a sale.

The driver pulled out onto the highway, heading away from the city. Occupied and anxious, he swerved to miss potholes while maintaining his speed.

After several minutes the woman spoke. "Would anyone like some fruit?" It was as if they were a family on holiday. Chellamuthu wasn't sure how to answer. It was always fruit that got him in trouble.

The smaller boy didn't flinch, perhaps also hesitant, until

Chellamuthu realized the youngster was not only scared but couldn't hear.

"Yes, please," Chellamuthu answered. "We both would."

The woman retrieved oranges and grapes from a bag at her feet. When the boys had finished those, she passed over several *Bondas,* a potato mixture deep-fried in batter. There was plenty. She had come prepared, a fact that caused Chellamuthu to wonder how long they'd be driving.

As the car rattled across the rough road, the motion of the ride, together with the jostling of the baby beside him and the contentment of a full belly, made Chellamuthu sleepy.

He ground his teeth, squinted his eyes, and forced himself to watch the road.

He'd traveled enough with his father to work in the outlying villages that he had become good at judging both travel distance and time; they had even made a game of it. When Chellamuthu paid attention, he could also remember where he'd been and how to get back home. If that was ever a skill that mattered, the time was now.

Once they stopped, as soon as the right opportunity presented itself, he was determined to make a run for it.

Kuppuswami didn't travel on to meet his brother, Chellamuthu's uncle. Nor did he go straight home. Instead he retraced his morning steps to the corner of First Street and Otapalayam Road, to a vendor of what he considered to be both the sweetest and strongest palm toddy in all of Erode, perhaps all of India.

It was early. He was their first customer.

He dropped his money on the makeshift counter and waited for the man to scoop a nearly full coconut shell of the liberating liquid.

He would go home early and of one thing he'd make certain.

He'd be good and drunk when he arrived.

Every baby in the car was wailing, and had been for the better part of an hour. Babies were harder to shut up with fruit than boys. Chellamuthu was rocking the child in front, while the woman behind him was attending to the babies in back. As if it weren't enough commotion, the young deaf boy, seeing the tumult, felt the obligation to join with quiet sobs.

The driver, not even holding a baby, looked to be the most on edge.

Chellamuthu had been watching him for several minutes, and he'd been repeatedly glancing at his mirror. Just as they were beginning to leave this city and head to another, the Jeep slowed. They turned down an alley on the outskirts of town and stopped in front of a massive metal gate. The man honked twice with two sustained beeps. His sigh almost formed words: *Praise Vishnu.*

"We're here."

The man's lips parted ever so slightly, the corners turning heavenward, as if all of them should be as thrilled to have arrived.

Instinctively Chellamuthu glanced across at the passenger door for an opportunity to flee. Yes, there was a baby on his lap, blocking his way to freedom, but he could twist, drop the child on the seat, grab the lock and handle. If the driver tried to grab him in the process, the baby would fall to the floor and, well . . .

He checked the driver—and then lurched toward the door.

He didn't get far. His little back had barely inched away from the seat when firm fingers bit into his shoulder, roping him backward and lashing him against the seat.

When Chellamuthu twisted to look up, the man was actually smiling, as if he'd seen this movie a dozen times and this particular scene was his favorite.

His grip loosened.

"You don't need to run. You're *safe* now," he said with a thin voice.

The Jeep had stopped, but the baby's screams hadn't. The driver raised his chin and then tapped the horn again with his free hand. He rolled down his window. "*Madaya!* Open the damn gate!" he hollered, as if the baby's cries were filling up the car inside and might suffocate him.

Chellamuthu edged forward, pressing against the man's hand that now rested on his shoulder.

The gate was a massive thing, attached to a surrounding stoic cement fence. A line of metal pickets on top bent inward, reminding Chellamuthu of the fence that surrounded the park in Erode, with one difference: this fence was meant to keep people in.

The woman in the back, who Chellamuthu just realized had been humming to calm the infants, placed the baby on the seat beside the others and reached for something in the back.

"Wake up. We're here," she said.

"How is she?" The man in front asked, glancing at the rearview mirror.

For the first time, Chellamuthu realized there had been another passenger riding like luggage in the space behind the back seat.

He heard movement, a petite moan, and then the tussled and sooty hair of a little girl rose above the seat to peer forward. She had gray skin, bony cheeks, and saucered eyes. Rather than curiosity, her gaze lugged loneliness.

She was about the age of the younger boy, perhaps four, maybe five. She reminded Chellamuthu of Manju, his baby sister, though this girl was older.

She coughed, winced, and coughed again.

When she spoke, her voice was tiny, and if it hadn't come at a rare moment of silence between screaming babies, he would not have heard it at all.

"I need to go home."

The woman stroked her on the head, like one might pet a cat. "It's all right, child. No reason for concern. You are home."

There was a clank outside, announcing they'd been heard, and as everyone turned their eyes to the walled compound, the gate began to swing open.

CHAPTER 6

Eli Manickam penciled in the last of the letters on the board and then used his finger to draw an imaginary line below each one as he read the words aloud, checking for errors. He'd learned from sad experience that carelessness encourages calamity.

Not today. The sign was perfect.

Lincoln Home for Homeless Children
Madukkarai, India

He would have Rajamani, his orphanage superintendent, paint and hang it tomorrow to replace the aged and fading one out front.

As he admired his work, a drop of sweat fell from his chin to the wood. He wiped it away with his sleeve and then dabbed at his spindly beard. With the humidity it was foolish to wear the sweaty thing, but what choice did he have? When his hairline began to recede, he grew his hair longer in back to compensate. It wasn't working, making him look instead as if his hair on top was slowly sliding toward the rear. To provide balance, he'd grown the beard. Then it all turned gray—an apt reminder, perhaps, that one's time on earth is limited and must be well spent.

He stepped to his desk where a letter waited to be opened. He eyed the addressee: Mr. Eli Manickam, Commissioner of Children's Services.

Eli was his Christian name and rightly so. His grandfather had been converted in the town of Madukkarai by Christian missionaries, and as was the custom in India, practicing Christians blessed their children with fitting Christian names. It was also a tradition that made it easy to identify a stranger's religious affiliation—Hindu or Christian—after a simple introduction.

The contingent of Christians in Madukkarai was small when compared to the number of Hindus, but that was true for all of India. Not that Eli cared. To him, what mattered was that the believers followed their hearts and found their calling. He was proud of his beliefs and what he'd accomplished. Like everyone else, he had his own struggles, his own crosses to bear, but he was overcoming them.

He scanned the letter's postmark—*United States.* He could guess the opening line without even looking but sliced the envelope open anyway.

> *Dear Mr. Manickam,*
>
> *Our names are Fred and Linda Rowland from the United States. We are writing to let you know that we are a loving couple desperately hoping to adopt a little girl . . .*

Impeccable timing.

He twisted to face the old typewriter that sat on a stand beside his desk. While Rajamani could type for him, Eli preferred writing his own letters, especially those to prospective parents. It was easier that way for him to keep them all straight.

After rolling in a copy of blank orphanage letterhead, he grimaced. It was the printed motto staring back that always gave him pause, a constant reminder of past mistakes. It was the reason he'd double-checked the new sign so carefully.

When the orphanage was first organized, he'd crafted two slogans. But it was difficult to decide between them so he'd printed both, one below the other. At the top of the page the first read, "Unto every child a loving home."

Brilliant!

The second slogan . . . well, that was a problem. Eli's English was adequate but seldom flawless. He had always loved an old Tamil phrase of his father's: *naam nalla petroraaga erundhal, num pillaigalum nalla petroraaga erupargal.* But he'd neglected to have his translation checked before sending the letterhead out to the printer. It was weeks later, after several thousand pieces of the starched pages had been delivered, that an acquaintance showed Eli his oversight. Although it should have read, "Be good parents to your children, so your children will become good parents," every piece of the orphanage's correspondence proudly proclaimed, "Best parents for the child, but not the best child for the parents!"

At the time, there was no money to have it reprinted. And besides, Eli was too thrifty for that. By the time there were sufficient funds, Eli had grown accustomed to it.

"It serves as the ideal reminder," he'd told Rajamani a thousand times since, "that men are imperfect, that we all need redemption—that even the man running the Lincoln Home for Homeless Children could make mistakes."

Rajamani had never seemed certain if he should agree or disagree.

Speaking of Rajamani, Eli heard someone climbing the stairs to his second floor office. A knock followed.

"Come in," Eli called out.

Rajamani entered. "Commissioner?" he said.

"Yes?"

"It's the new children—they are here!"

When Kuppuswami stumbled home drunk in the middle of the afternoon, Arayi sighed. It meant he hadn't found work. But if he'd been drinking, then where was Chellamuthu? She wanted to ask, but when the man drank to near unconsciousness, the only words he would mumble were usually crude.

Of course his current state also brought good news: when he drank this much, he was long past violence. The bad news was that he couldn't tell her where to find her son.

It was exactly like the boy to run off, and past experience meant that he could be anywhere—playing at the park, swimming in the river, stealing food, causing mischief with friends at any number of places in the city.

She wasn't worried.

"Selvaraj, have you seen your little brother?"

"I haven't."

"Would you go down to the river and see if you can find him?" Her words were stiff, tense.

"The river?" the older boy protested. "There's a million places there he could be."

"Son, go to the river now and look for your little brother!"

Selvaraj left.

She wasn't worried.

Later, with still no sign of the boy, Arayi walked down four doors to her brother's hut.

"Has anyone seen Chellamuthu?"

They hadn't. She noticed Krishna outside.

"Krishna, have you seen your cousin?" He shook his head.

Arayi could see Mrs. Iyer, the landowner, watering her plants beside her front door.

She hated to trouble the woman. "Excuse me? Have you seen my son?"

"Chellamuthu or Selvaraj?"

"My younger boy, Chellamuthu."

The stately woman stopped, considered her day. "No," she said, "I haven't seen him. Is he okay?"

"Yes, yes, yes. I'm sorry to be a bother. Thank you."

She left the woman to her watering and returned to the hut.

She pulled a few sticks from the pile heaped against the outside wall, near where the cooking stove sat, and began to stack them for a fire. She would boil rice and beans, and then she'd make his favorite curry. He would show up soon, probably wet and dirty and with a thousand excuses. His father would smack him—which he would deserve—and they would eat dinner, offer praise to Shiva, and go to sleep with full stomachs and by tomorrow everyone, including the boy, would forget that he'd run off again or that his mother had been looking for him.

She wasn't worried.

Once the couple in the Jeep had delivered their parcels—four crying babies, a voiceless boy, a sick little girl, and Chellamuthu—the man and woman couldn't drive away fast enough.

After they'd gone and the gate had closed, Chellamuthu realized he couldn't remember what the pair in the Jeep had looked like—what they'd been wearing, their features, the color of their hair, how heavy or thin either might have been. He'd been so focused on the road and the distance traveled that he'd paid little attention to anything else.

It was as if the two had never existed.

The sun would soon set, so while Chellamuthu could still see, he studied his surroundings, in case he'd need to describe the place to the police after his escape. Though the outside had looked like a fortress, the inside was actually quite functional.

The cement wall sheltered a rectangular courtyard. Hugging each of the long walls were two rows of smaller rooms, perhaps a half dozen along each side, built against the outside wall, but with doors that opened into the center common area. Anchoring each end of the yard were two larger structures, two levels high, with adobe shingled roofs and cement-plastered walls. In the far building, Chellamuthu could hear children playing.

The most obvious feature in the courtyard was a fountain, where two determined Indian women were bathing toddlers and babies. It sat adjacent to the main gate but still against the wall, and it swept around in a semicircle to form a concrete basin. It was two meters across and perhaps half a meter deep.

Even more mesmerizing than the concrete pool was the metal spout that poked through the wall to feed it. At home, Chellamuthu hauled buckets of water from a nearby well for use in their cooking and cleaning. Here, a woman twisted a handle on the wall, and water gushed out like an eager spring waterfall.

"Boy, what's your name?" a woman at the fountain was calling, and when Chellamuthu turned to confirm that she was talking to him, she raised her voice.

"Yes, you, child! Come for your bath!"

He wanted to run, but to where?

"Hurry!"

He lowered his head and shuffled his filthy feet forward. He'd watched for long enough to know the routine: strip, squat, wait. Bathing by assembly line.

He stepped to the concrete patch that bordered the pool, pulled off his shorts, and crouched. The process wasn't new. They were the same instructions his mother would give when she didn't have time to take him to the river—only at home, his mother didn't use soap.

Here it was applied abundantly.

Twice the woman dipped her bucket in the pool and twice Chellamuthu was lathered up like a dog before receiving a thorough rinse. This wasn't bathing for fun. It was cleaning with a purpose.

Once she'd finished and Chellamuthu reached for his shorts, a second woman brushed his hand away. She was holding a new pair, along with a matching shirt and leather sandals.

What is this place?

"I shouldn't be here," he said to the woman as he pulled on his new clothes. "I was taken. I have to go home!"

Her face jiggled. "Stay quiet, child! It will be better for you," she added, as she pushed him toward a large room where the sounds of playing children bounced into the courtyard through two open doors. Inside, he found bright yellow walls, a swept dirt floor, two tidy rows of straw mats—and children. This was the room where they slept and played.

In the corner, against the outside wall, as if standing guard beside the children, was a metal door, latched closed with a keyed padlock.

The younger boy who'd been in the Jeep with Chellamuthu was already sitting on a mat with crossed legs and sauce-dipped fingers. A banana leaf on the ground beside him held a mixture of rice, beans, and *poriyal*, a savory blend of shredded cabbage, lentils and coconut.

"Sit down and eat, son," an immense man in a khaki uniform directed. He pointed to an empty mat where a woman had just placed food. "The commissioner will be here soon." While the man owned a deep voice, every syllable smiled, as if tickled by the caterpillar mustache that clung to his upper lip.

When Chellamuthu didn't move, the man encouraged him. "It's all right. My name is Mr. Rajamani. I am the superintendent here. If there is anything you need, let me know."

Had he not just been torn from an Erode street and forced away by strangers, Chellamuthu may have imagined he was a guest at some fine public inn. Since the man had asked so sincerely, Chellamuthu decided to answer—despite the woman's advice. He waited for their eyes to meet.

"I need to break out."

For a moment, Rajamani's forehead creased, and his eyebrows crawled together. Then the man laughed from deep within his round belly, as if the boy had just told the funniest joke in all of India. He was still chuckling as he swept himself from the room.

Chellamuthu ate beside the wordless boy in silence. Between mouthfuls, Chellamuthu tried to count the children. Perhaps a dozen played in the room with a few more outside. Several were babies; some were toddlers; less than a handful looked to be four or five. None were as old as he was. However, with so many stumbling in and out, some getting their baths, others wandering in to eat, it was hard to tally them exactly. Chellamuthu's best guess: twenty.

In his observations, he noticed other details:

1. The children seemed content.
2. They had plenty of food.
3. He could see no doors to the outside except one beside the main metal gate in front and the locked door in the room where the children slept.
4. There were electric lights in several rooms, a convenience he'd never had at home. Another observation was more troubling:
5. The sick little girl from the Jeep had vanished.

There was one more fact that kept sounding inside his head, insisting it not be forgotten, a notion he'd been mulling since his arrival. Though he had no idea who had taken him captive or in what city this place was located, if he believed his instincts, one thing was certain: he was standing in a compound full of children three and a half hours from home.

CHAPTER 7

The night sky over Erode was dark and brooding, as if the developing squall had heard about the missing boy and was rolling in to watch the show. Arayi had Selvaraj build a large fire in front of the hut, both as a symbolic beacon should her little lost son wander home and to accommodate the crowd of relatives and neighbors who were gathering as word about the missing boy spread.

"Tell me again what happened?" Arayi pleaded to Kuppuswami, who stood in flickering shadows against an outside corner of the hut. The man's flaring nostrils and shaking legs not only announced that he needed something solid to lean against but that he hoped to get away from one more person asking the very questions Arayi was again repeating.

"I've told you," he growled. "I asked the boy to wait by the building. When I came out, he was gone."

Kuppuswami was ornery when he drank, but when people kept

him from drinking—which had been the case since early afternoon—he could get downright spiteful.

Lightning flashed. Thunder rumbled. Low-hanging clouds began to pepper the dirt with rain.

Arayi turned her face heavenward for hope, but the somber sky dripped only despair. Her throat tightened. Her heart quickened. She tried to suck in air but her lungs, now too full of worry to make room for anything else, refused to cooperate.

"Sister, you don't look well," Jaya said as she approached. "You must sit."

"How can I sit?" Arayi screamed back. "Somewhere out there in the dark is my Chellamuthu, lost, hurt, and crying. Or worse . . ."

It was a thought that must have been too heavy, because the instant it entered Arayi's head, her knees buckled, her palms slapped the earth, and her tears mixed with the drizzle. Then the lonely Indian mother, encircled by a crowd of friends, trembled uncontrollably as she threw up in the mud.

Chellamuthu's home in Erode, like many homes in India, had no plumbing. So after he'd finished eating and had been shown the mat where he should sleep, the boy walked outside into the courtyard and looked for a spot to go to the bathroom.

Eli Manickam, head of the orphanage, reached Chellamuthu just as he was squatting.

"Stop! Wait!"

Chellamuthu jerked to attention and yanked up his shorts.

"Child, what's your name?" Eli asked.

The boy's response was timid, almost whispered. "Chellamuthu." He knew he was in trouble. He just wasn't sure why.

"Chellamuthu, come with me."

The child glanced to the ground at the place he'd selected. Truth was he really did have to go. His face asked the question without speaking words: *Can this wait?*

Eli took his arm, and they walked back inside to where the children slept. Though the light had been turned out in the room, enough natural light from the moon seeped in through the open doors. Eli paused at the far wall and pointed toward the ground. Chellamuthu hadn't noticed it before, but along the wall in the dirt was a shallow, cement-lined trench with a blue plastic bucket of water that waited patiently nearby.

"This is where we go to the bathroom," Eli explained.

"Inside?" Chellamuthu asked, a question caked in disbelief.

"Yes. When you have to go to the bathroom, crouch here over the trench. When you are finished, take this bucket of water and pour it into the trench to wash everything through the hole to the outside. Do you understand?"

The boy's gaze followed the cement trough, and sure enough, it led to a hole in the wall the size of a melon.

"Would you like to try it?" Eli asked.

Chellamuthu nodded. He'd done well to wait this long.

Eli twisted away slightly as Chellamuthu pulled down his shorts, bent over and grunted. When the boy finished, Eli set the bucket nearby so Chellamuthu could pour water over his backside with a small cup that floated inside. When he had finished cleaning himself, Chellamuthu pulled up his shorts.

"Now watch this!" Eli said as he dumped the rest of the water into the trench, sending the waste along like trash in a tsunami until it reached the end of the wall and dropped with a splash through the opening to the ground outside.

Genius!

Chellamuthu grinned. This meant one could go to the bathroom inside, in the middle of the night, without needing to go out in the dark! And with a single bucket of water, the stink was washed away. The downside was its lack of privacy, having to squat in an open room, but that was a negative he could live with. Progress always comes at a price.

"Do you understand now?" Eli asked.

Chellamuthu nodded.

"I'm Eli, Eli Manickam. I'm the commissioner here. You said your name is Chellamuthu?"

Another nod.

"I'm glad we could meet, Chellamuthu. We'll talk more tomorrow, but tonight there is one more thing I need you to do."

Chellamuthu listened.

"Take the bucket out to the fountain and fill it up," Eli added, "so it will be ready for the next person."

Chellamuthu obeyed. He carted the bucket outside to the far end of the compound, dipped it into the water, and then started back in the direction he'd come. He could see the commissioner watching and so, despite passing right by the front door that led beyond the wall, he didn't bother trying it.

On his way back, as he passed one of the smaller rooms that bordered the outside wall, he thought he heard muffled voices. He rested outside the room for just a second, pretending he was getting a better grip on the bucket's handle. This time the sound coming from inside was more distinct.

He could hear a child crying.

In Erode, one of two sounds usually woke Chellamuthu at dawn: Banerjee chopping coconuts or the neighbor's crowing rooster six huts away.

This morning, in this strange place, it was babies—lots and lots of babies.

All of the children had gone to sleep on *pias,* straw mats laid out neatly in a double row, but by morning the room looked as if a cyclone had blown through. Kids were everywhere.

Seemingly on cue, the women who had been bathing children at the fountain the night before whisked in and began to put the room back together.

"Chellamuthu, come here," the older woman said. He was surprised she had remembered his name and was even more startled when she handed him a baby.

"I'm Mrs. Sundar. You're the oldest here now," she instructed. "There's no reason you can't help."

Since she'd also brought a basket of sand pears and was already giving them to the children, Chellamuthu took a pear in one hand as he placed the baby over his other arm. It was just like at home when he'd carry his sister.

It wasn't long before Eli entered. This morning he was wearing a *gerua*-colored *lungi*, and with his graying beard, as he looked down at the children, he almost looked like a wise swami.

"We'll be singing next, children, so after you clean up, gather by the fountain."

Singing?

Even the toddlers squealed. *It was song day!*

There were perhaps a dozen children old enough to sing on their own, and when Eli motioned for them to huddle close, they followed like a line of little ducklings.

The first song, called "ABCs," was foreign, though Chellamuthu soon realized they were singing the English alphabet.

The second, according to Eli, was an old Christian tune he'd loved as a child. He blew a note on a tattered wooden flute, but before he could even lift a hand, a few of the children had already started.

Deep and wide, deep and wide,
There's a fountain flowing deep and wide.
Deep and wide, deep and wide,
There's a fountain flowing deep and wide.

Chellamuthu wasn't certain why they were now singing about the fountain, but it was one of those tunes that invites itself into your head and then stakes a claim. *"Old Christian" was a very good songwriter.* The children continued, their enthusiasm hitting full stride.

Only a boy named David
Only a little sling
Only a boy named David
But he could pray and sing

Only a boy named David
Only a rippling brook
Only a boy named David
But five little stones he took.

With each line, their voices grew louder.

And one little stone went in the sling
And the sling went round and round
And one little stone went in the sling
And the sling went round and round

Arms began to swing in wild circles. Chellamuthu joined in. This *was* a good song!

And round and round and round and round
And round and round and round
And one little stone went up in the air
And the giant came tumbling down.

As they belted out the tune's final line, all of the children dropped to the dirt as if dead. It caught Chellamuthu off guard and for half a second, his heart raced. Then one of the younger boys climbed back onto his feet. "Can we do it again? Please!" the boy begged Eli.

Eli's smile was slight. "Yes, we'll do it again."

The next time, Chellamuthu also fell to the ground. He rolled and laughed with the rest of the children. It wasn't until later, when he was back in the large room playing with two of the boys, that he realized he'd forgotten to check the main door out front to see if it was left unlocked.

Tonight, he told himself. He'd pretend to go to the bathroom, and when he refilled the bucket, he'd check the door. The idea stayed in his head but not for long. The infectious tune and haunting words were keeping his brain busy . . .

Deep and wide, deep and wide,
There's a fountain flowing deep and wide . . .

The first out-of-town relatives arrived before dawn, besting the sun by half an hour. They were Gopal, one of Kuppuswami's older brothers, and his two eldest sons from the village of Ammanpalayam, an hour southeast of Erode.

Arayi was already awake and pacing in front of the landowner's home.

"We came as soon as we heard," Gopal announced, greeting his sister-in-law with the customary pressing of palms together near his chest, along with a nod of his chin. "We made the early bus. Others are following soon."

Indeed, dozens of friends and family had sent word they were coming to join in the search.

The landowner had placed a table outside, and a young Indian woman was setting it with fruit, flatbread, and *idlis,* a platter of steamed pancakes made from rice. While Gopal and his sons ate, Arayi drew Mrs. Iyer aside. "I can never repay you."

"There is nothing to repay. Now, let's get the map and the list so we'll be ready."

The kind woman gathered papers from the table. She drew a circle around the bus station on the map.

"We should start here. We'll search the closest areas first, and then people can spread out from there."

She reached toward a stack of pictures that had just been delivered and readied one for Gopal. It was the only picture Arayi had of Chellamuthu, a photo taken a year earlier when he'd attended the government school for three short weeks before Kuppuswami pulled him out to work in the fields. The landowner had insisted on paying to make copies so that each of the searching groups could show a photo of the boy to those they encountered.

Gopal approached Arayi. "Kuppuswami?" he asked, a single word that towed the weight of a heavier question.

"Not here." Her answer was awkward, hesitating. "He's been . . . taking this hard."

Gopal didn't push. With his younger brother, some things were simply understood.

"Where do we start?"

The women had sliced up the city into pieces like they would a jackfruit. The first groups would begin with the bus station, the train terminal, the park, the market, the hospitals, and then all of the neighborhoods in between. After that, they would fan out into the less populated areas, checking rivers and roads, fields and groves, ponds and canals.

A boy doesn't simply disappear for no reason.

It would be hot and grueling, but certainly, with so many people coming, someone would turn up something! It was just a matter of finding one person who saw something out of the ordinary.

One person.

"Stay calm," Gopal assured. "We'll find him. We'll find Chellamuthu."

It was late morning when the door beside the gate clanked open and a boy walked in, escorted by Rajamani.

The youngster, half a head taller than Chellamuthu, had lanky hair and a hefty chin. He seemed child-curious, with inquisitive eyes and a mouth that couldn't wait to smile.

The boy spied Chellamuthu in the courtyard and rushed right over.

"I'm Vikesh. What's your name?"

Chellamuthu glanced past him for a cautious second until Rajamani had left the courtyard.

He answered in a half-whisper. "Chellamuthu."

Vikesh pointed to the open yard. "You want to play?" he asked. At eight, few boys are strangers.

"Play?"

It was a peculiar question for an arriving child at a place like this.

"Yeah, play. Why not?"

"Aren't you scared?" Chellamuthu wondered.

Vikesh glanced around. There were only small children. "Scared of what?"

Of what? "Of never seeing your family again."

It was a question that bumped Vikesh back half a step. His face scrunched. His volume rose. "What are you talking about? Rajamani is my father. He brings me here to play."

The moment hung as Chellamuthu assembled the pieces in his brain. *Was he the only one who'd been kidnapped?* The word from Vikesh that stuck out, the one Chellamuthu finally grabbed hold of to make sense of the situation, was the last—*play.*

Chellamuthu's worry softened. His head tilted forward. "What do you want to play?"

Vikesh shrugged. "We could pretend we're soldiers protecting the Khyber Pass."

It was an excellent plan. For the better part of an afternoon, two boys, one free and one captive, single-handedly defended their country's honor by decimating legion after legion of enemy soldiers trying to enter India through one of the oldest mountain passes in the world.

When Rajamani announced that playtime was over, that it was

time for Vikesh to leave, the boys' pleas melded together. "Can we play a little longer?"

The two were assured that India's sovereignty would be safe for a few more days until Vikesh could return. Then, as quickly as the boy had appeared, he was gone.

Later that evening, after Chellamuthu had finished eating and carrying pans to Mrs. Sundar, he noticed Eli standing in the yard near the fountain. With valor from the day's battles still pulsing in his veins, he marched over and tugged at the man's lungi.

"I was taken. I have a family!" he declared with a strength that surprised them both.

Eli tipped toward the child like a deaf grandfather to make sure he'd understood.

"I'm sorry, Chellamuthu. What did you say?"

Another breath of bravery. "They stole me. I was with my father . . . on the street. I knew one of them. They said they had food, then they threw me in a van. I ended up here."

Eli turned. Alarm spread across his face like a third-world plague, not only at the child's words but at his determination.

"Chellamuthu, the children here are orphans. They are brought here because they have no family. Are you telling me that you do?"

The boy nodded.

Eli scratched amply at his chin, let the moment stretch. He stooped near the boy.

"Son, I am going to check into this. I will contact those who brought you here. I will investigate fully. It will take a few days, so be patient. Can you do that?"

Did he have a choice?

"Thank you, Chellamuthu, for being courageous. We'll resolve this. If you have a family, I will find them. That's what I do."

Eli stood. "Now, have you seen Rajamani?" he said, as casually as if he'd just stumbled into Chellamuthu in the courtyard. "I need to speak with him right away."

Kuppuswami hadn't returned home since the relatives began to arrive. How could he? He could barely tolerate living with himself under normal circumstances. To drape on the added load of disappointment, especially from family—the burden might crush him.

There was no escape but to the streets, the gutters, the solitude, which he could bear as long as he could stay utterly plastered.

In India, that part was easy.

However, now that he'd quit trying to find work, money to buy palm toddy was harder to come by. Worse, the toddy sellers, for crazy reasons he could only understand when he was sober, insisted he pay up front. The setback left a single solution: he would make his own. It involved two simple steps:

1. Extract sap from a palm tree.
2. Wait.

In real life, it meant that he had to climb to the top of a palm and cut a flower. He could then fasten a bucket beneath the flower stump to collect the milky sap.

An amazing property of palm sap is that it begins to ferment immediately, due to natural yeasts in the pores of the collecting pots. Within as little as two hours, a bucket will hold an aromatic wine that is not only intoxicating but deliciously sweet.

In Kuppuswami's case, making his own palm toddy was both good and bad. The good part was that it was virtually free. The bad part was that Kuppuswami had to be sober enough at least once a day to make the climb to the top of a palm tree to retrieve his buckets.

One of these days, if he wasn't careful, he'd fall from the top and snap his neck.

CHAPTER 8

With each passing day, Chellamuthu worried less about the door beside the gate. Eli would soon discover the truth, and all would be made right. The mix-up would be straightened out, Chellamuthu would be returned to his family in Erode, and he'd be left with the most incredible story to tell his cousins and friends!

It was dusk when Chellamuthu was drawing water from the fountain for Rajamani that the boy again heard the cries of a child. They were coming from the room with the large, white door. He stepped close and flattened his ear tight to the wood. Someone was inside.

Chellamuthu glanced back at the fountain and then to the open room where Rajamani was working but not watching. Chellamuthu set the bucket down on the dirt and reached for the handle.

It twisted. Without thinking, he pushed the door open and slipped inside.

The crying halted.

Beside the door, high in the wall near the ceiling was a lone window that opened into the courtyard. With the sun all but set, it took a moment for Chellamuthu's eyes to adjust.

Lying on a mat against the wall was the little girl from the Jeep. The light spilling in from the window seemed to take pity and gather around her. Anyone could see she wasn't well.

"Are you sick?" Chellamuthu asked, as he inched forward, his foolish words spilling off his tongue before he could stop them. He didn't give her time to answer. "What's your name?"

She shifted her weight slowly, silently.

"It's okay. Maybe I can help," Chellamuthu coaxed.

"Anu," she mouthed, with large eyes and a voice like fractured glass that might shatter into a million pieces at any moment.

As he took a step closer, he could see where she had thrown up. While the stench made Chellamuthu want to cover his mouth, it also tightened familiar fingers around his ankles that held his feet. He remembered his sister Manju, her sickness . . . his mistakes.

It was odd. With family far away, even the bitter memories were now sweet.

"I saw you in the Jeep," Chellamuthu said.

She didn't answer.

"I want to help," he added. Then, remembering her plea about needing to go home and hoping it would lift her spirits, Chellamuthu shared his good news.

"I told the commissioner, Eli, the one in charge, that I'd been kidnapped. He promised to find my family. I'm sure he can find yours, too."

Her face was wet, shiny, and fevered. She was too frail to respond. He was about to ask if she would like some water when the door behind them opened.

"Chellamuthu, what are you doing in here?" It was Rajamani, and he didn't sound happy.

"I heard crying and came to help."

As Rajamani glanced down at the girl, his own face saddened. When he spoke, his tone leaked regret. "She's been sick again," he said, stating the obvious. "I'll call someone to help clean her up."

"What's wrong with her?" Chellamuthu asked, ignoring that she was right there listening.

"Don't know. She can't keep anything down."

"Why is she in here?"

Rajamani touched Chellamuthu on the shoulder. "We weren't sure if she was contagious. We couldn't risk putting her in the room with the babies."

"Will she be all right?"

"We've been watching her, doing all we can. You didn't touch her?"

"No."

"Well, go wash up anyway and get to bed. We'll take care of her."

Chellamuthu turned to leave but paused at the door.

"Mr. Rajamani?"

"Yes?"

"Can I come back tomorrow, just to see how she's doing?"

Rajamani glanced first at the sickly girl, face down now on the mat and barely breathing, then at Chellamuthu, staring anxiously from the door.

"We'll see, son," he answered. "We'll see."

Chellamuthu hardly slept. He was thinking about home—and about Anu. His sister was the same, refusing to drink because it would make her vomit. He hadn't worried at the time, since his mother had taken charge. Today, by the time the sun had come up, he knew what he needed to do.

Eli was sitting beside Anu when Chellamuthu pulled open the door. The boy didn't wait to explain. "I can help. I saw how my mother helped my sister."

He set down a rag and bucket he'd taken from the kitchen, dipped the cloth in the water, and bent down beside the girl. She didn't move.

Chellamuthu continued. "She just squeezed some drops on her lips for almost all day, like this . . ."

The rag was full of water and when too much dripped into the girl's mouth, she gagged, coughed, and groaned.

Eli reached for the rag, as if he was about to shoo Chellamuthu away, but reconsidered when he took another glance at the girl.

"Chellamuthu," Eli said, reaching down for the boy's hand to make certain he was listening. "You should know that the doctor was here early this morning. He wasn't encouraged. He said that Anu is a very sick little girl."

He didn't need to say more. Chellamuthu had already pulled away and was dipping the rag in the bucket.

Vikesh and Chellamuthu wrestled in the dirt, though the dirt seemed to be winning. When the gate beside them clicked open, the boys' eyes turned—whoever it was had a key!

The man who entered was older, like Eli, but to young boys every adult is old. In place of a traditional lungi, he was dressed in a white buttoned shirt with dark slacks, like the businessmen Chellamuthu had watched coming and going from the International Bank building near where he and his father waited to transfer buses in downtown Erode.

This man was heavy, with open nostrils and a thick nose that adeptly balanced a pair of black glasses wrapping around his cantaloupe-sized face. Also like Eli, his hair was turning gray, but there was little of it, leaving him completely bald on top.

He surveyed Chellamuthu like a man buying a prized goat at the market.

"You're new," he said. "What's your name?"

His voice was smooth and rich, like English tea with cream. The air about the man practically wore a badge: *Indian Banker Boring.*

Should Chellamuthu answer?

The man glanced at Vikesh, who didn't hesitate. "His name's Chellamuthu."

"Is that right?" The stranger edged forward. "How old are you, Chellamuthu?"

Vikesh would have answered, had he known, but Chellamuthu didn't give him time.

"I'm eight." In truth, he wasn't sure. Birthdays were seldom celebrated by the poor.

"That's perfect." The man turned to Vikesh. "Is Eli here?"

"I think he's in his office."

As the stranger walked away, Vikesh dropped to a knee and stretched for Chellamuthu's ankle, hoping for a quick takedown. "Come on!" Vikesh called out. "Let's wrestle!"

Chellamuthu jerked away. He wasn't finished watching. His nose pointed toward the man's back. "Who is he?"

"Him? That's Maneesh Durai. He owns this place."

Chellamuthu's face puckered. "I thought Eli did."

"Maybe they both do." Vikesh added, "Eli runs it, but Maneesh helps with the money. He's a banker or something. They're friends."

Maneesh had slipped inside the building, but the upper window was open. The boys could hear the men talking, though it was tough to make out their words.

"Come on," Vikesh pleaded. "Let's . . ."

"Shhhh!" Chellamuthu pressed a finger to his lips. "Ah . . . I . . . I'm pretending we're spies, and we've sneaked up to enemy headquarters."

Vikesh crouched. His eyes adjusted to the notion. *Much better! This was a game he could work with.*

The two knelt against the building and listened.

The men's garbled words reminded Chellamuthu of picking through dirty trash looking for an item or two still fresh enough to eat. The first name Chellamuthu heard was *Anu.* It was followed by something about *sickness* and *travel.* Next was talk about numbers, but neither boy understood what they meant.

More jumbled words.

More waiting.

Then a word floated down from the window, a word they both recognized. Perhaps it was clearer than the rest because it was familiar. The boys definitely heard a name . . .

Chellamuthu.

"How are things at the bank?" Eli asked, making obvious conversation. He was already seated.

Maneesh prattled about the office, looking over their kingdom, taking in changes. He plucked an envelope from the desk, flipped it over absently to scan the postmark, then returned it unharmed. "Bank's the same," he answered. "The rich are getting richer, and the poor are helping them. I'm caught in between."

When Eli offered no smile, Maneesh moved in for a closer look. "You seem tense."

"Do I?" Eli asked. His voice was low, worn, fraying at the edges. "It's the sick girl, Anu. I was up all night again."

Maneesh took a chair beside him. "Is she getting better?"

"Not yet, but I'm hopeful."

"You and your hope. I guess that's why we work well as partners. You dream. I make sure we stay afloat."

Spoken like a banker.

"I think we're doing more than just floating."

Maneesh offered no hint of apology. "India has millions of starving orphans. America has parents yearning to adopt. We match them up and earn a profit. Nothing wrong with that. The more we earn, the more children we can help. And we're gaining status in the community. People are noticing. Everybody wins."

More than a banker, Maneesh was almost a politician.

"But don't you get tired of . . ." Eli paused. Had the word escaped him, or could he not bring himself to say it?

"Tired of what?"

" . . . the corruption. Everyone in India wants payment. To keep the engine running, money is passed, favors are granted, eyes look away. I'm starting to choke on the fumes. Doesn't it all make you . . . I don't know . . . *weary?*"

Maneesh's eyes actually brightened. "It's the way India works, my friend. Everybody has a price. We can't change human nature. We can only use it to our advantage."

"Our problem isn't human nature," Eli answered, never looking up. "It's human behavior."

Arayi paced by the fire as she waited for the last searchers of the day to return. It was a constant battle to keep dejection from clawing at her bleeding heart, as if she were fighting a determined tiger with nothing but a twig.

Friends and relatives had searched for Chellamuthu for days with few leads.

A man by the river had remembered a boy playing apart from the others and thought it could have been the lost child. But when he was shown a picture, he couldn't be certain—skinny, naked Indian boys playing in the mud can all look alike.

A merchant selling fish in the market near the hospital swore he'd watched a man tie up a screaming boy and carry him away into the crowd. But no one else in the busy square saw any such thing, and when pressed further, the man confessed he'd made up the story to draw attention and sell more fish.

The most promising lead was from a woman walking with her sister near the government building where Chellamuthu had disappeared. They had watched a van speed away that day with two or three children inside, but the woman admitted that from a distance she couldn't be certain. It might have simply been a young family in a hurry. The woman's sister, who was closer, had since returned to her village and hadn't been found to see if there was anything further she could add.

The dead ends were piling up.

Arayi's breathing deepened. She circled the fire one last time, then sank to the earth as the fatigued flames slowly flickered and died. With knees pulled against her chest, she watched glowing embers blacken into dirty ash as the last of any hopeful smoke drifted away into the dark and empty sky.

Like most boys, Chellamuthu preferred to swim in the river, as opposed to drawing a picture about it. What child wouldn't want to run instead of sit, play instead of study? While most of the children at the orphanage planned to spend the day drawing, Chellamuthu and Vikesh had already outlined a battle plan of their own—until the rain invaded.

Morning storm clouds had marched across the sky in search of a child's afternoon they could ruin, and when they spotted Chellamuthu waiting for Vikesh to return with his father, they parked themselves over the Lincoln Home for Homeless Children and poured out their rain.

When it became apparent that Vikesh wasn't going to make it back, Chellamuthu gathered up some of the colored pencils and paper, braved a run in the rain to Anu's room, and sat by her side to draw.

He'd been coming every day anyway, holding the moist rag to her little lips—and even Eli agreed that something seemed to be working. She'd sat up several times and had started to eat again, in small amounts, anyway. Chellamuthu wanted to believe that he was making a difference, that the girl *was* improving. But at times, when she would cough and cry and ache to be in another place, truth whispered that she was barely holding on.

At the moment, she was asleep.

Had Vikesh come, the two boys would have undoubtedly drawn pictures of tanks, trucks, and guns set against a heroic background of Indian soldiers fighting to their last breath. Had Chellamuthu been back in Erode and had his mother asked him to draw, he would have rolled his eyes, hurriedly scribbled something, and then begged for permission to run outside.

Sitting now beside a sick girl who only reminded him of home, Chellamuthu decided to draw his family. His eyes narrowed, his jaw tightened, and his fingers gripped his pencils with intent. Not only would the drawing help him to remember what his family looked like but he could also show the sketch to Eli to prove that he'd been telling the truth.

He started first by outlining the background: a familiar grove of trees. Next he penciled in each family member, in the same position the photographer had posed them at the wedding. His brother stood to his left, his father to his right, all three wearing satisfied smiles to match their new clothes.

Once the silhouettes were drawn, he focused on the detail. He penciled in Selvaraj with arms bigger than his own and a much older face, even though the brothers were separated by just three years. He drew his mother wearing the lavish silk sari she'd borrowed for the wedding from her second cousin in Bhavani. Arayi had looked so pleased with her family that day, so at ease.

His father was the hardest. At first Chellamuthu drew a smile but then replaced it with flat, stern lips.

Much better.

When uncertain about a particular detail, he would close his eyes and listen to the drumming of the rain, hoping it would help him remember—and it did. As he drew his own pants, he colored them with bulging pockets of money, the gift he'd given to his cousin at the wedding. And then, as if Shiva had looked down and smiled on his effort, the name of his recently married cousin popped into his head:

Suresh!

To help him remember his cousin's name, Chellamuthu drew Suresh and his new wife as silhouettes in the background to the left of his family. To balance them out on the right, he drew Aunt Jaya and Uncle Nataraj. But he couldn't stop there. By the time he'd finished penciling in his many aunts, uncles, grandparents, and cousins, he and his family were standing in front of a crowd of relatives so large that they filled every corner of the page.

He held up his masterpiece to admire it in the light. His figures weren't all drawn with the proper proportions, and the contentment he'd hoped to capture in his family's faces was difficult to see. His original backdrop of trees was now muddied with people and the colors he'd used for their clothing often strayed past well-intentioned lines. To the average person, the picture would be amusing but worthless, hardly deserving of a second glance.

But to Chellamuthu, alone and lonely, a captive at the Lincoln Home for Homeless Children—a place he didn't belong—the portrait was worth every rupee in India.

This was him . . . his family.

Perhaps it was the incessant pounding of the rain still beating its forlorn rhythm on the roof that worked the boy's emotions free. A lump had formed in Chellamuthu's throat and was migrating toward his chest. His picture looked fuzzy now, but when he reached up to wipe at his eyes, a cough startled him.

He hadn't noticed that Anu was awake or that she'd been watching. Though she didn't speak it, concern trickled from her petite brow and squinting chocolate eyes. If his emotions had any intention of putting on a parade, he forced them to retreat with a silent threat of death. He wouldn't cry—not in front of a girl.

He leaned over and placed his drawing between two clean sheets of paper, as if nothing had happened, then he stood and held them close to his chest. He would run hunched over to protect his drawing from the rain and then hide it beneath the mat where he slept to keep it safe.

Before he left, he spun around to share a secret with Anu—one he knew she'd keep.

"I'm going to find a way out of here!"

Maneesh was approaching the main gate when Eli stepped outside. Eli had been waiting, watching.

He would start with the good news. "I may have found a home for Ajeet."

Maneesh glanced up. His eyes grew wide as stones. "The deaf boy? That's great! I thought we'd never . . . I mean, I expected it would take more time."

Now the bad news. "The fee will be lower. I had no choice."

"How low?" His question itched with curiosity.

"Half."

The calculator in Maneesh's head was already clicking. "It's okay. We can make it up elsewhere. It could be much worse, considering he's . . ."

"Deaf?"

"No need to say it that way. You should be happy. You've saved another boy."

This wasn't the topic Eli had been waiting to discuss. He steered their words back on track. "Do you remember why we started the orphanage?"

Maneesh used his hands to gesture, in case his words weren't convincing enough alone. "You wanted to save children, and I . . ."

"You wanted to save yourself. You had just become a Christian."

"I saw the good you were doing—still are doing, like with Ajeet."

"Maneesh, have we lost our bearings? Have we gone astray?"

"Why would you ask that?"

"How many orphans did you pass on your way here? Those missing arms or legs, or those with disfigured faces? Yet the only children we take are . . . *adoptable.*"

"Not true. You just found Ajeet a home."

"Yes, but we didn't know he was deaf until he got here."

Seconds paced. When Maneesh spoke, he used unvarnished words. "Eli, if you want the truth, nobody wants disabled children. If we took them, we'd soon fill up and wouldn't have room for others. Look, we're doing a lot of good, just like you wanted. Don't apologize for it." Maneesh paused. He glanced across the courtyard. "Now, if we can just find a home for the older boy."

Eli clenched his eyes. "Chellamuthu?"

"Yes, older children are always more difficult—but I have faith in you, Eli. Cheer up—our future is bright. The Lincoln Home for Homeless Children is changing lives."

CHAPTER 9

Arayi was hunched outside over a dirty pot, scrubbing it clean with handfuls of sand. She needed to get rice boiling to feed the early searchers who would soon be returning.

"Excuse me."

Arayi turned. It was the landowner's servant. The girl bowed in greeting. "When you have a moment," she said, "Mrs. Iyer would like to speak with you."

Arayi forced an awkward smile, weighted with worry. The mother understood what the invitation meant. It had been several days, and the number of friends and relatives searching for Chellamuthu had dwindled. People had to return to their work, their families, their lives. The landowner was also a busy woman, and she couldn't keep providing help. Arayi would soon be left all alone.

When Arayi reached the door, it was open. Mrs. Iyer was seated inside at a table. She directed Arayi toward the chair.

"Thank you for coming. I've been meaning to speak with you for a couple of days now."

Arayi sat slowly, not wanting to let her eyes meet those of the woman. Arayi intended to thank her for her kindness, but she knew the minute she opened her mouth, tears would break loose, drowning her gratitude and good intentions. So instead, she kept her gaze down and said nothing.

The landowner continued. "I have noticed there are fewer people coming each day to search."

Arayi couldn't deny it. Her scowl agreed.

The landowner scooted her chair closer, perhaps to make the delivery of her words more manageable. "Life is resilient," she added. "It trudges on in the world around us, no matter how deeply our hearts ache."

"Yes, I guess it does." They were the first sounds Arayi had uttered since arriving.

"I want you to know . . ." Mrs. Iyer stopped midsentence, as if her words had bolted through the open door with no intention of coming back. Silence nudged in, and for the first time, Arayi noticed that the woman beside her was also fighting tears.

Both women breathed.

"I want you to know," Mrs. Iyer finally declared, "that I am not giving up." She paused, using the moment to retrieve her courage. When she spoke again, her words chased away the lingering silence with resolve. "I took the picture of your boy, Chellamuthu, and I am having large posters made. I will be paying to have these placed around the city, as well as to be displayed on the sides of many buses. Someone must have seen something. We just need them to see his picture."

Arayi's head was shaking. Her fingers were trembling. "Why are you doing this for me?"

Mrs. Iyer's chin rose. "I had a son," she said. "He was also lost."

Arayi didn't mean to gasp. "Lost? I'm sorry. What happened?"

Her words hesitated. "When I say *lost,* it was permanent."

"I don't understand."

The woman paced her delivery, as if she needed to dust off her explanation. "My son—our only child—was just two years old when disease swept through our village. It found our home. My son . . . he struggled for weeks, clinging to life, until the fight became too great."

"I didn't know."

"I don't speak of it. I tell you now because for many years I was bitter, angry at my husband, the village—everyone. You see, my boy was not the only one to get ill. I, too, was bedridden. But rather than mercifully taking us together, the illness was more cruel. It not only left me heartbroken at the loss of my son but also left me barren. There was no greater hardship."

"I am so sorry," Arayi replied, but the woman was not yet finished.

"For years I stayed away, isolated. I couldn't bear to be around children, to hear them, especially babies, to look at them, hold them. I had recovered my strength, but the disease had cankered my heart. Resentment, pity, shame . . . all were growing in the cracks of my soul like mold. We lived near Tirupati at the time, before moving to Bangalore, at the base of the Eastern Ghats, where the mountain range begins. It was a village alive with children, and every time a child cried, all I heard was the sound of loss and of death."

Arayi's head tipped. "But you love children. You sit out front for much of your day and greet them with kindness!" The lines on her face begged the woman to continue.

"One night, the neighbor's child was crying until all hours," she replied. "I woke up exhausted and upset, not from the innocent cry or from the lack of sleep, but from the crippling load of regret and guilt that was smothering me in the dark. I could no longer bear it. While we lived beside a great mountain, the pain I was asked to endure was even taller—it was too high. Regardless of my prayers and offerings, I could never climb over it."

"But you did!" Arayi answered. "You obviously did."

"NO! I didn't," she snapped with an intensity that surprised them both.

"What are you saying then?"

"On that day I was up before dawn, went into the yard, threw myself on the ground, and begged Lord Shiva to take my life, to let me pass on so I might return as an insect or a snake, as anything to end my current suffering and try again. I knew assuredly that I was through climbing."

Arayi tightened her already folded arms.

"What happened next?"

The landowner shrugged. "It was simple, really—the sun came up."

"The sun?"

"Silly, I know. But as I lay there helpless in the shadow of that towering mountain, unwilling to move, the sun peered over the peak, and I realized that my hardship wasn't about climbing a mountain at all."

"It wasn't?"

"It took me the entire day watching the sun plod across the sky, but Lord Shiva helped me understand that my only journey of concern was to be like the sun, to make it through the day offering as much light and warmth and consistency for others as I could—one single day. Each day. That was all." She drew a steadied breath. "So from that day on, I have continued to get up in the morning and offer that light, as much as I am able, in my own small way."

Arayi sat tall. "That is why you greet the children with friendship and love, never pity or regret! And no one knows the pain you've conquered."

"Not *conquered.* I've never reached the summit of my mountain, Arayi. Instead, you could say I've been hiking around it, one day at a time, for twenty-five years."

Arayi had many questions, but they crowded in her throat.

Mrs. Iyer stood. "Arayi, I wish I could tell you that Chellamuthu will return home. I pray to the gods that he will. I know from experience that your own mountain is blocking so much light that all you can see is darkness. I called you over to tell you that you are not alone. In my trudging, you should know that I've bumped into plenty of others on the same journey. Now, I'm not suggesting it makes the pain easier, but it does, perhaps, make the walking a little less lonely."

The landowner's servant entered the room.

"The searchers," she announced. "They are back."

Eli's home in Madukkarai was a short two blocks from the orphanage, though it was a place where he spent little time, especially since his wife had passed away a year and a half earlier. He'd have preferred now to sleep on a cot in his office, but Maneesh insisted it wouldn't look right, since the women they'd hired to help with the children stayed overnight. Maneesh was always the one apprehensive about what others might think: form, prestige, decorum, the proper way of doing things.

Eli was getting tired of it. Tired of life. Tired of loss. Tired of all of the work. Tired of fighting a corrupt system. Tired of watching children struggle.

Mostly, he was tired of remembering.

Saving children was never going to be easy, but it shouldn't bring such pain.

He rubbed at the scars on the back of his neck, which always ached this time of year, and then edged close to his desk. He placed his heavy fingers on the typewriter's keys. Tonight, before going home, he had one last letter to write.

Dear Mr. and Mrs. Rowland,

Thank you for asking that we help you find a female child for adoption. God has heard your prayers. It is with pleasure I inform you that we recently had an orphan girl of approximately 40 months arrive at the Lincoln Home for Homeless Children. Her name is Anu. I am including a picture (sorry it's a bit blurry).

We found her begging on the streets. She had no father and no mother, since both died leaving only the child. God has helped her to find a real father and a mother in you, in the great country of the United States.

She arrived sick, but with time should be well enough to travel.

I am including the required paperwork. Please return, along with payment of $5,000 to help cover the many costs of adoption in our country. You should be welcoming your daughter shortly.

May God bless you.
With kind regards,
Eli Manickam, Orphanage Commissioner

Two babies were wrapped and ready when the taxi pulled to a stop inside the compound. Mrs. Sundar held both. The deaf boy who'd arrived with Chellamuthu stood behind her. He was wrapped in silence.

Eli bent down close to the babies. "Go and make something of your life!" he said. He began speaking to the boy, Ajeet, but the child was glancing forward, not paying attention, and so Eli settled for a pat on the shoulder.

Three more children on their way to a real life.

Mrs. Sundar and her sister would carry them by car to the airport in Chennai. From there, she'd travel with them alone to New York via London. The young boy was old enough to hold one of the babies, if needed, but the trip would still be all that Mrs. Sundar could handle.

It would be all right. Saving an additional airfare would mean bonuses for all—happiness spread around.

Speaking of happiness, Maneesh passed Mrs. Sundar an envelope. "I believe that's everything. The paperwork is in order, but should you encounter problems at the airport, give them whatever is needed."

She understood. She'd done it before.

"These children will be a blessing to their waiting families," Maneesh announced to all, but his tone echoed thin. He turned too quickly to Eli. "Are more coming?"

"There are always more coming, Maneesh. Always more."

And without another word, Eli walked across the compound, into his office, and closed the door.

When Arayi arrived back home, a box was waiting with a letter taped to its side. Selvaraj said it was left by Oma, one of Arayi's older brothers. She tore open the envelope and read.

Dear Auntie,

We are sad since hearing about the disappearance of Chellamuthu. We have visited the temple in Karur, praying often for peace. Regrettably, I have not been able to come back to Erode with Uncle to help search. My new employer, the Utility Board in Karur, will not allow that I take leave so soon. We have little in the way of wealth but were blessed by generosity at our wedding. Since by Lakshmi's good fortune I have secured employment, take the money we received at the wedding, an unusually large amount, and use it in your search for Chellamuthu. We have placed his picture in our shrine and will continue to plead for strength, peace, and his speedy return.

Your nephew,
Suresh

After reading the letter, Arayi pulled open the box flaps. Inside, placed side by side, were three tight rolls of rupees. She untied the twine that held them, and as she counted, confidence lifted in her voice. She turned to her son. "Selvaraj, please take these to Mrs. Iyer right away. Tell her we need to order more posters!"

The boy hesitated.

"What is it?" she asked.

Selvaraj dropped his shoulders. "It's been weeks, Mother. More posters won't help. Chellamuthu is never coming home."

It was early in the morning, just as Chellamuthu and the other children were waking up, when Eli stepped into the room and motioned for the boy to come close.

"I have some news," he said. "We need to speak. Can you follow me?"

Something was wrong. Was Anu okay?

Chellamuthu tried to read Eli's face to learn if the news was good or bad, but the man had turned. The boy trailed behind him as they crossed the yard, wishing they could walk faster. When they entered the building and climbed the stairs, Eli pointed to a chair and then sat to face him.

"I finally spoke with the couple who brought you here, as well as the people who took you, and I believe there has been a misunderstanding."

Chellamuthu leaned into the news with relief. It was more than a misunderstanding. But whatever anyone wanted to call it was fine if it meant he could finally go home.

Eli continued, "Chellamuthu, you were right. You are not an orphan. You have a family." It was Eli's turn now to lean close. "But I misspoke when I told you that we have only orphans here. That's not entirely true. We also take in children from difficult family situations."

Difficult family situations? The words circled around Chellamuthu like vultures waiting for death.

"This will be hard for you to understand," the man added, "but you are here because your family—Chellamuthu, they sold you! They could no longer provide for you, and so sending you here was their best option."

Chellamuthu's head fell back as the blunt force of the news pummeled him between the eyes. *Liar! It wasn't true!*

"No!" he shouted. "NO!"

But despite his denial, the door of doubt had been cracked open, and the painful possibility had already nosed in. His head shook in defiance. His words quivered with panic. "We need to call the police!"

Eli wiped down his beard. His reply was measured, deliberate. "Chellamuthu, we can't go to the police."

"Why not?" the boy asked, his voice barely scratching to hold on.

"If we go to the police, they will arrest your family for abandoning you, for selling you. Do you want your family to get arrested? Your father and mother will go to jail!"

The words were weary and burdened, like heaving a full sack of rice to a boy.

"If the police ever speak to you about how you got here, you *must* tell them you are all alone, that you have no family to look after you. Do you understand? It's for your own family's sake! In the end, it's what they wanted for you."

The room's walls seemed to bend and sway, as if they could cave and crumble at any moment. Eli continued, "I know it's going to take some time for you to fully understand. All I'm asking is that you consider what I've said. As you do, also ask if you've ever been hungry here? Have you always had enough to eat? Good clothing and a dry place to sleep? Has anyone here ever hurt you?"

The silence waited.

"Did you have those things at home?" Eli asked.

Tears were poised to fall. "Yes, I did," he defended. "I did!"

Eli arched back, though his eyes fell to the boy's feet. "If that's true, then why are your feet scarred?"

Chellamuthu tucked them beneath the chair out of view. "That was my fault," he blurted. "I didn't obey. I kept running off. I stole fruit. It was me—not them!"

His words froze, naked and exposed. All that could be heard was the sound of his own breathing.

Was it possible? Could his father really have sold him? Thirty rupees . . . the man in the van had said thirty rupees!

Eli was patting him on the back now to console him, but it felt like the hacking of Banerjee's machete.

His legs trembled. His throat burned. He was certain his heart was about to rupture.

Eli's tone suddenly brightened. "Those who are brought to the Lincoln Home for Homeless Children are actually very lucky. You don't realize it now, but you will have opportunities that boys who remain in India can only dream about—education, employment, perhaps even wealth. You're going to have an astounding life, Chellamuthu. You will. And some day you will come back here to thank me, to show me what you've done with the blessing God is handing you."

Like dirty smoke from the factory near Erode Junction, the words settled around Chellamuthu and choked him.

He wasn't listening to Eli's promises. He was still arguing with himself.

No! His family hadn't sold him—it was all a lie.

Rajamani pulled at the ends of his mustache, as if it might tear off. *What do I do with the boy?*

He had wanted Chellamuthu to help him repair the commissioner's desk by holding the corner while Rajamani screwed in a new leg. However, since his meeting with the commissioner, the boy had plopped onto his sleeping mat and refused to move. He'd been like a statue, silent, motionless, even looking away when addressed. When Rajamani touched him on the shoulder, he'd angrily brushed away the man's hand. He'd even refused to eat!

Rajamani had promised the commissioner that the desk would be fixed before the end of the day, and that gave him less than an hour.

"CHELLAMUTHU!" Rajamani called out from across the room, with words as tall as the man was wide. "Come with me now!" He hated to be firm with Chellamuthu, since the child was generally so well behaved, but there comes a time of necessity.

As Chellamuthu slowly stood, Rajamani commended himself. As he'd always said, *A firm hand compels a compliant heart.*

His self-congratulatory back-patting had barely started when Chellamuthu looked heavenward and screamed—a shrieking, painful, lamenting, gut-wrenching scream!

Children jumped, faces twisted. Both toddlers and babies nearby began to cry.

Like a boy possessed, Chellamuthu reached for the banana leaf holding his untouched dinner and flung it across the room. Then, to the horror of wide-eyed children trying to create distance, the boy began pulling out the mats from beneath their feet and tearing the straw into pieces like a ravenous tiger.

Eli, who'd heard the commotion from across the yard, rushed in to help.

With children tumbling to the floor like spilled *sevai,* the men stepped slowly, cautiously, approaching Chellamuthu from opposite sides.

Rajamani reached him first. Chellamuthu's eyes bulged and his nostrils flared. His legs were planted wide. He was panting, teeth bared, like a desperate, cornered stray. While it was a fevered rampage, it was short-lived, as the boy's passion was no match for Rajamani's size. Once constrained, fury beat a hasty retreat, leaving only room for anguish.

Tight arms fell limp. Tense shoulders dropped helpless. And when Rajamani loosened his grip, the boy slid through his fingers like sand to the floor. He was sobbing in front of the children, Eli, Rajamani, and himself.

Rajamani turned to Eli. "I am sorry, Commissioner. I will make sure this never happens again. He will be severely punished. I will see to . . ."

"No!" Eli cut the man's words in two. "He's not to be punished."

"Sir?" Rajamani asked, his narrowing eyes still holding onto the question.

Eli was stroking at his beard, staring down at the crying boy. Rajamani knew this meant that the man was thinking. Eli looked up. "Tomorrow, give him extra vegetables with his rice and beans—and send someone to the market to get all of the children some sweets."

Rajamani's head bobbed. Eli continued, "These children are blessed to be here at the Lincoln Home. It's a fact we need to celebrate more often."

"Certainly," Rajamani answered. "I'll get this place cleaned up."

Eli wasn't listening—or if he was, it didn't show. As he made his way to the door, he seemed preoccupied. Before leaving, he turned to Rajamani and spoke, as if needing to give voice to a notion he was debating in his head.

"A time will come!" he said.

"I beg your pardon?" Rajamani called back.

"A time will come, Rajamani, when these children will recognize the gift we are giving them."

The astrologer hunched over his charts like a fox might hunch over a squirrel, only this man was flipping through page after page, making calculations, noting data about planets, stars, and orbits. In addition to his books, he'd brought his own little table to spread them on, a round folding top with carved planets orbiting its circular wooden edge.

He had arrived half a day late, though Arayi did not complain. She boiled water and served him tea and asked if he was comfortable. This man was in high demand, and she was lucky that he'd made the time. He was wearing a light orange shirt and a white lungi, and other than the large gold medallion that dangled around his neck, featuring the astrological signs, there was nothing special about the man—except his reputation.

His name had been passed to her by Sulabha Nalini, her friend at the temple. "There is *no one,*" the woman had said, so emphatically anyone would have believed her, "who reads the charts with more certainty than Devadas D'Souza."

He was also the most expensive astrologer Arayi had used. But can a mother ever put a price on her son? One found a way to pay, even if it required missing meals. Luckily, Arayi had saved a small amount of the money Suresh had sent to search for Chellamuthu. It was time now to put it to good use.

"Tell me about your missing boy," he'd directed, carrying confidence the way an old woman carries home well water. He expected more than just the boy's birthday. He'd wanted the time of his birth, the day they first noticed him missing, birthdays and birth times for both the boy's parents and his siblings. The man was thorough, she'd give him that.

After several minutes poring over his charts, he faced Arayi. "What would you like to know?"

She'd assumed her questions were obvious. She voiced them now aloud. "Is my son, Chellamuthu, still alive? Will he be coming home?"

The astrologer didn't appear nervous or under pressure to divine the answers correctly because, as he'd explained on his arrival—and as anyone with the slightest understanding of the heavens understood—this was science. Heavenly bodies serve as the fruit of karma, shining their influence on a person throughout their earthly life. To divine that influence, one simply had to know how to read the charts.

Now that she'd asked, now that she was waiting, now that she'd paid, he checked a few more pages in his notes, just to be certain. "I am only the messenger," he said. "All I can do is read the stars and planets and their orbits and then tell you what they say."

"I understand," Arayi replied. She paused, watched, waited. He said nothing. "Then what do they say?" she finally asked directly.

He lowered his head and clutched his medallion.

"I'm sorry to tell you. Your son, Chellamuthu, is dead."

CHAPTER 10

Chellamuthu closed his eyes, pretending to be asleep. His back was facing the courtyard door as he measured steady breaths. Long after the lights were turned out, hours after the children quit stirring, Chellamuthu quietly rose, grabbed the blue water bucket beside the trough, and hauled it toward the door.

Eli was lying about Chellamuthu's family. He had to be, and Chellamuthu intended to prove it.

Tonight would be like his pretend wartime missions with Vikesh where they'd sneak across enemy lines to break out captured soldiers, except tonight his mission was real. He was headed to the fountain.

His plan was simple. When helping to rinse clothes in the basin, he'd noticed the spacing of the spout and the tap as they poked through the wall. If he could just reach the lower handle by jumping from the bucket, he was certain he could grab the spout with his legs and then use it to climb up onto the wall. It would be like the monkey bars at the park in Erode—except instead of falling into soft sand if he slipped, the landing tonight would be unforgiving cement.

As if his plan wasn't exacting enough, he'd have to carry it out in virtual silence, since the room where the women slept was just a few steps away. And while the night was cloudy, masking the moonlight, the darkness also made it harder to see the handle when he jumped.

It didn't matter.

He climbed. He leapt. He stretched toward the handle and grabbed.

His body thumped against the wall, though he didn't wait to see if anyone stirred. He swung his legs until he could wrap them around the spout. Then, quicker than he could say *monkey bars in the park,* he pulled himself up into a standing position on the spout to lean against the wall.

As he gripped the steel posts on top and peered through them, he fought the urge to shout, to wake up the sleeping children below to announce what he'd done.

His elation died a quick death.

As he stepped up onto the top of the wall, still holding the posts, something stabbed in his foot. There was the sound of cracking. The top surface of the wall circling the compound was embedded with shards of broken glass.

Everyone in the compound was asleep. No one heard him cry out in pain. No one watched him wince as he lowered himself back down to the spout. No one could see the blood drip, drip, drip into the fountain.

He rinsed his stinging foot in the water, limped across the yard, and then held a shirt against the wound in the dark until he drifted off to sleep.

The next morning, when Mr. Rajamani shook him awake, Chellamuthu told him a story about cutting his foot on a sharp stone near the fountain in the dark while filling the bucket with water for the trough. When Rajamani pulled off the rag, a drop of crimson tracked down the boy's foot to his heel and then jumped free to the ground.

"This doesn't look good. Let me go get some ointment."

Chellamuthu counted the slow, steady drops as they hit the dirt. *One. Two. Three.* It still stung, but it wasn't his foot that made him uneasy. What he couldn't figure out how to stop was the ache that pounded in his chest.

Maneesh banged the poster against the startled table. "Do you know about this?" he asked Eli, wagging a finger at the face of the boy staring up from the paper. He didn't give him time to answer. "I was in Erode on bank business. These are plastered all over the bus station. Eli, he's not an orphan! His family is looking for him."

Eli wouldn't pretend. A simple nod sufficed. "I know," he said, his words too calm for the moment.

Maneesh wasn't ready yet to lower his voice. "Did you not think that as your partner I would need to know this information? How did we get him? Why is he here?"

"Don't fret. We'll get paid for the boy."

"Paid? Eli, we could get arrested."

"If there's a problem, bribe someone—like you always do."

"This isn't about paying off the police."

"But it is! In India that's what *everything* is about. And to answer your question, the boy is here because there are children besides orphans who deserve saving."

"SAVING? Eli, his family is looking for him!"

"Did you see his feet?"

"What about them?"

"They've been burned, scarred. Not only that, when he arrived he was starving and lice were practically building a city in his hair."

Maneesh sat. He appeared tired of being the only one with a raised voice. "Eli, you don't know the circumstance behind the boy's scars. Besides, when we were children, we were *all* skinny. We *all* had lice. This boy was taken from his family. That's not right!"

"So bribes are all right, but helping to save a battered boy is not? I have scars on my back that argue otherwise."

"That's different."

"Different? I was no older than Chellamuthu when I was forced to carry bricks in that godforsaken factory. When I was beaten so badly I almost died—all possible because the owner paid for the privilege of having the police look the other way. The difference—if that's what you're looking for—is that I'm saving children, not torturing them for my own gain."

Maneesh rubbed his thumbs against his fingers, a nervous habit when his brain was going but his words weren't yet ready. He'd heard the story a hundred times.

"I admit," Maneesh said, in a tone calmer than Eli expected, "there are aspects of our work that aren't black and white. But don't stir your colors together too self-righteously, or you'll end up covered in muddy gray—and we'll both end up in prison."

"It won't happen. I know you. You'll simply pay them all off."

Maneesh's voice was low, like gravel. The man was downright pensive—out of character.

"That, my friend, is a prison of a different kind."

On song day, Chellamuthu didn't sing about ABCs, flowing fountains, slinging stones, or boys named David. When the children around him fell to the ground at the end of the song in smiles and giggles, Chellamuthu turned his slumping shoulders back to the room and his mat. *What was the point?*

"I don't feel good," he'd told Rajamani, who was leading activities that day—and he didn't. For days Chellamuthu had combed over every last inch of the Lincoln Home for Homeless Children looking for a way to escape. The main door and gate were always locked. The door in back that led outside was padlocked, never open. He'd looked for a place to dig under the fence, but had no tools and would be discovered anyway. He'd watched for food deliveries, hoping to sneak into an empty truck, but most deliveries came by auto rickshaw and unless you were a small rat, there was no place in them to hide.

Time was running out. Children were being adopted. If he didn't get out soon, he'd be sent to a strange country, a place much farther away than three and a half hours, a place from which he'd *never* return home.

"Chellamuthu, hurry!" It was Rajamani rocking him awake. Fear was sweating from the man's face. "I need your help."

Chellamuthu had been dreaming of home, of working in the fields with his father and two uncles and, for a few seconds, wondered why his father was shaking him in front of all the workers. When the boy realized where he was, that it was actually Rajamani and not his father, he pulled away and rolled over. It was the man's next words that grabbed Chellamuthu by the heart, lifted him up, and placed him in a dead run behind Rajamani in an effort to keep up.

"It's Anu!"

Rajamani carted a pan from the kitchen and called back to Chellamuthu as they crossed toward the room where Anu slept. His words were hurried and halting. "The commissioner is away . . . taking babies to the airport. I checked Anu . . . she's throwing up again . . . not drinking. I worry that she c . . ." He paused mid-word, not letting the notion out.

Chellamuthu's pace quickened.

Rajamani continued, "The women have gone home so I have no help . . ."

The man reached the door and yanked it open. Chellamuthu followed him inside.

The girl was heaving. She had a bucket, but it was high and she was too weak to keep herself propped up. Rajamani pulled it carefully away and replaced it with the shallower pan.

"Easy, child," Rajamani said, leaning in close. "We're going to get you some help."

He turned to Chellamuthu. "I'll go call the doctor. There's water in the corner. You've got to get her to drink. Please. I'll be right back."

The smell of sickness swirled from the bucket she'd been holding, and as Chellamuthu moved it beside the door, the stench almost caused him to vomit right along with her.

She was dry heaving now into the pan; there was nothing left to come up. Her face was pale, her gaze withdrawn. She was about to faint. If she did, it could be too late.

Chellamuthu remembered that Arayi would hum to calm Manju. While he considered his mother's example, he opted for something more natural for him—he talked.

"Anu, I know you hurt. I'm sorry. It's like I told you, so did Manju, my sister, when she was sick . . . but you *have to* drink, or you'll get sicker."

He reached for the rag from the water bucket. Though her face was down, she must have understood, because when he held out the dripping rag, she pulled it from his fingers and pushed it to her lips. It didn't stay long. She pulled the rag away to heave, spitting up what little water she'd swallowed. It was a painful cycle: heaving, resting, then motioning again for him to give her water.

When Rajamani returned, he seemed pleased that she was sucking water from the rag. "Good, good. I reached the doctor, and he is coming." Rajamani took the pan, poured it into the original bucket, and then faced Chellamuthu. "The smell can't be good for her. Empty the bucket and then come right back."

It was a disgusting job, cleaning up after a sick little girl, but it was Anu, which made it okay. It was a curious thought that had stepped onto the stage in his head, because it also replayed pictures of his mother when she'd held sick Manju back at home in their hut.

He stopped and set down his bucket.

"She stayed up all night with Manju while everyone slept," he whispered to no one, as though seeing it for the first time, as if he hadn't been in the room with her that night.

The vision was a gift, a child's first grasp of a mother's devotion. But it was also a curse, for as Chellamuthu stood in darkness, hours away from home and uncertain if he would ever see his mother again, regret clawed at his heart. Empathy, he'd learned, can be lonely.

Chellamuthu reached for the bucket and hurried on his way. Anu would be waiting. If he stood in the yard any longer thinking about home, his emotions would flow like lava, and he'd promised himself that wouldn't happen again.

He scurried across the yard, into the room, and to the far wall. He covered his nose to keep the smell at bay and then emptied the little girl's vomit into the cement trough. Next, he picked up the waiting blue bucket full of water and poured it into the cement furrow with force to wash away the stink.

As the water swirled with the bile and carried it through the hole in the wall to the dirt outside the compound, a place where no one could smell the stench, a second moment of clarity flickered. He bent closer to examine the hole.

His mother had often said life was like that, answers so close they were too big to see. For days he'd been marching around the compound looking for a way to out, but he'd been searching in the wrong places. His escape had been waiting patiently inside, just meters from where he slept.

Chellamuthu's heart beat the sound of impending freedom. He'd be escaping after all. But instead of climbing triumphantly to freedom by scaling the wall, he would humbly inch through it. Like a sewer rat, he'd be crawling out a hole.

In darkness Chellamuthu poured three pails of water down the empty trough. If questioned, he'd claim he wasn't feeling well. Would anyone make him bend over to verify?

Even with the rinsing, the escape would be disgusting. Sometimes the roads we choose in life are just messy. He lowered his body face down into the trough and began to scoot toward the opening.

A child in the room stirred. Chellamuthu waited, breathed, waited. As he hugged the cement and inched forward, the persistent smell of excrement smothered him, urged him to vomit. Desperate thoughts raced. *Wait! Should I go feet first?* Doing so might help with an upright landing, but he wouldn't be able to see if it was far to the ground.

Again there was movement in the room. This time he could hear steps coming toward him.

Bhagavan! Help me!

Chellamuthu didn't raise his head, as that would clearly have given away his position. The noises told him everything he needed to know: a discouraged sigh, the dragging away of the empty bucket, then silence. Whoever it was, they were heading to the fountain to refill the blue bucket and would promptly return to use the trough.

Perhaps Chellamuthu should have sprung to his feet, raced to his mat, and pretended to be asleep. Instead, he stretched his arms out over his head, arched his back, and used his toes to scoot his body into the opening. It was now or never.

Unless the hole was shrinking, perhaps in an attempt to chew on the boy, Chellamuthu had completely misjudged its size. When his shoulders hit the edge, they stopped like a cork.

Not good!

Chellamuthu twisted, pulled his shoulders in, twisted some more. As he wriggled in the dark like a muddy worm, the feces-covered cement scratched at his skin. He grunted, wrenched, pulled, contorted, grimaced, prayed, and grunted harder. If he didn't make it out soon, he could be dead before he was discovered.

In his panic, he'd been sucking in deep gasps of air. Then an enlightened thought skipped into his brain.

I should be doing the opposite.

Like a Yogi beginning morning meditation, Chellamuthu shut his eyes, relaxed his muscles, and exhaled with a steady, sustained breath, purposely forcing out every measure of air from his lungs. When nothing more would come and he was certain he'd pass out if he waited even a second longer, he garnered all the strength that his constricted little body could muster and *pushed.*

Had someone been watching from outside, it must have looked like the building was birthing a small boy. In a single, sliding movement,

Chellamuthu popped out, flipped over, and landed backside down on the pile with a splat.

He wanted to cry like a newborn, perhaps so someone would carry him away and clean him up, for when he extended his hand to push himself up, it squished into a shallow layer of putrid waste.

He was sitting in the bottom of a slight furrow created from the constant splash of liquid that had eroded away the dirt. It led down a small rise to a ditch that ran beside the road, a road with buildings lined up along the opposite side—and they had lights on.

Chellamuthu pondered the scene, wondering what he should do, where he should go, hardly believing that he'd actually made it out undetected.

By the time he heard the splashing sound from above, it was too late. A stream of tainted, smelly, warm water poured over him, as if warning the boy never to try escaping that way again! It oozed around him, cuddled him.

He sat in the dark, polluted, exhausted. His skin was itchy, scuffed, and raw, and another child's urine was now dripping in his eyes.

Chellamuthu didn't care.

He was free!

CHAPTER 11

Eli was whispering to Rajamani in the courtyard when Maneesh entered. They were hoping not to wake any of the children.

"I got your message," Maneesh said. "What's wrong?"

Rajamani excused himself and hurried away. Eli turned to greet Maneesh.

"This must be bad," Maneesh added.

"Why would you say that?"

"Rajamani rushed away like I have smallpox."

"We need to sit."

Maneesh followed Eli inside. "There's something I need to tell you about Chellamuthu, the boy who . . ."

"I know who Chellamuthu is. What about him?"

"He's gone!"

Arayi had wept most of the night after the astrologer had delivered the terrible news of Chellamuthu's death, after he'd packed up his carved table and his astrological charts, conveyed his deepest condolences, finished another good day's work, and headed home to eat dinner with his own family.

At first she'd believed him, and for several hours she mourned desperately for the loss of her little son. But she awoke before dawn the next day unable to shake a feeling that had soaked into her muscles and bones overnight. It insisted that the man was wrong. Perhaps he'd mixed up two stars, misread a line in his chart, inadvertently switched a planet.

Something. She couldn't put her feeling into words, except to say that at times a mother senses truth in ways that can never be logically explained.

A few days later, she sat in the home of Jagdish Prasad, another astrologer. She needed a second opinion.

Arayi had come to his home because it was less expensive, because the charts, she'd been assured, should read the same anywhere. He didn't have an ornate carved table, nor did he wear a crafted gold medallion. He used only a few charts, two maps, and a single book. He claimed to have learned the skill from his late father and was happy to use it now, for a tiny fee, to help others—in this case, a grieving mother.

He took less time than the first man, but he claimed to be just as sure in his conclusion. "If I am reading the signs correctly, and I believe that I am . . ."

Arayi fought the urge to cover her ears, to run from the house before he could deliver his reading. At least then she could cling to her hope, her instinct-fueled belief that Chellamuthu was still alive. If this man delivered the same message, then a mother's love—that force that overshadows all of the stars and planets and surely holds the universe together—wouldn't be real. The sun must cease to shine. Stars would fall from the sky. Planets would leap from their orbits, and the universe would implode.

Life itself would lose all meaning.

"Your son," the astrologer announced, "is not only alive and well . . ." He lifted the open book into better light. " . . . he is coming home at this very moment and will return to you soon."

Arayi exhaled. Could it be true? "How soon?" she pleaded. "How soon?"

Another check of the charts.

"Your son will be home by tomorrow night."

In the darkness outside the orphanage, Chellamuthu considered his two choices: walk toward what appeared to be the city center and look for someone who might be able to help or shun any people and head toward the edge of town, hoping to get far enough away to stay out of danger. He opted for the latter, resting for only a moment beside a rundown warehouse that sat across from a towering cement factory. At least he intended it to be only a moment.

It was the rumble of eager trucks pulling out of the yard with their weighty loads that stirred him awake—just in time to greet the sun rising over the busy building.

"*Muttal!*" he mumbled, annoyed at himself for not creating further distance in the dark when he'd had the chance. Now his only choice was to stay hidden, out of sight, until the sun set again in the evening.

His stomach wasn't convinced. He'd eaten little the previous day, and thankfully so, since he'd barely squeezed out through the opening.

The price now, however, was a complaining belly that sounded a lot like the heavy trucks.

And it wasn't just the rumbling that jabbed at his gut, but Eli's words. *Haven't we always given you plenty to eat?*

"Shut up!" Chellamuthu answered aloud, as he inched forward to get a better look at a man across the street.

The worker held a long green hose behind a chain-link fence, and as the cement trucks rounded the corner and stopped, the man would thoroughly spray down every truck, as if he were washing a parade of dirty elephants. Chellamuthu scratched at his scalp. The water looked . . . *wonderful.*

It wasn't enough that his stomach was being ornery, but every inch of his body was joining in to complain. His skin was more than just smelly, it was beginning to rash.

He'd tried last night to listen for a river, a place where he could scrub off the stink. They must have a river, he reasoned, because the street he'd been following was named Chenkatti Bridge Road. Every bridge he'd ever known had crossed water.

He strained his ears again and listened, just as the landowner had shown him. There were sounds all right, but nothing familiar. No Banerjee. No drunken father. No Manju. No cousins. No Erode. And no Kaveri.

If I could just get to the river, I could get home.

"Hey, boy!"

Chellamuthu spun around. A man in uniform was approaching—a policeman, perhaps, or a security guard from the cement factory. Chellamuthu said nothing.

"Come here, boy."

Perhaps he should have asked what the man wanted, or at least waited to find out. But the way he'd called him *boy,* raised the hair on Chellamuthu's neck.

Instead, the *boy* turned down dusty Chenkatti Bridge Road—and ran.

And ran, and ran, and ran.

"What if he goes to the police?" Maneesh said, pacing furrows in the courtyard dirt.

"He won't."

"Why not?"

"He believes that if he does, his family will go to jail."

"Where did he get that idea?" Maneesh asked.

Eli glanced at his partner. Why bother to explain?

"So you decry and belittle bribes," Maneesh needled, "but lies are fine?" It wasn't really a question.

"Perhaps it's not a lie," Eli replied. "Besides, you said yourself that everything has a price. I'm willing to pay it. We're helping them break free from poverty and pain. The boy will recognize that soon enough and come back."

Maneesh huddled in close. "I've been wondering, Eli. Are you trying to help children escape, or are you hoping to escape yourself?"

"Let's not do this again. I'm giving them a future . . ."

"But it's costing them their past. You're playing God."

"You don't know what you're saying," Eli replied.

"Don't I? Are there more? Besides the boy?"

"More what?"

"More children who've been taken from their families? Children who aren't really orphans?"

Eli's voice stiffened. "I've never forced a child to stay."

"You're fooling yourself—that's deception of the worst kind."

Eli stood. "Judge all you'd like, but if a child is kidnapped from hell and carried to heaven, should we condemn the kidnapper?"

Maneesh returned only a slight shake of his head as he headed to the door. "The difference," he added, "between a hero and a fiend is often razor thin. Be careful where you step, Eli."

Maneesh slipped outside, but before he closed the gate, Eli called out.

"There's something else about the boy's family you should know."

Chellamuthu's legs finally gave out on the edge of town, near a field of cotton where he stumbled to a stop and fell into the lukewarm shade of a tamarind tree. He was hungry and tired and thirsty and filthy—and lonely.

"Why can't you rain now, when I need it?" he asked the cloud-filled sky. But his words were shadowed by a bigger question: Why had his life taken this terrible turn? His mother would say that we choose our destinations when we choose our paths, that all choices have consequences. She had counseled him on many occasions to follow knowledge, duty, and devotion. He'd preferred following the path to the park, the river—stealing. Was he now being punished? Was this his reward for disobedience?

It was early afternoon when he gathered both the courage and the strength to stand. He'd decided he would walk back to the road and beg a ride, and he'd go with anyone, *wherever* they were going.

When he stood, a shimmer caught his eye. It was off the road a distance, and while there was no sound of water, it was deep and wide and waiting. It was larger than a pond but smaller than a lake, and though this body of water could never compare to the Kaveri, it welcomed him with outstretched arms.

Chellamuthu made his way to the edge, and oddly, as he waded into the water to rinse his deprived body clean, the silly song from the Lincoln Home bounced into his head:

Deep and wide, deep and wide,
There's a fountain flowing deep and wide.

The basin must have been fed by an underground spring, as the water was cool and clear, and he gulped big swallows until he was certain he would be sick.

He had no soap like the women at Lincoln Home, so instead, as his mother had once taught him back in Erode, he reached for something else that would take away the filth—handfuls of sand. He stripped off his shorts and shirt and used the sand to scrub at his arms, legs, neck, and chest. He even pressed handfuls of the gritty mixture into his hair and scalp, rubbing and rinsing it away until he felt clean. As an afterthought, he scooped up a fingerful of the grit and polished his teeth.

Once his body had been sufficiently scoured, he focused on his clothes, kneading them against both sand and rock, as he'd watched his mother do at the river, until they were equally clean.

Since there was no one around—and even if there had been—he placed his clothes on the twigs of nearby bushes to dry and rinsed his naked body again in the water, just because he could. Then he poked along the shore, hoping to find berries or something he could eat.

He recognized the plant immediately. It had broad leaves, purple flowers, hairy stems, and the scent of lemons. It was the same plant his mother had sent him to find so she could treat Manju. Knowing it was perfectly safe, he pulled off a leaf and pushed it into his mouth.

Chellamuthu parked himself on the ground near the water and pulled up his bare legs. He stared at the scars on his feet, put there so he'd remember the pain and make wiser choices. He should have taken the leaves back to his mother right away when Manju was so sick, rather than selfishly riding the elephant. He knew that. Perhaps if he had gone right back, his father wouldn't have burned his feet. He wouldn't have been taken. He wouldn't be lost, alone.

Choices have consequences.

Chellamuthu pushed his feet into the soft mud to cover the marks—but guilt is hard to hide. The mud seeped into the cut still healing on his foot, reminding him of a more recent shame, a persistent pestering that had been clamoring in his head and pinching at his heart since the stinky trough had given birth to his freedom.

He had left Anu.

She was ill and alone, and even after he'd promised to bring her water and help her get better, he'd left without telling her why. Would she understand? Would she be okay? Would she survive anyway? Why did it matter, now that he was free?

It was the scars that offered answers. He pulled his feet from the mud and stretched for the water to wash them clean. He longed to be home, if only for a moment, to tell his father that he no longer had to be disappointed in his son.

The scars were working!

Chellamuthu coiled around to face the plant. He would eat soon enough. Right now he needed a stick. Glancing around, he saw one in the mud nearby that would do nicely.

As he knelt beside the plant, the rustle of its leaves seemed to whisper a familiar word: *dharma.*

Arayi had kept the fire going until early the following morning—just in case. Despite the day's heat, she fell asleep in the hut and didn't wake until Jaya returned with Manju in the afternoon.

"I don't know who to believe," Arayi cried to her sister. "Is there no one who can tell me what happened to my son?"

Jaya couldn't answer. Or wouldn't.

It was time for Arayi to start cooking dinner, but she had no more fuel. She'd used up all of their wood the night before.

She stirred what was left in the fire—it was nothing but ash.

Kuppuswami sat in the dirt and slugged down the last of his palm toddy. It wasn't enough. He was still conscious, still aware, still unable to squelch the ache smoldering in his chest.

As he lay back down alongside the road, he pondered what to do.

Where does one turn when palm toddy isn't strong enough, when its arms are too short to reach down and choke out all the pain?

Kuppuswami had been walking along the proverbial edge for years. For many traversing a similar road, stumbling along life's brink, a crisis often serves to wake them up, pull them back to safety, save them from themselves. For others, like Kuppuswami, faltering on rocky crags, tragedy steps in like wind to nudge them off the edge of the cliff.

The broken man crawled toward the field of a neighbor who grew *ganja,* a cannabis plant that was technically illegal in India but could be grown and used for "medical and scientific" purposes, if the right people were paid. Kuppuswami could imagine no better medicine.

He picked a handful of the mature leaves and spread them on the ground in the sweltering sun. As soon as it was ready, he would roll it, light it, smoke it, and let it deaden the agony that was too heavy for him to carry alone.

While he waited, Kuppuswami studied the scar on his leg. Maybe if the *ganja* didn't work . . . he would find a real cliff.

Chellamuthu crouched in the dark outside the Lincoln Home for Homeless Children, peering at the begging bundle of leaves he'd left outside the gate for Anu. He was hidden behind a crate that had been dumped outside a building across the street, but he couldn't expect to stay unnoticed for long. He had come back without a plan—only resolve—and so far, it wasn't enough.

Hours earlier he'd watched Eli swing the door open, the metal pushing the roll of leaves and stems aside like garbage. His foot might even have brushed against it as he locked the door and then strode off into the night. How could he not see that help for Anu was right there, so close, pleading to be let in?

Chellamuthu had hoped that after Eli had hurried away, Mrs. Sundar would head for home and see the bundle of leaves on the ground. The problem was, she didn't always go home. It was just as common for her to stay the night . . . and even if she did see the leaves, there was no guarantee that she'd realize their purpose.

Chellamuthu's stomach growled its displeasure. Other than some rancid *adai* that he'd fished from a garbage can hours earlier, he'd had little to eat, and his body was letting him know.

What was he thinking? Why had he even bothered to come back?

The sound of scraping feet startled him. A man with a lantern was rounding the building from behind.

Once the children were finally asleep, Mr. Rajamani said goodnight to the women on duty and waddled to the door. He was six steps away when the pounding started. It wasn't a timid knock, but an authoritative one—the kind policemen use on official business. Perhaps it was news about the missing boy?

When Rajamani pulled the door open, Chellamuthu marched inside as if a delivery this time of night was normal. He didn't bother with a greeting. Instead, he held out a bundle of leaves.

"You have to boil them. That's what I watched my mother do, boil them 'til the water's green. Anu has to drink it two times a day, whether she likes it or not, 'cause Manju didn't like it, but Mother made her drink it anyway. And then boil the roots, but not too much, and mash them up and give her little bits with her food. If you do all this, she'll get better."

Stunned, Rajamani took the bundle. Then, as if Chellamuthu had never escaped from the compound at all, he hiked across the yard and through the doors to where the rest of the children slept.

Eli had gone home early with a piercing headache but had asked Rajamani to keep him informed if anything unusual happened. This likely qualified.

Rajamani followed the boy's steps across the yard and peeked inside the door. Chellamuthu had peeled off his shirt and was sitting on his mat, taking huge bites from an apple he'd retrieved from a basket beneath the table.

Rajamani scratched curiously at the edges of his moustache. Then, instead of fetching Eli, he dashed to the room beside the main office and rapped on the door.

"Akkā, wake up! Wake up! Hurry and boil some water!"

CHAPTER 12

Chellamuthu reached for the cup of fresh tea Mrs. Sundar had brewed for Anu.

"Can you take it to her by yourself?" she asked.

He wanted to hurl it back at the woman. Why did she ask, knowing that he was the one who brought back the leaves and that he'd been carrying Anu her tea every day this week? Why treat him like a child?

"Yes!" he answered, stomping his foot to the ground.

She smiled. "Then here you go."

As always, he walked it carefully across the yard, knowing it would take several minutes before it was cool enough to drink. For the first three days Anu hadn't been able to finish it without vomiting. The last four, however, her bucket had been clean. If she kept improving, Eli said she could move in with the rest of the children by the weekend.

Chellamuthu expected to feel heroic by helping Anu recover. Instead it was just hard work. Perhaps this was a secret that heroes don't share: Courage comes from doing common things. He wished his mother could see that he was helping. It was the first time he'd followed through with something so important. Knowing her son was making a difference would bring her joy.

When he reached Anu's door, it was closed. He balanced the cup carefully in one hand while turning the handle with the other. The room was quiet.

"Anu? It's me. I have your tea."

Arayi scraped her right knee against a seam in the stone floor, breaking her skin and causing it to bleed. She shifted her legs but stayed kneeling. She'd been at the Sri Kongalamman Temple in Erode since dawn. She had come today, yesterday, the day before that—and she would be here again early tomorrow.

She saw no alternative as the number of searchers dwindled to near zero and the astrologers had all been wrong. There had been no sign of Chellamuthu for weeks, no clue as to his whereabouts or disappearance, and the uncertainty was tearing at her heart like a lion. Hearing nothing was like having a wound that was picked open every day, with never a proper chance to heal. Without knowing what had happened to Chellamuthu, she would never find peace—*ever.*

Her penance had been to shave her head, worship at the temple, and leave offerings of food wrapped with a mother's pleadings that she hoped would flow to the ears of the goddess Kongalamman:

Bring back my son. He needs to be home.

Rather than rise to heaven, her words dropped like loose gravel covering the stone floor and making it painful to kneel.

Just before 8:00 in the evening, as the temple prepared to close, Jaya tiptoed in. She touched Arayi's arm. "Sister, it's time to go."

Jaya helped her stand.

"Manju?" Arayi asked, with sudden alarm. "Is my daughter well?"

"Yes, she's fine. I left her with Selvaraj."

The two stumbled to the entrance where Jaya steered her toward the steps. "Let's sit for just a moment," she said.

Arayi sat, waited.

Jaya inhaled. "Sister, we—all of the relatives—will continue to offer prayers and offerings that Chellamuthu will return safely. Every time we go to worship, the name of Chellamuthu will be in our minds and on our lips and in our hearts. Always! But, my dear sister, we are also praying for you, that you also may find your way home."

"What do you mean?"

"On the day Chellamuthu was lost, a mother was also lost." Jaya pressed close. "I just want you to know that we also pray for *your* safe return."

Sadness hung in the humid air, holding Arayi's lungs tight, forcing her to draw a breath to answer. "Jaya, if my son indeed continues to live, I won't be there to teach him about prayer walks and *pujas.* I will never hear him chant the *Gayatri Mantram.* How will he learn on his own about the offering of praises? Will he know to celebrate the four days of *Pongal* or the *Shivaratri?* Who will teach him these things? Who will teach my son?"

Hers was a voice drenched with desperation, like flailing hands hoping to stop a fall toward pointed rocks but grasping at nothing.

"Jaya, how will Chellamuthu find goodness?"

Jaya let the question settle as she gathered her words. "I don't bring answers, sister. I don't know. Perhaps there are times in life when we must simply let go and trust."

Trust who?

Arayi opened her mouth to answer, but sadness smothered her

objection. Her head drooped as Jaya continued. "There is one thing I do know. You have a daughter and a son still at home, and so many others . . . family who need you back."

Arayi clenched her eyes, swallowed her distress, and then softly wept.

Jaya wept beside her, holding her close.

When time nudged, they stood, steadied each other, and then stepped shoulder to shoulder onto the road.

Two sisters.

Heading home.

A smile had followed Rajamani around the courtyard all morning, so when Vikesh arrived—a boy who should have been in school—Chellamuthu wondered if something important was about to happen. Perhaps it was time to celebrate *Diwali,* the festival of lights. At home, his mother would arrange a row of small clay lamps in front of the hut, filling each with a touch of oil and a small wick and then letting Chellamuthu light them. Other children would sometimes set off firecrackers. But the best part of Diwali was that children would get sweets.

But it couldn't be Diwali, because there had been no special lights placed around the orphanage. No clay lamps. No candy. Chellamuthu was sure of that.

What, then?

Chellamuthu was trying to get Vikesh's attention when the door opened and Eli paraded in leading a tall, slender white man—a *very* white man. In fact, his skin was so pale that Chellamuthu wondered if the man was ill. His hair was a muddy red, his freckles looked like spice on rice, and in his hand he carried a small case. He pulled it open, bent back the lid, and placed it on a narrow folding table that reminded Chellamuthu of the fruit seller's cart at the Erode bus station.

The odd-looking man faced Eli and waited.

Eli looked out at the children as if expecting to quiet them, but except for a handful of fussing babies in the background, they were already at rapt attention with eyes cemented forward.

With a nod from Eli, the man took a step and bowed to the children, as if they were Indian royalty. "I am Chubby the Clown," he said in a squeaky, matter-of-fact voice, and then he waited, as if expecting the children to laugh. However, he was speaking English, and since the children spoke only Tamil, Eli stepped up to translate.

Chubby politely thanked them for attending before taking from his case a dangly piece of what looked to be red yarn. Chubby held it to his lips and blew.

Everyone but the babies gasped.

As it filled with air, the red string sprouted to the thickness of a *Himangi* cucumber, growing in his hands to nearly a meter in length.

Mouths opened. Eyes widened. Some children edged forward to get a closer look, while others scooted away in fear.

"It's a *balloon,*" Chubby said. Eli struggled to find a proper name in Tamil, ultimately settling on *great rubber tube of wonder.*

Chubby then knotted the end that had been touching his lips and with a flick of his wrist, tossed it out toward the children.

IT FLOATED!

While some gasped, others giggled.

As the wondrous object drifted toward the ground by Anu, who'd been feeling well enough to come, she reached out to knock it back toward him.

Chubby the clown could have packed up his case and trotted out of Lincoln Home right then and the children would have talked about the great rubber tube of wonder for days. But the man was just getting started. He selected another balloon, this one blue, and within the space of a breath, blew it into a second floating cucumber—and then more magic followed. He grabbed the first and twisted it with the second, and right before the children's eyes, he formed a flower.

He stepped to Anu, called her *princess,* and gallantly handed his creation to her. She giggled—the first laughter Chellamuthu had heard from the girl.

And for the greater part of an hour, Chubby, the white, skinny, red-headed clown who spoke only English wove his magic balloons into monkeys and trees and lions and fish and crocodiles and elephants and bears and beetles and swords and crowns—and the laughter and shouts of those inside the Lincoln Home for Homeless Children wafted over the outer wall and soared up into an awe-filled sky.

Chellamuthu forgot about Erode and his family.

Anu forgot about the pains still stabbing at her side.

Rajamani took pictures of Vikesh and Chellamuthu holding their prizes and then let them play for longer than usual in the yard.

Later, as Chellamuthu lay on his mat in the great room holding his balloon snake—an irony for certain—he remembered that Chubby had promised the snake would protect him. It was a notion about snakes that he'd never considered.

That night, the first in a very long time, Chellamuthu slept soundly. He dreamed of climbing trees and chasing tigers and eating bananas and licking his mother's curry from his freshly dipped fingers.

By morning, the snake that was to protect Chellamuthu was withered and limp. It had died in the night. Some of the other children's balloon animals lasted longer, but by the third day, all were gone. And it was on that third day—cloudy and dreary—that hope, like Chubby, hurried out the front door.

Chellamuthu was sitting with Anu and a younger toddler who were attempting to stack a pile of rocks they had collected when Anu closed her eyes and slumped forward. Chellamuthu shouted for help, and Rajamani was instantly there. The man picked up Anu, made certain she wasn't choking, and carried her to the white-doored room.

The doctor arrived an hour later and stayed until the sun had almost set. Eli wouldn't allow Chellamuthu to wait inside, so the boy stood close enough in the courtyard to see the worried doctor leave with a lowered head and sagging eyes.

Chellamuthu lingered in the shadows until Rajamani spotted him. After scolding the boy for not minding his own business, he divulged that Anu was awake and improving. The man delivered brave words, but they floated to the ground like Chubby's balloons, burdened with doubt.

Chellamuthu lay on his mat until most of the children were asleep and then crept beside Anu's door to listen. He had to know for himself how the girl was doing.

Maneesh had arrived. He and Eli were inside.

Chellamuthu peeked through a crack. The men's backs were to him, but he could hear their voices.

"What more can we do?" Maneesh asked, waving his hand in the direction of the girl.

Eli turned slightly. Chellamuthu could see him pinching at his lips by lamplight. "There is one other option," he said.

"I'm listening." When Maneesh leaned closer, so did Chellamuthu.

"We send her now," Eli answered.

"To America? Like this? She'll never survive."

Chellamuthu was nodding with him in the dark. Maneesh was right.

Eli wasn't finished. "Once the parents pay, and the child is sent . . ."

"I don't believe what I'm hearing," Maneesh interrupted, with noisy breath. "You're the one now concerned about the money?"

Eli faced the sleeping girl. He spoke softly, as if his voice was swathed in cotton. Chellamuthu pushed the door open just a crack more to hear. "You misunderstand, my friend," Eli said "I don't care about the money. I'm trying to save Anu."

"Then what are you saying?"

"I'm saying that once the family has paid, they'll keep her, help her. American hospitals and American doctors mean more advanced tests and treatments. It's risky for Anu to travel, but it may be the only way to really help her."

Maneesh turned, mouth open, hands in the air in either protest or surrender. But Chellamuthu heard no words.

"How soon can we have documents ready?" Maneesh finally asked, apparently conceding.

"It will take at least a week," Eli replied. "In the meantime, I'll keep giving her the medicine the boy brought back. It's the only thing that seems to help."

"Agreed then. Do it. Make the arrangements."

"No!" Chellamuthu shouted as he pushed through the door.

The men spun in unison. Maneesh was the first to step forward. He raised his arm to stop the boy, then grabbed him by the shoulder to twist him around.

"Let him be," Eli said, stooping down to meet him. "Chellamuthu, if we don't try, she could die. By sending her to America, she'll have a chance to live."

"But you don't know that! I heard you say that you don't know."

"I won't lie to you. We *don't* know—we can never be certain. That's how life is. Sometimes all we have is hope."

It wasn't good enough. "What if she dies?" he asked.

Just then Anu stirred. Her eyes opened as she motioned for water. While Eli reached for the cup in the nearby bucket, Maneesh ushered Chellamuthu toward the door. "Let's let her rest, shall we?"

He pushed Chellamuthu outside and shoved the door closed. Chellamuthu pressed his ear up against the wood.

The first voice was Eli's. "We still have plenty of the plant. I'll have Rajamani give her a good dose now, and we'll keep her on it for a week. I'll push the family. If all goes well, she'll soon be in America."

Maneesh still didn't sound convinced. "Are we saving her or killing her?"

Eli didn't hesitate. "We're saving her, Maneesh—we're saving them all."

"Hello? Anyone here?"

Arayi circled around to the front of the hut to find a boy calling. He was about twelve and stood beside an old bike whose basket cradled half a dozen packages. He glanced up and studied Arayi's face, as if it would help him verify that he'd found the correct house. Just to be certain, he pulled a written list from his pocket.

"I am looking for . . . Mrs. Arayi . . . ?" He checked for the last name, but it wasn't necessary.

"Yes, yes, that's me."

"I have a delivery for you," he said, as he reached for the wrapped box on the bottom. "We apologize for the delay."

Before her son disappeared, receiving a parcel would have been unusual for the family. But since the frightful event, packages had been arriving with regularity from relatives and friends. Their contents varied: sometimes food, sometimes a few rupees. Most often, well-wishers sent flowers, candles, incense or a small figurine of a god to include in the family's humble shrine.

Arayi thanked the boy and then carried the parcel inside. She sat cross-legged on the ground to unwrap what looked to be a book. It was clad in heavy brown paper and was taped so thoroughly at each end that it took seconds of wrestling to finally convince the tape to let go. When it did, the contents slid out and dropped into the woman's lap in full view.

Arayi pushed the wrapping paper aside. Her eyes squinted, widened, and squinted again, as if they couldn't believe what they were seeing. Once her head had signaled to her heart that something was wrong, it began pumping blood so fast that the woman felt faint and had to touch the ground so as not to tip.

It was their family portrait, taken by the photographer at Suresh's wedding, mounted in a gold-leafed frame that Chellamuthu had helped his mother select.

Emotions, already in full sprint, spun around to clarify: *Should we be happy or sad?* Even the pain that had started pressing against her ribs seemed confused.

In a city of so many people, it was doubtful that the proprietor who'd sent the box would have known about little, lost Chellamuthu. Had the man known, he surely would never have dropped off the gift so casually.

Arayi had forgotten it was coming, and considering what had happened since that night, it was a treasure, a picture of her family—with her son Chellamuthu—that she would hang on the wall of her hut to help her remember better times.

Of course, it was also a scourge. The mischievous boy smiling back from the wall would constantly remind Arayi that she would probably never see her Chellamuthu alive again.

She clutched the photo against her chest and rolled over in a ball on the dirt floor—perhaps to hide the picture, perhaps to protect it. She let go with a single hand and smashed her palm against her lips. No matter how bad it hurt to not scream out, she wouldn't let the neighbors hear her cry again.

CHAPTER 13

Fred and Linda Rowland believed in second chances. How could they not? It was a second marriage for both, and this one was working. Not that there weren't differences, with both carting around their share of baggage. They'd simply learned that life was easier when two grabbed onto one handle.

"Are we ready for this?" Linda asked as Fred signed his name to the wire transfer that would send $5,000 of their hard-earned money directly to the Lincoln Home for Homeless Children in faraway India. The payment would not only deplete their emergency and vacation funds but wipe out all the money they'd saved for Christmas. And perhaps the next Christmas as well.

Fred's head lowered as he turned. "I'd imagined that girls would be more expensive. I just didn't realize it would start immediately."

He wore a stern face, and the listening bank manager glanced at Linda to see if he was joking. Linda smiled.

When Fred and Linda were first introduced—teaching at the same high school—she wasn't sure about the man either. He always appeared to be so irritated. It took her weeks to realize that his features, like those of a bulldog, were simply stuck that way. They laughed about it now, but on their first date, when he'd pasted on a fake smile to overcompensate, he'd looked so awkward and uncomfortable that she'd asked him to take her home right after dinner, certain he wasn't feeling well.

Both had long since grown accustomed to his façade, a look that had served him well, considering his occupation. Fred Rowland was a boys' PE teacher.

It wasn't that he couldn't have achieved more in life. When they'd met, he had already earned a master's degree in exercise science from ASU and a doctorate in biology from Stanford. He could have taught at almost any university. But when all was said and done, Fred Rowland, the man Linda fell in love with and married, was a man with a tolerant heart who wanted to make a difference teaching boys.

There was more. In addition to PE, he taught biology and early morning driver's ed. In his spare time, he coached the Mountain View High School All-State Wrestling Team.

If Fred was the gritty bulldog, Linda was the social poodle. The tiny blonde was attractive but unassuming, ambitious but teachable, focused but inclusive. In reality, Linda could have run a small country if given the chance. She was also a believer, a woman of faith who wasn't afraid to jump into a problem and get her hands dirty whenever God was slow to do His part—which was fairly often, in her estimation.

After teaching high school, she moved on to the university. When she grew weary of the bureaucracy (too many smart people in too small a space), she decided to try her hand at sales and was soon the managing broker at a local real estate firm.

There was nothing she couldn't do—except have children.

After eight years of trying—prayers, potions, pills, and positions—they gave in and adopted their first baby, a boy, Rux, from Arizona, whose birth mother was only fifteen. A year and a half later, another call came—why were they always at 2:00 a.m.?—and a second boy, Josh, from Nevada, was added to the family.

Like most mothers, she yearned for a daughter to giggle with, take shopping, stay up with until all hours talking boys, first kisses, pierced ears, and fashion. When the third call came from a corporate attorney in Albuquerque asking if they were interested in adopting another child, her hopes bloomed. The man had learned of Fred and Linda through a mutual friend, and when Linda asked why he seemed so insistent, he confided that the teen mother placing the baby for adoption was his granddaughter and that she wanted the baby to go to a loving family.

Linda's first question was obvious. "Is the baby a girl?"

It was still early in the pregnancy and ultrasounds hadn't yet determined the gender. By the time they had, Linda had already made space in her heart and her home. The baby, a boy they named Jarem, joined the family.

With three active boys, the Rowlands considered themselves done—until a family they'd met when adopting their first child (adopting parents are a tight-knit group) called to announce they were finally getting a baby girl through an orphanage in India. They encouraged Linda to at least inquire.

It took three weeks for Linda to collect enough nerve to write a letter, and even after it was mailed, she wasn't sure she'd be ready for the response. When it came and a little girl's picture dropped out of the envelope, Linda cried for two days.

It was finally happening! They would fax back the application, wire their payment, and hopefully within a few short weeks their family would be complete.

Linda squeezed Fred's hand. A little girl in India needed them. More important, they needed that little girl. Finally, after so much hope, so many prayers, and such painful longing, Linda Rowland would be getting a daughter.

Anu spent most of the week resting in the room behind the white door. Chellamuthu knew she'd be leaving for America soon, and not knowing if the news would make her happy or sad, he said nothing.

On Saturday night before the children went to sleep, she told Chellamuthu that she was feeling better and asked him if he would go to the kitchen and get her more *Kootu*.

On Sunday morning, when he walked over to ask if she'd be strong enough to sing with the children by the fountain, her room was empty. Chellamuthu checked the kitchen, the lower office, and the room where Rajamani kept his things. He asked Mrs. Sundar, who was folding clothes in the courtyard, but she claimed to be too busy to talk and shooed him away a bit too quickly.

One last time, Chellamuthu ran back to the room where the children slept, thinking perhaps Anu was resting under a mat in the corner and that he'd just missed seeing her. When she wasn't there, Chellamuthu even climbed the stairs alone to check in Eli's office, a place where the children were forbidden to go.

One thing was certain—Anu was gone.

Three hours later, well after singing time should have started, the door beside the gate clanked open, and Eli and Rajamani trudged in.

"Shall I gather the children by the fountain?" Chellamuthu heard Rajamani ask in a somber tone.

"In a moment," Eli replied. He had already spied Chellamuthu approaching.

"Where's Anu?" Chellamuthu asked impatiently, before the man had a chance to speak.

"Please, come with me," Eli answered. Every inch of the man looked fatigued. His eyes were blood-red, as if he'd been out all night drinking. After they arrived in his office and sat, Eli edged close. "Chellamuthu, I have something very important to tell you, and I need you to listen to my words carefully. Can you do that?"

The boy dropped his chin to agree.

"I'm sorry, but Anu . . . left last night."

"Left? To where?"

Eli inhaled so deeply that Chellamuthu wondered if the man's chest might burst. Then, like a used balloon, it deflated until there was barely anything left. "Chellamuthu," he said, pausing again as if every word deserved individual attention, "Anu . . . went to America last night."

Like blows coming from his father, the words stung even before making contact.

"To America?" Chellamuthu asked.

"It was unexpected," Eli added. "We didn't realize the family would be taking her so quickly."

Chellamuthu shuddered. It was not what Eli had said but the way he'd said it, as if he'd rolled a piece of bitter melon in sugar and was now passing it off as candy.

"While we will miss her, it was also a blessing. She was unwell and in pain. Now she doesn't have to worry. She is with a family who loves her. She can run and play and laugh, just like the rest of the children. Yes, Chellamuthu, Anu is very happy in America."

And then he leaned so close Chellamuthu could sniff his breath. It smelled sad. "Do you see what I'm telling you?" Eli asked, waiting to be certain. "Do you understand?"

Chellamuthu tensed. He hated it when adults asked him that question. He sat motionless—without so much as a nod—holding the answer between his lips until his head could reason with his heart. Chellamuthu detested Eli for lying to him, for telling him that Anu had gone to America when Eli knew—when they both knew—that Anu had died in the night.

And yet, wasn't that Eli's point? He had told the truth without ever uttering the words aloud. He was letting Chellamuthu choose the level of heartache he could bear. He was coloring misery with hope. His cruel lie was compassionate.

"What time did she leave?" Chellamuthu asked.

Eli's eyes tightened. "It was shortly after the children went to bed," he said.

"Did it take long for her to get to America?" Chellamuthu asked.

"No, Chellamuthu. The journey was very quick."

"Was she happy?"

"She was very happy—and peaceful."

Chellamuthu reached inside to pull out another question, but he found the bucket empty.

Without saying another word, without crying, he climbed down the stairs and returned to the mat where he retrieved the picture he'd drawn of his family. He took a pencil from the box Rajamani kept on the desk and, in a space between his brother Selvaraj and his sister Manju, Chellamuthu drew the face of Anu.

Then, as carefully as he'd retrieved it, he placed the picture back between the two blank sheets of protective paper and hid the treasure again beneath his mat.

Anu was finally happy in America.

Eli pulled the old typewriter close, the trusted servant that had written so many letters to help the children in the orphanage find a home.

This letter would be no different.

> *Dear Mr. and Mrs. Rowland,*
>
> *I am writing about the girl you were to bring into your loving family. I am sorry to tell you that she did not get better. Even with our constant medical attention, she has passed away.*
>
> *While this news brings sadness to us all, God is not without purpose or a plan. Another child at Lincoln Home for Homeless Children desires to be part of your loving family. Chellamuthu was abandoned as an orphan and has no family. While he is a male child, he is very young.*
>
> *Chellamuthu is just . . .*

Eli's fingers hovered over the keys while his brain considered what to type. In truth, he didn't know Chellamuthu's actual age. But also, in truth, typing the number that was tingling the tips of his fingers would be a blatant lie.

As a lifelong Christian, he was well aware of the ninth commandment. *Thou shalt not bear false witness.* Yet also as a lifelong Christian, he believed as Matthew had preached, that one should not turn away a little child, for of such is the kingdom of heaven.

If he typed an accurate number, the family—any family—would reject the boy, sight unseen. Eli knew from experience that it was almost impossible to place an older child.

However, if he lied and put down the age they wanted to hear, it was unlikely that a family, as they stood with welcoming arms at the airport, would do anything but accept and love the child. In this case, lying meant he could save another boy.

He typed the rest of the line:

> *Chellamuthu is just 3.*

Was it worth it? Could he live with such deception? Eli reached behind his neck to scratch at his scars.

Absolutely.

And if God disagreed, well, he could cast Eli down to hell when judgment time came. But for now, while his heart was still beating in his body and his lungs were still pulling in air, he would do whatever it would take to save a child.

He finished the letter.

> *I commend your goodness, your desire. Orphans have no one to watch over them. They need to be cared for and loved. It can be a thankless job, but it is one that comes with its rewards.*
>
> *He who keeps the orphans keeps them from harm, watches over their lives, their comings and goings. He keeps them like a shepherd keeps his flock.*
>
> *To that end, may God bless us all as we turn tragedy into hope.*
>
> *With kind regards,*
> *Eli Manickam, Orphanage Commissioner*

CHAPTER 14

When Linda Rowland was frustrated, she would bake. She found that the straightforward directions of most recipes helped clear her head, that mixing batter was an activity she could do with Rux and Josh, and when they were finished, they'd have something that was both appreciated and delicious.

With Eli's letter sitting open on the table, Linda had orange rolls cooking in the lower oven, cranberry pumpkin bread baking in the top, and she was now mixing chocolate chip cookie dough that she was starting to eat raw.

Adopting children was always a roller-coaster ride, but with this latest go-around, Linda was getting nauseated. Her heart now ached for the girl who would never leave India, but she also fretted for the boy who was still there waiting.

For good or bad, when God had baked Linda, he double measured her compassion. Questions swirled with the aroma of the breads.

Was all this mess just part of God's master plan? Was this boy,

Chellamuthu, meant to be part of our family? How am I to know for certain?

A friend of Linda's from church insisted that God was *always* in charge. If that was true, then why, at times, did he seem so unorganized?

"How do we know, Fred?" she asked as they sat that evening at the table eating warm rolls she'd just pulled out of the oven. "How do we know if this is actually God's doing or just . . . bureaucrats?"

Fred smiled. "Maybe He uses bureaucrats. Perhaps they're cheaper, easier to manipulate."

She wasn't ready for his humor. "You're okay with another boy, then? When do we stop—at a football team?"

She didn't have to ask. The answer was leaking from his eyes. "I teach PE," he said, with a grin. "What's one more boy? The issue is that *you* need to be okay with it."

Her head shook back and forth, like a puppy with a toy. "Argh! How am I supposed to know? God can be *so* frustrating?"

"Maybe we aren't," Fred answered.

"Aren't what?"

"Supposed to know. Perhaps there are times He trusts us enough to move forward without giving us every little answer."

"Little?"

He waited for more, but she was grinding her teeth.

"Nothing to add?" Fred wondered.

Her reply was curt and clear.

"I think I'll make some muffins."

The next communication from Eli wasn't a letter. It was a telegram. Linda tore it open as if it contained money. Her eyes darted line to line. Hopefully this was good news about their son.

> Dear Mr. & Mrs. Rowland,
>
> Thank you for your patience and faith. May God bless you and your loving family. In our country there are many fees to arrange the proper paperwork. Unfortunately, it has been more costly than expected. Kindly send another $400 as soon as possible to cover these unforeseen costs.
>
> Soon you will welcome your son into your caring family.
>
> Kind regards,
> Eli Manickam, Orphanage Commissioner

Linda's jaw clenched. Her posture stiffened. "It's not right," she murmured.

The letter didn't just smell fishy. It was downright rotten. Had such a request happened just once, she would have ignored the issue. Last time it was money for the girl's medical expenses. Now it was unforeseen costs for the boy. She knew full well that this was the nature of foreign adoptions, to throw money into a hole of hope and then pray that one day a child would pop out—but there was a limit.

"Take my money," she said, "but don't you dare start jerking around my boy."

At church on Sunday, a lesson had been given about a girl praying to God to protect the birds that her brother was trying to catch in his traps. While it was a common Christian story that Linda had heard many times before, the ending always made her smile.

At first the little girl prayed that the birds wouldn't fly into the traps. Next, she prayed that if they did, the traps would malfunction. Lastly, the girl went outside and kicked all of her brother's traps into teeny little pieces.

Linda didn't need to call Fred. He'd back up her decision. The time for prayer and patience was past. It was time for Linda to start kicking some traps.

She hurried to the phone and punched in the number of her friend Jessica. After the niceties, she skipped right to her question. "Jessica, how's your brother the senator doing?"

"Busy. Why do you ask?"

"Honestly? I need a favor."

"What's up?"

"I know the senator is always swamped, but we've already paid this orphanage in India nearly $5,500, and I just got another letter asking for $400 more. I don't want to be unreasonable, but I get the feeling they're trying to take advantage of us, and I was hoping that, well . . ."

"You'd like me to see if he'll make a few calls? Rattle some chains?"

"That would be amazing. Is that possible?"

"Did you vote for him?"

Linda laughed. "I'll vote for him twice next time."

"I'll see him tomorrow. Don't stress—he loves assignments like this. I'll have him call the consulate, and they'll get to the bottom of it. Now, if I remember correctly, he flies back to Washington on Friday. Can you get me copies of your paperwork?"

"I'm on my way! I'll bring them now—and I hope you know you're my favorite friend in the world!"

Linda made three copies of everything and then drove toward town. She glanced in the rearview mirror and brushed back her hair. "Don't mess with Blondie," she snarled to a man half a world away. "You have no idea who you're dealing with."

CHAPTER 15

Maneesh sat at Eli's desk waiting for him to arrive. He added up pending payments, studied a list of current children, then sorted the names of hopeful parents.

When the phone rang, a woman in the adjacent room answered it and then entered. "Sorry to interrupt, sir."

"What is it?"

"The phone. They asked for Mr. Eli, but he isn't here, and I thought you would want to take it."

"Why, who is it?"

"The police, the head constable. He wants to come and visit. He says he's bringing someone from the American consulate!"

Chellamuthu awoke early, used the cement trough, and washed his face in the fountain. Vikesh would arrive soon, and the two had already drawn up grand battle plans.

Then a car outside the gate honked. Nobody came. It honked again—long and loud.

"I'm coming. I'm coming!" Eli rushed from his office but jarred to a stop when he saw Chellamuthu standing there. "I was just coming to get you," he said to the boy.

Mrs. Sundar stepped from behind Eli lugging two large suitcases, as if she and Eli had decided to run off together. She glanced down at Chellamuthu and passed him a polite smile—one that also appeared to carry a secret. She leaned in to Eli. "Tell me again which ones?"

Eli cupped his mouth so Chellamuthu couldn't hear. As Mrs. Sundar listened, her eyes scooted back to the boy and then toward the room where the children slept. She nodded her understanding. "I'll be right back."

Eli swung the gate wide and a van entered. While the driver loaded the two suitcases into the vehicle, Eli bent down.

"I have exciting news for you, Chellamuthu. We have found a family in America who wants to adopt you. Do you know what that means?"

Chellamuthu wrenched back. "But I already have a family!" he protested.

It was an argument Eli would never win. "Chellamuthu, you are going to have a remarkable life. Trust me. You will see. Now get in the van. You get to ride on an airplane!"

Mrs. Sundar returned with a baby in each arm. One of the younger toddlers was trailing her, lassoed by the woman's words of encouragement.

It was all happening so fast. Why hadn't they warned him? Why couldn't Eli have said something about this last night? Why hadn't Chellamuthu run when he'd had the chance?

"I don't want to go," he declared, hardly believing the words himself as they spilled from his mouth. "I'm playing with Vikesh today!" he protested, as if that would be sufficient reason to let him stay.

"Chellamuthu, it's normal to be nervous," Eli said in a half-hearted attempt at sympathy as he lifted the boy up onto the seat. He motioned for him to sit against the far window.

The van was clean, and the driver was smiling. But neither fact prevented the smells, sounds, and suspicions of Chellamuthu's first kidnapping from sitting right there beside him. When he twisted around to crawl out, Eli was blocking his way.

"I can't go to America," he said. "We're defending the Khyber Pass."

The driver smiled. Eli smiled. After Mrs. Sundar climbed in beside the children, the doors slammed closed. The van had just started to move when Chellamuthu hollered, "Wait! I forgot something! Please . . . I . . . I have to go to the bathroom!"

Perhaps it was the utter despair that scratched in his voice or the panic dripping like tears from his eyes that begged Eli to reach into his heart and grant the boy a last request. "Please, hold up for a second."

When the driver obliged, Eli pushed the door open to let Chellamuthu step down. "Hurry—and while you're at it, get your sandals."

Chellamuthu ran across the yard and would have kept running if there had been any place to hide. Instead, he stopped beside his sleeping mat, pulled up on the corner, and retrieved the picture he'd so carefully drawn of his family. It was still sandwiched between two sheets of plain paper, and while he hated to fold it, he had no choice.

He trudged back to the waiting van, and without any further delay, the vehicle pulled out from the yard and onto the street that led toward the airport. Eli was busy now checking through the paperwork to make sure all was in order. Mrs. Sundar was rocking one baby, dangling her fingers in front of the other, and vocally assuring the restless toddler sitting at her side that all was well.

Chellamuthu glanced back at the walls and building that had been his home. The van was half a block away and gaining speed, so Chellamuthu couldn't be certain, but just as the Lincoln Home for Homeless Children disappeared into the clutter of the surrounding buildings, he thought he saw Vikesh at the outer door reaching up to knock.

His next words were a whisper.

"I didn't even get to say good-bye."

A day earlier, standing beside both Eli Manickam and a district judge in Coimbatore, four different women took money to swear they were the sole living parent of their named child—two babies, a toddler, and an older boy—recently placed at the Lincoln Home for Homeless Children.

Each affirmed she was an unfit mother and completely unable to provide proper care while expressing a heartfelt desire that her child be given up to a better family in a country with more opportunity. Three of the women actually cried.

Once the judge was also paid, the proper papers were signed, stamped, and prepared.

Eli dabbed at his face with his sleeve. Saving children was not only arduous, it could be expensive. Greed, it turns out, has long fingers.

Although Eli and the children were ready to leave the country, the cogs of paperwork at the American consulate in Chennai weren't quite as easy to grease. It had taken hours of sitting in sticky waiting rooms before three of the four children were cleared and permitted to board the flight.

But there was a problem with the last boy—an older boy with a runny nose and scarred feet.

Ring, ring, ring . . .

Linda stirred. Fred didn't move.

Ring, ring, ring . . .

She lifted her head and glanced at the clock. *3:07 a.m.*

Ring, ring, ring . . .

She rolled up from the bed and grabbed at the receiver. Her voice was shaky and faint. "Hello?"

"Hello, ma'am. Is this Linda Rowland, wife of Fred Rowland?" The voice reaching through the phone was both low and formal, sounding almost like a marketing call. All Linda could think was, *What a terrible way to start a conversation at three in the morning.* He continued, "I'm very sorry to call so late . . . err . . . early. It's urgent, and with the time difference, well, I had no choice."

Time difference? "Please, who is this? What is this about?"

"Mrs. Rowland, my name is Matt Conway. I'm calling from the consulate general's office in Chennai, India."

"What is it? Is everything okay?"

"I'm not sure. Are you adopting a boy from India named Chellamuthu?"

A breath. A pause. "Yes. What's wrong?"

"Ma'am, I'm sorry to be the one to tell you this, but I'm processing the paperwork, and it says that Chellamuthu is three years old."

"Yes, that's correct. The boy we're adopting is three. Does that matter?"

The sound of the man exhaling raced more than eight thousand miles through the phone to land in her bedroom clear as day. "The boy is standing here in front of me, and regardless of what the paperwork says, there is no way in hell—excuse my language—this boy is only three."

"Well . . . how old is he?" It was Linda's turn to sigh.

"The kids here are sometimes smaller, so it can be hard to tell. Best case, ma'am . . . maybe seven or eight. Realistically . . . more like nine."

Fred was sitting up now. "Honey, what is it? What are they saying?"

Linda didn't move, didn't flinch, couldn't speak. How could she take a boy who was already older than her other children? She'd read the articles. She knew what problems that could cause.

Mr. Manickam had said that the boy was three!

"Ma'am? Are you there?"

A second passed . . . and then a dozen . . . and a dozen more. The man must have known they were still connected because Linda was both puffing and growling into the phone.

"Ma'am? Would you like us to still send you the boy?"

The pressure in her chest was racing for her throat. It would take but a moment before the mix of anger and sorrow would begin to wrestle with her heart, making it difficult to stay composed.

"I'm sorry, Mr. Conway," she finally said. "Please give me your number. I'm going to have to call you back."

Eli approached the man at the desk one more time, serving him the same argument. "As I said, it was a simple mistake in the paperwork.

His birthday is off by a couple of years. Don't penalize the boy for that."

The man quit typing, glanced up, looked Eli square in the eyes. "A couple of years? Are you telling me, sir, that you really believe this boy is just five?"

Eli's entire body shrugged. "Perhaps six."

Seeing the man wasn't buying, Eli nervously checked his watch. An hour longer and they'd miss their flight.

"Look, Mr. . . . Manickam," the man said as his smile grew wider. "Nothing's changed. It's like I told you already, and I don't expect to have to tell you again. If Mrs. Rowland calls back and says she is okay with his age, then I'll let the boy board."

His voice deepened. "But if she's not, I can tell you as sure as Indians love their curry, this boy won't be leaving India."

Linda rocked gently back and forth as she sat beside Fred on the edge of the bed. She'd wept. She'd paced. She'd cussed. She'd screamed. She'd come full circle and wept again. It didn't take long to rest and reload.

"It's not right! First, he was supposed to be a girl. Then, he was a three-year old boy. Now, we find out our 'baby' is eight! EIGHT! If we take him, there will be problems. He'll be older than our boys. He doesn't speak English. He'll have bonding issues. He'll never have the chance to be cradled in my arms as a baby. How can we take an older boy, Fred? How could these people do this? It's not right! It's just not."

Her complaining voice was beginning to stumble.

"I think we've established it's not right," Fred added, purposely keeping his own voice calm. He draped his arm across her shoulders, hoping to head off more tears. "The question we need to answer, however, is *What do we do now?*"

He took the momentary lull in her frustration to make one point clear. "Linda, whatever we decide, we shouldn't feel pressured. Mr. Manickam misrepresented the child's age, pure and simple."

"He lied!"

"Okay, he lied—and if we decide to say no, to walk away, that doesn't make us horrible people. We do have other children to consider."

"Plus it's not fair to the boy," Linda added, a point she'd missed in her previous objections.

"It isn't fair to anybody," Fred confirmed.

There was only her breathing. Her arms folded across her chest. "What we decide now will change the rest of his life—and ours. We can't mess this up. This isn't gym class. The bell isn't going to ring and send everyone home."

"There is another way to look at it," Fred added, brightening.

"What's that?"

Fred straightened. "If he was three but we found out that he was missing an arm, would we still take him?"

Linda didn't hesitate. "Naturally."

"What if he had diabetes?"

"Sure, but . . ."

"Linda, he's eight." He let it sink in. "I can think of worse ailments."

She hated it when he was right. Her face didn't smile, but it also didn't frown. Without a word, she picked up the phone and dialed. Fred's eyebrows arched.

Had they decided?

"Mr. Conway? This is Linda Rowland calling back." Her question was simple. "When will our son be arriving?"

It was only after she'd placed the phone back in the receiver for the second time that night that she looked heavenward. She even pointed her finger.

"God, if this isn't your doing," she said, "this momma is gonna be ticked!"

On the plane, Eli was holding one baby and Mrs. Sundar was cradling the other. The toddler sat between them. Eli let Chellamuthu sit by the window, and as the plane took off, the man seemed to be more entertained watching Chellamuthu than anything else around him.

"We'll be flying to Germany," he said as they gained altitude. "We're meeting two families there at the airport who are adopting the babies. From there, we head to America."

Chellamuthu looked up through swollen eyes but said nothing.

"It will be quite a long ride," Eli assured him. "You might want to get some sleep."

As an afterthought he added, "Let me know when you have to go to the bathroom. They have one onboard, but I'll need to show you how to use it."

Chellamuthu glanced toward the rear of the plane in the direction Eli had pointed. He pictured a cement trench, a sloshing bucket of water, and a carefully placed hole in the tail of the plane where the waste would drop through onto those watching from below.

That would be something.

He might have to pretend he needed to go, even if he didn't.

It was late afternoon, and with the weather clear, Chellamuthu spent the next hour gazing down at the melding lines of rivers, roads, towns and cities, wondering if it was the same view that Shiva and the other gods had as they watched over India.

With the passing of each distant city, he also wondered, *Could that be Erode? Is Mother on the ground looking up?*

He closed his eyes. Erode was getting farther and farther away.

Will I ever find my way back?

The woman was perhaps forty, stirring a kettle of sambar over a fire. She didn't look like an astrologer at all, and for a moment Arayi hesitated.

"Can you tell me about my son?" Arayi asked.

"Only if you pay my fee."

Reluctance held Arayi but only for a moment. She handed the woman money.

"Wait here," she instructed, leaving her cooking kettle on the fire to head inside.

She returned with a ream of loose paper, pages scribbled with writing. While the others had at least played the part, this woman barely tried.

"Sit here on the ground beside me."

"How long have you been an astrologer?" Arayi asked as she sat.

"I have had an interest for years. I learned from my grandfather. I've only been practicing since he passed. A few months." The woman moved, swayed, chewed a mouthful of betel nuts in rhythm. If she read Arayi's disappointment, it didn't show.

"You said your son is missing? You want to know if he'll return?"

A nod.

"I need the times and dates."

As fast as Arayi could recite them, the woman flipped her pages. She thumbed them like a deck of cards, forward and back. Reading quickly and then moving on. Forward and back. Back and forward. Each page evidently leading like a puzzle game to information on another.

"It's interesting," the woman finally said.

"What's that?"

"The signs all say that your son is fine. I've had others where that wasn't the case."

"What does that mean, fine?" Arayi leaned forward to get a better look at the pages. She didn't mean to hope, to let it grow, to blossom so quickly. It would be too painful again if . . .

"Where is he, where?" Arayi asked, interrupting her thought.

"The signs don't say, but it's not here."

Not here?

"Then where? Do the signs say where he is, or if he will be coming home?"

She apparently didn't need to recheck her papers. "He will return to India, that is certain, but I can't say if he will find his way home or not."

"How can that be? Surely if he returns to India, he would come home. When? When does it say he will return?"

The woman's head was shaking. "I don't know, but when he does, the signs are clear." The woman raised her arms to the sky. "He will fly. When your son returns, he will fly!"

"Fly? FLY?" Arayi stood, her voice rising with her. This woman was talking gibberish. She'd been swindled again. "What does that mean, he will fly?"

"These are the signs. I can't force you to like them. *He will return. It doesn't say when. When he does, he will fly!*"

Arayi didn't bother saying good-bye. The astrologers had *all* been wrong, and this crazy woman was the worst of the bunch. She was tired of them taking her money.

That was it. She was finished.

"I feel like a kid on Christmas Eve," Linda said as they pulled into the airport parking lot. She thought the comment especially funny, considering it actually *was* Christmas Eve.

Fred was too focused on finding an empty parking spot to offer applause. A light snow was falling, and the wipers were going. Rux, Josh and Jarem, all relatively quiet, were buckled into the back seat.

"At least he'll feel at home," Fred added.

"What do you mean?"

"There's over a half a billion people in India, and we have close to that many cars here in the parking lot!"

With the holiday traffic and slick roads, they were already late. They had agreed to meet Eli at baggage claim, and as they now arrived with two children in tow and pushing one in a stroller, Rux asked an intriguing question. "How will we know it's him?"

Linda bent down and unzipped his coat. She was about to explain when an Indian man stepped out from behind an approaching throng. A woman, whom most travelers would have assumed to be his wife, trailed three steps behind carrying a sleeping toddler. In between them, as if corralled, walked a tattered scruff of a boy.

"I think we'll know," Linda said, as time stood beside her to watch.

Although she could never give birth to children of her own, Linda had always imagined this moment—the first seconds when she laid eyes on her newly adopted children—to mirror the emotion a mother must feel when she cradles her newborn baby in her waiting arms.

Linda knew her son, all right.

From behind a passing flurry of hurried holiday legs, as if hiding in a people-forest, a confused and frightened, licorice-haired boy peeked at them. His blue cotton shorts clung to boney hips. A shabby, sleeveless shirt draped over his slumping shoulders. His bare feet were filthy, unlike the leather sandals held in his left hand. Bloodshot eyes revealed that he'd been crying, and his running nose begged for a tissue.

Outside, it was snowing.

Inside, the weather was still unpredictable.

While Eli greeted Fred and made introductions, Linda stayed low to try and catch the boy's eyes.

In Linda's perfect world, he'd run to her with outstretched arms, thanking her in broken English for bringing him to America, for including him as part of their family, for giving him a proper education and upbringing—for loving him.

Linda guessed this little boy's world hadn't been perfect for a very long time.

Always curious, Rux interrupted again, this time with a pointing finger. "Why is he so black?"

While Linda had told her children that they were getting a new big brother, it had never crossed her mind to include the boy's color.

"His skin is dark," she said to Rux, with Josh now listening, "because he is from India, a country where most people have dark skin."

"Why?" Rux persisted, needing something more.

When they got home she would pull the encyclopedias off the shelf and give them a proper explanation about the color differences of children in China, Africa, Europe, Latin America, and more. Right now, she had a son to meet.

"He has dark skin," she said to Rux, jumping right to her point, "because God is an astounding artist, and like you, he loves to paint with many different colors."

She didn't wait for Rux to ask why again.

"Take my hand," she said, "and let's go meet your brother."

"I'm sick," Chellamuthu had whined to Eli as they reached the airport's baggage claim.

He was positively sick—with worry. He was freezing. He was famished. He was half a world away from home and about to be abandoned in a distant country with a grumpy-looking man and a woman with banana colored hair.

He was more than sick—he was terrified.

"I want to stay with you," he had pleaded with Eli on the plane, words he'd never thought he'd speak.

When the yellow-haired woman gave the child she was holding to the frowny man and then reached down, Chellamuthu wrapped his arms around Eli's leg, gripped tight, and began to scream.

People stopped to stare.

In Erode, before he was taken, one of the older boys from Kannaian Street had told Chellamuthu that children in America were often forced to work in labor camps as slaves. Chellamuthu didn't believe him—until today. Why else would these strange-looking people want to take him away?

The yellow-haired woman backed up, watched, waited. Eli touched Chellamuthu on the arm, crouched down, and pulled him off just enough so that the two could see each other's faces.

"I don't want to go! Please don't leave me here!" Chellamuthu pleaded. He was trembling, wheezing, choking on panic. "I'll watch the babies, and I'll clean up all of their messes. Take me back, take me back, take me back. I'll never try to run away again. Take me back. Please, please!"

Eli waited for the boy's breathing to slow. "Chellamuthu, son, please listen carefully to what I have to tell you. You are young and won't understand—especially now—but listen anyway. Your life's path will never be the same now. You are being given a gift tonight, and you need to hold it tight. Here in America you will get an education. You will have opportunities that other boys in India can only dream about. Chellamuthu, your adoption is a blessing! Live a good life, make something of yourself, and then help others, perhaps even those back home. Do you understand what I'm saying?"

Every word screamed that he was about to be abandoned. Chellamuthu whipped his head sideways. "I can be good at home. I can help people there."

Eli tried again. "Do you remember when you climbed out the sewer hole at the orphanage?"

Chellamuthu calmed enough to offer a solitary nod. Perhaps that's what this was all about. He was being punished. "I'm sorry! I will never do . . ."

"Chellamuthu, that was a great day!" Eli added.

The boy stopped.

"It was a great day, Chellamuthu, because you came back—you returned to help another, and I was so proud of you. It showed me that you have courage, and strength, and initiative—but most important, it showed me that you have a kind heart, that you *can* love. Late that night, Chellamuthu, when Rajamani came by and told me what you had done, I knew that you were going to make something of your life. And I realized right then that I needed to give you an opportunity right away."

Chellamuthu clutched tighter. Eli continued, "The day will come when you will thank me."

The man sucked a deep, uneasy lungful of air.

"It's time, Chellamuthu. It's time."

While Chellamuthu screamed, Eli and the pasty, yellow-haired woman stripped him away like they were peeling a banana. He gritted his teeth, clenched his fists, and wriggled his body in her arms—and it worked! Eli stepped forward, turned, and reached for him, as if he'd changed his mind and had decided to take him back to India.

Chellamuthu stretched out his arms and grabbed on for safety. Eli had saved him after all. But then he realized through watering eyes that he'd just scrambled into the arms of the frowny man and was now being hauled away.

One more time Chellamuthu was being taken. Once more he was being discarded, deserted.

As he struggled, the strangers carted him outside where everything was covered in a harsh white. Snow! Chellamuthu had never seen snow except in pictures. At any other time in his life, he would have smiled and run and giggled and played—and it would have been magical. Tonight he shivered.

When they reached their car, they strapped him in the back with the other children and tightened up the buckle on the seat so that he couldn't move. He'd been right—he *was* being taken as a slave!

Eli had lied. Again.

Today wasn't special. It was empty. It was just like the day he was taken in Erode, the day Anu died, the day he was rushed away from Lincoln Home so quickly that he couldn't say good-bye to Vikesh.

It was like the evening when his feet were burned, except tonight the fiery poker was jabbing at his heart.

Chellamuthu's fingernails dug into his own palms. His throat was sore and scratchy. Eli had left him all alone, and now Chellamuthu wanted to hit him in the face so hard it would knock him to the floor, much as the man with the knife had done to Chellamuthu in the van when he'd been kidnapped.

But now, swirling with the anger to become one, like his mother's curry mixing with rice, was an overwhelming rush of sadness. Kuppuswami, Arayi, Selvaraj, Manju, Anu, Vikesh, Eli, perhaps even India itself—after tonight, he would never see any of them again.

CHAPTER 16

At home, Linda steered Chellamuthu toward the bathtub and mimed for him to climb in. He must have understood because he began to undress. She hollered to the younger boys that it was time for their bath but turned to find Chellamuthu in the center of the tub, naked and squatting, as if he expected to be hosed down.

His eyes flashed curiosity when she twisted on the water, set the temperature, and motioned him to sit. His curiosity morphed to wonder when Rux rounded the corner carrying an armful of plastic boats.

"Can we add bubble bath?" Rux asked Linda, as they traded giggles. "That will totally freak him out."

A squirt and squeal later, eager bubbles lathered laughing boys—including a soapy and stunned Chellamuthu.

"Keep it in the tub," Linda reminded, as the frothy foam looked ready to spill out. *Where was Jarem? He was missing all the fun.*

"Jarem! Bath! Now!" she hollered.

It was then she noticed her second oldest—*no,* now her third oldest—standing outside the door peering through the crack. "Jarem, hurry! Come on, climb in!" she encouraged.

The boy didn't move. His arms crossed his body with hands jammed into his armpits. He was biting at his lower lip.

"What is it?" Linda asked, reeling him close with wagging fingers. He arrived slowly, sheepishly. "What's wrong? Don't you want a bath?"

He shook his head back and forth so quickly it almost rattled. And then she noticed his gaze locked on Chellamuthu.

Jarem leaned in and whispered into her ear. "I don't want to touch him."

"Why not?"

His little words were bathed with concern.

"Because, Momma, I don't want to turn black!"

In the middle of the night, when Chellamuthu awoke, he was lying on cold brown carpet. It took a moment to realize that he was no longer at the Lincoln Home for Homeless Children. There were no stirring babies, no grass mats, no Rajamani, no cement trough, no blue bucket—nothing familiar at all.

And he was freezing. He understood now why the other boy in his room wasn't also sleeping on the floor. Perhaps Chellamuthu would likewise climb under the load of blankets the woman had left on the bed, but first, it was lunchtime in India, and he was starving.

When he glanced out the bedroom door into the hall, the house was quiet, so he crept to the large room where the white couple had tried to communicate with him earlier. After an hour of speaking, pointing, and repeating—often in a loud voice, as if that would help him to understand—he took away that their given names were *Mom* and *Dad.*

More critical, he had noticed a bowl of brightly colored candy on the table, and he was hoping it was still there.

The home was large enough to house several families, though at the moment there seemed to be just the one. The style was also strange, with rugs glued to nearly every speck of floor, including the stairs. Like the orphanage, this place also had a fountain for washing—several of them—and each could be filled by merely turning a handle. More incredible, if one turned the handle on the left, hot water came out without one ever having to build a fire.

When he had to go to the bathroom, in place of a common trough they had toilets, just like those that Eli had taught him how to use at the airport. But rather than a long row, this house had toilets in three separate rooms. And every one of those rooms would lock! *Why did they need so many toilets?*

With everyone asleep, he wondered if tonight wouldn't be the perfect opportunity to escape. Except that he was already cold, and when he looked out through the large window, he could see that the falling snow was now high enough to easily reach his knees. Instead, Chellamuthu lingered at a tree sitting inside the house, some kind of decoration he was still trying to figure out. It was lit with hundreds of twinkling lights and was covered with glass balls and strands of gold, and while he couldn't be sure, he'd gathered that a holiday was coming, similar to *Diwali.*

Around the tree were stacks of brightly wrapped boxes that he hadn't remembered earlier when he was shuffled off to bed. He stepped back. The scene was actually quite beautiful, and he wished his mother could be here with him to see it. She loved celebrations.

He faced the table holding the candy bowl—and sighed. *Dad,* the grumpy looking man, had eaten all but two pieces. Chellamuthu popped them into his mouth, savored their sweetness, chewed, and swallowed before heading toward the *kit-chun,* the room where *Mom* had prepared food when they arrived.

On his way, he noticed their shrine. It was placed on a table beside the couch, and it was, in a word, *pathetic.* All of their tiny gods were carved out of wood, every one stained to look the same. They weren't ornate or intricate or colorful at all. There was no place for incense, no silver cup for water, no spoon—all things a good shrine should have.

He studied the figures more closely, looking for anyone familiar. He checked for *Ganesh,* the god of intellect with his elephant head and stout trunk; *Durga,* an incarnation of *Parvati,* the divine mother with her ten arms astride a tiger; or *Shiva,* the preserver with his matted hair, third eye, and blue throat.

Nothing close.

Here there were only sheep and cows and men holding long sticks. There was a bowing mother, a kneeling father, and a baby sleeping in a cradle. This was the worst shrine he had ever seen.

Still, he couldn't help but think of his devout mother and the countless times she'd hauled him by the ear from the river or park to the temple to worship. And even though he didn't recognize any of these homely gods, he paused for just a moment in front of the sad, little shrine to utter a short prayer in the room's dim light.

One problem: there were so many deities to whom his family prayed, it was hard at times to keep track of the best one. Which god would best help a kidnapped boy from India who was now stuck in America? It was a problem that had never come up before. For most prayers, he had preferred Shiva, but now he had to wonder.

Could Shiva even hear him when he wasn't in India?

He decided to quietly chant the *Gayatri Mantram* his mother had taught him.

On the absolute reality and its planes,
On that finest spiritual light,
We meditate, as remover of obstacles
That it may inspire and enlighten us.

After he recited the mantra twice, he moved on to a more personal plea. "Great Shiva," he prayed, "I'm far away. I have no way to get back home. Help me. Watch my family. Keep them safe. Shower them with health and peace and happiness. Help them to know I am alive. And please, Shiva, help me . . . get me back to India."

He wasn't actually finished praying yet, had a few more thoughts to add, when he looked up and noticed a bowl of oranges on the far counter—large, ripe, beautiful oranges. He scooted over and picked one up. It didn't take long to peel. After he finished the first, he ate a second, and then a third. He'd counted eight to begin with, which left just five, and not knowing if they intended to feed him in the morning—or if ever—he gathered up those remaining into his arms and headed back to his room.

As he passed the shrine, he remembered he'd forgotten one of the most important parts of worship—leaving the gods an offering of food. He carefully placed an orange between the two sheep and the sleeping baby, a simple act that caused another question to raise its hand.

Is it okay to pray to Shiva for help, while at the same time stealing oranges?

When he returned to the room, the boy they called Rux was stirring. Chellamuthu hurried to pull back the blankets and climb under them. The fabric was chilly against his skin, but in just a few moments it began to warm.

Will I ever get used to the cold? Will I ever get used to America?

With that question on his mind, he wiped his sticky fingers on the clean bedding and then pushed his remaining oranges to the bottom of the blankets where they'd stay hidden, right beside the picture he'd drawn of his family.

With a full stomach, he closed his eyes, pulled up the blanket, and drifted off to sleep.

CHAPTER 17

Linda's favorite quotation, fastened to the mirror in her closet where she dressed, was from *The Phoenician Women,* by Euripides.

"This is slavery, not to speak one's thought."

If it was true, Chellamuthu was veritably in chains. To pick at the lock, Fred and Linda started with the basics. They would point to an item and say the word as slowly and clearly as possible—"*cereal.*" Then, with an enthusiastic assortment of jerky hand movements, like a bad game of charades, they would encourage the boy to repeat it. When Chellamuthu pronounced the word correctly, the two would smile and clap in unison. *We have a winner!* When he came up short, sighs of silence directed everyone back to step one.

The first words Chellamuthu grasped were easy.

Eat. Drink. Bathroom. Sleep.

Linda loved that he called her *Mom* right away, until she realized he thought that was her name.

It wasn't teaching him the single-word bodily functions that had her frustrated; it was helping him to understand everything else. It was the same question she had posed to Fred a day earlier. "How do you convey to a nodding child that *everything is going to be all right,* when he's about to get his teeth drilled at the dentist for the very first time?"

It was more than just drilling. Over the course of a week, at three separate doctor's offices, Chellamuthu's arms were poked, his blood was drawn, X-rays were taken, pills were prescribed, and vaccines were administered. As Linda anxiously watched, her son was probed like a terrified space alien. It was a wonder every morning to find her boy hadn't run off in the night.

"Will he survive here, Fred?" she asked, as Chellamuthu scowled angrily back now from the barber chair as his hair was shaved to help treat for lice.

"He'll survive," Fred confirmed.

"Perhaps, but he's like a little volcano. So much anger pent up inside. One day he's going to explode—or worse, he'll shut down. It will all just harden into rock around his heart."

"That's insightful," Fred replied. "You should make that into a cross-stitch."

"I'm serious."

"Well, unfortunately, I've coached enough boys to know we're at the easy part."

"What do you mean?" she asked, with a turn of her head.

"Little boys grow up to become teenagers."

Rather than sit on the floor to eat dinner like normal people, Chellamuthu's new family sat in hard chairs around a large wood table. In place of conveniently scooping food onto a banana leaf, to be neatly discarded when the meal was over, they used glass plates that required washing after *every* use.

Silly.

Instead of picking up food with their fingers, a quick and easy way to get it from the table into one's mouth, they used an assortment of forks, spoons, and knives.

Clumsy.

For all of the stories he'd heard from his uncles about how America was so *advanced,* Chellamuthu had yet to see it. For example, in the several meals he'd been served since arriving, they'd never once had rice or beans. More unbelievable, there was no sign of curry!

It was like they'd never heard of it!

While the food at Lincoln Home had been constant, perhaps even repetitive, at least it stood up and talked back. It was pungent and flavorful, tangy and mysterious. It had opinions and it shared them, whether you agreed or not. In contrast, American food was . . . lonely.

Most bizarre was breakfast. It was poured every morning out of a cardboard box into a bowl and soaked in cow's milk to make it edible.

Not that he wasn't grateful. Chellamuthu understood the necessity of eating whatever was around in order to survive. He'd lived it—and starving people can't afford to be picky.

But when he opened the cupboards in the kitchen, they were all full. They had enough food in the house to hold a wedding. Perhaps two!

As near as he could tell, America wasn't starving. Just the opposite. People were eating three meals a day, plus snacks. Lots of snacks. There was so much eating going on in America, in fact, there hardly seemed time for anything else.

"Chellamuthu?"

It was the mom-lady calling. She always spoke so fast, running her sounds together, impossible to understand—*and it was in English!* Still, he'd been able to learn the rhythm of a few basic phrases without knowing the words themselves. He guessed what she was saying now, but he remained in his room until she repeated herself. The second time was always louder. It was like a game.

"Everyone to the kitchen. It's time for dinner!"

Chellamuthu wedged into his desk on the first day of school surrounded by a crowd of eager first graders—all short, very short. Like at the Lincoln Home for Homeless Children, he was a good head taller than any of his classmates in the room. Unlike in India, these kids' craning necks and wide eyes screamed that he was the first dark-skinned peer ever to join the class.

The teacher stood, wrote what Chellamuthu presumed to be her name on the chalkboard, and then addressed everyone. Despite her bubbly tone and encouraging gestures, often aimed in his direction, he couldn't understand a word the woman was saying.

When she finally quit speaking, the children, starting with a boy in the first row, rose beside their desks and one at a time addressed the class. They seemed to be sharing details about their lives and families.

It caused Chellamuthu to remember his father.

Several months prior to Chellamuthu's kidnapping, Kuppuswami had secured a six-week job in Tiruppur at a factory that extracted sesame oil from pressed seeds. When the machine jammed, which was often, it helped to have someone with small hands reach inside and clear away the excess husks—and so he had dragged along his son.

Chellamuthu had been happy to oblige. The job was not only easy but it provided bits of sesame paste he could eat at will, and while not particularly tasty, they filled his stomach.

More memorable than the work was the bus ride to the factory. It was on their walk to the station the first morning that Kuppuswami realized he had enough money for only one fare. Rather than return to beg rupees from relatives, the proud man improvised.

After a quick detour through the market, Kuppuswami scoured up a sturdy cardboard box. His reasoning was simple: a man with a boy will cost two fares. A man carrying a box will cost just one.

He stopped at the corner before the station and commanded Chellamuthu to climb inside.

The only way the boy would fit was to lie sideways with his knees pulled into a ball, his head tucked forward.

If it had been just once, Chellamuthu wouldn't have complained. Unfortunately for him, it had worked so well the first day, Kuppuswami insisted that it continue. After all, saving the cost of a child's fare would mean half a dozen cups of palm toddy when the workday was over.

Of course it was painful to be scrunched up in a ball in the dark, unable to stretch—but he'd learned after that first day that there was something worse.

The part of the ride that had turned into near torture hadn't been the confinement but the silence. Lest he be discovered, Chellamuthu hadn't been allowed to make a sound for the entire trip. The *boy-in-the-box-on-the-bus* in India couldn't communicate.

Chellamuthu's thoughts were interrupted when the girl to his right, who had been speaking to the class, sat down.

His turn.

The teacher was pointing her finger at him. When he shifted his legs that were lodged up against the bottom of his desk, it lifted momentarily off the ground and landed with a clank.

The class laughed.

His stomach was pushed so tight against the back side of the desk, it was difficult to squeeze out.

As Chellamuthu stood, he glanced momentarily at the four corners of the square room.

If he spoke in his native language—his only choice—not a single person would understand.

It turned out that boxes come in many sizes.

The teacher was smiling now, encouraging him, flinging reassurance at his feet. He had to say *something.* He uttered a few words, all in Tamil.

"My name is Chellamuthu," he said. "I want you to know that once upon a time in India, I rode with my father on a bus in a box."

The children, having no clue what he was saying, began to giggle.

He continued anyway. "I was surrounded by people—talking, laughing, and joking—like today, and nobody at all knew that I was even there or what I wanted to say."

Linda was just starting dinner when the doorbell rang. On the porch stood two college-age men, one holding a camera.

"May I help you?" Linda asked.

"I'm Chuck. This is Wayne."

Linda paused, squinted. "May I help you?"

Chuck sighed. "Uh, didn't Donna call?"

"Donna who?"

His shoulders dropped. "I'm sorry. Donna's our editor. She was supposed to call. We're from *Hometown Life,* the town paper. We're here to do a story on your son."

"My son? Which one?" Linda suspected she already knew the answer but asked anyway.

"The boy from India."

"And you think he's somehow newsworthy?"

Chuck snickered through his nose. "Have you looked around? Your son is the first person from India ever to live in Mapleton. So yeah, we think our readers will find the story interesting."

Linda invited them in.

Before sitting, Wayne asked if he could start with a picture of the boy.

"I suppose that would be fine."

Linda opened the door to the basement where the boys were playing and hollered for Chellamuthu. When he came up the stairs and noticed the man with a camera, he froze.

"It's okay," Linda consoled, surprised he was being timid. "He just wants to take your picture." She tugged him toward her so they could stand together.

Even with Linda close, his steps were cautious. He eyed the men warily but particularly the man focusing the camera. No matter how Wayne prodded, Chellamuthu wouldn't smile.

It was only after the interview was over and the men had driven away that Chellamuthu's head raised. He faced Linda. "*Pōlīs?*"

Linda shrugged. She didn't understand.

It took a moment for him to remember the English pronunciation. "Police?" he asked again, in a stuttered tone. "I . . . stay?"

Their lack of communication had been frustrating, at times even comical. This was the first time it brought Linda nearly to tears. She let her arms fall around her son and pulled him in tight. Though it was a one-sided hug, it almost felt real.

"You stay," she confirmed. "You stay."

While Linda's push was to teach Chellamuthu new words, Fred lobbied for the area he knew best. "Words matter," he conceded, "but to keep a boy focused and motivated, get him involved in sports."

Linda couldn't disagree. But which sport?

The encyclopedia noted that the most popular sport in India was cricket. That would be a problem, since the only cricket they'd ever seen was the kind you smashed with your shoe when it came into the house.

What, then?

After dinner, Fred loaded his two oldest boys into the car and drove them down to the Mapleton Indoor Recreation Center to introduce Chellamuthu to the pool.

In the locker room Fred noticed Mark Christiansen, a science teacher from school.

"Does he swim?" Mark asked, as the boys trotted out toward the pool.

Fred smiled back with his coach face. "Guess we're about to find out."

Chellamuthu had heard of swimming pools, certainly. He'd just never been to one in person, not living next to the Kaveri. *Did they not have rivers here?*

When things were unfamiliar, Chellamuthu watched those around him, to see what they would do. He observed as Rux hurried to the pool's steps and climbed down in the water, not waiting for anyone.

Chellamuthu walked to the edge and looked in. Like the rivers in Erode, it was blue—but were there snakes?

When he was certain all looked clear, Chellamuthu followed Rux's example and took his first step into the pool.

The water was warm, as if a piece of the Kaveri had been carefully boxed between cement walls.

What kept it clean?

Another step down.

Rux was already splashing toward the opposite end, calling for Chellamuthu to follow.

Down another step.

He could swim to Rux—it seemed safe enough. But in this tiny square of a stagnant river, what was the point? There was no destination: no trees, no rocks, no cliffs, no plants. Nothing but a large box of water.

It was up to his chest now, lapping at him.

"Come on!" Rux called again.

Chellamuthu filled his lungs with a long, deep breath as he would have done back home. Instead of leaping, however, he stretched out toward the deep end, pushed off, and then let the water swallow him whole.

It was peaceful, almost like a dream, floating motionless beneath the surface. It shut out all the noise and chattering that had been making him crazy. He pretended that if he surfaced, he'd find the deep blue Indian sky welcoming him home.

The water here stung his eyes, and so he closed them. That was even better. He could almost hear his friends laughing, feel the river's pull, smell a hint of curry drifting in the breeze to join the fun.

And then a childish notion once again echoed in his head.

If only I were a fish.

If he could choose to hide somewhere, he'd hide down here beneath the surface forever, let the water protect him from the threatening snakes: fear, frustration, isolation, loneliness.

If only I were a fish, I could swim back to India.

His lungs were beginning to burn. He didn't move.

Then, as in the river back home, someone grabbed his arm. He was yanked to the surface, pulled in a panic to the side, and then plopped to the safety of the concrete shore by his American father.

Never a choice. Always being rescued.

He motioned to Fred that he was all right and then signaled the same to Rux, whose face dripped with distress. When Rux realized that Chellamuthu wasn't drowning, that there was nothing to worry about, he coaxed his brother to jump back in.

Chellamuthu shook his head. He'd had enough. He headed toward the room where they had dressed, all the while feeling the stares of strangers tracking him, watching, wondering.

There was a man at the train station in Erode who had trained a monkey to strum a small guitar, making music for the passing crowd who would gather, giggle, and clap.

Maybe I should find a guitar.

But tonight it didn't matter. He was too busy considering another thought that had leaked in between his ears.

Why did he always have to come up for air?

When Chellamuthu walked in from school, Linda was holding a radio, though it wasn't playing music. "Come!" she said, as she beckoned him to sit beside her at the kitchen table.

She pressed two buttons and then bent down toward the machine. "This is a recorder. It's used to record your voice. We want you to speak to it."

She poked it a second time with her finger and then turned to watch his reaction.

"This is a recorder. It's used to record your voice. We want you to speak to it."

Chellamuthu could hear her talking, but her lips weren't moving—instead her words were spilling from the strange little box. His own lips parted. His forehead furrowed. He watched as she repeated the demonstration.

"You speak into this machine, and it will record whatever you say."

A few more button pushes, and it once again repeated her words perfectly.

Her drumming fingers meant that she now wanted him to try. Her nod told him she was ready. He leaned toward the device and opened his mouth but hesitated, unable to collect his words.

"Just say anything," she encouraged as she again pushed the buttons.

He started by trying to remember a few of his best English words.

"Hello . . . I talk . . . now."

"No, no. Speak in Tamil," she said.

"Tamil?" he asked with astonished eyes.

For Chellamuthu, whose every waking hour consisted of brothers, parents, teachers, classmates, and even total strangers asking him to try to speak in English, her request for Tamil was like jerking away debris from a clogged and swollen river.

What would he say? Where would he start?

It wasn't just the relief of being able to speak without the shackles of strange words, it was that he could say anything—and the machine would remember.

Chellamuthu sat up, scooted forward. He might even have giggled. For all he knew, this machine might speak Tamil back. His eyes glowed.

He would start his story at the beginning. It would take some time, but neither the mom-lady nor the machine seemed in a hurry.

He breathed, then reached out and clutched the table with determined hands.

"Ennoda appa amma kitta erundhu enna kadathitanga . . ."

CHAPTER 18

When swimming didn't seem to take, Fred decided it was time to introduce Chellamuthu to the world's greatest sport: amateur wrestling.

"Quite simply," he'd often repeated to Linda, even when she had left the room and was no longer listening, "there is no better way on earth to teach a boy self-discipline, mental toughness, and sportsmanship."

And who better to tackle the task than the high school's own wrestling coach?

At the end of each day, Fred picked up Chellamuthu from the elementary school and hauled him back to the high school gym for team practice. For the first two days, he made Chellamuthu observe from the bleachers. On day three, he let the boy suit up and invited him to step onto the mat. With Fred instructing, Chucky Hogan, the best lightweight wrestler on the team, helped Chellamuthu practice basic moves.

To Fred's surprise, and perhaps Chellamuthu's, he was a natural.

Chellamuthu was still smaller than any of the boys on the team—

even the featherweights. But by the end of the week, he had mastered take downs, tie ups, rolls, and switches. It turned out he could Double Leg Snatch with the best of them.

Chellamuthu didn't say much when wrestling, but as Fred observed, when wrestling, not much needs to be said.

By the end of week three, Chellamuthu had made so much progress that Fred called in a favor and signed up his son to wrestle in an exhibition club match the following weekend.

Linda, Rux, and Josh all cheered from the stands as Chellamuthu wrestled in his first competition, and while he didn't take first, he scored points in two close matches and won a third, to receive an overall third-place ribbon.

For the first time, Linda noticed a gleam of contentment in her oldest son's eyes.

On the way home, Chellamuthu spoke Tamil in the car, asking questions and then waiting, as if expecting an answer. When none came, he tried to use his English words. He was holding up his ribbon.

"Show . . . mother?"

Linda turned. "I can see it," she replied. "You did so well!"

Chellamuthu drew the ribbon close. "No . . . home, India!" he said. "Show . . . India mother?"

Fred tapped the brakes. He glanced toward Linda. "What did he just say?"

Linda was already twisting in her seat. "India mother? You have a mother in India?" she asked with wide-eyed words. She nudged him with her hand to make sure he was watching. "India mother?" she repeated.

"Mother. Yes. India. Show . . ." He was holding up his ribbon alongside a rusty smile.

"Father?" Linda asked.

The boy's head was nodding like a bobble-head doll. "Father, yes. And *Anna,* . . . err . . . brother . . . sister."

Linda glanced at Fred. His hairline couldn't have gone any higher. Plenty was being communicated with their few peppered words.

Their newly adopted son wasn't an orphan at all.

Linda began typing the moment she walked in the door. She'd been kicking the words in their shins the entire drive home. This couldn't wait. When she finished, she had Fred check for mistakes and then climbed into the car and drove directly to Western Union.

> *Dear Mr. Manickam,*
>
> *When we adopted Chellamuthu, you told us he was an orphan. You have not been honest again. He has told us that he has a mother, father, sister, and brother in India. We love him and consider him our adopted son, but we need to immediately know his background and if there is truth to what he has now told us. Any information you can provide is important. We insist on your immediate reply.*
>
> *Fred and Linda Rowland*

"Come fold clothes!" Linda hollered, speaking like a caveman—though doubting the words were in a caveman's repertoire.

Chellamuthu ignored her. Playing trucks with Rux was way more fun. If he pretended he didn't understand, it would buy a little more time.

A minute later she was back. "Please, boys."

Why did they have so many clothes, anyway? Life was so much easier in India, where a boy needed only a pair of shorts.

"Come. NOW!"

Rux dropped his truck and headed up the stairs. Chellamuthu was still considering his options. While his two mothers lived on opposite sides of the world, they were the same in many ways.

"No swimming in the river until you help Uncle." "No TV until you make your bed."

"Eat your curry." "Finish your peanut butter sandwich."

"Hold Manju." "Watch Jarem."

"We're going to temple." "We're going to church."

"Where's your father?" "Where's your father?"

Mother working late in India. Mother working late in America. Rushing here, driving there, cooking this, cleaning that.

It was worse with his new mother, since she was so . . . *stubborn.* Always insisting she was right. Why did she have to be that way?

Even when she came home late and both she and Chellamuthu were tired, she'd still make him study his words. When he was hungry after school and wanted cookies, she'd make him wait until after dinner, or worse, try to give him carrots.

It always had to be her way.

Fred, his dad, was more fun. He was teaching Chellamuthu how to wrestle. But even that really didn't matter. If they took him away from this family tomorrow, so what? He would get used to it quickly enough.

Experience had taught him well. Whoever he got close to was taken away, and it always cut deep.

No more—the scars were finally growing thick.

When he heard Linda's footsteps coming down the stairs, he stood. As he'd said, she was always *so stubborn.*

"I . . . coming! Coming!" he called out, a touch of disgust trailing in his voice.

When Eli wouldn't respond to Linda's telegram, she tried a registered letter.

When he ignored the letter, she picked up the telephone.

It turned out calling was both expensive and fruitless: Mr. Manickam was always busy, often away, never willing to come to the phone.

If Eli wouldn't address the problem, she'd find someone who would. She'd call a United States senator, again—or at least the sister of a senator.

Linda spoke with Jessica, who spoke to her brother the senator, who agreed to again have his office contact the consulate general's office in Chennai. He wasn't hopeful they could help, but he was prepared to try.

A week later, at five in the morning, the phone rang. The voice was distant, but familiar.

"Mrs. Rowland? Sorry for the early hour again, ma'am. It's Matt Conway. We spoke briefly several months back when you adopted your son."

Linda sat up.

"Sure, Matt, sure. How could I forget?"

"Yes, ma'am. Well, I'm following through on your request to the senator's office to track down information about your son."

"Yes, yes. Thank you so much."

"We will do all we can, but like my Alabama grandma used to say, these guys can be slicker than an oyster soup sandwich. Unfortunately, all we can do is make an official request to the Indian authorities for the matter to be investigated and . . . well, many of the laws here turn out to be mere suggestions, depending on who pays whom, if you know what I mean? I just wanted you to be aware."

"Thank you. Please let me know if you hear any news."

She was about to hang up when he interrupted. "Ma'am? How's the boy doing?"

Despite the fact that all this man had ever done was wake her up in the middle of the night with bad news, she liked Matt Conway.

"The progress is slow, but it's forward. Thank you for asking."

"Good to hear, ma'am. Give him my best. Y'all have a good day."

Linda shut off the alarm. It would be going off soon anyway.

The dead ends were piling up. Options were running thin. Then she remembered one last avenue.

Two days earlier, by sheer luck, she'd run into a woman she'd met twice before at gatherings for adoptive parents. The woman, who'd also arranged for a child through Lincoln Home, had recognized Linda waiting in the supermarket checkout line. As Linda rehearsed her newfound concerns with Eli Manickam, the woman had remembered receiving correspondence from the orphanage signed by someone else when they'd had a dispute about her final payment. She promised Linda she'd look for his name, and yesterday she'd called with his information. Linda was on her way out the door and had scribbled it down on a scrap of paper she dropped into her purse.

She pulled it out now and placed it on the table. It was a long shot. She understood that. But what worthwhile thing in life wasn't?

A plan was taking shape as she examined the name. She would write a letter to this man, tell him Eli Manickam hadn't responded, and plead to his goodness for some answers. Her questions were simple:

Did Chellamuthu have a family in India? If so, why did Eli say the boy was an orphan? If their son had a family, why did they give him up? Could information about the family be provided, so her son would have it when he was older?

This man was her last, best shot. Hopefully he'd take pity and help.

She rolled a piece of paper into the typewriter and paused for a moment before typing the addressee's name. "At least," she mumbled to herself, "I finally have someone to write to besides Eli Manickam."

With a renewed sense of optimism, she pushed the keys.

Lincoln Home for Homeless Children
Attention: Mr. Maneesh Durai

Chellamuthu knew from experience in India—three whole weeks in the public school in Erode—that paying attention to a teacher was trying. Sitting now for hours at a time, weeks on end, when he could only understand one in ten words, was excruciating. It was not that he didn't want to learn. It was that when the teacher spoke, every sentence sounded like the syllables were jumping places on purpose just to tease and torture.

There was, however, one word that he'd learned to recognize and appreciate early—a word that his ears trolled for whenever the teacher spoke, a word that all the students equally adored: *Recess.*

When the weather was cold and snowy, the students spent their recess inside—a punishment, it seemed, for both the children and the teachers. However, when the days finally warmed and the snow that covered the matted grass melted and the flowers pushed their little yawning faces to the sun, the world tipped back into balance again and every breathing person attending Vineyard Elementary rejoiced—including Chellamuthu.

It didn't take long for the boy to learn that outdoor recess in elementary school meant one activity: *Kickball.*

The game was easy enough, having rules similar to cricket (with several notable exceptions). Instead of using a small, hard ball that could injure elementary schoolchildren when it hit them in the face, the game was played with a bouncy, overly anxious rubber ball about the size of a watermelon.

Rather than pitching, the large red ball was rolled at home plate, bowling style.

Instead of using a bat, the person who was *up* kicked the ball with as much force as they could muster, usually toward the outfield.

If the ball wasn't caught in midair, which counted as an out, then the square box of bases would be run, and a point would be scored for the team.

To get a runner out, whoever had the ball would either throw it to pummel the runner between bases, or chase them down and punch them with the ball before they reached the next base.

When the kicking team reached three outs, sides were switched, and the game ended when the school bell rang.

Easy.

Since Chellamuthu was so much older than his first-grade classmates, at recess he stayed with kids closer to his size, mostly third graders. At the first outdoor recess of the spring, Chellamuthu watched as the captains selected their teams. He wasn't chosen.

The next day, he stood closer. He barely received a glance and was again overlooked.

On the third day at lunchtime, Chellamuthu sat on the grass watching two of the better third-grade teams play. Minutes into the game, the ball glanced sideways off the kicker's foot and bounced to Chellamuthu as a foul.

"Here!" the boy at the mound screamed, before spitting in the dirt toward Chellamuthu. "Kick it here!"

Chellamuthu was wiry but strong. He pretended he was back in India with Selvaraj, the time they were trying to kick tamarind pods against the wind. Only his target today was significantly larger. Chellamuthu's foot connected with the ball square and solid. It not only soared over the pitcher's head, it cleared second base and rolled into the far outfield.

"Whoa!" the boy at the mound hollered, praise understood in any language. "That's what I call a kick!" He was wearing a red T-shirt and must have been in charge, because he talked to the captain of the opposing team and an argument ensued. Chellamuthu was only able to pick out occasional words.

"No . . . Yes."

"NO! . . . YES!"

"Not fair . . . Fine!"

One thing was obvious, they were arguing over him!

"Yes!" the red-shirted boy hollered again. He'd evidently won the argument because he directed Chellamuthu into position on his team, aiming to a spot between first and second base—and the game continued.

Chellamuthu tried not to grin. Like any boy, in any state, in any country, on any continent in the world, he ached to fit in. He couldn't care less about the language barrier. He just wanted to play the game, kick the ball, make friends, and belong.

The next ball lumbered through the infield, was easily caught for the third out, and the teams switched positions. While the players waited for their turn to kick, the team captain tried to strike up a conversation with Chellamuthu—if that's what it could be called.

"Name?" he asked, as he elbowed Chellamuthu.

Chellamuthu understood the word. He'd also learned that he needed to answer slowly. "Che-lla-mu-thu."

A few of the other boys on the team laughed.

"Me Todd," the boy grunted in reply, slapping himself in the chest.

More laughs—and for a moment the experience felt familiar. Chellamuthu didn't mind the mockery. He had friends—and it was wonderful!

When his teammates cheered, he cheered. When they spit, he spit. When they pointed that it was his turn to kick, he pounded the ball into the outfield and scored a run. By the time the bell sounded, their team was ahead by double digits.

On their way back to the school, Todd's eyes narrowed and the sides of his mouth turned up. He pulled Chellamuthu to a stop.

"Teacher?" Todd asked, looking into Chellamuthu's eyes for recognition of the word.

"Yes, teacher," Chellamuthu repeated. He knew that word. "Mrs. Wyness," he confirmed, pointing at the school and repeating her name.

Todd shook his head. "Wrong!" The boy's face was stern, but his eyes grinned.

"*Wrong?*" Chellamuthu asked, his accent stiffening.

Todd made sure the two were facing one another, that Chellamuthu could watch his lips. He spoke slow and steady.

"It's Mrs. *Wide Ass,*" Todd said, holding an expression now so serious there could have been a death in his family.

Chellamuthu paused. It was true he'd had a hard time learning her name. Could it be that he'd been saying it wrong all along? "*Wide Ass?*" Chellamuthu questioned.

"Yes! Fantastic!" Todd assured.

A couple of the boys in the circle began to snicker, but when Todd shot them the stare of death, they wiped the grins from their faces.

"Principal Dickens?" Todd asked, fishing for a second bite.

Chellamuthu nodded like he was getting free candy. He knew the man. He'd sat in his office twice. He'd learned his name when his mother brought him to enroll.

Todd enlightened with convincing lips. "It's Principal *Dick Head.* Repeat it!"

Chellamuthu did so, mimicking the words with equal conviction.

"Can you remember?" Todd was tapping his head so Chellamuthu would understand.

Of course he could remember! He wasn't stupid.

There appeared to be more words Todd was eager to teach him. *What a good friend!*

As Chellamuthu learned his new words, he also praised Shiva for the chance he'd had to kick the ball so far, to show the children he was a good player. This was all going much better than he could have imagined.

"This next word is the best of all," Todd said, his eyes glassy like a snake's. "Look at me. Watch my lips."

Chellamuthu waited anxiously for the new word. Each was a gift.

Todd's gaze roped the ring of waiting boys and pulled them in tight. Eyes grew so wide some looked like they'd pop.

He waited until all were listening.

"The word is . . ."

The phone was ringing when Linda entered the house.

"Mrs. Rowland?"

"Yes?"

"This is Principal Dickens."

Her voice quickened. "Yes, what is it?"

"Everything is fine. We just had a little incident here at the school this afternoon, and I wanted to make you aware."

"Incident? What do you mean? What happened?"

The man skated around his words. "Your son was using some . . . well, colorful language and the students were laughing, and so he kept repeating it all louder and . . ."

"What did he say?" Linda asked, interrupting.

"Frankly, I'd rather not repeat it. He's sitting here in my office, and I was hoping you'd be able to come down and pick him up. Is that possible?"

Linda swallowed a sigh. "I'll be right down."

The kids were already in bed when Linda arrived home. She'd been meeting late with a client about a new listing and while she'd signed the deal, it had dragged on longer than expected.

Fred pointed to the envelope from the Lincoln Home for Homeless Children that was open on the counter.

"What does it say?" she asked, pulling the letter out.

"You read it. It's short."

Dear Mr. and Mrs. Rowland,

I am sorry to know of your plight. There are many lost and orphaned children in India, and many who have been adopted through our organization. I will do my best to get information about your son, but it may be difficult. You have given me little. Can you provide the name of the boy's town, village or state, or any school he attended? Please send and I will investigate.

I do not know how much information I can get from Eli. He has not been well. Let us hope we will all soon learn more about your son.

Sincerely,
Maneesh Durai

"That's it?" Linda asked. "He's asking *us* for information? We've told him everything we know."

She was looking at Fred as if he had a pocketful of answers.

"It seems to me," he said, "Mr. Maneesh Durai is politely telling us to go fly a kite."

Linda carefully read the letter again, studying each word. While Mr. Durai had no obligation to help, still, they were adoptive parents, paying customers. They deserved more. Even so, there was something about his phrasing that seemed peculiar. It could be the language barrier, the way he'd translated Tamil phrases in his head into English sentences on paper—or was it more than that?

She couldn't be certain . . . but something didn't smell right.

CHAPTER 19

Linda was at work when the school called again. With three weeks left before summer recess, Angie Wyness, Chellamuthu's teacher, was asking if she could meet with Fred or Linda.

"Is there a problem?" Linda asked.

"I feel like we need to talk," she answered.

Linda hung up the phone, pinched her lips, and then repeatedly clicked her pen. She'd been an educator since the invention of dirt. She was fluent in *teacher.* When the woman said they *just needed to talk,* Linda knew it was time to panic.

They met the following day.

"I'm concerned with Chellamuthu's comprehension," Mrs. Wyness said. "He's confusing his letters. He's connecting the wrong sounds with letters. He's often guessing at unknown words, rather than sounding them out."

"But that's normal," Linda objected, in a tone that sounded like the defensive parents she'd always abhorred.

"If he were only five or six, like most of the students in my class, then I'd have no worries. But he's much older, and I'd expected he'd be farther along by now. The biggest problem isn't just that he doesn't grasp what I say, it's that he doesn't seem to care."

Linda pulled in a slow breath. She took even longer to exhale.

Mrs. Wyness continued, "Don't get me wrong. He's very smart. When he's doing problem-solving activities on his own, like puzzles or activities that don't require speech or reading, he's the best in the class. It's just . . ."

"I get it. I understand," Linda said, her words already waving white flags. "What do you suggest?"

"I hate to say it, but I really think he needs to repeat the first grade. If he doesn't, it will just get worse."

The muscles in Linda's face weren't sure whether to cue up for a laugh or a cringe. "Have you ever, in all your years in the classroom, flunked a first grader?" Linda asked.

The teacher didn't answer. She must have presumed the question was rhetorical.

"You're right. I know you're right." Linda added as she stood. "But I can't have him repeating here. It would be too embarrassing for him. I'll see if I can enroll him at Fairview, maybe work out some tutoring, maybe . . ."

"Mrs. Rowland, there's something else."

Linda hovered, then sat. "What is it?"

"He's a good kid, but with the language, and being from India, well . . ."

"Tell me."

"The kids tease him. In place of Chellamuthu, they call him *Jello-mutant, Cello-player, Hello-MooMoo,* and . . . well, those are the nice ones. I get cross with them, of course."

"Of course."

" . . . but his Indian name is hard to pronounce, and kids are kids. They say some pretty insensitive, stupid things. I'm not justifying their behavior . . ."

"Certainly not."

" . . . I just wanted you to know."

Linda had always hated the hurt in a parent's eyes when, as a teacher, she'd relayed similar news. She'd just never realized how much it stung. Now that it was her own son, her own heart, she had to do something to dull the pain.

She'd make one more stop on the way home.

Fred was reading on the couch when Linda burst in. "I have news," she announced, but in lieu of eager eyes, she was packing worry.

Fred lowered his newspaper.

"I quit my job," she said.

Her words drained shamefully onto the carpet. She looked as if she were admitting guilt to capital murder.

Fred arched forward, cupped his ears. She *loved* her job. He must have misunderstood.

"Say what?"

If he sounded gruff, he didn't mean it. His tone, like his face, often wore its angry coat. It was more comfortable. He folded the paper and dropped it on the floor.

Linda sat beside him. "We should have talked about it, I know. I'm sorry. I am. I know it's a bit rash. It's just, well, the kids at school are calling him names, Fred—and our son flunked the first grade! I've never heard of a child flunking first grade . . . so I decided to take a year off."

When Fred said nothing, she kept pedaling.

"But we can afford it, because we won't have childcare . . . and I'll cook more! And it will give me more time with all our children. And . . ."

Linda was hunching, hyperventilating, holding back tears.

"Honey, relax!"

"Fred, I'm a teacher," she said. "I'll be damned if a son of mine ever flunks another grade again. I just won't allow it. I won't."

Fred picked up his paper. There was only one good answer. "It makes sense to me."

" . . . Wait, what? Which part?"

"All of it."

Gratitude seeped from the woman.

Fred fiddled for the sports page. "I presume you'll tutor him at home," he said. "When will you start?"

Before answering, she leaned in and gave Fred a longer than normal kiss, scrunching the innocent newspaper against his chest. Neither cared.

Then she twisted her attention toward the basement stairs and the sound of playing boys.

"Would you call Chellamuthu?" she said. "I'm starting right now!"

Marcus Campbell, the principal at Fairview Elementary, was an old acquaintance of Linda's. The two had taught together at East High about the time Fred and Linda first met. It was time to catch up, time to ask a favor.

"Hello?"

It was late in the afternoon. The receptionist had gone, but a light was on in Campbell's office. The nameplate on the door was polished brass with lettering twice the size of any she'd ever seen.

Short-man syndrome?

Enrolling Chellamuthu at Fairview to repeat the first grade had drawbacks. Most important, it was farther away, which meant Linda would have to drive her son both *to* and *from* school every day. It also meant that none of his friends in the neighborhood would be attending the same school.

Attending Fairview also had advantages. Most important, *it was farther away,* which meant that the students at the school not only didn't live close but they would never have heard the name *Chellamuthu.*

Linda hoped it wouldn't matter. Between now and the start of school, exactly three months away, she would execute her newly formed plan. Chellamuthu would hate it. Fred and the kids would hate it. Linda would *absolutely* hate it. Every day, all summer, from breakfast to bedtime if necessary—for a dozen hours a day, if that's what it took—Linda was going to teach her son to read, write, and speak English. Teasing children be damned (bless their hearts). Linda Rowland was stepping in to take charge.

She knocked on the principal's door.

"Linda, it's great to see you again," Marcus said as he welcomed her into his office. "How's Fred? Is the old coot still teaching PE?"

"Can you picture him doing anything else?"

The man laughed.

They both sat.

He checked his watch. "Hey, I know you're short on time, so let's get right to it. Since our phone call, I've been thinking a lot about your request to enroll your son here. I'm on board with it, but I'd like to add a little stipulation."

"Stipulation?" Linda edged forward, leaning into the word. Two more inches, and she'd slip off her chair. She would have growled if she had thought it would make a difference.

"Perhaps that's not the right word," Marcus added. "Let's call it a *strong suggestion.*"

"Get to it, Marcus!"

"You need to enroll your son, and we . . . well, we desperately need a PTA president."

Linda squinted disbelief. "Are you *strongly suggesting* that person be me? This is feeling like a shakedown."

Perhaps obeying orders, his smug expression didn't move.

"Well?" she asked.

"I wouldn't say that. I'd call it . . . *two old friends doing each other a favor.* It's a marvelous opportunity, actually. I scratch your back, you scratch mine."

"It sounds like I'm the one doing all the scratching."

She wiped her fingers on her blouse.

She waited.

He waited.

The clock on the wall waited. *Tick tick tick.* Clearly, it had all day.

When Linda finally grunted her agreement, Marcus shot from his seat. He reached out his hand like a used car salesman to seal the deal, to welcome his new PTA president. Why, he almost danced!

"It's gonna be great, Linda, a *win-win* for everyone. Just like old times at East High."

She pulled at the hem of her blouse again. "If it's a win-win, why do I feel like I need a hot shower?"

At her car, Linda yanked on the handle with resolve. She might have lost the battle, but she was making progress on the war.

"The war . . ." she repeated. In an instant, she knew what she had to do next.

Fred had coaxed her into watching a war movie last weekend with a scene of the D-day invasion. It was heartbreaking to see so many lives lost, simply because of obstacles blocking their landing on the beach.

It was the same with Chellamuthu. His obstacles were not death, dying, or drowning—she didn't mean that—but they were still very real. There are times, she reasoned in her head, when we have no choice but to fight through life's barriers.

She climbed in, closed the door, grabbed the wheel, and pressed back against the seat.

For a smooth beach landing, however, it is necessary to first clear obstacles from the sand.

She pushed in the key and started the car.

She would need to convince Fred first. Then she would need to communicate the idea to her son. Her beach-clearing plan was simple. Before Chellamuthu started school again—actually right away—it was time they address a glaring problem.

It was time for Chellamuthu to choose a new name.

Fred Rowland loved lists. He once made a list of the reasons everyone should use lists. He carried his on a school-issued clipboard that never left his side. He ate with it, slept with it, watched TV with it. He once tried to shower with it. Linda drew the line when he brought his clipboard to bed.

Tonight, with the family huddled around the kitchen table, they were making a list for Chellamuthu.

Names.

With their children watching, occasionally helping, Fred and Linda scoured the *Encyclopedia Britannica, Volume I,* as well as any issue of *National Geographic* that even pretended to mention the Indian subcontinent. Possibilities were written, sorted, repeated—*Rajah, Jute, Kumar, Ira, Ravi.*

With each one, they glanced at Chellamuthu to gauge his reaction. A raised eyebrow was better than a tipped head. Frowning lips were worse than crossed arms.

They'd hoped to settle on a name that was noticeably Indian, to retain his heritage, but one that wouldn't provide easy fodder for the taunts and jeers of thoughtless school children.

While Rux kept voting for his favorite, *Anaconda,* there were two names that Chellamuthu seemed to prefer.

The first, *Taj,* came from the Taj Mahal, and while Fred and Linda knew little about the famous landmark, they read that it had been built by the Mughal emperor Shah Jahan in memory of his third wife, Mumtaz Mahal, and that it was often listed as one of the seven wonders of the world.

The second name, *Khyber,* a possible middle name, came from an article in *National Geographic* on the Khyber Pass. "If it's important enough for *NG* to dedicate the center spread to it," Fred declared, "it works for me."

But would it work for Chellamuthu?

Fred repeated the new name slowly, so his son would understand.

Taj Khyber Rowland.

It should be like asking an American boy if he'd want to change his name to John Wayne, Elvis Presley, or Nick Fury. What was not to like?

Would Chellamuthu agree?

Everyone faced the boy and waited.

Chellamuthu needed time to think. He didn't need to speak English to know that his start in America had been rough. Children at school laughed when he spoke, some sneered, and he hadn't seen another dark-skinned kid since landing.

He looked around at the faces of his new family. If he couldn't understand their words, how would he ever grasp their culture?

Do they really eat peanut butter because they like it?

He wanted to fit in here in this strange new place, but would changing his name make a difference?

It wasn't until Fred took the large world-globe down from on top of the cabinet in the family room and set it in the middle of the kitchen table that his predicament began to sink in.

"Here," Fred said, motioning to the room around them and then to a miniscule spot on the globe in the western United States, perhaps hoping his son would comprehend the correlation.

Fred then spun the globe all the way around to the opposite side.

"India," he said, as he tapped a finger to the map.

Chellamuthu grabbed the globe and twisted it around to find the two spots again—*United States, India.* India wasn't just far away, it was on the opposite side of the cursed world! The only way he could get farther away from home would be if they packed him into a rocket ship and shot him out into space.

He twirled the globe around a third time, using his fingers to measure the length of the separating ocean with his fingers.

Too far to walk.

Too far to drive.

Too far to swim.

The impenetrable stone fence around the Lincoln Home for Homeless Children had been daunting. The deep ocean barrier surrounding every shore of America was impossible.

Fred's clamoring object lesson rang clear: America didn't need a fence. Chellamuthu was never going home.

Bam, bam, bam.

In his dream, Eli was once again carrying bricks as a child, working at the factory where he'd been enslaved. This time it was different. Instead of being beaten across his back with a switch, Eli wielded a hammer and was breaking apart the bricks as fast as they could be cast.

Bam, bam, bam.

At first he was alone, smashing the bricks with impunity, single-handedly. Then, other children began to appear, each carrying their own hammer.

Bam, bam, bam.

"MR. ELI! We have a problem. Sir! Wake up!"

Rajamani, panting and wide-eyed, was shaking Eli awake at his desk where he'd fallen asleep.

"There are policemen at the front gate. They are with a man from the American consulate. They insist on an inspection."

Eli blinked, rubbed at his eyelids, commanded they open. "An inspection? Of what?"

"The Lincoln Home!"

He straightened. "Why?"

"I don't know, sir. I told them I'd get a key to let them in. Then I came to wake you."

Bam, bam, bam.

Adrenaline pulsed. "That's good. Thank you, Rajamani." He jerked open a drawer on his desk, rummaged inside. "Is Maneesh here?" he asked, his terror rising.

Rajamani waited. "No, sir. I haven't seen him in a few days."

Eli pulled a key from the clutter in the drawer. He pried open Rajamani's fingers and placed it in the center of his palm.

"Take this and unlock the back door in the room where the children sleep. Gather the children—not the babies, just those who can speak. I'll open the front gate for the inspectors to let them in."

Rajamani was confused. "Gather the children? What should I tell them?"

Bam, bam, bam.

Eli's panic was now in full view.

"Open the door . . . and then tell them to RUN!"

CHAPTER 20

When Chellamuthu walked in from wrestling practice, Linda already had dinner on the table. After the family had finished eating, she pointed toward his room. "You need to clean your room and make your bed."

When Chellamuthu didn't understand his new mother—which was most of the time—he had two choices: shrug in ignorance, which caused her to repeat what she'd said, each time louder, as if the problem were his hearing; or nod with enthusiasm, giving her the impression he'd understood her English to perfection.

Each option had its advantages. While the latter was preferred, the long-term consequences were unpredictable. Tonight, he was too tired to play the game. He shook his head back and forth, hoping she'd go away.

No such luck. Linda repeated her command with more volume than expected.

Chellamuthu met her volume with more rigorous head wagging.

Linda, obviously exhausted from her day's work, signaled for Rux to take Chellamuthu by the hand and show him what to do.

No hand-holding was necessary. Chellamuthu stood and followed Rux into their room. There, waiting for them on top of their bare mattresses was a stack of freshly washed sheets.

Chellamuthu's mouth ripped open. He shoved Rux aside and rushed to the bed.

"No. No! NO!" he shouted in English, as he tore apart the pile of linens. When he found nothing, he raised the mattress with two hands and scoured beneath.

He had already learned that hiding food wasn't necessary, that it annoyed his mother when she found it. But he'd never told her about the picture he'd drawn of his family.

Everyone holds secrets that need protecting.

Chellamuthu had received a flashlight for Christmas, and on occasion, after Rux had gone to sleep, he would pull out his drawing from beneath the mattress and shine the light across familiar faces.

Last night, he was too cold to climb out of bed, and so he placed his carefully folded picture between the sheets at the foot of his bed, promising himself to put it back under the mattress in the morning.

He'd forgotten.

Now, shaking the uncaring sheets like a wolf might shake a rabbit, he was screaming phrases in Tamil that no one in the room—or likely the city—could understand.

Enga! Enga!

What had she done with his picture?

Linda dashed in, at first confused by the fevered scene, until a vague notion of her potential wrongdoing soon gelled. Her chin lowered. Her eyes squinted. Her guilt-ridden face flushed with fear. She motioned for her son to follow her.

They trekked together to the laundry room for a joint investigation of the crime scene. When she lifted the lid of the washer, both peered inside.

What they saw wasn't blood, but it might as well have been.

On the inside of the drum were four small scraps of limp and tattered paper clinging to the side for dear life—but there was no life left in them. Each was about the size of a mangled thumb, with the faint remains of lost lines that nobody, including Chellamuthu, could make out.

He carefully peeled the scraps away from the drum, cuddled them in his hand, and trudged silently back to his room, where he laid them like wounded soldiers on his desk. He tried to reassemble them, but the ragged pieces were no longer breathing. The largest was possibly the top of Selvaraj's shoulder, the smallest was Anu's little face. The remaining two were nothing but smudged strokes, muddied color, and faded scribbles of unidentifiable family.

Once again, everything was lost.

Linda repeated her apology, somberly made his bed, and then slunk from the room. When she returned twenty minutes later—always the problem solver—she carried colored pencils, sheets of paper, and misplaced hope. She doodled with a pencil in midair, miming that he could sit down and resurrect his lost masterpiece.

He took the pencil and touched its colored tip to paper, but he couldn't form the words—in Tamil or otherwise—to explain why the task was now impossible.

When he'd first drawn his picture with all of his aunts, uncles, cousins and other relatives peppered into the background, he'd left one off. It was true he had seven uncles on his mother's side—but he'd once had eight.

The missing man had moved with his family to the village of

Nadipudi, near the Bay of Bengal, when Chellamuthu was just three. The uncle and his family had come back to Erode once since their move, on their way to perform a *Yatra,* and had made plans to visit again—until a cyclone hit. The vicious storm had attacked the region of Nadipudi with such fury that, within minutes, swollen, debris-laden waters had crested over their village and wiped it clean away, like a woman might casually wipe spilled tea from a table. No trace of his uncle or the family had ever been found.

Chellamuthu hadn't included his uncle in the drawing because he couldn't remember what the man looked like.

The problem had now spread.

When Linda held out a second sheet of well-intentioned paper, Chellamuthu knocked it away. He couldn't draw his family again because he was having problems remembering their features. His memories, like his paper in the washing machine, were churned, torn, and dying.

The picture had been serving as his anchor, helping him cling to India—albeit precariously—by connecting him to his past. With his last thread now frayed, broken, and dangling, his own untethered existence would also soon wash away and drown.

It would be as if his family had never existed.

The house was still when Chellamuthu slid out of bed.

Fred and Linda had been teaching him to pray, and while it felt awkward without a shrine, tonight he was making an effort.

He ground his teeth, set his jaw, struggled to form the words.

Lord Shiva . . .

He coughed as the sounds stuck in his throat.

What was the point? His family didn't know he'd been kidnapped. Even if they did, he was half a world away. They could never afford to come and get him.

The truth hissed in his ear like a snake.

Shiva can't do anything.

Chellamuthu stood without finishing. At the desk he picked up the remaining scabs of paper and with fingernails tearing like fangs, he shredded them into bits of negligible scraps. He pinched them between his fingers and flicked the wad into the garbage.

A storm was swelling. A wave that had been rising off-shore was cresting now toward the room—it was coming for him.

He didn't care. He wouldn't swim. He wouldn't gasp for air.

Chellamuthu was done fighting, paddling, remembering, trying.

He wiped at the tears dripping down his face and then climbed into his box-shaped bed. Loneliness draped her spindly fingers around his neck and squeezed as Chellamuthu released a final breath.

But the grip loosened.

In the shadowed and shivering room, the boy coughed softly and then reached forward to pull the blanket over his head as if he were folding closed the flaps on a cardboard box.

With his face covered, Taj Khyber Rowland drifted off to sleep.

CHAPTER 21

1990, Ten Years Later

Taj stared into the trophy case that guarded the school's main auditorium. It was a rare quiet moment, because when the bell rang in exactly three minutes, organized chaos would settle in with shoving students trying to be first inside.

The spot where Taj stood would get especially crowded. The senior class photo had just been posted and every let's-talk-about-me student in the school would be trying to find himself or herself in the picture.

For Taj it was easy.

Of the nine hundred and thirty-one students in the Mountain View High School Senior Class of 1990, all were white but one—a single black sheep in a very white flock.

That wasn't what perplexed him.

As he leaned close to the glass, a voice behind him began to sing.

"One of these things is not like the other . . ."

Taj didn't need to turn around. The gravelly vocals of his best friend, Rod Lewis, flung their arms around Taj and held him tight—like always.

Rod pushed in beside Taj, squished his nose up against the case, and let his gaze rake back and forth across the photo. "Where are you again?" he asked, pretending to swoon.

He was a kid who valued one-liners, and Taj loved him for it.

Rod didn't wait. "There you are—front row, surrounded by cheerleaders. Honestly, when I die, I want to be you!"

"Is there something strange about this picture?" Taj asked, ignoring the praise. "Besides the fact that I'm dark?"

Rod's eyes billowed. The world was his stage. "You're DARK?"

"Do you have a serious bone in your body?"

"My *mandible* is serious most of the time."

"That's not even a real bone."

"You should have listened in anatomy."

"I'm not kidding," Taj insisted. "There's something odd that I can't figure out."

Rod didn't need a second look. "You're standing between two hot, happy, delicious cheerleaders—what adjectives did I miss?—and both girls love you. You're wearing a varsity letter jacket—swimming *and* wrestling. You're the student body president, the most popular kid in school, with an amazing best friend. And you've moved out—*against your parents' wishes and while still in high school*—and are living in your own apartment with *college kids.*"

Rod slammed his head to Taj's chest. "I love you, man!"

Taj bumped him away. "I'm serious."

"Dude! Look at the picture! The only thing odd is your face. You look like someone just shot your dog. You're the saddest king of the world I've ever seen."

Only Taj's mouth moved. "I don't have a dog."

Rod was losing patience.

Taj continued. "Is Lily dating me because I'm a novelty?"

"Novelty?"

"The only Indian in four counties."

"Indian? Taj, you're as American as Twinkies—chocolate Twinkies, but Twinkies nonetheless. I can't speak for Lily, but . . ."

"I can speak for Lily!" A petite blonde pushed her way between them. Her engaging eyes wore little makeup, didn't need it.

"You guys talking about me? Don't stop."

She tossed them a teasing smile, let it dangle. Lily could land about any boy in the school, but she had chosen Taj. She already had her arm around him, pulling him close.

"Yes, we are!" exclaimed Rod, not wanting to waste the question. "I say you're smarter than you are beautiful, but Taj disagrees. What do you think?"

Rrrrrring. Rrrrrring.

Doors burst open. Students filled the hall. Taj, Lily and Rod filed into the auditorium and took their usual seats on the front row. Once the student body was settled, the principal stepped to the mic.

"Thank you all for coming. To introduce the assembly, please welcome your student body president, Taj Rowland."

The walls in the guidance counselor's office were drab, dim—weary. Bill Baker, the counselor who had called Taj out of class, sat at his desk as he gestured toward the boy to take the waiting chair. For Taj, the surroundings were fitting, since he would have described the man as *ordinary*—height, weight, hair color, personality. Taj wouldn't have been half surprised to glance at the man's family photo and find 2.3 kids, a white picket fence, and a dog barking back. At least the guy had a sense of humor.

"Taj, thanks for coming. Have a seat. Give me a second." Baker flipped opened a file folder.

Taj sat, stretched, leaned back. When he lifted his feet toward the desktop, Baker raised his head. "Don't even think about it."

Taj swiveled. "I have swimming practice, so coach wondered if we can make this quick?"

"You're right," the counselor answered dryly, as his eyes let go of the paper. He leaned forward. "This is only about your future. Let's get through this right away, so you can get back to something more important, shall we?"

It was hard not to appreciate the man's sarcasm. Taj leaned in to meet him. "Fine. What do we need to talk about?"

Baker picked up the top paper. His lips flattened as he studied the figures. "You're on schedule to graduate, but your grades are slipping. Is there a problem?"

When the man's eyes lifted, Taj was ready. "Did you ever have parents?"

Baker didn't crack a smile. He'd heard them all.

"Parents—yes, I have parents."

"Unless you're too old, you'll remember they can be difficult."

"I'm thirty-two."

Taj was nodding with his entire body. "My point."

"Parents are parents. We all deal with them." Baker said. "Speaking of which, I understand you're no longer living at home, that you moved out a month or two ago. How's that working out?"

"Who told you? My dad?" The pitch in Taj's voice shifted.

"We do work at the same school. Let's just say it came up."

A shrug from Taj insisted he wasn't concerned. His nervous hands claimed otherwise.

Baker continued. "Are your jobs going well? You're working two of them now to pay for your apartment—right?"

"Is there anything you don't know, oh Great One?"

"I know that you haven't applied to any colleges yet. You better have a good reason." It was lean-forward time.

"That must be tiring." Taj noted.

"What's that?"

"Being stuck in a job where your only two choices are to lean forward or lean back."

It was the first time Baker smiled. "Yes, it is, and for the record, when nobody is watching, I'll even spin around—but you didn't answer my question. Is college not in your plans?"

How could Taj explain? "I looked at a bunch, but I guess I just couldn't decide." Taj felt his mouth twitch, as if he had more to add but wasn't sure he could trust the man. "Actually, I'm not sure I'm ready for college."

Baker set down the folder. "That surprises me. Are you sure?" He started to lean back but caught himself. "If you're not ready for college, how about a trade school?"

Taj shifted with him. "Like, to be a mechanic or something?"

"Sure, if you like, or an electrician . . . you know, a trade."

Taj would get to the point. He didn't have all afternoon. "What do I do, Mr. Baker, if I have absolutely no clue what I want to do with my life?"

"You become a high school counselor." The line was delivered too quickly, as if he'd used it before and had been waiting for a chance to throw it out there again.

Taj didn't smile, didn't laugh.

Baker shrugged. "Tough audience. Come on! It's funny. Smirk or something."

"Sad if that's the best you've got."

Baker pushed close to his desk. He blinked twice. "I'll be serious, which I know will be incredibly tough on you. Taj, I envy the people who have direction in their life—I do. I wasn't certain what I wanted to do after high school either, and it took me two master's degrees and a doctorate before I figured it out."

"Do you find that a bit ironic, since you became a guidance counselor?"

"Believe it or not, I enjoy my job. Trust me when I tell you there's something out there for you. We just need to figure it out."

Taj could think of a million punchlines. What was the point? He spoke softly so Baker would have to strain to hear. "What do you do when you don't fit in?"

Baker's eyes squeezed together. "Taj, you're the student body president. You're one of the most popular kids in school. You're . . ."

"I'm not talking about school," Taj interrupted. "I'm talking about . . . life."

It was a big question with even bigger answers. For a moment he seemed to have the man stumped—but this time Baker leaned forward with intent, as if he'd been tapped on the shoulder by the idea fairy.

"I have a thought," he said, reaching for a stack of papers at the edge of his desk. "Ta-da! Here it is. There's a study-abroad program that may be the ticket. They offer three different cities and work through local universities, so you get college credit. It will give you time to figure things out while still staying channeled toward a higher education. It's also a cultural immersion program, meaning you'll learn about the country's customs and history. I can tell you that other students have really enjoyed it."

Taj wasn't sure if the man was being serious now or just brushing him off. "Study abroad?" Every inch was skeptical.

"You have a better idea?"

Taj didn't. "I doubt my parents will go for it."

"You won't know until you ask."

"I don't see them very often."

"Taj, your dad's right down the hall—and that, for you, must be tiring."

"What's that?"

"Avoiding your dad when you're both at the same school. Would you like me to talk with him—about the study-abroad thing?"

There was no room for hesitation. "No! I'll do it."

Baker backed off. "Cool. No problem."

"What cities?"

"What?"

"The study-abroad—what cities?"

Baker checked the brochure. "Looks like Montreal, Mexico City, or London."

Taj's next question would be easy. "Which city is the farthest from here?"

"London, but that's not how I suggest you . . ."

"And they speak English there, right?"

Serious time was over. "Now you're just messing with me."

Mr. Baker checked his watch. "Go to swimming practice, Mr. Rowland—and don't forget the brochure. On your way out, could you send in the next student?"

"Hi! What's up?" Lily asked, as she snuggled in next to Taj, who'd been waiting in the school's bleachers overlooking the football field. Her perpetually happy tone bubbled like soda water.

"Thanks for meeting me," Taj said. He'd tried to infuse at least a spark of enthusiasm into his greeting, but his words frowned.

Lily stopped. Her eyes drooped as her arms folded over her stomach.

"*Thanks for meeting me?*" she repeated. She stood, fell half a step back to get a better look. She was blonde but not stupid.

No hello. No hug. No smile.

"Are you . . . breaking up with me?" she asked, as her upper teeth began tugging at her lower lip.

Taj twitched. He rubbed at his neck. It wasn't emotion that betrayed him but the lack of it.

"Look, Lily, it's not you . . ."

"Don't you dare!" she interrupted, her tone jumping to her defense. "Don't say another word."

He expected that, like the others, she'd storm off, cussing both his reputation and herself for not seeing it sooner. To his surprise, and perhaps hers, she sat back down beside him. Perhaps she was punishing him, making him stew in the sentiment.

Seconds ticked.

"Was I a trophy? A conquest?" she asked.

"No, 'course not."

"No? Because it sure feels like you had something to prove."

The sound of passing cars mingled with Lily's subdued sobs. Taj watched, waited.

"I guess I was stupid for thinking I'd be different," she finally said. "I thought we had something going that was . . . I don't know . . . *special.* I've been so blind."

"I'm sorry," he answered but in a tone that didn't sound sorry at all.

Lily fished a tissue from her purse and wiped at her running makeup. But then her head tipped. "You never cry?" she asked.

"What do you mean?"

"In all the years we've known each other, even when we were just friends, I've never seen you cry. Even that time wrestling, when you dislocated your shoulder, in all that pain—there were no tears."

Taj shrugged. "I can't help it. I just don't cry."

Lily wiped at her nose. A patch of pity held her words together when they spilled out. "That must be very painful," she said, slumping at the realization.

Taj's entire face wrinkled. "Painful? To not cry?"

Lily shook her head. "No—painful keeping everything all bottled up. If you continue, one of these days you'll burst."

It was nearly midnight when Taj pulled into Silver Shadows Apartments and locked up his motorcycle. The place was dark, dog-eared, and inexpensive, heaven for any student on a budget. His bike—more a scooter—was in worse shape, a dumpy old thing that barely ran, but it was all he could afford, and it served its purpose.

After school, he'd driven straight to his first job, taking tickets at Movies 8, and from there to washing dishes at the Whistle Wok. Living on one's own wasn't nearly as glamorous as it sounded.

The worst part was that he had to be back at school by 6:20 a.m. for an early student council meeting. It was no wonder his grades were slipping.

The second-floor apartment was dark, which probably meant his roommates were not yet home. If he showered quick and got right to sleep, perhaps he wouldn't wake up when they came in.

When he climbed the stairs, he found Fred, his father, waiting.

"What are you doing here?"

"Taj . . ."

Fred pulled his head away from the door where he'd obviously dozed off. He stood, but it took a moment to collect his composure.

"What do you need?" Taj continued, too tired to wait.

"You quit wrestling?"

"I didn't have the time . . . I . . ." *Wait.* They'd had this discussion. "I stopped showing up weeks ago. I'm guessing you aren't really here about that, are you?"

Fred's cheeks sagged in the weary light. "We—your mother and I—we're hoping we can talk you into coming home. It's been hard on your siblings . . . not having you there, having to explain why you left. Rux is acting up now. He thinks he's also above the rules."

Taj rocked forward. "Hey, I understand rules. If you'd have listened, I was in charge of the dance. It was my job as student body president to stay late with everyone else and clean up. I told you that."

"You had a curfew."

"And I told you before I left that I'd be late."

It was worn and well-trodden ground. Taj checked his watch.

"Look," Fred continued, "I don't want to argue. I came to apologize for our misunderstanding and to ask you to think about coming home."

Taj didn't answer.

Fred continued selling. "You could quit one of your jobs and even take the car on occasion and . . ." He paused, perhaps to get right to the main point. "Taj, we miss you."

"I spoke with Baker," Taj said, carefully sidestepping.

"Baker?"

"The counselor at school. He said you two had talked."

Fred's eyes lifted as he connected the dots. "Bill Baker. Sure, we chat on occasion."

"He suggested I might want to think about a study-abroad program—perhaps as a way to figure things out."

"Study abroad? Instead of the university?"

"It *is* a university." Taj added, "It's just not here."

Fred's head slanted sideways, as if dragged down by his frown. "I'm not sure what you're saying."

Taj would be blunt. "Yes, actually, I'd like to come home."

"That would be wonderful," Fred replied.

Taj had more to say. "I need to save a bunch of money."

"Why?"

"Come fall, I'm going to London."

CHAPTER 22

"Ladies and gentlemen. We are beginning our descent . . ."

The flight should have been liberating—leaving the U.S. behind, venturing off to a new country on his own. Instead, Taj had fallen asleep over the ocean, and his reward was a stiff neck and a numb arm.

He'd never flown on a jet, at least not that he could remember. For certain he didn't swim over as a child from India, but he held no memory of the journey.

"Sir, could you straighten your seatback?"

Taj obliged and then unfolded his letter. The instructions were clear: wait at baggage claim for a man in a green suit. He would transport students to the University of London for living arrangements.

Of the forty-eight students participating in the program, sixteen converged at the airport within an hour of Taj's landing. They huddled like lambs around Mr. Huddersfield, a green-suited man who addressed them in a British accent that sounded more like Mr. Bean than Mr. Bond.

Huddersfield herded the group onto a bus, fed them pastries and punch, then drove them an hour to the university in northwest London, where the students who had arrived earlier waited.

It was late, and Taj was tired.

"Thank you for your patience," Huddersfield grunted as they assembled in the large classroom. "Come down when I read off your name. You've been assigned with another student to families that live close. Since you will be using public transportation to get to and from the university, we want you to travel in pairs. That way you can get lost together."

He waited, but no one laughed. Sleepy crowd.

"All right then, let's start with Jonathan Sansone." A boy beside Taj stood. "You will be living with the Norwich family. Your traveling partner is Eric Fiala, who will be living with the Edwards family." When the pair approached the front, Huddersfield turned back to the class. "Students, in most cases, a host family member is waiting outside and will accompany you back to your home. For the few who are not, Miss Howland has made arrangements for your travel."

Taj listened, waited, and watched. Names were read. Numbers dwindled. With half a dozen students still seated, Huddersfield glanced directly at Taj.

"Taj Rowland."

He waited for Taj to stand. "You will be living with the Tamboli family. Your traveling partner is . . . Kelly Cooper, who will be with the Harrisons."

Besides Taj, there was one boy left in the room. He stayed seated. Instead, a slender girl with dark, shoulder length hair stood in the back. She spoke to Taj as she walked past.

"I'm Kelly," she said. "Don't look so surprised." She then let out a laugh that seemed too big for her petite and yet perfectly proportioned body, as if to say, *I'm not laughing with you, I'm laughing at you.*

Huddersfield spoke to Kelly first. "The Harrisons live near Upton Park. They are a very nice older couple with deep English roots. They host every year, and you'll find them quite delightful."

Taj's turn.

"Mr. Rowland. We noticed your picture when selecting host families and thought you'd enjoy the Tambolis. This is their first time hosting, but they come highly recommended, and I'm sure you will find them most accommodating."

Taj swallowed. "You noticed my picture?"

Huddersfield glanced across the room at Miss Howland, as if the selection was her idea. His words stumbled. "I just meant that they're . . . you know, uh . . . they're Indian. Like you."

"I'm American," Taj blurted, his words bellowing their protest.

"Well, yes, I know," Huddersfield replied, swirling his hand toward Taj, hoping to highlight the obvious. "But you *are* of Indian descent, correct?"

"I guess," Taj replied. How could he explain it to the man? Taj had never met another Indian, let alone lived with an entire family of them. "Do they speak English?" he asked, as his fingers drummed against the desk. "Because I don't speak Indian."

Kelly leaned in before Huddersfield could answer. "It's Hindi."

"Pardon?"

"Indian isn't a language. They likely speak Hindi."

His eyes lifted. If the girl's intent was to make a bad impression on her first day in England, she was doing a jolly good job.

Huddersfield's chin bobbed in agreement. "Yes, Mr. Rowland. They speak English." He rustled his papers. "We thought you'd be excited."

"I'm sorry. It's fine."

Huddersfield was already pointing with his misshapen finger toward their luggage stacked against the far wall. "If it doesn't work out," he added, "let me know, and we will make a change. Their son is waiting in the foyer."

Taj pushed through the door first. Kelly was right behind. A thirty-something Indian man began to wave at them as if they were standing on floats in a parade.

When Taj glanced back at Kelly, she winked. "Let's go, Captain America," she said. "I think that's our ride waiting."

Taj longed for silence. Even from the back seat, the radio clamored, street horns bounced against the window, pointless conversation seemed to incessantly drip.

Pranay Tamboli was talking too fast to notice. It didn't help that Kelly was nodding, prodding, inviting their driver to clarify every mundane answer to every unnecessary question in excruciating detail.

During the drive to Upton Park, the neighborhood where the family lived, Kelly and Taj learned that Pranay was the third oldest child; that his parents, Hari and Rachna Tamboli, had immigrated from New Delhi in 1953; that his father, who had been working in a British hospital in India, was recruited to London by the National Health Service to train as a doctor.

Why stop there?

His parents had had an arranged marriage; he loved watching rugby, specifically the Saracens; and now that his parents were retired and getting older, his young family had moved in with them to help.

When Kelly asked Pranay if he had a favorite British band, Taj shifted his attention outside.

London. Proper, prim, and picturesque. The streets teemed with activity—buses, cars, people—all scurrying about as if everyone were late for tea and biscuits with the queen. It matched the photos Fred had marked for Taj in a story featured in *National Geographic.*

Pranay turned off Green Street to avoid traffic.

Even the neighborhoods were quaint. Long lines of connecting homes, block after block of them, like rows of colonial soldiers standing shoulder to shoulder at attention. If one fell, the man on either side could stumble.

Most of the homes were two stories high and almost as wide, each one distinguished from its neighbors by changing styles of brick or wrought-iron fences enclosing front courtyards. Nearly all featured a bay window that stretched to the upper level, most outlined with slender colonial pillars.

Brick chimneys protruded from every connected home at evenly spaced intervals, generally pushing through the roof above common walls that separated dwellings beneath. While the façades were often painted in different colors—generally a shade of white—if a man had too much to drink at the local pub and wandered into his neighborhood in a drunken stupor, he'd be hard pressed to remember which door he called home.

"We're getting closer," Pranay said.

But the closer they got, the more the scenery changed. Not the buildings themselves, but the people. If one were comparing the surroundings to Fred's *National Geographic* pictures, they might have questioned if they were even on the same continent.

As they neared Uptown, nearly everyone around them—strolling the sidewalks, driving past in stubby little cars, hurrying into the shops that lined the brick paths—was Indian.

When Kelly inquired, Pranay proudly explained that the borough was home to one of the world's largest communities of Indians living outside of mother India.

Minutes later the car braked in front of a better-kept home with a bricked courtyard.

"This is where you'll be staying," Pranay announced to Kelly, and before anyone could step from the car, a kindly, gray-haired couple, noticeably English by their accents, strode down the front steps to embrace Kelly, like she were a daughter coming home from college.

The Harrisons, one of the few English families still living in the neighborhood, first shook hands and then hugged everyone, including Taj. They invited the group in for tea.

Thankfully, Pranay declined, insisting they had their own impatient tea-sipping family at home waiting for their new addition.

Ten minutes later and three blocks down the street, Pranay parked for a second time. He turned off the key and twisted around to face Taj.

"They will be most astonished."

"Your parents?"

"Yes. They decided to host a student from the States to provide a little American culture for my son." His snowy teeth stretched halfway around his face. "Won't they be surprised to learn we have instead been sent an Indian!"

Paintings of tigers, elephants, and olive-skinned women with red-dotted foreheads hung in abundance on the walls inside. The furniture, mostly carved, was cuddling intricately embroidered pillows of plush, vibrant colors. Strange figurines, both brass and wood, some with elephant heads on human bodies, watched from the shelves and mantels.

Taj sniffed at the stuffy air. He had removed his shoes, seemingly an Indian custom, but after hours of traveling, his feet reeked.

He'd seen *Oliver Twist.* This wasn't London.

"We apply for an American, and they send us you?" The deep booming voice, Indian accent prevalent, rattled down the hall.

It was followed by an old man. "What shenanigans is the school trying to pull?" he asked, wielding a carved wooden cane.

Taj shuffled backwards.

"Quiet, Papa," an old woman scolded, trailing him from behind. "You'll scare the boy and wake Amil."

Though the man's words were stern, his face was not. It bent quickly into a broad smile.

"I know, I know," he admitted, before Taj had even uttered a word. "I make a terrible liar." He pointed at Taj's nose with his cane. "Greetings, my son. We are honored to have you in our home."

The old man's wife, equally gray, equally eager, equally Indian, edged in front, not wanting to be forgotten. Pranay proceeded with the formalities. "Taj, I'd like you to meet my parents. My father, we call Papa Hari. My mother, Momma Rachna. Parents, this is Taj Rowland from the United States."

"And yet the man forgets his own wife!" said a younger, attractive Indian woman who had approached from behind. She placed her palms together in front to greet Taj.

"Shyla, I didn't see you," Pranay exclaimed. "Certainly, I would never forget the most beautiful woman in the world—who happens to also be my wife."

"Liars. All terrible liars," Shyla added. She turned back to Taj.

"With this family, you have to nearly shout if you expect to get in a word. It's a pleasure to meet you. How was your travel?"

Taj had yet to speak. His lips dropped open, as if they'd forgotten how to form words. Every muscle was jet-lagged.

Liars, she had said.

Should he lie also?

In reality the experience thus far had been . . . *smothering.* Had he been delusional? Why again had he come to London?

A roomful of foreign faces waited for a logical answer. It was all so *surreal.* Like that children's book, *Alice in Wonderland,* where the girl dreams she's traveled to a mixed-up, backward land.

"Does he speak?" Hari asked, looking back at his son.

Taj blinked, focused, breathed. "I'm sorry. Yes, my trip was . . . well . . . long."

"It's true, then," the old man added with a bit of glee. "You look Indian but sound American."

"Show the boy his room," Momma Rachna insisted, in motherly fashion. "Then, once he's settled, everyone come to the kitchen. I will have something ready to eat. He must be starving."

Taj hobbled behind Pranay down the hall until he halted at the second door.

"Your room is here. I hope you find it pleasant."

Taj had heard stories about sketchy living conditions. He glanced around: *Bed. Light. Carpet. Desk.* Everything here was modern and clean. The room even had an attached bathroom, an amenity the school hadn't guaranteed.

He shuffled forward.

Sink. Shower. Tub. Toilet.

Taj reached out and pulled the handle. It flushed.

"It works," he said to Pranay as the water swirled, as if both should be surprised.

It was Pranay's turn to step back. "I'm glad you like it. I will check on dinner."

Taj had barely unzipped his suitcase before Pranay was back.

"Mother has prepared *samosas* and *bhajis* in the kitchen. We can't wait to hear about your family, where you are from, and why you have chosen London for your university studies."

Taj's ears were ringing. His eyelids were sand. He trailed Pranay down the hall, but three steps from the kitchen, his legs stopped moving.

"Mr. Taj, is something wrong?"

Taj could hear voices—strangers—just around the corner speaking gibberish.

They were laughing, joking, eating who knows what. It had been hours since he'd slept. His head was pounding, and someone had now turned on eerie Indian music to which the old man was tapping his cane on the ground. Taj's brain was still processing the car ride. It hadn't planned on working overtime.

London was supposed to be fish and chips, soldiers wearing tall black hats, a clock in a rather large tower that someone had named Ben, and Monty Python—where was Monty Python?

Tonight, incense was burning.

He needed air but coughed instead.

"Thank you. It's kind. But I am just . . . I am . . . *tired.* I think I'll go to bed."

Before Pranay could object, before the family could interrupt and then shuffle around the corner to try to convince him otherwise, Taj fled back to his room, exhaled relief, and then closed and locked his door.

CHAPTER 23

Since Papa Hari's favorite Indian restaurant, the Mumbai Palace, was west of Upton, Taj had reluctantly agreed to go directly from the university to meet the family for dinner.

"Bring Kelly," Pranay had insisted. "We will provide you both with a traditional Indian welcome dinner."

Taj mouthed an okay with his lips, which must have confused them, because his brain was already affirming there was no way in hell. There had been nothing in the brochure about living with Indians and unquestionably nothing about pairing up with a girl whose undies were cinched too tight.

When he stepped from Pranay's car, Kelly was waiting beside the Upton Station sign. Pranay had just started to pull away but jolted to a stop when he noticed her. He stuck his head out and hollered.

"Miss Kelly! Miss Kelly! We are inviting you to dinner tonight. Taj will tell you all about it. It will be very delicious."

Kelly smiled. Pranay flapped his fingers. Taj could barely lift the corners of his mouth.

Pranay wasn't finished. "You two grab a hackney, and we will pay for it."

As he drove off, Kelly turned. "What's a hackney?"

Taj followed his shrug down the stairs toward the train platform. "I'm not sure, but I'd wash your hands if you grab one."

Kelly, undeterred, confirmed with a woman on the platform that he meant a taxi.

"Are you all right?" she asked. "You seem a little . . . what's the technical term? . . . freaked out."

"Do you just spit out whatever pops into your head?"

"Pretty much. I call it a gift. So you're asking me to dinner?"

"No . . . I . . ."

"Well, I accept."

She was grinning.

"You're joking, aren't you?" he said.

"You're adorable, you know that? In a strictly platonic, stern-faced sort of way."

"It's going to be a long semester." It was a thought that he normally wouldn't have spoken aloud. At the moment, that didn't seem to matter.

"Lucky you! Our train is here," Kelly announced. "We get to chat the entire way."

When school ran late, thrusting Taj and Kelly into London rush hour, finding a hackney proved harder than Pranay had implied. It meant when the two finally arrived outside the restaurant, they were twenty minutes late.

Kelly rushed. Taj dragged.

"Are we sure about this?" he called out, his words ringing with reservation.

When Kelly pulled open the door, rhythmic Indian folk music dashed past, bounding off into the night. Her eyes gleamed.

"Come on, party pooper!" she commanded. "We're letting all the fun out!"

At first, the confused attendant inside tried to seat the pair, assuming they were a couple who had come in for dinner. Taj repeated the name Tamboli three times before the server's head wobbled as his arm swept toward a banquet room in the back.

The family was already waiting—and more. The room was packed with Indians of all shapes, sizes, and hues—friends, neighbors, relatives.

Music played. People danced. Food was being placed in the middle of the table.

The two stopped cold—Kelly, who reveled in the splendor, Taj, who was filled with panic.

He'd never seen such a large room filled with so many people where every breathing, bronzed body looking back was dark. Like him. It should have been exhilarating. Instead his heart pulsed, his fingers curled, his chest constricted, as tiny beads of sweat, running away in full retreat, traced channels from his armpits to his waist.

A familiar feeling was gurgling in his gut—the urge to flee.

He turned to leave just as a welcoming hand rested on his shoulder.

"Taj, come in! Come in! We are just getting started." Pranay pulled him forward, like a man reeling in a reluctant catch.

"We've saved two seats at the head of the table."

Taj touched Kelly on the shoulder. "You go first. I'll sit by you on the end." He wasn't joking.

Kelly winked. "I promise you, sweetie, they don't bite."

There was no time to argue. Papa Hari was already banging his cane.

"Good evening, friends! We are happy to welcome our American guests here tonight to sample the best Indian food north of the Gogavari."

Everyone cheered but Taj.

He looked across the parade of waiting Indian dishes. Did they laugh? Standing in for a plate, a cut banana leaf was spread at each place at the table. A waiter was already dishing rice onto each leaf, and Taj hadn't even asked for any.

He hated rice.

The dish directly in front of him bore a strong resemblance to stewed weeds. Had they never heard of cheeseburgers? What about steak and potatoes? Vegetables had pulled an obvious coup, invaded the kitchen, and jumped into everything with reckless abandon.

When Kelly nudged, he picked up the bowl-o-weeds and passed it directly to her. She wasn't shy. She took a spoonful, dumped it onto her rice, and was about to pass it back when he motioned with his head to keep the bowl moving.

"Wait," she said, her eyes forming a question. "Have you really never had Indian food? I thought you were joking."

Taj shushed her quiet. "Why and where would I have had Indian food?"

Kelly's eyes traveled from his head to his feet—and then back for a second look. "Oh, I don't know," she deadpanned.

That was the problem. Looking Indian didn't make him Indian. Why couldn't people understand that? Outside doesn't determine inside. Ignoring the misleading color of his skin, underneath he was pasty white!

He didn't belong here.

In truth . . . he didn't belong anywhere.

Pranay, sitting across the table, sensed the boy's reluctance. He hunched over to highlight the delighted dishes.

"Here we have *gobhi aloo,* which is cauliflower and potatoes sautéed with garam masala. Beside it is *baingan bharta,* which is *baingan*, or eggplant, as I believe it is called in the United States, cooked with tomatoes and onions. And the restaurant's specialty, *palak paneer*, which is cottage cheese cubes in a spinach gravy."

He waited for Taj to respond, as if he expected him to gleefully clap.

Taj wasted no time. "Why, it looks so . . ."

Kelly must have seen the glimmer in Taj's eyes as he searched for the right word, because beneath the table, the tip of her pointy shoe caught him squarely in the calf.

" . . . healthy," she said, finishing his sentence.

Pranay was too enthused to notice. "Oh yes, it's very, very healthy and very, very good."

"That's a lot of *verys,*" Taj noted, as Kelly kicked again with more force.

It wasn't just the array of thick, gravied vegetables that had Taj perplexed but the way people were eating. A spoon had been placed in the serving dishes, but the utensils for eating had eloped. A quick glance down the table answered the dilemma. Everyone was stirring the food together on their banana-leaf plates with their fingers and then scooping it into their mouths—even the messy stuff.

It was like a bad day at scout camp.

"Go ahead!" Pranay insisted, pointing toward the waiting serving bowls in the center. "Don't be shy."

"There are just so many," Taj said, almost mocking. "It's so hard to decide."

Kelly's eyes locked onto Taj, as if she could read his mind—and it all apparently amused her.

"Watch," she said as she pushed all four fingers into a serving of rice so yellow it must have been radioactive. She carried it to her mouth mockingly, as if to say, *that's how it's done, little boy*—but then she paused. Her head fell forward.

She chewed. She tasted. She swallowed. Her eyes widened.

"This is the best . . ."

She didn't finish. Instead she mixed the rice with a swirl of the waiting sauce beside it on her plate that was happy finally to be included. She lifted it again to her mouth.

It started with nodding, more chewing, and then the near moaning of words like *unbelievable* and *spectacular.* Taj was certain it was all a charade to make fun of him—all because he'd made the mistake of telling her on the ride over that he'd never eaten Indian food.

Pranay stood, outwardly alarmed that Taj still had nothing but bare rice in front of him. He called down the table for Rachna to pass a platter of chicken, the one with breast pieces so red they looked sunburned.

Taj watched, waited. It was firing squad by Indian food, and he had nowhere to run. He was about to pass the platter along to Kelly when the rising steam reached out and latched onto his cheeks with all its fingers.

He pulled the dish back and sniffed it.

His head tilted. His lips drooped. A question mark of wrinkles formed in his brow. The scent that swirled around his neck had started rubbing his shoulders, reminding him softly that once, a very long time ago, they had met.

"Are you going to take some or just hold it all day?" Kelly asked.

"Wait just a minute," Taj answered, more curt than he'd intended.

He picked up the spoon and stirred the sauce, as if expecting it to speak. *And it did!*

He couldn't place where he'd had this dish before, and it was maddening. It was like bumping into someone on the street you remember as an old friend, or the very least an acquaintance, but no matter how hard you try, you can't place the person's name or from where you know them.

"I've been here before," Taj muttered, not letting go of the platter.

"I thought this was your first trip to London," Kelly questioned, confused.

Taj didn't reply. He was busy sliding a piece of the saucy chicken onto his rice.

He reached for a fork—it was missing. Knowing she was watching, and not wanting to cede satisfaction to her *I told you so* grin, he tore off a piece of the chicken with his fingers and took his first bite.

The spices in his mouth grabbed hands and began dancing in rhythm across his tongue—*cumin, garlic, peppers, ginger, tamarind, cinnamon,* and more. They weren't just dancing—they were cheering, clapping, celebrating, singing, reminiscing. They were pulling out wallets and showing each other pictures of their kids.

"What is this?" he said to Pranay, his mouth still melting with confusion.

"That, my friend, is the finest chicken curry in all of London."

Curry!

Taj set down the breast and licked at his fingers. He couldn't help it. He might just have to suck on them all evening.

Where had he tasted this before?

He let his tongue roll across his lips to catch any morsels that may be trying to escape. This was more than just a meeting of old friends;

it was finishing their words, laughing at inside jokes, recognizing a camaraderie that hadn't aged with time. Blood brothers.

Taj picked up the chicken and took another bite, only this time with tightly closed eyes. He licked again at the coriander, the chili, the cardamom, and the bits of curry leaf. It must be a taste remembered from his childhood—that was the only answer that made sense—but he found the growing recollection oddly curious.

The mingling spices, the familiar taste, it felt like a whisper arriving with the wind, more message than memory.

"Taj," it seemed to say. "It's time."

Traveling to and from the university each day meant taking the Tube, London's subway, between Upton Park and Euston Square, an hour-long ride, morning and evening, sitting beside travel mate Kelly Cooper.

Her inky hair loved to drape forward across her flushed cheeks. Her Barbie-like blouses happily hugged her curves in all the right places. Her slender fingers were always ready to illustrate her words, of which there were plenty.

If people on the train stared, Taj knew it wasn't at him.

The first few weeks of riding with a stranger were awkward. She was attractive, yes, but at times acidic, like a sparkling glass of refreshing iced vinegar. She was a girl who spoke her mind about *everything,* a girl with a lot on her mind.

"Tell me something about you I don't already know," she said, with words too cheery for the early hour. It was one of her favorite games to play on the train.

"I despise people who talk too much," Taj deadpanned, keeping his eyes tight.

"Wow, a joke! We're making progress. We may become friends yet. My turn. In high school, I was a champion spelling bee-er. Now you go."

Taj tried again. "My favorite thing to do in the morning is to think quietly without interruption."

"That's good," she gave him a shoulder squeeze. "However, the game is things we don't already know. *Buzzzzz.* You lose. I'll start again. Let's see . . . I belong to a small group of people who actually know the meaning of the word *esoteric.*"

Taj had been resting his head against the window. When he straightened, she was waiting like an impatient puppy looking for a treat.

"You're exhausting," he said. "If you really want to become a psychologist and expect your clients to ever come back, you're going to have to learn to be . . . agreeable."

"People aren't looking for *agreeable,*" she retorted. "People crave honesty."

He raised his finger, was about to argue, but let it fall back into his lap.

"If you want me to be honest, then," he said, harnessing bluntness in place of wit, "I'd be fascinated to know if anyone has ever asked you out on a second date?"

It was one of those questions that sounds funny and clever in your head but jumbles into malice when it breaks itself free. Taj started to immediately gather the pieces.

"That came out wrong. I just . . ."

She glanced back without a flinch, not speaking a word, seeming to mull the notion over in her head, and for just a split second, Taj might have detected sadness.

"I'm sorry," he said. "It's just, you're smart and . . . sort of intimidating, and I can see . . . well, how you might scare guys off."

Still nothing.

"I guess I should just shut up now," he added.

Her finger touched her lower lip. "Are you saying you prefer shallow girls?" she asked.

"No . . . I . . ." Taj glanced at his feet.

"Seriously," she insisted, "what kind of girls do you date?"

"How do you turn every conversation into a psych session?"

"This is your topic, not mine. So, what kind of girls do you date?"

He was no match. "Blonde."

"Why did I know that? Did you date a lot?"

He would have hoisted a white flag if he'd had one. He knew from experience she'd be relentless.

"Quite a few." He glanced again at the floor. "But I was never really fair to them, if you want the truth."

"The truth! Now we're getting somewhere." It was like giving a dog red meat. She latched on to it instantly. "What do you mean?"

He'd seen that look. "Do you want your five cents now or later?"

"Later. What do you mean, not fair to them?" she repeated.

Taj arched back in his seat, waiting for her eyes to meet his. "I'd chase, flirt, take them out, date them just to . . ."

"Just to what?"

Did her eyes just smile? "I think to prove to myself that they liked me because of . . . *me.* Not because I was a novelty."

"You mean because you were the only Indian?"

He feigned a smile. "The only one around for miles."

"It's interesting you say that."

"Why?"

"Here in London, especially living in Upton with the Tamboli family, you're not unique at all. You're actually pretty common—and yet . . ." she paused, as if for dramatic effect, " . . . yet, people here still seem to like you. A lot. Crazy, right?"

She had a way of doing that—making him consider notions he hadn't—and she wasn't through.

"You said most of the girls you dated were blonde?"

"They were."

"Why would that be?"

"I don't know."

"Sure you do. Dump the doubt and admit it."

"You never filter, do you?"

"Takes too much energy—and stop avoiding the question. Why don't you date dark-haired girls?"

"Girls like you?" he confirmed.

"Yes, like me."

He knew the answer. Worse, he knew that she knew it. He glanced across the half-empty train, as if hoping someone would scurry by and rescue him. Nobody came.

"Because the dark-haired girls looked too much like me."

"And you didn't like what you saw?" she confirmed.

Taj didn't answer.

She could have quit there but didn't. "Would you date a dark-haired girl now?"

"Are you asking me out?" he asked with a smile.

"Me?" It was her turn for surprise. "NOOOO! That's not where I'm going with this at all. No offense."

"Now you're just being rude—getting even."

"Would you?" The girl was Webster's definition of determination. "Date a dark-haired girl?"

Taj fidgeted with his watch. "I think when I get home . . . ," he said, still putting the words together in his head, " . . . that I'd like to try to date . . . an Indian girl."

Kelly's lips creased upward.

"Good answer." And then she reached out and squeezed his leg, as if she instinctively understood that a simple touch would communicate more than any words.

"You're like so many people, just hiding, waiting to be found."

"What does that mean?"

"Hide and seek. You played it as a kid, right?"

"Sure."

"If you were like me, your competitive side wanted to find the best hiding place ever, somewhere no one would ever think to look, a place from which you could emerge triumphant after all the other kids had been found."

"So?"

"The problem is that hiding can also be boring, empty, lonely, even scary. True?"

"I guess."

"I remember sometimes, in the middle of the game, starting to panic a bit as the minutes ticked by and the other hiders were discovered and released one by one. You're no different, Taj. I think the softer side of everyone simply wants desperately to be found, to be accepted, to belong. So quit holding back. Quit hiding. Reveal your true self. Let Taj Rowland be found."

When the train stopped, they stood, and as people crowded around the door to exit, he leaned close. It was his turn to whisper.

"You're going to make one hell of a psychologist."

CHAPTER 24

After class, on the ride home, Kelly jumped up when the train reached Plaistow Station, one stop earlier than their normal exit. She twisted toward Taj.

"Oh, I forgot to tell you. This is where I need to get off. I'm meeting my mum and dad at West Ham Park. They're watching Archie, their little grandson. I told them I'd help. We're all going out for crumpets after. You want to come?"

"What's a crumpet?"

"I'm not completely certain. It's either a musical instrument or an English pastry. Either way, I believe they slather them in melted butter."

Did she ever quit? Taj followed her out the door.

"Why do you do that?" Taj asked, as they hopped up the stairs to the street.

"What?"

"Call them Mum and Dad when they aren't related to you?"

"Because they love it . . . and I guess they feel like family. Don't the Tambolis feel a bit like family to you?"

Taj had never considered the notion. "My mom and dad back home hardly feel like family to me, let alone strangers here in London."

Her eyes drew together, nearly crossed with confusion. "You don't get along with your parents? I wouldn't have guessed that."

"Why not?"

"After talking with enough people, one learns to tell who's loved. It shows in people's relationships. Guess I'm just a little surprised. Why do you say you don't get along?"

Taj had quit making therapy jokes. He was actually growing to enjoy their conversations.

"My mom always works. My dad, he's a real treat. He carries a clipboard everywhere with his to-do list. When I was in high school and it was time to wake me up, he'd come in and grab my hand, raise it in the air, and hold it there all the while asking, 'Taj, you awake? Taj, you awake? Taj, you awake?' Over and over and over. How would you like to wake up to that every day? It was miserable. I was just one more thing he needed to check off his list."

Kelly said nothing but seemed instead to count their footsteps against the pavement as they walked.

Step . . . step . . . step . . .

"No comment?" he asked. "That's not like you."

"Just thinking."

"About what?"

She hesitated. "I'd get woken up in the morning too."

"And . . . ?"

"Let's just say . . ." Her pace slowed, and it was the first time he'd noticed she wasn't using her hands to help hold her words. " . . . my stepdad would come into my room after my mother had gone to work."

Her voice trickled to a whisper. "I would have preferred your dad's clipboard."

Step . . . step . . . step . . .

Every word Taj tried to form rang hollow, felt petty. "Kelly, I'm so sorry," he finally sputtered.

"I've been living with my older brother and his wife for the past four years. All is good now."

Step . . . step . . . step . . .

"Is that why you're studying to become a child psychologist?"

She didn't answer.

"Look, there's Archie. Come on, I'll introduce you."

For the neighbors living around West Ham Park, the place was nearly eighty acres of bliss. It contained a botanical garden, tennis courts, soccer fields, cricket nets, and a track, with the highlight for anyone under ten being a children's playground that was second to none—a massive modern play area encircled by a protective wrought iron fence.

The Hamiltons hadn't yet arrived, but their daughter, Millie, was waiting with Archie, her son. Kelly greeted her like a sister, made introductions to Taj, and then Millie waved good-bye as she rushed off to meet her husband for a business dinner.

"You're a dear!" she called out. "And you're so FIT!"

"NO, YOU'RE FIT!" Kelly hollered back, but Millie was gone.

"What was that all about?" Taj asked.

Kelly grinned—often a bad sign for Taj. "Do you think I'm fit?" she asked.

"I'll bite. Yes. You're *very* fit."

Archie was tugging her off to the slide. She didn't prolong the torture. "*Fit* in England means *hot, stunning, beautiful*—so thank you!" She batted her eyelashes twice and then chased after Archie.

While Taj waited for the Hamiltons, he grabbed the metal fence with his fingers, pushed his face against the posts, and leaned in to watch. Kelly was climbing the steps to the slide with the boy, and while Taj would never tell her in a million years—because he'd never hear the end of it—she was not only *fit,* she was going to make one remarkable—though demanding—mother.

Archie was young, just three or four, and as Kelly held his hand and helped him climb, a line of small boys backed up behind them—all Indian boys.

They weren't just waiting at the slide. They were everywhere: Indian children—running in circles, playing tag, chasing each other around with no cares in the world.

It was all instantly familiar.

It wasn't just that they were Indian children—this was East London, that would be expected. It was deeper. Beyond the slide were Monkey Bars, a Teeter-Totter, Jungle Gym, and Merry-Go-Round. They weren't in the right order, not where he'd remembered they should be, but all still there.

"*. . . You distract him while I climb the fence . . .*"

Taj glanced at the ground near his feet and then behind him, as if half expecting to see a crouching, dirty boy.

His feet stood in London, but his head had bolted elsewhere.

"*. . . If the guard catches you, he'll beat you like a sewer rat . . .*"

If Taj had to describe to someone what had been happening lately in his head, the best he could piece together was that his brain had been switching channels. It would be like watching your favorite sitcom and right in the middle of a funny sentence, when you'd least expect it, the picture would change. The new images would be like snippets of old movies strung together, and while strange, jumbled, and confusing, they were also vaguely familiar.

"Taj? Hello . . . Are you okay?"

He looked up to find Kelly, to feel her arm gently poking his shoulder. "Taj, you zoned out there. You tripped to zombie land."

"Sorry, sorry. I'm fine. I'm back now." But his brow was still rippled, his eyes still those of someone straining to see in the dark.

"Taj, the Hamiltons are here."

Only then did he notice the confused couple standing right beside Kelly.

"You must think I'm on drugs," Taj mumbled, before deciding that was perhaps not the best way to introduce himself, given that he would be helping Kelly watch their grandson.

Kelly stepped in to save him. "I could go for a crumpet or two right about now. How 'bout you all?"

Archie bounced excitedly on cue, evidently an avid crumpet lover. Kelly herded everyone toward the street.

"Sorry to bow out," Taj said, "but I think I'll head home. I have a lot of . . . homework."

Kelly was blinking. "Wait, you're walking back by yourself?"

"Why not?" Taj asked. "You do it all the time."

"Yes, but I'm a teeny white girl, and you're a big, strong Indian man. You're usually terrified."

Taj smirked, then turned away. She was right. He did hate walking in the area alone, especially once it was dark.

Tonight was different. Fear be damned—he needed time alone to think.

He was only a few steps away when Kelly hollered again. "Excuse me, Taj?"

He spun around. "What?"

She pointed behind her. "You'll end up in Scotland. Home is that way."

Wait, what?

He glanced around at the park, the location of the slide, and then past Kelly toward Green Street. He was generally good with directions, seldom got turned around. Odd.

"Right, good. Thanks."

As he walked past, he considered telling her to wipe away the silly grin, but she'd only slap him with a witty comeback. He'd already accepted that she could beat him in a verbal duel any day of the week.

Besides, a new question echoed in his head, demanding an answer: *Why did it feel like home should be on the opposite side of the park?*

Taj ignored the light sneaking in from the hall that seemed determined to keep him company. Still, it proved bright enough to highlight his surroundings—elephants, tigers, beaded pillows, paintings—all India, all keeping him company. It had taken time, but the sitting room, once foreign, now felt warm, even awkwardly anxious, as if waiting for a first kiss.

The lock clicked open. The light flipped on. Pranay hurried inside but paused when he realized someone else was home.

"Taj?"

"Yeah?"

"What are you doing in the dark?"

"Thinking."

"Where is everyone?"

"Your parents went to pick up dinner. Shyla took Amil to buy shoes. They should be back soon."

Pranay parked in the opposite chair as his gaze frisked the room. "Are you all right? You usually avoid this place."

"Pranay, I'm Indian!" Taj announced, as if he could hold in the discovery no longer.

The man smiled. "Yes," he replied. "Most of us can see that."

Taj edged forward. "I'm not sure you understand. I don't mean that I have dark skin, that I was born in India. I know all of that."

"What then?"

"I don't know, but . . . I think I might have family there."

Pranay's nose wrinkled. "You said you were adopted in the U.S. as a child? From India?"

"Yeah."

"But you can't remember anything?"

"Tiny flashes. More bits than pieces."

"Well, what do you remember?"

Taj answered with feeble eyes. "Fragments . . . crazy things that come at the most unusual times. It's like I'm asking my brain to remember what I've spent a lifetime demanding it forget. It's as if the memories are there, in the shadows, waiting like a frightened child to step forward. The thing is . . . I think they want to be discovered."

"Then discover them. Let them out." Pranay stood. "I'll be right back."

When he returned, he carried a map of India. He spread it across the coffee table and motioned Taj close.

"You've never been to India?" Pranay asked.

Taj shook his head no. "You?"

"Certainly. Many times."

"What's it like?"

"Crowded."

"Besides that."

Pranay glanced at the map and then around the room, as if waiting for the décor to step in and help explain. "How does one begin to describe India? Besides the hordes, she can also be . . . peaceful but hectic, soothing yet sad, incredibly poor while holding the wealth of the world. Taj, India is thousands of years of devotion, energy, thought, study, commitment, love, and loss, all woven into a single, colorful fabric. She's a complicated woman—but once you relent and let her take your hand, you will never be the same."

Pranay rested a finger at the map. "Does anything seem familiar? Do you remember what part of India you are from?"

Taj studied it, an entire country spread before him, peppered with the countless names of villages, towns, cities—long, short, foreign, confusing.

"No. I don't recognize anything."

"You were given the name Taj," Pranay continued. "Perhaps you are from Agra, in the state of Uttar Pradesh, home of the Taj Mahal?" He aimed at the spot.

"My adopted parents picked that name because it was one of the few Indian words they could pronounce."

Taj touched the city that was his namesake, but then let his finger trace a widening web to neighboring names—*Surat, Nashik, Indore, Patna, Nagpur, Balangir, Kolkata.* All cities of millions, according to the map, and all places he'd never heard of.

"How many people live in India?" he asked Pranay.

The man scratched at his ear. "Nearing a billion—give or take a few hundred million."

"A billion?" Taj repeated. *Such a hopeless word.*

"And nothing looks familiar?" Pranay asked a second time.

"The truth is," Taj mumbled, with a reply so sad and sullen the entire room seemed to frown, "I could be from anywhere."

Pranay reached for Taj's shoulder. "You can't lose hope. If India wants you back, listen. Keep searching. She will come to you."

As Taj studied the vast landscape of India that spread before him on the table, a larger question circled in his eyes. His voice begged like a child. The questions were standing in line in his head.

Who are my real parents?

Where am I from?

How did I get to the United States?

"Pranay?"

"Yes?"

Taj reached out and grabbed the man's shoulders, as if he could answer.

"WHO AM I?"

CHAPTER 25

To his surprise, Taj was thoroughly enjoying his classes at the University of London. It wasn't Oxford or Cambridge, but at least the professor's accent would let him pretend.

"Students! May I have your attention? We'll be learning about cartography. Who can tell me what that means?"

"The study of carts?" a boy called out from the front row.

It should have been funny, but he was from Italy and with marginal English skills, leaving the professor uncertain if the student was joking.

Taj came to his rescue. "I don't suppose it would be the study of cats?"

"No, Mr. Rowland, that would be *cat*-ography. Anyone else?"

It was Kelly's turn. "What is the study of maps for $400, Alex?"

"That's correct—as usual."

Of the five classes on Taj's schedule, this was the only one he shared with Kelly. Though the pair sat together, they were strikingly different: one a listener, the other a talker; she loved a healthy discussion, he preferred to sit back and take notes. When Taj did speak up, it was usually to make the class laugh.

As the professor grabbed his chalk, Taj opened his binder and picked up his pen.

"Students, the first maps appeared more than five thousand years ago and served to record places of interest. They were pictorial, meaning the mapmakers used drawings or symbols to show small areas, like a hunting ground, a trade route, or a city."

The professor turned on an overhead projector that displayed a broken clay tablet.

"This is a map from the Babylonian era, about 600 B.C. Notice how it shows Babylon scratched in the center, surrounded by the Euphrates River, mountains, and the ocean. If anyone is interested, you can see this actual artifact in the British Museum. It's on Great Russell Street at the opposite end of our campus, just a few minutes from here."

Taj set down his pen.

"As you can see, students, early maps were crude compared to our modern maps. Our modern maps usually have north at the top. Not so with early maps. They had no rules relating to orientation and were seldom accurate or to scale—but they did serve a purpose."

Taj raised a hand. "If they weren't to scale, if they weren't accurate, how did they help?"

"Good question. They really just defined a relationship. To do so, they didn't need a lot of detail, didn't need to be accurate. They just needed to point you in the right direction, establish a bearing and a path. These ancient maps worked well enough precisely because they *were* small and simple, not elaborate. It's a good lesson for life, don't you think?"

English accent or not, the professor was brilliant. He kept going.

"Sometimes, just focusing our view, taking a new perspective, makes all the difference."

Taj eyed the wall clock, checked it against his watch. The last twelve minutes of class were like waiting on death row. When the professor finally announced they were excused, Taj's books were already packed and halfway out the door. He chased after them.

"Let's go," he called out to Kelly. He was bouncing like a school girl.

"Where?"

"The British Museum."

"Why?"

"I . . . um . . ." The idea was darting around so fast in his head it was getting dizzy.

"Use your words," she instructed calmly.

He took a breath. "To see the map. I've been remembering things, places, images, smells, faces."

"Yes, so you've told me."

"Well, I've decided that I want to go back to India and find my family."

"Now?"

"No, of course not now. I have to finish school first, get back to the U.S., save some money. Look, the *when* isn't as important as the *why*."

"Don't leave out the poor little *how*."

"The other day Pranay spread a map of India out on his table, to see if it would help me remember anything."

"And . . ."

"It didn't work. It was too big, too overwhelming, too much."

"But . . ."

"The lesson today, it all makes sense. I don't need a large map of the entire Indian subcontinent. I need a small one, a map of the place where I'm from—my hunting ground, the town where I grew up. Just like he said, it doesn't have to be perfect or to scale or have everything in its proper place."

Kelly was biting at her lower lip, still not understanding.

"Where are you going to get a map of your town in India if you can't remember the name?" she asked.

Taj's eyes sparkled. They could have been diamonds.

"I'm going to draw one."

The map was crude, but if he believed his professor, it wouldn't matter. More important, it could help him find his boyhood home. Since coming to London, images, memories, fragments were piecing themselves back together. It was time to write them down.

While the clay tablet he'd studied at the museum had the great city of Babylon at its center, his own map's center was a bit more humble—a series of circles representing dirt-floored huts. He couldn't remember how many, what the huts had looked like, which one was his, or if they'd sat in a ring or in rows. He did remember that a large cement building stood beside them—a home where a kind lady sat out front.

There was the park, he'd already noted that, a large children's park with a high fence, and while he couldn't say how far it was from home, he believed it was to the west. The river that he'd drawn across his paper with a blue colored pencil flowed from north to east, cutting across the paper's top right corner as it escaped off the edges. It was a great start, but now Taj was confused as to where to put the bus station.

He was sitting on the train headed home, staring at his map. Kelly had decided to stand.

"You look like you're on the nib of a smarmy, knicker-twisting revelation," Kelly said.

"You've been in England too long," he retorted, hardly glancing up. His eyes continued to dart from the park to the huts to the river.

She watched. "Don't hurt yourself."

When he didn't answer, she nudged him with her shoe. "A threepence for your thoughts?"

Taj breathed, exhaled. He pushed his pencil back into his backpack before looking up. "Seriously. You've been in England *way* too long."

"What have you learned from your map so far?" she asked.

"Would you like to sit, doctor?" he asked, patting the open seat beside him.

"I'm good. Been sitting all day. So what have you learned?"

"I've learned that I'm an Indian," he answered, matter-of-factly.

The train had stopped, and more people than usual were getting on. An older man sat in the empty seat beside Taj.

"I'm sorry, what were you saying?" she questioned.

Taj repeated it louder. "I said I've learned that I'm from India. I'm an Indian."

Kelly cupped her palm to her ear. "I'm sorry. It's so noisy. Say again."

This time he nearly screamed. "I'M INDIAN!"

As the train's new riders returned baffled glances, her smug smile patted him on the shoulder to tell him she'd heard perfectly well the first time.

"I'm sorry," she said, before he could say a word. "I couldn't help myself."

"You enjoy that, don't you?"

"Very much. But never without purpose. I wanted you to see what it felt like to actually shout it out. So?"

"So what?"

"How did it feel?"

At times she could be maddening, like an annoying know-it-all little sister. She was opinionated, irritating, and loud. And when the year was over and they parted ways to head home, he was going to miss her immensely.

"It felt . . . *true,*" he answered. "And wipe that smile off your face."

When the train reached Upton, Taj almost floated above the concrete. The two would walk together for a block before heading to their separate homes.

"You've inspired me with your map," she conceded.

"What do you mean?"

"When you first showed it to me, I thought it was . . . I don't know . . . too simple."

"That's the beauty of it."

"I know, I know. I realize that now. In fact, I've decided to make my own."

"Your own? But you already know where you're from."

"True, but it doesn't mean my family isn't just as distant." She was nodding her head, as if having flashbacks herself. "I've felt just as far from my parents as you, and I was only sitting on the other end of their couch. I'd like to change that—at least with my mother. There is simply something beautiful and profound about mapping out your life with a crayon."

Taj's continual string of questions for Pranay ranged from easy to hard, from the trivial to the profound. On occasion, like tonight, when everyone was home and the family joined in, it could become a circus.

"Why are there so many Indians in London?" Taj asked, sitting beside Pranay and Papa Hari at the table as they sipped tea.

Papa Hari shook his cane. "The British ruled India for nearly two centuries. We all moved to London to get even."

"And in Papa's case, it's working," hollered Momma Rachna from the foyer.

"Here's one," Taj said. "Why do we eat with our fingers? How come we don't use knives and forks?"

Papa faced his son and whispered, though even the man's quiet voice could be heard from anywhere in the house. "We are converting the boy," he said to Pranay, with glistening eyes. "You notice that he said '*we.*' He is almost one of us."

"I'm serious," Taj asked.

"Answer the boy's question, Papa!" Momma called out.

Papa Hari tipped his head toward Pranay, letting him answer, though his narrowed eyes announced he'd chime in if needed.

"We don't use knives and forks," Pranay replied, leaning forward, "because we are not at war with our food. We don't need weapons. We have learned it is better to surrender to the flavors, to caress and embrace them. You see, eating for Indians is a passionate affair. Picking up the food with our fingers evokes a closeness, a feeling of warmth, a connection. It would all be lost if we started stabbing and cutting."

"That's very poetic," Taj replied. "What about your carved figurines? All these little statues?"

"What about them?"

"They're your gods, right? Why so many?"

Papa Hari rapped his cane on the floor, as if to jar it awake. "Why not? As Hindus we love our variety. We exclude nothing. Yes, we have many gods: Vishnu, Shiva, Saraswati, Lakshmi. In fact, many devout Hindus also worship cows, monkeys, trees, mountains, rivers, even the ocean. In the end, Taj, we believe that God and the many creations in the universe—no matter their form—are one."

"It's confusing."

"I would say *encompassing.*"

Taj was quiet, hesitant.

"What is it?" Papa Hari asked.

Taj picked up a carved bearded man with four faces and a lotus flower growing from his head. He studied it, placed it beside the others.

"I must have had some of these same gods when I was a kid. They seem so familiar."

"You don't have them now?" Pranay asked.

"I'm a Christian."

"Excellent," Papa Hari chimed in.

"Excellent?" Taj breathed surprise. "You don't care that . . ."

Papa Hari interrupted. "Taj, there is a declaration in our sacred texts that reads '*Vasudhaiva kutumbakam,*' which means 'The whole world is a family.' Does your belief help you to become a better person, to grow, to progress? That is our only concern."

Silence sailed in, but it was caring and comfortable, embraced by everyone.

"What are your plans?" Papa Hari finally asked, taking his turn at a question. "What will you study once you return home?"

"Business, I think."

"And what will you do in business?"

Taj shuffled his feet. "This is going to sound crazy . . . but I've wondered about setting up, you know, a business to import things from India."

"Not crazy at all," said Pranay. "If you are serious, I have a friend in India who may be able to help. He is also a Christian, like you, about ten years older. His name is Christopher Raj. He's a good man."

Pranay reached for a piece of paper and scribbled the information down.

While Taj waited, he elbowed Papa to get his attention. "Could you pass me more *chikki,* please?" He pointed to the plate at the end of the table.

"More *chikki?*" Papa asked with a grin. "Yes, my friend. You are Indian indeed."

The Tamboli family had welcomed Taj and Kelly to London with Indian food, and so it seemed fitting to say their good-byes in the same manner.

"Can you reach the *aloo gobi?*" Taj asked as he poked Kelly's shoulder and then pointed down the table. "And I know what you're thinking . . . not a word. Is that humanly possible?"

Kelly didn't technically speak as she passed him the plate, but softly hummed Bob Dylan's "The Times They Are a-Changin'."

Taj scooped a healthy portion onto his waiting rice, then stirred it with his fingers like a child mixing mud.

"Your parents are gonna love your new table manners," Kelly said. "Especially on spaghetti night."

"You just couldn't stay quiet," he quipped, his mouth trying to smile while full. "Oh, and don't let me forget . . . I have something for you."

Her eyes widened. "For me?"

"Don't get too excited. I'm cheap."

Once they were finished eating, he washed his hands and then walked her out front to where a vendor was selling Indian folk music CDs on the sidewalk.

"I noticed these on the way in." Taj purchased two and handed one to Kelly. "To remember me." Then he added with a grin, "I'm sorry, I didn't have time to wrap it."

From the sidewalk where they were standing, they could see down the alley to the restaurant's east side. A slatted fence partially corralled a protruding dumpster that looked anxious to break out. Music showered the scene from an open window near what must have been the restaurant's kitchen, a fitting reminder to anyone passing that affluence and poverty are often separated by only a few feet.

Taj was never sure what triggered the memories—smells, sights, sounds. He only knew they came at the most unexpected moments. His eyes watched. His ears listened. His nose tugged him closer to the smell of rotting food.

"What is it?" Kelly asked.

He didn't answer. He was walking.

"It's happening again, isn't it?" She'd seen that look in his eyes. "What are you remembering?"

"Food," he answered, " . . . and a dumpster."

Kelly trailed down the alley after him.

Taj lifted the lid, let the smell of well-seasoned decay smack him in the face. When he let go, the lid slammed closed.

Just like at the park, he couldn't help but glance around, as if expecting to see a skinny, shirtless, fleeing boy.

"I remember," he continued, "eating from a restaurant dumpster, kind of like this one. Why would I remember that? Why now? It was mostly little rice balls, leftovers tossed out with banana leaves."

He turned to Kelly, repeated the revelation as if it would make it more palatable, more believable. "I ate from a dumpster!" The words had no place to land.

"Do you remember where? Can you place it on your map?"

His head almost rattled. "It's all so bizarre. How does any of this fit into reality?" he asked.

"What do you mean?"

"I can't quit wondering how or why I ended up here, in London, right in the middle of all the Indians. Is it all chance—the Tambolis, that class, my map, the memories? It's all a little crazy, don't you think?"

"I don't believe in chance."

"Then what does it mean? Seriously, where do I fit in? What am I supposed to do with all of this? Am I meant to go back to India to find my family?" He faced Kelly directly. "You're the doctor—or you're going to be. How do I make sense of it?"

A warm stillness slipped in, like an arm around a shoulder.

"Taj, these are answers that won't come from a doctor."

"What do you mean?"

"When God works in our lives, those without faith like to call it chance. Those who believe call it a miracle. I don't know where you land on that scale, but I'm suggesting God is not as distant as you may believe."

"So do you think heaven is sprinkling bread crumbs that I'm supposed to follow to India? Wouldn't it have been easier to just leave me there in the first place?"

"We seldom get answers all at once. Parts of life will always be confusing."

"Then what do I do?" he asked.

She reached out and held his wrists. "It's not a race. Just work out your life one puzzle piece at a time. You'll figure it out."

"I will?"

"You will. You have a map."

CHAPTER 26

When Taj arrived at the airport, Fred and Linda were waiting with open arms and a hand-painted welcome sign.

"Son, it's so good to have you home."

Although he'd been gone for only two semesters, not quite a year, everyone agreed that it seemed longer. Mapleton felt smaller, his parents moved more slowly, the world around him had aged. He also found it peculiar to see no traffic, no smog, no honking horns—and no Indians.

They stopped at his favorite place for lunch, The Corner Café, ironically not on a corner, and while he told them it was good to be back, he didn't have the heart to let his parents know the food tasted bland.

When they asked which parts of his trip he liked best, he told them about his classes at the university, living with the Tamboli family, and his new friend, Kelly Cooper. He did his best to describe the brightly colored clothes, the narrow alleys that burped the smell of curry, and eating chicken tikka masala with nothing but his fingers.

If his parents noticed he was antsy, that he would fidget in his chair, gaze past neighbors who lingered to visit, or glance at his watch as if he had some place he needed to be, they said nothing.

He wasn't ready to tell them that he'd remembered places from his childhood, that he was constantly curious about his birth family, that he missed living in a country he could barely recall. He also wasn't ready to tell them about his map.

It wasn't that he was afraid of what they'd say or think or even that they'd misunderstand.

Perhaps it was just the opposite.

What if his family encouraged him? Showing them his map, wondering together about his origin, his history, that was one thing—actually stepping onto some unknown road to discovery, that would take a different kind of courage altogether.

He was eager to try—he was. The question he hadn't yet answered was more direct.

Was he prepared to accept what he found at the road's end?

Sitting in a classroom listening to a professor lecture at Western Valley University was surprisingly similar to listening to a professor lecture at the University of London—without the cool accent.

As Mr. Baker, his high school guidance counselor, had promised, his university credits transferred without a ripple. With a year of college general education already in the books, Taj declared his major in business management and penciled out a plan.

He would have loved his first action items to be "visit India, find family, tip the world back into balance." Just one tiny problem: zero money.

Worse than being penniless, he owed his parents $2,700 for London expenses. Then last night, they'd informed him that he was going to need to buy his own car. After dinner, he opened a letter telling him that his semester's tuition was now due.

Reality crushed dreams like soda cans.

Taj took a long, hard look at his map and then sandwiched it in the pocket of a 3-ring binder that he buried beneath a pile of books on the shelf in his bedroom. It was unlikely his brothers would touch anything labeled Business Law—Class Notes.

Next he turned to the Help Wanted section of the local paper. He spread it out and circled three jobs that looked promising.

If he was ever going to make it to India, he would need to save a bundle of money.

"Desire without a plan is only a dream," Fred would always say.

Taj dialed.

"Hi, I'm calling about your ad in the newspaper. I believe I'm a great fit. When would be a good time for me to come in for an interview?"

"You've settled in nicely," Carter said to Taj. "It's a pleasure to have you on board."

His boss was barely older than he was and way too enthusiastic about a company that sold skin cream. Taj had been hired to work in their call center, a sea of identical cubicles holding fifty or so customer service representatives who provided phone support for direct sale, multilevel marketers living around the country.

Taj hated that word. He hadn't *settled* anywhere! He still harbored big dreams of exploring faraway lands, battling menacing dragons, storming walled castles, and rescuing any willing princesses who needed saving.

Then again, even heroes can use soft skin.

The company loved hiring students, and though they paid next to nothing, his boss would work around almost any school schedule.

Taj positioned his headset and then checked the screen. Per company policy, he was supposed to make personal calls only during break time. To police compliance, call managers would listen in on occasion. Today's eavesdropping manager had yet to arrive.

He punched in a number.

A familiar voice answered. "Hello?"

"Does London feel like a dream to you?" he asked without any other introduction.

"Taj? How are you?" Kelly replied.

"A little crazy, but you probably already guessed that."

"So nothing's changed. How's school going? You back at it?"

"It's fine, I guess. Everything's just moving too slow. It's like life is mocking me. I have no money, school debts, had to buy a car—Kelly, I'm never gonna get to India!"

"So you're calling for a pep talk?"

"Putting it that way kind of takes the pep out of it. I'm just frustrated. What good is a map if I can't follow it?"

There was no hesitation. He expected none. "You know I'm going to say what's on my mind, right?"

"I've learned to love that about you."

"I have a solution for you. Inhale. Relax."

"That's the best you can do?"

Kelly took a heavy breath herself. "Look, Taj, you drew your map, which was amazing. Pat yourself on the back. But honestly, putting pencil to paper is the easy part. I mean what were you expecting? That you'd get home to find a pumpkin carriage with singing sparrows waiting to swoop you up and carry you off to India?"

"I don't care if they sing."

"Here's my advice. First, be patient. Life doesn't happen overnight. Give it time to simmer, to come together. That's what makes life flavorful. Does that make sense?"

She didn't wait for an answer. "Second, be persistent, tenacious."

"Wait! Don't patience and persistence conflict?

"Not really. Persistence takes patience. I'm trying to tell you that life is hard for everybody. It's tough, complicated. Having a map is wonderful, but following it, gritting it out through the mess to see where it leads, that's the magic."

"Is this when I cheer?"

"Not yet. If your dream is to go to India, say a prayer, feed the desire, move your feet—you'll figure it out. I believe in you. And Taj?"

"Yeah?"

"Now you can cheer."

It was late when Taj arrived home from work. When he walked into the kitchen, Linda's conversation with Fred stopped cold.

Taj glanced from one parent to the other. "What?" he asked, assuming he was in trouble.

"Should I tell him?" Linda asked Fred.

The man shrugged permission.

Linda faced Taj. "I had a dream about you last night."

"About me?"

"Yes."

"Was I rich?"

"I'm not sure."

"Famous?"

Linda squinted. "I . . . I don't think so, but I'm not certain."

"What, then?" Taj asked, as he poured a heaping bowl of cereal. He picked up his spoon and waited. Fred waited. Linda crouched lower.

"I dreamed, Taj . . ." It was as if she was sharing secrets of the universe. " . . . that you got married."

Taj bit on the spoon to suppress his smile. His lips wouldn't listen. "That's great, Mom," he said, "but I'm not dating anyone."

Linda's eyes rolled. "Not now, but eventually."

Taj took another bite. He still had studying to do. "That's . . . *special.* Thanks for sharing." He didn't even try to sound sincere.

Linda leaned closer. "Taj, you don't understand. I didn't just dream you got married . . ." The woman's voice almost wrinkled. ". . . you married an Indian girl!"

Taj waited until no one else was home to dial the number Pranay had written down. He listened. The reception was crackly, but on the fifth ring a voice answered, an Indian man.

"Hello?"

"Hi, my name is Taj Rowland. I'm calling from the United States. I'm hoping to get in touch with Mr. Christopher Raj."

"Speaking. How may I help you?"

"Pranay Tamboli, in London, suggested I call. I'm thinking about starting a company, and he said you might be able to help."

"What kind of company?"

"Import-export."

"From India to the United States?"

"That's the plan."

The man hesitated. "What did Pranay say I could do for you?"

"He said you know people, have connections."

"What exactly, Mr. Rowland, are you looking to import?"

"Well, I'm not certain."

"Not certain? Have you been to India?"

"Not that I remember."

"Not that you remember?" His words echoed confusion. "Sir, I would think you would remember India. How old are you, Mr. Rowland?"

"I'm . . . well . . . early twenties."

"Early twenties?"

Why did he keep repeating everything?

"Do you have lots of money, Mr. Rowland?" he continued.

"No, not really. I'm a college student. I have a little under three years left to finish my degree."

"And I presume you don't speak Hindi, Tamil, Bengali, Tulu, or any other of the many languages of India?"

"I'm still working on English."

"Well, I must ask, why do you want to start an import-export company?"

"I'm not entirely certain."

With the poor reception it was difficult to tell, but it almost sounded to Taj like the man was laughing.

"Is this a prank call?" he asked. "Are you prank calling me, Mr. Rowland?"

"No, I assure you this is not a prank call."

Christopher continued. "Then let me see if I understand. You want to export something from India, but you don't know what. In fact, you have never been to India that you can remember. You don't speak the language. You are in your twenties. You have no money. And you don't know why you even want to start this company."

The man had pretty much nailed it. Taj did his best to sound confident. "You paid attention."

"This is the moment, Mr. Rowland, where most people in India would hang up on you."

Taj waited. There was no click. "But not you?"

"I am not sure why, but I like you—and I trust Pranay Tamboli."

"Thank you." Taj responded.

"So if you are going to start an import company," Christopher continued, "you must first decide what to import. Perhaps you should think about it. I will think about it also. Then we could talk again."

It was a reasonable approach.

"Sounds good. But, Christopher, it's very expensive to call India from the United States. I'm using my parents' phone, and I'll need to pay them back. Would it be all right if, once I put some ideas together, I sent you an e-mail?"

"A what?"

"An e-mail," Taj repeated.

"What is an e-mail?"

It was Taj's turn to pause. "Christopher, this is the nineties. You claim to know a lot of people and have many connections, and yet you don't know about e-mail? Are you pranking *me,* Christopher Raj?"

Concern rose in the man's voice. "No, I assure you, I am not pranking you." He sounded sincere. "I have never heard of this e-mail."

"Christopher?" Taj said.

"Yes?"

"This is the moment where most people in the United States would hang up on you. But I'm not going to. Do you know why?"

"No."

"Because I like you as well—and I also trust Pranay Tamboli. I will begin to look for ideas of things we can import. You learn about e-mail, and we will keep in touch. It's been very nice talking to you, Christopher Raj."

Taj was about to hang up, but he needed to make one point clear.

"Christopher?"

"Yes?"

"It's true I don't have much, but it doesn't matter. I can tell you right now, we are going to make a lot of money together, you and I. I just wanted you to know."

There was silence, and for a moment Taj wasn't sure if he'd lost the connection.

"I look forward to it," Christopher finally responded. "Very much. Good-bye, Taj Rowland."

"Good-bye, Christopher Raj."

With the exception of Kelly in London, Taj had never told another soul about his desire to date an Indian. It had never mattered. In fact, in all his years growing up, Taj had never met an Indian girl even remotely close to his age.

When his mother related her dream—him marrying an Indian girl—he wrote it off as *crazy things mothers say.* And then a young man, Vasu, an Indian consultant recently hired by the call center to provide IT support, strolled into Taj's cubicle. When he announced that Taj should meet his Indian cousin, Taj softly hummed *Twilight Zone* music.

"She's beautiful," Vasu had declared. He pulled out a picture. Beautiful she was.

"She's intelligent," he had added. "She scored very high grades in school." Smart also.

"And she's magnificent in the kitchen!"

Could life get any better?

Two days later, to prove his point, Vasu dropped off a plate of the tastiest *kummayams* Taj had ever eaten.

What Vasu had neglected to mention—bless him—was that his cousin, Esha, had been in the U.S. for barely six weeks, spoke virtually no English, always kept her beautiful face covered with a shawl, and if she did drop her veil, even for a minute, she wore an ornate gold piercing the size of a silver dollar in her nose.

Esha would make someone an outstanding traditional Indian wife—just not Taj.

Two and a half weeks later, Taj relented for a second attempt, this time a blind date with an Indian girl arranged through an acquaintance of his mother. *Where were these Indian girls suddenly coming from?*

He'd only agreed when he learned that, while she was Indian, she had grown up in the United States.

Terrific! Until after he'd taken her to dinner at a pleasant little diner located up the canyon. In the few seconds of time between his politely closing her door and walking around to slip behind the wheel, she had unbuttoned her shirt to her waist and was now eying him with wanton eyes and a bare chest.

While he was flattered, it was not the type of dessert he had in mind.

When a third disaster followed a month later, a date involving curry ice cream, Taj gave up hope. Trying to date an Indian girl was like picking an exotic island vacation from a brochure. Every time he arrived, he found that he'd actually booked Alcatraz.

"I have another cousin," Vasu announced at work a few weeks later. At least the guy was determined.

"Thank you, Vasu, but I've changed my mind. I'll only be dating striking blondes who speak English."

"You are very funny, Mr. Taj," Vasu said, as he headed back to work.

Taj had never been more serious.

Could there be a more boring class in the entire world than International Financial Reporting Standards? The professor was droning on about reporting techniques for intangible assets as he wheeled a large, squeaky, white board to the front of the room. He selected a red marker and began to illustrate the concept with way too much enthusiasm.

Taj raised his hand.

"Do you have a question?"

"What's that board you're writing on?" Taj asked.

"This? It's called a whiteboard. You use these special markers called dry-erase. It lets you write in colors, but it erases easily. It's much cleaner than chalk. They're becoming quite popular now. Why do you ask?"

"Just curious. Never seen them before."

The professor turned to the rest of the students. "Does anyone else have a question about items in the room? Desks? Blinds? Light fixtures? I mean, why spend time on a topic that will *actually* be on the test?"

He cast a glance back at Taj as if to ask, *Anything else, wise guy?*

Taj shook his head. "I'm fine." He then picked up his pen and began to make notes—but they had nothing to do with intangible assets.

E-mail Christopher, he scribbled. *See if we can make whiteboards in India.*

Taj waited a few minutes after his American literature class to clarify with the TA what reading material would be covered on the test. Students from the following class were already taking their seats.

"Taj? Taj Rowland!"

It was a pleasant voice, a friendly voice, a female voice.

Taj twisted around to greet Lily Evans, his old high school girlfriend. Her hair was longer, darker, more brown now than blonde, but the glow in her eyes was unmistakable.

She held out her arms for a hug. Taj obliged.

"It's so great to see you," she said. She both beamed and bubbled.

"You, too!" he replied, and he meant it. He pushed back to get a better look. "You look great . . . really . . . *fit,*" he added, swallowing a smile.

The two stepped out into the hall to avoid disturbing the gathering class. She learned that he'd loved London, that he was living at home to save money, that he was working full-time and taking a full schedule of classes, all while trying to start an import company. He learned that she was studying elementary education, that she'd decided to teach third grade, that she was living with roommates near campus, and that she volunteered at a rest home every other Saturday.

The class Lily was supposed to be attending had already started. As it became apparent their conversation was coming to an end, she reached out warmly and held his arms, as she had done when they'd talk in high school.

"Are you dating anyone?" she asked, watching his eyes for a reaction.

"Well, there is Esha," he said, not even trying to stop his upturned lips.

"What's so funny?"

"Nothing, it's just . . . I've had a couple of blind dates lately that I can't even begin to describe. Bottom line—no, I'm not dating anyone."

"Then we should go out sometime." Her words were genuine, intriguing—and surprising.

"Really?"

"Sure, why not?"

"Last time we spoke, I think you may have called me *shallow.*"

Lily laughed. "I did not . . . besides, perhaps you've changed."

"Why do you say that?"

"I don't know. You just seem different somehow but in a good way."

The girl was adorable, he would give her that—too adorable. "How about Friday night?"

"Yes, that works. It's a date."

They exchanged phone numbers. He scribbled her address on the back of his class notes and zipped them safely in his pack. As she pulled open the classroom door and hurried inside, she mouthed him a message. He couldn't hear the words, but he'd understood her perfectly. He was watching her mouth because he couldn't get over the girl's amazing lips.

"See you Friday!" she said.

Between work, school, and time studying at the library, Taj was seldom home. Since both of his parents were usually at work, he was surprised when he dropped in between classes to pick up a book and found Linda in the kitchen.

"Taj, I have great news," she said. "You know our new office building?"

He nodded. She was working for Coldwell Banker now, and they'd just moved into the upper level of a two-story building on University Avenue.

"Guess who's moving in to take the main floor?" she asked, as if he were a game show contestant.

"Child Protective Services?"

"No."

"Youth in Asia?"

"No."

"Children Against Guessing Games?" This was getting ridiculous.

"No, Bombay House," she answered.

"I was just about to say that."

Linda was almost giddy. "It's a new Indian restaurant, and I met the owner. He's a nice young man, not much older than you. He's been in school, I think in Hawaii, but he's decided to open a restaurant here. His name is Daniel. I told him all about you coming from India, and he's invited us to the grand opening."

Actually, it *was* good news. Taj had been searching for a good Indian restaurant since returning from London and so far, he'd been nothing but disappointed.

"When?"

"At the end of the month. But if you have time, drop in before. He said he'd be there and would love to meet you. I'm thinking you two will have a lot in common."

"Because we're both Indian?"

"Yes, and because . . ." She thought for a moment. "Well, yes, because you're both Indian."

If the guy cooked half-decent Indian food, it was good enough for Taj.

Bombay House was no match for London's Royal Mumbai in atmosphere, but it held its own in the kitchen. It took only one visit with Daniel Durai, the owner, for one thing to become instantly clear: *the Indian dude could cook!*

Daniel had lived in India as a child and then moved to the area with his family when his father came to earn a doctorate degree. When his father took a job teaching in Singapore, Daniel headed off to culinary school in Hawaii.

After graduation, the next step for the Indian chef seemed obvious, and Bombay House was born. For Taj, a business student, it was the restaurant's location that he found most curious.

"Why open a restaurant in a town with no Indians?" he asked his new friend.

"You're here. I'm here. I'll cook for the two of us."

"Seriously."

"There's no competition. That makes my food the most delicious Indian cuisine for miles!" His grin was as wide as his face.

Since the grand opening, Taj had raved about the food often enough that Lily insisted on a visit. When they dropped in on a Thursday after class, Daniel was there to greet them, as he was for all his customers.

"Taj Rowland, my good friend. I'm guessing you'll have the chicken coconut kurma?"

"How often did you say you come here?" Lily asked.

Daniel clasped his palms together and offered Lily a courteous bow. "He comes often but never with such a beautiful woman. Welcome to Bombay House."

"I like this place already."

After the pair was escorted to their table and orders were taken, Taj excused himself to wash his hands. He ambled to the back near a hallway only to be collared by a recently hung picture. There on the wall was a portrait of Daniel's family—an Indian family.

Taj stepped closer.

The dark-haired girl standing to the left of Daniel and beside her parents was wearing a long, blue dress and a gold-colored blouse. She was about his age, perhaps younger, with delicate cheeks, a narrow chin, and petite fingers clutched together in front.

Light bounced. His lips parted. His jaw lowered. His eyes blinked. She was like an Indian princess. Royalty. Deity.

As he studied her, the clattering of dishes from the kitchen at the opposite end of the hall fell silent. The buzz that had been ringing from the ballasts in the fluorescent lights overhead turned into a musical hum—a familiar melody, but he couldn't place the name. The sterile acoustic ceiling tile could have been clouds, the floor in the hallway a beautiful forest path.

She was protected under glass, like a priceless museum piece, but that didn't stop him from leaning close and touching the surface.

Had he met her? Why did she look so familiar? Was she staring at him, or past him?

His heart pumped fire. His burning lungs reminded him to breathe. He glanced at his hands—they were trembling.

"Cotton candy," he whispered.

He was answering his English professor from hours earlier. She had asked her students to write a descriptive paragraph about something in their life, and then, once it was written, reduce it to a single sentence. When that was complete, shorten it to a word.

It was a ridiculous assignment, and he'd not understood it—until now.

"I just put that up this morning," said Daniel, startling him.

"I can see that . . . you have sisters." It was more statement than question.

"Yes, I've told you that, haven't I? One older and one younger. I'm the handsome one there in the middle."

"And your younger sister, she's the one on the right?"

"Yes, that's Priya."

Priya. What a beautiful name.

Taj hung on every letter. "Where is your family?" Taj asked, hoping it sounded as if he were making conversation.

"This picture was taken in Hawaii, at my graduation when . . ."

"No, I mean where are they *now?* Where do they live?"

Daniel took a breath. "Well, . . ."

Hurry! Speak faster!

" . . . they're still in Singapore. My father teaches organizational behavior there at the university."

"Singapore," Taj repeated. "How far away is Singapore?"

"I wouldn't walk."

Taj offered a courtesy smile. He turned back to the picture. *Christmas . . . was that a better word? Thanksgiving . . . fireworks . . . birthday . . . heaven . . .*

"Taj?"

Kittens . . . motorcycles . . . chocolate cake . . .

"Hey, Taj!"

Taj turned.

"Are you okay?" Daniel asked.

"Sorry. Does your family ever come to visit?"

"It's expensive, so not very often. Why? Would you like to meet them?"

"That would be nice."

Daniel tapped on his watch. "I'd better check on your food. I think it's about up." He motioned toward Lily. "And you have a beautiful woman waiting."

He was already turning when Taj reached out. "Wait! Daniel?"

"Yes?"

"Would you mind giving me Priya's phone number?"

It was bold, even stupid.

Daniel was a man who appreciated a good joke, but he couldn't hold back his laughter. His head tossed from one shoulder to the other. "You're hilarious, Taj."

"Don't laugh too hard. I'm going to marry your sister."

It was only Taj's unwavering gaze that wiped away Daniel's smile. The man stepped back. It was like a broom handle had smacked him square across the face. His voice faltered.

"You're interested in Priya? BUT YOU'RE ON A DATE!"

Taj let the moment hang, as if deciding which way to let it fall. When he finally grinned, Daniel slapped him on his back.

"You got me! That was a good one! I admit it; you really had me going there!"

Taj laughed.

Daniel laughed.

When Taj returned to the table, Lily asked what they'd been talking about—she had been watching him from across the restaurant. Taj changed the subject to his arriving *chicken kurma.* He assured her it was mouth-watering, and it must have been, because from the time the food arrived their conversation remained quiet.

After they'd finished eating and were leaving the restaurant, Taj paused after opening her car door. He told her he'd forgotten something that he needed to ask Daniel and promised he'd be right back.

He left off one minor detail: if he didn't go back inside and speak with Daniel about Priya this instant, he was sure his chest would implode.

He found Daniel at the cash register, though the words Taj had planned to say weren't the same ones that came out of his mouth.

"Hey, I'm doing a group assignment for history on . . . Asian civilizations. My portion is actually on Singapore. What are the chances, right? Well, I was wondering, is there any way, if I wrote or called your family, maybe one of them could answer a few questions?"

When Taj climbed into the car and Lily asked him if everything was all right, he couldn't convince his lips to stop grinning. The sun shone brighter, the flowers grew taller, the birds chirped in stereo.

"What a great time I had," he said as he folded a napkin into his pocket. "The food was delicious, the atmosphere pleasant, everything was superb. But now, what I could totally go for is . . ."

"Yes?"

"Does anyone around here sell cotton candy?"

CHAPTER 27

"Hello?" A man answered.

"Good morning, sir. Is Priya there, please?"

"Who's calling?"

A breath. A pause. "My name is Taj Rowland. I'm a friend of your son, Daniel."

Silence. A cough. "Why are you calling my daughter?"

"I saw her picture," Taj replied, "and I'm also Indian. I thought we might have a lot in common."

The receiver sucked in his words before he could snatch them back. His eyes rolled. Had he really just said, *I'm Indian?*

"Are you wanting to date my daughter?" the voice inquired. "Is that what this is about?"

Give the man a star for astuteness. "I was just hoping to speak with her, sir."

"What is your name?"

Taj sat, squinted. He wouldn't have been surprised if an interrogation light suddenly clicked on.

"As I mentioned, it's Taj Rowland."

There was no hesitation. "Mr. Rowland, let me make this clear. Our family believes in arranged marriage. Do you know what that means?"

"I'm not asking to marry your daughter . . ."

"It means I'm asking you never to call my daughter again. Do you understand?"

No, Taj didn't understand. He just wanted to speak with the girl. What could be wrong with that?

"Sir, I just want to . . ."

"Good-bye, Mr. Rowland."

Click.

Taj spoke to the phone. "Well, I'd say that went pretty well."

He laid the bruised and bloodied receiver back into its cradle, then slid onto the couch to ponder his next move. Music from a radio in Rux's room was squeezing through the cracks around the door. The song was familiar.

Taj opened the door to the hall so he could better hear the words. It was his favorite group, a song that had sold millions of copies. He could sing it in his sleep—beautiful lyrics about love and loss and sorrow and hope.

By the time the chorus started, Taj had his next step planned.

When people can't find the right words to express the feelings that are pulsing through their veins, they turn to someone more qualified: a poet. It was true—Hallmark would back him up on it.

Today, however, Taj had a better idea. He checked for his wallet, grabbed keys to the car, and headed out the door. He drove first to the mall, then to the post office.

Instead of trying to call Priya again and risk her father's wrath, Taj would send an innocuous gift to the girl. Who could object to that? But not just *any* gift.

As he handed over his package, Taj wished the postman a very pleasant day—which it was. Taj even tried to give a tip to the man, which he refused, citing federal regulations.

"How long will it take for the package to arrive?" Taj asked.

"Eight to twelve days," came the reply.

Taj smiled. It wasn't gold. It wasn't pearls. It wasn't chocolates. But in less than two weeks, if he believed the good man postmarking the box across the counter, a silk-haired, dark-eyed goddess currently living under guard with her family in Singapore would unwrap *romance.* A stranger—Taj Rowland, from the United States, a man she'd never met—had just mailed her the most moving, irresistible album of love songs known to the modern world:

Air Supply: Greatest Hits.

Breaking up with Lily was harder the second time. This time his heart hurt.

It was confusing. Lily was funny and gorgeous and smart. She had direction and dreams, not to mention impeccable lips, which he'd had the pleasure of kissing on several occasions. As Taj tallied her traits, his head kept asking why in the world he shouldn't give it more time. It could all still work out.

Then his heart piped in.

This wasn't about Taj. It was about Lily. It wouldn't be right to drag it out, to hurt her worse down the road, to pretend he cared when he knew that every second he spent with her he'd be thinking about someone else.

Just like the first breakup, Lily cried. Unlike the first breakup, Taj put his arm around her, told her how amazing she was and why. He explained, as best he could, that he didn't want to lead her on, that she should never *settle.*

His brain kept calling him *stupid.* He was doing this without ever knowing if anything would work out with Priya, a girl to whom he'd never spoken—who lived in Singapore, for heaven's sake!

"Thank you, Taj," Lily said, "for being honest."

She pulled a tissue from her purse, a familiar moment. "I want you to know that I meant what I said," she continued.

"Which part?"

"You still seem different to me—and I mean that in a good way. You've changed."

She dried her eyes. He gave her a hug. They parted friends. As he drove away, a familiar song was playing from the radio.

He wasn't sure whether to shut it off or turn up the volume.

The encircling words wrapped around him but more like a rope than a blanket. The words of the song's title were repeated over and over in the lyrics.

Perhaps they chafed tonight because he sensed they were true.

"All Out of Love."

Eight days. Sixteen. Thirty-two.

Weeks. Months.

Nothing—no word from the girl in Singapore.

Taj thrived on effort, on success, on accomplishment in his life.

Somewhere monotony had slipped into the room and was slowly smothering him to death with a pillow.

His routine had been reduced to ten repeating steps, items he could easily check off a daily list. Fred would be so proud.

1. Wake up.
2. Eat breakfast.
3. Go to school.
4. Eat lunch.
5. Go to work.
6. Study.
7. Eat dinner.
8. Study.
9. Get ready for bed.
10. Go to sleep.

Day in, day out. Day in, day out. Day in . . .

The weekends were barely different. On Saturday, Taj would work a double shift. On Sunday, work was replaced with church.

Hamster. Wheel. Round and round he went. Would it ever end?

Worse, every time he dropped into the restaurant to see Daniel, she was there—eternally peering out cheerfully from the wall.

He didn't dare tell Daniel about his recurring dream—or was it a nightmare? Priya would always be standing on a fog-covered rise, Taj running uphill to reach her—calling, begging, pleading to know if she'd received his package. No matter how hard he ran, or how loud he screamed, or how frantically he thrashed his arms, she would never turn, never acknowledge, never even look in his direction.

She was trapped behind glass.

"Hello, Christopher? It's Taj, Taj Rowland."

"Taj. How are you?"

"Frustrated. I sent you more ideas for items to export, and I haven't heard a word. It's been a good month, so I'm following up. Did you get them? I sent them by e-mail."

There was a fumbled pause.

"No, Taj, I'm sorry. I haven't seen them. I have to go to Chennai to get my e-mail. And I haven't done that. Can you just tell me what it says?"

Taj squeezed the receiver. "Chris, if I have to call to tell you what my e-mail says, that sort of defeats the purpose of e-mail, don't you think?"

He could almost hear the man nod. "I see your point."

"Well, good."

Christopher promised to do better. Taj agreed to be patient.

Next, Taj slid behind the wheel of his car, aimed toward the school, then pressed the gas to see if he could outrun the cloud that had been hanging over him for days.

As he passed Bombay House, he considered dropping in to tell Daniel about Priya's package, perhaps to even ask if Daniel wouldn't mind calling up his sister to find out if it was ever received.

But Daniel's laugh was hard to forget.

"You! Dating my sister? Of all people!" he'd blurted out when they'd joked together that day in the restaurant.

"I can't help but wonder . . ." Taj had asked, grinning. "Why is that so funny?"

Daniel patted him on the back. "Don't get me wrong. You're a good friend, and while you're Indian on the outside, you're American cream-filled all the way to your center."

"So?"

"So . . . Priya dating an American? Taj, my father would never allow it."

When Taj arrived home late—not unusual—there was an envelope waiting on his desk. He tore at the eager paper.

It was a wedding invitation. Kelly was getting married. He didn't bother even looking at the clock before dialing her number.

"You didn't tell me!" he said the second Kelly answered.

A laugh drifted through the line. "I'd decided it would be more fun to surprise you. Are you surprised?"

"I'm surprised you found a guy with enough patience. Who is he? I want to hear all about it."

She was like a teenager at girl's camp. "Do you remember how I was going to draw my own map?"

"I do."

"It meant doing things that I knew would be hard, very hard. I hadn't spoken to my mother in over three years, but I'd reached a point in my life where I needed to move past it, to step forward. I mean, how could I hope to help others professionally if I was a mess myself?"

"I don't think I'd call you a mess."

"Inside I was. In ways, we all are. Anyway, Taj, I'd had a restraining order out against my stepfather, and in order to see my mother, I had to work with an attorney—an attorney whose name is Jason."

"You're marrying an attorney?"

"A fantastic, hard-working, thoughtful, and kind attorney."

"Those are all oxymorons, but I'm happy for you."

"Here's the stunning part. If I hadn't decided to move on, to forgive my mom—and my stepdad—I would never have met my husband. That is both so profound and terrifying that at times it steals my breath away." Kelly paused. "But enough about me. How about you? How are you coming with your map?"

Silence betrayed him.

"Come on, let me hear the details," she coaxed.

"Life right now is like . . . a ship without a rudder . . . in a typhoon. I'm blowing around in circles."

True to form, Kelly wasted no time. "Your ship metaphor is a bit cliché, but if we're sticking with it, I'd suggest you need an oar."

"Here's the deal, doctor. I've already been paddling the hell out of my boat, and all it's doing is making me dizzy."

"In that case, Taj," she said, "quit paddling."

Taj's tone lifted. "What do you mean? I've read the books, seen the movies. We're told to never give up, fight to the bloody end, make our own luck . . . blah, blah, blah. Did you not get the memo?"

"I'm not suggesting you give up trying or even hoping. All I am saying is relax. Listen to the wind, feel the water. See where life's breeze wants to take you. Look, if God wants to give you a bigger oar or two, he will. He has plenty. There are times, however, when he's trying to blow us one way and we're paddling like crazy the other. Occasionally we just need to stop and be grateful."

He said nothing. He was busy thinking.

"Are you there?"

"I hope so."

"Are you coming?"

"To your wedding? I wouldn't miss it."

For dinner, Taj often grabbed something cheap from a vending machine at school, but when his Wednesday night class was canceled, he drove home instead to eat with the family.

"You'll never guess who I just sold a house to," Linda said as she passed the mashed potatoes.

When nobody jumped in to play, Taj took his best shot. "Oprah?"

"No, of course not. Daniel, who owns Bombay House. He's buying a cute little home about three blocks down the street. We'll practically be neighbors."

It was arguably interesting news. It had been two or three weeks since Taj had dropped in to see Daniel, but the man had said nothing about buying a home.

"When is he moving?" Taj asked.

"That's the thing. He was very particular about the closing date because of their milk boiling."

"Milk boiling?"

"It's fascinating. It's like an Indian house warming." Linda eyes widened. "Daniel was telling me all about it. It's regarded as second in importance only to a wedding ceremony. It has to be done on a certain day and time that's determined by astrological charts. Family comes from all over to attend. They boil the milk in a new container until it spills over, which they believe ushers in abundance, and as soon as it boils over, they break a coconut. It's at that moment the house becomes a home."

"Wait just a minute," Taj said, tilting back his head. "Can you back up?"

"To the coconut?"

"Before that. Did you say that family comes . . . from all over?"

"Oh, yes. It's very important. Daniel said many of his relatives will be there."

Taj lowered his fork. "Do you know if his parents and siblings are coming from . . ."

Linda finished his sentence. "Singapore? Yes, the entire family."

Taj straightened, almost laughed. His head lifted. Did angels just begin to sing hallelujah?

"The family will be there!" Taj repeated. By the third time he was shouting with two fists in the air. "THE FAMILY WILL BE THERE!"

Taj pushed himself back from the table, snatched his keys from the counter, and bolted toward the garage door.

"Where are you going?" Linda asked. "What's the rush?"

"I was begging for an oar, but I just got a motor."

Her entire face crinkled. "What does that mean?"

The door was already closing. He didn't have time to explain. He barked his reply, letting it scoot around the door just in time before it slammed shut.

"I'm inviting myself to a milk boiling!"

CHAPTER 28

Taj hadn't seen a room packed with so many Indians since London. It was more crowded than Free Appetizer Tuesday at the Bombay House. That proved both good and bad. Bad because he had only twice caught a distant glimpse of Priya mingling with the congregating relatives, giving him no chance to make eye contact and introduce himself. Good because the throng of friends and family made it easy for Taj to avoid her father.

Though house-warming ceremonies could be elaborate, depending on religious and family traditions, Daniel had kept his simple. As a Christian, he claimed it was more cultural than religious, though he was the first to admit the distinction for Indians was like conjoined twins—hard to separate.

The purpose, however, was clear: to purify the space, to cast out negative energy, to bestow health, wealth, peace, and prosperity on the home and its owners.

Like nearly all religious ceremonies, if taken solely at face value, it was rather odd. They were, after all, watching milk boil. Once you scratched beneath the surface, however, even Taj had to agree there was an undeniable beauty in the gathering, with so many friends and relatives all channeling their hopes, hearts, and prayers into the success of a single family.

When it was time, the crowd massed into the kitchen. Taj watched from the back. A prayer was offered, and then Daniel and his wife, wearing new clothes, poured fresh milk into a just-purchased pan which was heated on a brand-new stove.

Milk warmed, swirled, and bubbled. Eager family watched, whispered, and waited. Anticipation rose like steam. A shawled woman with a long neck held her breath. A man with a yellow turban and a parted beard took out glasses and fastened them onto his nose. A young girl, perhaps four, asked her father to lift her up so she could watch the house become a home.

Flames. Bubbles. Steam. Waiting. Waiting. Waiting.

Few sporting events were as tense.

When the milk finally frothed and billowed over the pan, every person in the room cheered—including Taj.

After eating a plate of wonderful food, as expected at the home of a man who owned a restaurant, Taj went in search of Priya.

He started in the basement: mostly children. Next, the back bedrooms: friends, family, no girl. Upstairs: empty rooms, since moving in any of the family's main furniture before the boiling was strictly forbidden.

Taj was beginning to worry that she'd slipped out until he rounded a corner of the living room in a rush and nearly crashed into her.

She was standing in a semicircle of relatives: mother, aunt, uncle, two brothers—and her father.

"I'm sorry," Taj said.

Daniel made the introduction. "Family, this is my good friend, Taj Rowland. His mother, Linda, is the real estate agent who sold us our home."

As Daniel presented his family, Taj tried to pay attention, but the only words he heard were, "Taj, this is my younger sister, Priya."

Her hand was warm and soft, her fingers slender but firm, and he held her grip much longer than he should have, especially with her father watching.

She was polite enough, shaking his hand with confidence, but her eyes never directly met his. Instead she gazed momentarily past him before pulling away to reach for her glass of water.

Taj turned next to greet her father, a man quite happy to make eye contact—and unless Taj was mistaken, the man's steely stare seemed to be asking for someone to please pass him an ice pick.

"It is nice to meet all of you," Taj said.

He was about to excuse himself when Priya's uncle spoke. "Join us. Daniel was just telling us about his restaurant."

"Thank you," Taj replied, flashing an unintentional grin as he stepped in beside Daniel and across from the girl.

"Daniel," the uncle said, "you never answered. How do people hear about the restaurant? What brings them in?"

The circle listened politely while Daniel expounded on the finer points of restaurant advertising. It didn't take long before Priya's aunt—Taj hadn't caught her name—grew bored with the business talk and shifted the conversation to her niece.

"Priya, are you enjoying your time here?"

"Yes, Auntie," Priya answered as she reached over and grasped the woman's hand. "It's wonderful. I especially love the clean air. It's just so . . . energizing . . . so soothing."

It was the first time Taj had heard her speak, and it was like being swaddled in Egyptian cotton sheets while listening to Mozart on a lazy Sunday morning.

Cotton candy.

"It's because we're near the mountains," the aunt replied.

Priya's finger touched her bottom lip, giving Taj an excuse to stare. "Yes," she said to her aunt. "I think you're right—so much sunshine, an endless supply." Taj could listen to her voice all day—flawless English, with just the slightest adorable accent—but he'd be lying if he didn't admit her answers were peculiar. He'd chalked up her word choice to cultural differences—until she'd answered that last comment.

His chin rose, but Priya wasn't finished. "The air and sunshine are great, but even better, we're all together as family. And, well, here I am. It's the . . . greatest." She gathered her small hands to her chest and patted her heart. "It . . . hits me . . . right here."

The aunt's head was bobbing—everyone's head was bobbing. Who wouldn't agree with fresh air, sunshine, and family?

As the dots connected in Taj's head he burst into laughter. Everyone in the circle stopped and turned.

"Taj, are you all right?" Daniel asked. "What's so funny?"

Funny? She was brilliant! The *air* is soothing? The sunshine is in endless *supply*? Did she really say *here I am*? Priya was not only telling him she'd received his gift, *Air Supply's Greatest Hits*, but was now quoting its song titles—and nobody had a clue.

Taj's eyes went immediately to hers, and for the smallest sliver of a second, she glanced back.

Taj straightened. "I didn't mean to laugh. I just find this conversation fascinating," he said. "She's right. It's terrific here. With the fresh air, *even the nights are better*."

Take that! Game on.

She looked at him directly for the first time, "Taj, are you in school? Are you *taking the chance*?"

"Yes . . . I'll graduate in business management, and then one day, I'd like to start my own company, but I must add . . ." His gaze ticked around the circle like a roulette wheel. It stopped on Priya. "*It's not easy.*" Another song title from Air Supply, this one from their first album. Would she know it?

She smiled. He smiled.

He knew when to quit. "It's been a pleasure meeting all of you—truly. I think I'll head to the kitchen to get some more food. I hope we have a chance to talk again." He was addressing the group but knew she'd get the message.

As Taj walked away, Priya's aunt leaned over to Daniel. The woman didn't realize Taj could still hear.

"Your friend seems like a pleasant young man, but he's a bit odd."

By late in the afternoon, Taj and a handful of relatives had helped Daniel move in his furniture. Taj was resting alone on the front steps when Priya stepped through the door and out onto the porch.

Taj stated the obvious first. "You speak Air Supply."

It caused a smile. "A little," she admitted. "I wondered how long it would take you to notice. Thank you for the CD."

He combed dirty fingers through his sweaty hair. "I'm glad to know you got it."

"How long have you known Daniel?" she asked.

"A while. A few months. He's a good guy—and he can cook!"

"Ha, yes, that he can." She glanced back through the front door before she stepped closer, as if nervous someone might be watching.

"Will you be here long? In town, I mean?" Taj asked. They were casual words with impatient eyes.

"I'm not certain," she said almost in a whisper. "My family is in town for another ten days, but I'm thinking about going to school here. It's one of the reasons we came out—besides the milk boiling."

Had he heard right? His voice jumped a pitch with surprise. "When will you decide?"

"I have an appointment with a counselor tomorrow."

"And your father is okay leaving you here?"

"Is it dangerous here?" she asked, laughing.

"No, I just . . ."

She knew exactly what he was asking. "My brother's here. Besides, I'll get a better education than in Singapore. In that regard, he can't object, can he?"

She glanced back over her shoulder again toward the house, and then answered the unasked question. "I believe he's napping."

Ask now. ASK NOW! His head was screaming to his lips. *Before her father wakes up and ends this conversation!*

"Can I buy you lunch sometime?"

Priya shook her head. "I can't date."

"You can't date? Why not?"

"My parents believe in arranged marriages, so we don't date."

It was likely the way he began fumbling with coins in his pocket because her lips tugged again into a smile. "I could perhaps go on a group activity, though," she said. "I mean, after my appointment with the counselor tomorrow, I'll need to eat. Right?"

Not just beautiful but pragmatic. She was extraordinary. Every muscle in his face was nodding.

"Meet me in front of the administration building tomorrow at noon. I look forward to getting to know you, Taj."

No problem that he had a class. For this girl, he'd cancel heart surgery.

"I'll be there," he said. "I will absolutely be there."

Their first group activity together, Taj decided, was a lot like the ball scene from Cinderella—but with no animation, dancing, or pumpkin carriage. He bought her a sandwich and drink, and they sat by the fountain on campus and talked and laughed and answered each other's questions in Air Supply lyrics before either of them realized how low the sun had sunk. She was late and had to run off, leaving him alone, and if he'd found a glass slipper where she'd been sitting, it wouldn't have been the least bit surprising.

It was all so perfect, it kept him wondering: Was she just being nice because he was friends with her brother? It must be, because no girl could be that warm and witty, fearless and friendly, brave and beautiful—and still actually like him. Something had to be wrong.

By their fifth clandestine date, they decided that calling their time together a group activity was silly, especially since her parents had gone back to Singapore and she'd moved into an apartment near campus with roommates who didn't care if she dated or what time she came home.

That was the night they kissed.

It was all going so well, Taj found himself waking up every morning with a smile already pasted to his face. He'd have to slap himself in front of the bathroom mirror just to confirm he hadn't been dreaming.

By their ninth date, just when Taj was beginning to accept that his life was real, Priya's call was like an unexpected punch to the stomach.

"Taj," she'd said somberly, "we need to talk!"

How could she? He'd invented *we need to talk!* He had a copyright on the miserable phrase. He'd broken up with more girls than England had had queens and could deliver the line in his sleep.

But that was the problem. He had never been the one on the receiving end.

Her words reached through the phone and pushed nails into his heart.

When he pulled up to her apartment, she was outside waiting. She climbed in with resolve. No reason to waste time.

"Taj, I've been doing a lot of thinking," she said. Also his line, and as she spoke it an itchy lump tightened in his throat.

"Are you ashamed of me?" she asked.

What had he said? What had he done? He parsed her words. He played back every recent conversation. He was coming up empty.

"Why would you think that?"

"Taj, you've never taken me home to meet your parents."

Relief draped around him like warm sunshine. He gripped her fingers so tightly that she let out a cry. He let go and then tried a high-five. He'd never been so excited to introduce anyone to his parents.

It was a short drive. There were no lights on inside when Taj pulled into the driveway.

"I'm sorry," he said to Priya. "They're old. They may have already gone to bed."

He pushed open the door from the garage, turned on a light in the kitchen, and steered Priya to the couch in the family room.

"Do you want a soda?" he asked, turning to the fridge.

"That would be nice, sure."

When he passed the hall, he could see Linda standing in the shadows, wearing her pink bathrobe and flagging him down like a stranded motorist.

"If Priya's going to run," Taj mumbled, "it will be tonight."

His shrug to Linda all but begged, *Please don't screw this up!*

Linda was pointing toward Priya. "That's her, that's her!"

"Who?" Taj asked.

"The girl you're with—I saw her as you walked past. I've seen her before. Taj, she's the girl I dreamed about."

Taj latched onto Linda's shoulders. The night was getting worse. It was a plea that started deep in his throat. "Mom! I don't know what you dreamed or why, but don't you dare breathe a word."

"Taj, please. I'm not stupid," she replied but in a voice loud enough to sufficiently prove his concern. While she scurried off to change, Taj went to prep Priya.

To Taj's relief, Linda returned dressed, thankfully minus her bathrobe. She gave Priya a squeeze, as if they were already friends. She sat beside her on the couch, forcing Taj to sit across in his own chair. Within minutes, the two women were chatting like girlfriends.

Each story Linda told started the same. "Let me tell you about the time Taj . . ." And then while Taj denied any memory, claiming the crazy woman was making it all up, Priya and Linda would laugh, and despite their making fun of him, he was euphoric.

"Wait!" Linda pronounced, with shining eyes. "I have something you should see."

She hurried to her bedroom and returned with a box. Inside was a bulging scrapbook. It contained pictures of Taj growing up, the article published in the town paper when he arrived, an assortment of birthday cards and awards he'd won in school.

It was every son's worst nightmare—home movies without the movies.

"Anything to do with Taj or India," Linda announced proudly, "I've saved in this book."

Taj moved behind Priya to look over her shoulder.

"Why didn't I know about this?" he asked Linda.

"It wasn't hidden," she said. "You were just never very interested."

As Priya turned the pages, Linda described the pictures. Most generated laughter, usually at the expense of Taj.

"Are we sure this is the best activity we can . . ."

Priya didn't let him finish. "I wouldn't miss this for anything."

More pictures. More laughter.

As Linda flipped over the last page, a clear plastic sleeve held a white audio cassette tape.

Linda pulled it out, examined it. "I'd forgotten about this. When we first got little Taj, we knew he'd forget his language, so we recorded him speaking."

"I'd love to hear it," Priya said.

"Let me find the player. I think it's in the cupboard in the utility room."

Linda returned with an old audiocassette player and fresh batteries. When it was ready, she pushed Play.

The sound was scratchy but started with the distinct voice of a child singing unintelligible words.

"I remember this," Linda exclaimed. "He sang the songs he'd learned in the orphanage."

Priya tipped her head to hear better.

"He's singing in Tamil?" she announced.

"How can you tell?" Taj asked.

"I speak Tamil. It's spoken in southern India."

Taj scooted forward. He was watching Priya. A smile softly wrapped her face. "It's a Christian song," she said. "You're singing that you love Jesus."

When the singing ended, the boy began to speak. Even with the static, anguish carried in his voice.

Priya's smile faded.

"Can you rewind that?" she asked.

Linda obliged and again pushed Play.

Priya edged forward, covered her mouth. She looked first to Linda but then faced Taj. Her hand gently lowered. "Taj, you're saying that—" Tiny wrinkles etched across her brow. "You're saying that you were taken, that you were kidnapped! That you have a family, a mother in India. Did you know this?"

They swam in silence.

Priya waited.

It was several seconds before Taj finally nodded. "It started in London. There are parts of my childhood—flashes, pieces, images—I've been remembering."

He turned to Linda. "Mom, did you know?"

Linda stopped the tape so they could talk, so they could breathe. She clutched the couch cushion with determined fingers, as if it might offer courage or perhaps protection. Her words, usually firm, were frail.

She spoke directly to him. "We first found out when you began to learn English. I still remember the first time that you mentioned your mother. I swore my heart was going to burst. All I could think about was the poor woman, the family, who must have been going crazy missing you. We knew nothing. Honestly. We tried to find out more. We immediately wrote to the man who ran the orphanage to get more information, but he wouldn't return our letters or take our calls. We pursued it through the embassy, but they told us there was nothing they could do. There were others in India we contacted, but nobody was willing to help."

"Why didn't I know any of this?" Taj asked.

"You were already so traumatized, we didn't want to make it worse. We couldn't get your hopes up. Perhaps we should have said something when you got older, but by then, what was the point? To us, you've always been our son."

Her eyes were glassy, blinking. Her lips quivered.

"As it happened, there was nothing more we ever found out." She wiped at her eyes with her shaky fingers that only served to smear her tears.

Taj stepped around to sit by his mother on the couch. "The man who brought me . . . do you remember his name?"

"That much I do know. His name was Eli . . . Eli Manickam."

Linda flipped back to the front pages of the album to the pictures they'd taken at the airport. There was one photo of a gray-haired Indian man holding a young boy. Taj pulled it from the album.

"I remember him," Taj said, as he looked at Linda. "I remember his beard, and he wore a white skirt thing."

"It's called a lungi," Priya added.

Taj turned back to Linda. "Do you have anything else, anything at all?" He hadn't told her about his map, his memories.

"Whatever we have," she said, "it's in the box. I haven't looked through it in years."

Taj scoured through the papers layered in the bottom. "Is this my passport?" Excitement stumbled from his lips.

"You had it when you came."

When he opened it up, pasted in the front cover was his picture—below was his Indian name.

"My name was Chellamuthu?"

"Yes," Linda explained. "We changed it from Chellamuthu to Taj so the kids would stop teasing you at school."

"In Tamil *Chellamuthu* means 'precious pearl,'" Priya said.

Taj rummaged through more papers in the box, mostly articles about India that Linda had cut from magazines. In the stack was a letter with an Indian postmark.

The return address was clear—Lincoln Home for Homeless Children.

"What's this?"

Linda flipped it over. It took a minute to remember. "That's right. After Eli wouldn't answer our letters, we found the name of another man in India, a man involved with the orphanage. We wrote to him, and he was kind enough to write back, though it was still a dead end."

Taj skimmed the words. Priya was reading it beside him. She leaned forward.

"Wait, can I see that?" she asked.

She took it from his hands to study it more closely. "That's so strange. This looks so familiar." When she turned it over, she gasped.

"What? What is it?" Taj asked.

"Are you okay, dear?" Linda added.

"This letter," she said. "It's signed by Maneesh Durai."

"So? Do you know him?" Taj wondered.

"Yes, I know him," she said. "Taj, this letter was written by my father!"

CHAPTER 29

At two o'clock in the morning, Taj was still sitting with Priya in his car outside her apartment.

"How is it possible?" Taj asked again, as if anything in the last hour had changed. "There are a billion people in India, half a world away, and I end up dating the daughter of a man tied to the orphanage who took me as a child from my family! Do you realize how crazy that is?"

Priya had no answers.

"What if he knew?" Taj asked.

"That you'd been kidnapped?" Her calm balanced his concern.

"What if he helped?" Taj added.

"I'd like to think he wasn't involved like that, but I don't know. I was just a child."

"What if we talked to him, see what he says, what he remembers, if he knows anything about me or my family? Maybe he could help me find them."

She'd already been over this. "Taj, we can't! My family believes in arranged marriages. I'm forbidden to date. My father's leery of you, anyway. If he weren't back in Singapore, well . . ."

"I can't help that he hates Air Supply," Taj added.

It was a needed smile. "He does hate Air Supply," Priya confirmed, "but that's not why. I think you scare him."

"Me? Scare *him?* Why?"

"Because you're assertive. You know what you want and go after it. You aren't afraid of people—and, of course, you called him on the phone and wanted to date his daughter."

"Those are all good things, right?"

"I'm sitting here, aren't I? Listen, just be patient. We'll ask him, but we can't do it yet."

"When?" It was an eager word that begged for an answer.

Priya spelled it out for him. "We can't talk to him until we know we're serious. There has to be no turning back."

"Priya," he said, his voice lowering to a whisper, "I would tell you I'm falling in love with you, but actually . . . I already fell. The moment I saw your picture at Daniel's. Does that . . . I don't know . . . freak you out?"

He clutched her fingers, their eyes intertwined. "Are you just saying this so I'll talk to my father?"

"No . . . I . . . didn't mean . . ."

She uncovered her grin. "I'm kidding. Taj! The thing is . . ."

"Yes." He was absorbing every glance, every pause, every movement.

"I'm falling in love with you, too."

Priya tugged at the door of Bombay House and peeked inside. With any luck, Daniel would be in the kitchen.

"Priya?"

"Oh, hi, brother."

"What's up?"

"I've been told the food here is tolerable. Can you hook me up?"

"Sure, what can I get you?"

She didn't need to look at the menu. "I'll have the coconut kurma and maybe take some chicken masala, for later."

Daniel halted. "You hate my masala."

"No, I don't."

"You tell me I use too much garlic, that you like Mom's better."

"All true, but I don't hate it. Besides, I'd like to see if you've made any improvements."

"Sounds reasonable. I guess honest feedback never hurts. Kurma to stay and a masala to go."

Priya's lips formed another lie. "Actually, I'll take them both to go. I have to . . . um, study."

Daniel's eyes narrowed. "You despise eating out of a styrofoam box—and since when do you need to study? You've always breezed through school."

She could feel her face blush and excused herself to go to the bathroom. When she returned, Daniel was placing her food in a bag. He dropped in a set of utensils wrapped with a napkin. "Can I have two of those . . . one for later?"

He tossed in another and then stepped around the counter. "Come on, I'll walk you to your car."

Beads of perspiration were mobilizing in patches on her forehead. "I'm completely capable of carrying my own food, thank you." She reached out and took the bag from him.

"Geez, whatever. A brother tries to be nice and look how he's treated."

"Sorry," she replied, "I'm just . . . in a hurry."

As the door closed behind her, he called out. "Let me know how you like my masala!"

When she reached the car, Taj was bouncing. "I'm starving. What took so long?"

Her eyes smoldered. Her fingers clenched.

"Next time, we're going to McDonalds!"

From: Christopher Raj
To: Taj Rowland

Taj,

This is Christopher Raj. I've finally figured out how to log on to e-mail. Can you hear me?

Chris

From: Christopher Raj
To: Taj Rowland

Taj,

Sorry you had to phone again. This time I really do have e-mail figured out.

I have an idea for a product. In India, many people sleep directly on the ground. Families with money purchase woven mats that not only provide protection but are also very colorful.

I imagine people in the United States would like them. Can we import and sell these sleeping mats? I'll keep this short as I'm not sure if they charge me by length.

Christopher

From: Taj Rowland
To: Christopher Raj

Chris,

We don't sleep on mats here. We prefer beds with mattresses. We do, however, go on picnics and take vacations to the beach. Perhaps your sleeping mats would make great beach mats.

What do you think? Please send a sample.

Taj
P.S. There is no limit to length when using e-mail.

Love is both comfortable and complacent, like a child's blanket that in a perfect world would last forever.

Every month, Taj and Priya talked about telling her family. Every month, it was easier to focus on school, schedules, and strategy, as they planned what their lives together might look like after graduation.

"We could come at Christmas!" Priya's father had said when he last called.

"It's freezing here, Papa, and there's no reason to spend the money now," she'd countered. "School is going well. I'm getting good grades. I'll be just fine." And she was. Taj was making sure of it.

Daughters are experts at persuading their fathers.

Another semester here, another holiday there. Here a spring, there a winter. Always putting off the inevitable, like a boy not telling his parents that he broke their heirloom crystal vase, as if it might magically piece itself together.

"I'll graduate in the spring. Why not wait until then?" Priya wondered.

Taj wasn't listening. He was staring out the window at the churning clouds. A storm was blowing their direction.

When it finally arrived, it was going to be ugly.

It was early March as Taj lounged on Priya's couch watching a rerun of *Jeopardy*. He knew all the answers. Reruns can make anyone a genius.

Priya was in the bathroom drying her hair. It was movie night at the dollar theater, and they were going to be late if she didn't pick up the pace.

The phone rang three times before Priya answered it.

"Hello?"

A pause.

"Oh, hi, Papa," she said, surprised.

A longer pause.

"No, I . . ." Concern peaked in her voice. Taj rose from the couch.

"You're what? No, no, you can't . . ."

He stepped closer.

"Papa! You haven't even . . ."

Her fingers clenched. Her eyes clenched. Her teeth clenched.

"That's not right . . . it's just . . ."

Twice her lips almost spit out a word. Twice it was swallowed.

"But you . . ."

Within a second, anger thawed into frustration, and frustration melted into tears.

What happened? Had somebody passed away? Taj sat beside her, pulled her close with one arm while taking her hand in the other.

"Priya, tell me what's wrong."

When she faced him, it wasn't worry still glistening in her eyes, it was terror.

"They'll be here this weekend," she muttered.

"Priya, it will be okay. We'll sit down and calmly tell them. It will be all right."

She was trembling. "You don't understand." She reached out and grabbed his leg to steady herself.

"Father said they're coming because they've found the man I'm going to marry."

CHAPTER 30

Taj walked into the restaurant first. They'd purposely waited until closing time, so that Daniel would have time to talk.

"Taj?" Daniel said, surprised to see his friend at such a late hour. "I'm not sure what we have left . . ."

Priya stepped up behind him.

"Hey, sister," Daniel acknowledged with a nod. "Hey, what a surprise, you guys are here at the same time."

Observant.

Taj got right to the point.

"That's why we've come, Daniel. We have something we need to tell you." Taj pointed to a booth. "Can we sit?"

Taj waited for Priya to slide in first and then scooted close beside her. It took Daniel a minute for his brain to register what should have been apparent.

"Are you two dating?" he finally asked.

"We are," Taj confirmed.

Daniel's chin rose. "How long?" he snapped, in a tone that caught everyone off guard.

Priya was next. "A while, Daniel. Look, I wanted to tell you, but I didn't want Mom and Dad to find out. You know how they'd react."

"I asked how long?" he growled.

"Almost two years," she answered.

When she dropped her head, he began shaking his. "TWO YEARS? Are you kidding me? You've been dating behind my back for two years?"

Was it anger or disgust filling up the room?

It was Taj's turn. "Daniel, we meant no harm."

Disdain gurgled deep within Daniel's throat. "You both must think I'm so stupid! Every time either of you came in, you were laughing at me behind my back. I was your friend, Taj! Doesn't that mean anything to you?"

He wasn't expecting an answer.

He turned to Priya. "And you, my sister. We're supposed to share these things, not hide them!"

His eyes had caught fire. His hands were twitching from the heat.

Priya tried again. "Daniel, we just . . ."

He swung his arm across the table, knocking a pitcher of water to the floor. It shattered into pieces, all running for cover.

Daniel hollered as he stood, his deep voice swaddled in anger and hurt.

"Get out!" he demanded. "Both of you! Get the hell out NOW!"

When they pressed the doorbell, the entire house bristled. Daniel answered and silently led Taj and Priya to the entry. The place should have been more welcoming, since rooms once full of folding chairs were now filled with handcrafted furniture, woolen rugs, and family pictures.

Today, entering guests were barely tolerated.

"Father's in the family room," Daniel grunted to Priya. "I suggest you meet with him alone. If you two saunter in together, he'll see that as a challenge to his authority—but do what you want. You're good at that."

"Is he still mad?" she asked Daniel.

"Furious. What did you expect?"

Priya exhaled the thick air. "Danny, listen to me. I am so sorry. I didn't mean to hurt you—or anyone. I should have told you. Just please forgive me!" She would have dropped to her knees had she thought it would help.

Daniel turned. Their eyes met. His shoulders slumped. The fatigue in his brow softened.

"What are you going to tell Father?" he asked.

"The truth. I'll tell him that I love Taj, that he loves me, that I can't marry a stranger, that we're in the United States, not India."

"He's a man of tradition, old and set in his ways. He won't take it well. He'll tell you that going against him will disgrace the family, that an arranged marriage worked for me, for your sister, that it will work for you also."

Daniel's wife rounded the corner from the hall. "Your father is calling. I think he's ready to speak with Priya."

Daniel nodded. "Tell him she'll be right there."

He turned back and spoke to both Priya and Taj. "Do you two love each other enough to turn your back on family, on tradition?"

Taj answered first. "Daniel, we're sorry for not telling you. As for family tradition, all I can tell you is that I've never met anyone like her. Whenever we're apart, she's all I think about. I can't imagine life without her—and she feels the same."

Priya reached out for Daniel's hand. "That sounds like the start of a pretty great tradition to me."

Daniel didn't argue. "I know this feels all *Ek Duuje Ke Liye,* but remember how it ends?"

Priya translated for Taj. "They're an Indian Romeo and Juliet." She turned back to Daniel.

"I don't pretend to know the future, our challenges, but I do know that I've made my decision and it's right."

"Then it's done." He gestured toward the family room. "He's waiting."

She was a step away when he reached forward and grabbed her arm.

"Priya, since I see you're set on this, that you've made up your mind, . . . there's something you should know."

"What is it, Danny?"

"It's Father and Mother . . ." The words cowered behind his teeth, afraid to come out. "Priya, theirs was also a love marriage."

Priya gasped. Her head rocked back. "What, that's not . . ."

Daniel brushed away her doubt. "They've kept it a secret, didn't want us to know. Considering all this, it might help."

The news was like unearthed gold. It couldn't be true! But she could see it glisten in his eyes. "How do you know this?"

"It's not important. I just do."

Priya's cheeks dimpled. It was her first genuine smile of the morning. "Thank you. I love you, Danny."

"Had you trusted me, I would have kept your secret," he replied.

"I know." She held his hand and squeezed.

"But being angry is exhausting," he added. "I'd much rather cook."

She let go of his fingers, leaned toward Taj, and kissed him. Then marched toward the living room to meet her father.

Priya's talk with her father was short—a surprise to both.

He told her that Taj was likely from a lower caste and that marrying someone from a lower caste would bring ridicule to the family. He described how arranged marriages were an Indian tradition, how parents know better than their children in such matters. He preached that obedience was critical and that arranged marriages were far more apt to last than marriages of passion. He said that the color of Taj's skin was too dark, that it would be easier for her children if she married a boy whose skin was lighter and closer to her own.

After he finished, Priya explained in a soft yet determined tone that she loved her father but she was going to marry Taj no matter what he said. She told him she was grateful he understood, from his own experience, what it was like to be able to marry the person you loved. When his eyebrows furrowed, it was hard to tell, even for a daughter, if he was shocked or outraged that she knew the truth.

"How did you . . ."

She wasn't about to let this escalate. She couldn't take the chance. There was an easy way to stop it cold.

"Papa," she said, interrupting. "Did you know that Taj was adopted from an orphanage in India?"

He tipped toward her. He clenched his determined teeth. "Priya, this is what I'm telling you! As such, we don't know his caste and never will. We don't know if you are marrying down. That is the reason why . . ."

"Papa, he was adopted from the Lincoln Home in Madukkarai."

If it was anger bubbling over before, it traded places with confusion and shock.

"How is that . . . ?"

"His name was Chellamuthu. He would have been seven or eight. Do you remember him?"

Her father's eyes darted, as if the news were too hot to set down. Air seemed to race into his lungs, turn around and race out—and then, for a moment, his eyes glanced heavenward. Priya couldn't be sure, but it sounded like a name.

He looked forward, past her. "*Eli?*"

"Father?"

It was as if she weren't there. "Dad? Are you all right? Is there anything else?"

His ghost-chased words were so dazed he could barely get them out. "No. No. You can go. Just go."

CHAPTER 31

Three days later, when Maneesh Durai opened the door at Daniel's house, he found Fred and Linda Rowland standing on his doorstep, both wearing traditional Indian dress. Taj stood behind them in a vibrant blue-and-purple sarong.

The family was invited inside, where Fred and Linda presented the Durais with an engraved silver engagement plate, filled with coconuts, flowers, turmeric, and beetlenuts. With Priya directing, Taj's parents recommended to the Durais that the families come to an arrangement concerning the marriage of their children.

With little said, the parents agreed, a date was set, the engagement was considered official, and wedding preparations were begun in earnest.

The reception held in their honor on a beautiful May evening in the rotunda at the City and County Building was an interesting intermingling of Indian tradition and western culture. Sadly, Air Supply music was not invited.

Priya was glowing. Taj was giddy. The stunning couple exchanged vows and ate cake. They circled a pretend fire and drank coconut milk. Curry danced recklessly with the fruit punch, while chocolate cake snuggled up to the *sharbat.*

Hundreds were invited. Hundreds attended.

Typical of Indian weddings, there was food everywhere. It was catered by Bombay House, naturally, and Daniel had promised the cuisine would be talked about for years to come.

Taj was dancing with Priya when Kelly and her husband entered. She was hard to miss—the woman was visibly pregnant. She and Taj hugged as best they could, swapped congratulations, then had as thrilling a conversation as anyone could have while being thronged by hundreds of happy dancing Indians.

She promised to call and catch up once Taj and Priya returned from their honeymoon. And then, as the festivities continued, Taj lost track of Kelly in the celebrating crowd.

An hour later, when he slipped out to move his car to thwart any sibling notions that shaving cream and tied-on cans would be funny, he found Kelly waiting for Jason, who had gone to get their car.

"You're leaving?" Taj asked.

"Truly, if I eat any more curry, it could kill the baby."

"Or give him excellent taste."

"Yeah, well, I can't chance it."

"It's so great to see you—*pregnant,* no less."

"Had you said fat, I'd have bludgeoned you with my stomach."

"You know, I'd almost like to see that."

Kelly's smile straightened. "On a serious note, how's that dream coming along?"

"To which dream are you referring?"

"I think you know. It involves a large continent and a certain map."

Taj rested against a pillar. "If I'm being honest, it's probably not going to happen."

"Why?"

"Take a good look. I'm married, barely finishing school. We're waist-deep in student loans. I'll be an old man before I get to India."

Kelly nudged him with her foot. "Come on, no one is asking you to walk to India. It doesn't cost that much to fly."

"Are you kidding? By the time we save any money, Priya will be pregnant—not that I have anything against pregnant women, mind you. I'm just saying that I have to face reality. Kelly, I've read this story and already know how it ends. It's a comedic tragedy. Trust me."

"Okay, drama boy."

"I'm not being dramatic, I'm being realistic. There's a time in life when you harbor hope and chase crazy dreams, and there's a time where you have to let it all go."

He noticed her jaw clench. It was a look he'd seen before.

"Do you have something more?" he asked.

Jason was pulling up the car. Kelly motioned that she'd be right there.

When her words marched out, they were swinging swords. "Two lessons that you need to get through your head. First, never make a pregnant woman mad, especially when she's eaten too much curry."

"I'll keep that in mind."

"Second, never give up hope. Plans change—I get that—but that doesn't mean we quit trying, that we sit down and whimper. Look, do you remember how I told you I met Jason?"

"Sure."

"Life is like that. It has a way of pushing, pulling, sometimes kicking us to where we need to be."

Taj must have sighed. He didn't think it was so obvious.

"You can sigh all you want, Taj, but there's goodness and purpose and reason out there. Believe it, embrace it, trust it. Life will always be hard, but if we do our best, if we persist, we can make a difference—and good will win out over evil, love will conquer hate, and butterflies and kittens will play together in the sunshine . . . That last line about kittens . . . it may be the curry talking."

Taj stooped to her side and yelled to Jason behind the wheel. "I'm going to kiss your very pregnant wife now!"

When Jason nodded his blessing, Taj planted a kiss on her cheek followed by a parting hug. "Knowing you has always been an adventure."

"I'm serious, Taj. Don't give up on your dream. Promise? It's time you discover who you really are!"

His was a forced smile. "Promise."

"Good. Now I'm off to Bedfordshire."

"Where?"

"Taj, Taj, Taj. Did you learn nothing in London? It's slang for bed. Oh, the innocence of a child."

"You, my friend," Taj duly noted, "are completely off your trolley."

Kelly climbed inside the car, blew a kiss good-bye, and drove away into the night.

CHAPTER 32

"I'm glad we've come to an agreement. It will be a pleasure to have you on board as part of our team. If it works for you, you can start on the first of next month. That should give HR adequate time to finish the paperwork."

When the man wearing the gray pinstriped suit extended his hand, Taj shook it with confidence. He looked him in the eyes. "I'm thrilled, Jerry, for the opportunity. It'll be great working with you."

On the outside, Taj was calm and assured. Inside, he wanted to throw his arms into the air and race around their office giggling like a three-year-old.

The telecommunications company was a short thirty-minute commute. He'd have a private office, an assistant, superb benefits, and decent pay. He'd be analyzing the company's departments, looking for ways they could streamline their operations. It was a dream job.

Priya was at the kitchen table when he waltzed into the room bearing the news. She was punching numbers into a calculator like an accountant on tax day.

"You, my dear," Taj announced, "are looking at the newest member of iLink's operational management team."

"That's so great!" Priya jumped up and wrapped her arms around his neck. "I knew you'd land it. I'm so proud of you." She wore excited eyes but carried cumbered words.

"Is something wrong?" Taj asked. She was always terrible at keeping secrets.

"We can talk about it later, after we celebrate."

"Seriously, what is it?"

"You should sit," she directed.

The man had been married long enough to know that *you should sit* meant *I have something to tell you, and you aren't going to like it.*

"What's up?" he asked.

"Family is important, right?"

Could there be a more loaded question in the world? It was a minefield. If he didn't watch where he stepped, it could get messy quick.

"Yes, family is important," he replied.

"Well, Emanuel is getting married."

"Your brother? When? Where?"

She plowed right in. "Taj, I think we should go. After all that has happened, I feel like it would be good to be there to support my family."

"By *go,* do you mean . . ."

"India."

His first question was obvious. "How do we pay for it?"

It seemed she'd already figured out that part. "We have $2,400 in savings. We can pay the minimum on our credit card this month in place of the full balance, and I get my check on Friday. Besides, you just landed a great job."

He'd asked the easy question. It was the next one that was troubling.

"When is the wedding?" Taj asked.

Her eyes were big, brown—and forlorn. She paused before answering. "We'd need to be there in six weeks."

His head started shaking immediately. "Priya, I start work in three! I just shook the CFO's hand. We made all the arrangements. I can't push them back now."

"Can't you just call and ask?"

"Honey, it's not the Rotary Club. Jobs like this don't arrive with the morning paper. You know how long I've been interviewing! There's a boatload of qualified applicants hoping I crash into a tree on the way home. We can't chance it."

Her silence held longer this time. She didn't look mad but rather like she was thinking.

"It seems to me that we've made a great list of the reasons we shouldn't go," she finally said. "Now, to be fair, let's list the reasons we should."

"Fine."

Priya had already mentioned the importance of family. He wrote it down.

"What else?" he asked.

"Well, you were born there and have talked about going back."

"Yes, but . . ." He'd accepted the silly exercise in the first place because prudence was on his side. No matter how she spun it, this job was critical and would trump all other petty reasons. But as he lifted his finger to begin his argument, Kelly's words scrambled into his head.

Don't give up on your dream, Taj. Promise?

"I know, but . . ." he said aloud. He was ready to disagree, to make a solid case she couldn't refute, but the words wouldn't cooperate.

Taj! Promise?

"But what?" Priya wondered.

If Kelly were here listening to this, she'd be slapping him about now. Two women ganging up, and neither realizing it.

It was true his job was perfect, that it made sense not to do anything that might disturb it. On the other hand, if not now, when? Once he and Priya started having children, it would never happen, and . . .

He didn't need to draw the conclusion. Priya had a point. Would it hurt to ask?

"Honey, you're right. I'll call Jerry and tell him a family situation has come up and that I'll need to delay my start date slightly. Hopefully they'll be okay with it."

Priya blinked. "Really?"

"No promises, but I'll call him. And don't sound so surprised."

"I know, but . . ."

"What?" he said, with shrugged shoulders. "Family is important, right?"

It was after she'd given him an extended hug, after they'd eaten dinner, while Priya was already organizing the clothes she planned to take, that Taj called to her from the spare bedroom, the one they were using for storage that was now packed with piles of boxes.

"Priya? Do you know which box has my old school notebooks in it? I'm looking for a specific binder. I think it was labeled . . ."

He pulled the lid off the box on the floor.

"Never mind. I found it!"

The binder was marked Business Law–Class Notes. He opened it to the back, to where his hand-drawn map was patiently waiting.

From: Taj Rowland
To: Christopher Raj

Chris,

I've found something we can import to India from the United States—me. I arrive in Chennai on May 19th and will travel to Coimbatore to attend my brother-in-law's wedding. My wife, Priya, arrives two weeks earlier to help her family with preparations.

I know we haven't met in person, but I was hoping you could be at the airport when I arrive and help me get to Coimbatore.

Thanks,
Taj

When his plane touched down in Chennai, on India's southeastern coast, Taj wasn't concerned. He'd lived with the Tambolis in London. He'd walked the streets of Upton. He'd heard their music, eaten their curry, admired their traditional Indian dress.

It didn't take long to realize that living in London had prepared Taj for India like holding an umbrella prepares one for a hurricane. There wasn't just a room full of dark-skinned foreigners speaking an indecipherable tongue, there was a thronging sea of them, of various hues, walking, talking, smoking, waving, laughing, arguing, selling, eating, drinking, bumping, pushing . . . and that was just at the airport.

Christopher Raj was to be there waiting so they could travel together to Coimbatore, where Priya's family lived—except for a single glaring problem: Taj had no clue what Christopher looked like.

What if the man didn't show?

Taj had been reading about Chennai on the airplane. It was the third largest city in India and the thirty-first largest urban area in the world. The article had called it the "Detroit of India," perhaps not meant as a compliment.

The airport was under construction—at least he hoped that was the excuse—and only a few of the temporary signs were in English. He wound his way through the maze of barricades to baggage, pulled his suitcase from the belt, and headed for the door.

If walking through the terminal induced culture shock, they should have placed a neon sign outside that read *Danger! High voltage!* A chaotic crowd, as if hired as the greeting party, waited just beyond the outside doors for anyone brave enough to wade the gauntlet.

"Hey, Ṭāksi? Ṭāksi?"

"Hōṭṭal? Hōṭṭal?"

When Taj stared blankly back, they switched from Tamil to English.

"You need taxi? Hotel?"

"I get your bag. This way!"

"No, come with me!"

"Good price!"

"No! NO!" Taj brushed them all away like roaches, tightened the grip on his suitcase, and glanced across the swell of shoving bodies.

He was praying he'd see his name written on one of the signs that flapped along the crowd's edge, but that meant making eye contact. Each time his eyes locked on an eager Indian stranger and then glanced away, it only served to encourage the rest, like serving blood to sharks. It didn't matter that his skin was their same color, that he looked just like them—except perhaps for his dark blue blazer. He was a wounded fish splashing about in the water, and they could smell the fear, taste the money.

"Here, mister! Taxi?"

"This way!"

"Here, sir! Here!"

"I help you! I take you where you need."

The air was thick, moist, hard to breathe. His armpits were already wet, dripping panic. Was the crowd circling, or was he just imagining? True, he wasn't wearing a lungi, but if he stepped forward into the crush of bodies, he was certain he would blend in and disappear.

He was ready to twist around, to retreat back into the relative safety of the terminal, and catch the next flight home.

"Taj Rowland?"

He turned. "Christopher?"

The man was certainly Indian—no surprise there: dark skin, about the same shade as Taj's; black hair, though cut shorter and not as curly; grandfather eyes, framed by large silver-rimmed glasses. He wore a royal blue polo that draped his wiry frame like an old T-shirt might drape a scarecrow—but he wasn't scary. He welcomed Taj with a smile so wide it likely touched both ears.

A picture of Taj was clutched between his skinny fingers.

"It is so good to meet you," Taj said, and he meant every precious syllable. "Where did you get my photo?"

"You sent Priya's flight information, remember? I met her at the airport, and she passed me your picture."

His English was good, his accent noticeably Indian. Taj wouldn't have cared if the man was speaking pig Latin. He had come as promised.

"This way," Chris called. "We'll take a ride to the hotel. In the morning, we'll catch the early train to Coimbatore. We'll get a better price on the taxi if we aren't standing right in front of the airport. Follow me!"

One had to appreciate the man's frugality.

Christopher picked up the suitcase while Taj lugged the backpack. They worked their way through the crowd to the outside curb and then down the street.

While the bustle inside the terminal had been startling, even eye-opening, anyone indoors had to be able to afford a ticket. Without a financial filter, the scene on the street as they walked farther away grew increasingly raw.

"Stay close," Christopher instructed, weaving between people on the sidewalk. He stepped over a man, dirty, prostrate and motionless, like a child might step over a flower—except the comatose man didn't smell like a garden.

It was hard to identify the many mixing aromas—gasoline, tobacco, incense, mildew, something fried in oil—all liberated by the heat. One smell clambered over the rest, stood on their shoulders. It was more pungent, more visceral—the smell of rotting urine.

Taj's eyes darted nervously to Christopher and then to the sidewalk near his feet, trying to both keep up and watch where he stepped. Why did he feel the sudden urge to wash his hands?

When they were a good block away from the airport terminal, Christopher motioned to a green and yellow, canvas-covered auto rickshaw, also called a *rick* or *autorick,* a motorized three-wheeled cart with just enough space in back for two. In the States, on a hot summer day, it might have been mistaken for a small ice-cream truck. In India, it provided the primary means of transportation.

Their driver wasn't shy. He hurled the suitcase beside his seat up front while the men climbed into the back. He didn't bother asking if they were ready. If a checkered flag had been waved, Taj didn't see it. The driver gunned, braked, swerved, honked—all while reaching out with one hand to grab the tipping suitcase and steering with his other.

And he wasn't alone. An entire swarm of drivers, brothers perhaps, all clones from the same driving school, buzzed around in synchronized chaos, honking, gesturing, hollering back and forth like courtroom attorneys. Taj didn't bother to ask what they were saying.

The hotel was more akin to an apartment building with a single entrance on the street. No valet, no parking. No mint waiting on a feather pillow.

"I forgot to ask if you wanted a private room or if you prefer we share."

"Are there two beds?"

"Yes."

"Sharing is just fine."

Taj passed Christopher some money.

It wasn't the Ritz Carlton. Taj couldn't say it even equaled a Motel 6. His brain was on overload, his body too jet-lagged to care.

The elevator was out of order, so the men hiked the stairs.

Christopher took one bed. Taj took the other. Within minutes, Christopher was snoring. Four hours later, dead tired but with open eyes, Taj's confused body clock couldn't figure out why it was so dark at noon.

He forced his eyelids closed, slowed his breathing, folded the lumpy pillow to cover his eyes. Nothing could keep his brain from jumping up and down on the bed and yelling like a teenager.

You made it, Taj! You made it to India.

By morning, little had changed. India was still frantically scurrying about outside the window.

Taj and Christopher walked to a small market adjacent to the hotel and ate their breakfast: *idlis* and fried potatoes. Christopher had tea. Taj drank a Coke.

Even early there was honking, never-ending honking. Christopher explained that it was a courtesy to let other drivers know you were coming. Seldom was it intended to be rude.

Beside them, against the building, sat an old woman with a young child, perhaps her granddaughter, and it appeared they had been there all night.

She watched Taj stare, then held up her hand.

Compassion tugged.

"Should I give them something?"

"Who?" Christopher asked, finishing the last sip of his morning tea. He turned his head. "Oh. I will leave it up to you," he said, "but I wouldn't give them money. You'll learn quickly that charity here must be . . . selective."

Taj took the last of his *idlis* and passed them to the woman.

While Christopher stepped to the street to negotiate their next ride, Taj couldn't help but glance around again.

India.

Still surreal. Still strange. Still a dream.

It was more than begging children. It was the sheer swell of humanity that burgeoned around him, a school that swam on all sides. In the street, right in front of the hotel, even as he waited for Chris, cars shared traffic with an oxen-pulled cart. Half a block down, a cow had wandered out into the busy road—*a cow!*—and as near as Taj could tell from his distance, little was being done to move it.

When Chris called, Taj grabbed his suitcase and scrambled in.

A car stopped behind them, and a man jumped out to urinate in the gutter. Taj was the only one who seemed surprised.

The driver of their rick honked twice and then pulled out into traffic.

A dog trotted past, so skinny that Taj wished he'd bought more *idlis.*

Honk. Honk.

Christopher faced Taj and smiled. He spoke a single word.

"India!"

CHAPTER 33

The train station was as brimming as the airport—too many people shoehorned into too small a box. The complex was never ending, cement platforms with trains of various colors, coming, going, some never stopping. It appeared common to find your train, run alongside an open door, and then jump on. Taj wondered how the elderly in India ever managed to travel.

And where were all these people going?

Christopher walked toward a blue-and-white-striped passenger train that was thankfully stationary. The cars themselves looked modern enough, though well used and dirty.

They had paid for a sleeper car, which appeared now to Taj to mean they wouldn't have to stand. There were two rows, three seats wide, in the car, with a narrow aisle up the center. One could sleep, all right, as long as it was done sitting up.

There were vents in the roof and windows along the side, but neither seemed a match for the rising May temperatures expected to push 100.

Christopher helped Taj lift his suitcase to the overhead rack and then pointed out their seats.

As the train jerked into motion, the men sat. It was the first real chance they'd had to talk. Taj learned that Christopher was about ten years older than he, married, with two young sons. He worked for the Indian Railroad in their management office, and though it sounded important, it meant his family still struggled. He lived in a tiny, rented home and was still in debt from his wedding eight years earlier. He was a third-generation Christian, a practicing Catholic—a rarity in a country that was 80 percent Hindu.

When he asked Taj about his past, Taj kept his answers short.

Married. No children. New job. Big plans for the future.

"It's ten hours to Coimbatore," Christopher added as their conversation waned. "You might want to get some rest."

Christopher, a man who apparently could nap anywhere, let the train's serenading rhythm coax his eyes closed.

Taj squeezed out into the aisle, then made his way to the back of the car. There was an open platform at the front and back of each car, with steps that descended nearly to the ground. Two vertical bars provided the only safeguard on the fast moving train.

Taj took a step down. Then another. He needed some air.

It was a precarious spot, considering a good grip on the railing was all that kept him from falling to his death on the blur of tracks just inches below.

Within minutes, a uniformed man approached.

"Coke?" he asked, holding up a bottle.

In America they'd be screaming at him to come back inside the train. In India they hoped to sell him a soft drink before he slipped. He bought a bottle and wiped the lid clean on his shirt.

Clickety-clack. Clickety-clack.

To call the moment *surreal* would heighten all future expectations and overburden the word. Taj had been longing to return to India for so long . . . now that he was here, staring out across its cities and landscapes, he was convinced he'd jar awake at any moment.

The train tracks cut a diverse swath across southern India, and from Taj's new vantage, he could sample it all—ornate stone temples and dilapidated huts, modern-day cars and broken-down bikes, pampered cows and emaciated dogs.

Mostly he noticed the people—old and young, male and female, a few with obvious wealth but most looking hungry and poor.

As the sun gathered strength, the smell from the sewage dumped onto the tracks became more potent. Taj should have stumbled back inside the stuffy compartment to try to get some rest. Today, however, his feet remained planted, his fingers holding steadfast to the rail. He'd missed more than fifteen years of this country and wasn't about to miss any more.

He stayed glued to his spot because, superimposed on his panoramic view, a story was unfolding. It was a book that Linda had used when teaching him how to read English as a child, a book by P. D. Eastman about a confused baby bird whose mother wasn't there when he hatched. All alone, the little bird set out on a journey asking the same question to everyone he met along the road—a hen, a dog, a cow, even a boat and a plane:

Are you my mother?

It was the very question Taj had wanted to ask the begging woman at breakfast, the reason he'd given her food. It was the very question poised on his lips to every bent-over woman, every shawl-covered head, every distant mother who now waddled beside the tracks as the train clattered past.

And they all could have been—every woman his mother, every man his father, every young man his brother, every child a niece or nephew. In a country of a billion, how would he know?

Are we related? he wanted to scream out. *Are we family? Please, tell me who I am!*

It became more than people. Large cities, small towns, everywhere in between.

Is that my village? Is this my hometown? Am I passing right by my childhood but this very moment?

It was a journey that should have left him teeming with optimism. He was finally in India, here with a chance to trace his beginnings, his roots, his identity. Instead, it burdened him with worry.

What if I can't find them? What if I fail?

Worse yet . . . What if I don't like what I find?

It was 4:30 in the afternoon when the train shuddered to a stop, when Christopher touched his shoulder.

"Taj?" he asked, with puckered eyebrows. "Have you been out here all day?"

Taj nodded.

Passengers edged past, anxious to reach their destinations.

"Is everything okay?" Christopher inquired.

"You have a beautiful country," Taj answered, stating the obvious but also avoiding the man's question.

Christopher waited, expected more. When Taj said nothing, Christopher patted him on the back, like a father might do to a son. "Grab your bag," he said. "Let's get you to where you are going. I'm sure they're waiting."

By American standards—the only gauge Taj held at the moment—his father-in-law's place might be called shabby. It was a single story, cement rectangle that had been slathered over the years, both inside and out, with countless layers of limestone paint.

Its flat roof held down plastered interior walls that divided the space into smaller lifeless rooms that, if one squinted, were hard to distinguish from one another.

An undersized iron gate guarded a courtyard of sorts where potted flowers struggled to add cheer. They sat on a tiled perimeter, about eight feet wide, that circled around the house and abutted a six-foot wall that separated the postage-stamp property from its surrounding neighbors.

In short, it was a house that yawned. Uninspiring. Boring. Dreary.

The neighborhood didn't help, equally lackluster, a mesh of one-lane streets—more like alleys—some paved, most dirt, none that would let more than a single car pass at a time. Similar homes puzzled together in the crowded community, all lamenting their misery at not being grand.

Of course, by Indian standards—a measure that Christopher assured him would soon become familiar—the home was firmly middle class. Yes, the roof was flat, but it was solid and not thatch. Indeed the house was only a single story, but it was designed for a second, and plans were already underway to begin the addition next year. Understandably it sat on a tiny parcel of property. This was India. What else could be expected in a country of countless people with little land to go around? More important, the place was family-owned, not rented, and the soil holding up the home's walls was Indian proud.

When Taj banged on the gate, Priya ran out.

The couple hugged like newlyweds, thanked Christopher for his hospitality, and then greeted Priya's relatives.

It was only after Christopher had gone that Taj realized he hadn't paid him for their train fares.

Priya had been sharing the smallest of the home's bedrooms with an aunt. With Taj's arrival, arrangements were made for him and Priya to take a room several blocks away, in an empty home that belonged to an acquaintance, a professor Maneesh knew from Singapore.

The home had never heard of American standards.

There was a bed, so that part was good, but the two-roomed structure came with enough dust and cobwebs to scare a haunted house. They swept out a battalion of bugs, most of which had likely died of boredom, and then the couple sat together on the bed.

"Are you thinking what I'm thinking?" Taj asked, glancing back at the waiting mattress.

"Not unless you're thinking we need to shower first."

She gripped his fingers, then reached up to let them drift across her neck. "I didn't tell you the best part," she said. "You get to help me prepare the *puttu* tomorrow. I was dreading having to do it myself."

Perhaps it was his hesitation that tipped her off, or the way his eyes wilted.

"Taj . . . ? I know that look," she said, in an interrogating tone that assured one day she'd be a good mother. "What are you not telling me?"

It was his turn to finger squeeze.

"Priya, I'm here to find my family." The naked words coughed themselves out. There was no way to dress them. He sensed she already knew.

She had but one question. "How?"

"I'll start with your dad. I'll go to the orphanage. I have the address.

Who knows, they may still have old records. Also, do you remember when we were first dating and I showed you my map?"

"The old scribbled one?"

"Yes, well, I brought it. Perhaps it will help. After that, I'm not sure."

"Before the wedding?" she asked.

He stood, inflated his chest, pushed at the air that was muscling into the room. "Not only before the wedding—*today.* I'm finally in India. I don't have time to waste. The thing is . . ."

He sat back down beside her. "Priya, I have a problem."

"What is it?"

"I can't go alone. I don't speak the language. I don't know my way around. You need to come with me."

"Impossible."

"It's four days until the wedding. It can't be that big a deal that you're here the whole time."

"Oh, Taj." Her shoulders slumped, as if he'd asked her to lug a brick-laden backpack. "I want to help, really I do, but I just can't."

"Why not?"

"I'm here for my family and, well . . ."

"Well, what?"

"Taj, this is India. The culture is different here. It's not like the U.S. Look, you were taught growing up that you could do anything, that the world was wide open if you simply exerted yourself and worked hard."

"Isn't it?"

"Not here. Not in Tamil Nadu. Not for a woman. They have customs and traditions and . . . limitations."

"I don't understand."

"My family won't like it if I go with you—and they have much more say here than they do back home. They're trying to get ready for the wedding. I promised I'd help. It's a big deal. It's important. Besides, they're already concerned about . . ."

"About what?"

"Us, the questions their friends will ask because of you, the fact that our marriage wasn't arranged, that they don't know your caste. Taj, they're concerned about what people will think, how it will affect their . . . well, their status."

"Status? Have you looked around? Why would their friends care? Why do they care what anyone thinks? Besides, it's your brother who's getting married, anyway."

"I *have* looked around. I grew up here, remember? It's exactly my point. They don't have much, so they cling to tradition. I know it's hard for anyone not raised here to understand. I'm just telling you, if I go with you, it will put a strain on my family, my parents, my father, on my relationship with them. Taj, please don't put me in that position."

Her dark eyes and downy skin never gave him a choice. "It's all right. You don't have to go." He stood for the second time. Resolve sparked in his eyes.

"What will you do?" she asked.

"It's too bad Daniel couldn't come," Taj said, as he stepped to the door. He looked out in the direction of the family home. His gaze narrowed.

"But that's okay . . . I'm going to ask your father."

When Taj entered, Maneesh was huddled in the corner with his brother crouching over a fire. They were whispering.

Taj should have waited. He knew that. But time was limited. His fuse was burning.

"Sir, I need your help to find my family."

Maneesh glanced back. One bushy brow lifted and then settled before he turned back to his conversation. The men were speaking Tamil. Taj waited until the words waned. He repeated himself.

"Mr. Durai. While I'm in India, I would like to find my family. I need your help. Please." He hadn't intended to beg.

Back home, when Taj had stood on the doorstep with his parents to request permission from the man to marry Priya, everyone assembled there understood that it was a formality, that they were going through the motions, that with or without his permission, the couple was going to get married. On the porch that day, Taj had caught a glimpse of his future father-in-law's eyes. At the time, they had flooded with panic.

Today, in India, however, the man didn't look away.

"I am sorry. There is nothing I can do to help you," he said.

But he didn't look sorry. He looked perturbed, and disdain spilled everywhere.

Taj stepped into the puddle.

"What do you mean *nothing?* You can do *everything.* I'm finally here in India. You worked with the orphanage who stole me. You can tell me if you know where I came from. You can take me to the orphanage to see if they have records. It's not that far away. We can get there and back in half a day."

Maneesh's brother had been eyeing the exchange. He faced Maneesh.

"*Teru nai,*" he mumbled in Tamil, and the men laughed.

Am I back in the first grade?

Taj wiped at his face with an arm. He'd been sweating since his arrival, and now it was dripping down his chest.

"Did you know about my kidnapping?" His fingers clenched. His back arched. His face twitched. "Were you involved?"

Maneesh pivoted. His voice rose to meet Taj. "We are in India!" he bellowed. "You are standing in *MY* house! You have no right to accuse me! I have a son who's having a *proper wedding,* and we have much to do to get ready, so unless you have come to help, STAY OUT OF MY WAY!"

The only sound was noisy breathing.

Priya's brother Emanuel hurried in from the other room. His face stretched with dread. Taj looked right at him. "Your father won't help. Will *you?*"

"Taj, calm down. We'll figure something out," he said.

Taj stabbed a stern finger, first at Emanuel and then toward Maneesh.

"Calm down? All I'm asking for is half a day. Why is that so hard? Am I not part of this family? Well, you know what? I don't give a damn! I'll go on my own! I don't need any of you."

It was a lie that made the veins in his neck pulse even harder, as they obeyed their orders to push blood to the face.

Taj bolted out the door and marched down the dusty street. Never mind that it was a strange country. No worries that he didn't speak the language. Not a problem that he'd just told his wife's family—the only people who could help him—to take a flying leap into the deep end of the Indian Ocean.

For all he cared, they could take their pettiness and . . .

"Taj! Please, wait. Wait up!"

Taj twisted. It was Emanuel. He was flapping both hands like a referee. "Hey, let's talk."

Taj's eyes were still burning, still hot. "Unless someone is willing to help," he said, "I don't see the point."

Emanuel steered him to the side of the street and against a building. Taj wasn't finished. "Look, I didn't come all this way to cause contention. I'm just trying to find my family. Is that really so terrible? Why can't you help me?"

While Emanuel's head shaking started immediately, it took a moment for the words to find their way out. When they arrived, at least they sounded genuine.

"Taj, I would normally go with you, but I'm getting married in *four days.* Seriously, there just isn't much that I can do considering the circumstances. I'm sorry."

"Did your father send you after me?" Taj asked, pointing back in the direction of the house.

Emanuel's head bobbing changed from back and forth to up and down.

"Why?"

A grin escaped. "Because you scare the hell out of him. Look, I know he said he won't help, and he seems upset and let you storm off, but if you want the truth, he's terrified."

"Of what?"

"The family's reputation. It's important in this part of India."

"How would finding my family mess that up?"

"Just you being here messes it up. Look, it's not your fault. I'm not blaming you. I'm just giving you the facts. They don't know your caste, you're in a love-marriage, you're not a traditional Indian."

"Are you worried about all this?"

"The family's reputation?" Emanuel grabbed Taj's sweaty shoulders with equally sweaty palms. "Taj, look at me and listen. *I'm having an arranged marriage.* I don't really know the girl. She doesn't know me. I'm not a naïve Indian. I've spent time in the United States."

"What are you saying?"

"Trust me when I tell you, I have much bigger concerns right now than what others may think."

Well, since he'd put it that way . . . Taj exhaled a warm breath. His wrinkled eyes relaxed. "So you don't love her?"

"How could I know? They say I will in time."

"Then why go through with it?"

"This is what I'm talking about. There are aspects of our culture that seem odd to outsiders, customs that need bigger words to explain. I didn't say I wasn't okay with my marriage. All I said was that I'm nervous."

"Can I ask you something else?"

"Sure."

"What's a *Teru nai?*"

Emanuel snickered. "Yeah, I heard that. He called you a *street dog.* From all the barking and growling back there, it sounded like you were both busy marking your territory."

Taj reached for a folded paper in his back pocket. "Before we go back, can you take a look at this?" He passed it to Emanuel. "It's a map I drew of the place where I grew up. I know it's rough, but do you recognize where it might be?"

Emanuel pulled it close, studied it. He stated the obvious. "A park, a river, a group of huts surrounded by a city—Taj, this could be anywhere."

"That's why I need to go to the orphanage and speak to Eli."

"Eli?"

"Yeah, the man there who took me to the United States, the person my parents dealt with when I was adopted. He's going to know things."

"Taj, I know who Eli is. My father worked with him years ago. When we lived here, before Singapore, he would come over to the house. He was a family friend."

Taj turned. His eyes begged. "Emanuel, I know you're getting married, but please, can you spare just a few hours and take me to see him?"

Emanuel's lips parted, a finger raised, but in place of words, there was only a sigh.

"What is it?" Taj asked.

"You can go to the orphanage, but you won't find Eli."

"Why not?"

"Eli is dead."

CHAPTER 34

Bringg, bringg. Bringg, bringg.

"Pick up!"

Bringg, bringg. Bringg, bringg.

"Please, pick up!"

Bringg, bringg. Bringg, bringg.

Taj was prying the receiver from his ear when a single word reached through to command that he stop. "Hello?"

"Christopher? Is that you?"

"Taj? What's wrong?"

"Chris, I need your help."

"What is it?"

Where should he begin? "I was kidnapped as a child in India, then sold to an orphanage, then adopted by my family in America. I'm back now to try and find my family. That's why I'm here."

That was probably a line the man had never heard before. A confused pause lingered.

"Chris? You still there?"

"Did you just say . . ."

"Look, I know I told you I was coming here for my brother-in-law's wedding and to talk about our business ideas, and while both are true, mostly I came to find my family. I don't know if I'll ever get back to India again, so while I'm here, I have to try. This could be my only chance. I have the address of the orphanage, but I don't know the language. My wife's family won't help me—they won't even talk about it. Chris, is there any way you can come back?"

Taj already knew the answer. Christopher, a man he hardly knew, had already taken the ten-hour trip over and back. He had a wife, two children, a job. He'd already rehearsed to Taj the difficulties of a run-down rental, of being deep in debt, and trying to keep his family fed on one meager salary. What was Taj thinking?

"Christopher," Taj said. "I'm sorry. It was wrong of me even to ask."

The man interrupted his own silence. "Taj, as a Christian, I've been taught to help those in need when it's possible, and as near as I can tell, you're as needy as they come. Let me make a call, but plan on seeing me in about ten hours and . . . fifteen minutes."

Stillness followed.

"Taj, are you there?"

His throat had filled with sand. He couldn't swallow.

"I won't forget this."

When Taj hung up, when he turned, Maneesh was standing in the doorway. He'd been listening.

The bus ride to Madukkarai took an hour and a half. On the way, Taj spread open his map for Christopher to study. His friend's reply was word for word the same as Emanuel's: "Taj, this could be anywhere."

Taj pointed to the notes he'd jotted below.

"I know that the map is crude, but look, I have the orphanage's address from my mother's letter. I also know my name—Chellamuthu—it was on my original passport. The man who ran the orphanage was Eli Manickam, and though Emanuel said he's passed away, that doesn't mean the place won't still have records. I have plenty of information; they should be able to look something up. True?"

Christopher answered with quiet words. "We will hope for the best."

Compared to other cities in India, Madukkarai was dingy and barren, a town with few friends, a place that made Coimbatore feel tropical. Their rickety old bus rolled into the edge of town, past an old cement factory, past the squatters who had set up tarps along the edge of the road, past open smoky fires and abandoned road construction and lean shops whose keepers eternally hoped for better times. Even the few new buildings under construction looked old.

Madukkarai was a place, Taj determined as he stepped off the bus at the center of town, that had never known the privilege of being called quaint.

Twenty minutes later Taj and Christopher were standing in front of a mold-tinged, white-plastered cement compound in desperate need of paint. Its address matched the one written on the bottom of Taj's paper—but there was no orphanage.

The Lincoln Home for Homeless Children was gone.

The large metal gate was now a wide open entrance, welcoming where it had once forbidden. Inside, the spacious courtyard had been skinned, quartered, and carved into separate plots for homes, a mishmash of new building that nearly masked the separate structure weeping at the far end of the compound where Taj had once played as a child.

The great stone fence, once proud and impenetrable, begged now from its knees, decaying, feeble and broken. The longest portion, seemingly unwilling to surrender, stretched along the north but was not nearly as tall as Taj had remembered. He pulled himself up, checked the top, and found it had been rendered toothless. The shards of glass were gone. The rusty nubs of steel posts, long since removed, were all that remained.

"Look at you now," Taj whispered. "Do you remember me?"

There was no answer.

While the compound had been sliced up the middle and subdivided into new housing, a small section of the old courtyard in front had survived the incursion. It was there Taj noticed the fountain.

He'd remembered it being rather grand, even ornate. Without notice, the words *wide* and *deep* channeled into his head, and he could almost hear the melody—but the fountain was neither. The concrete was chipped along the edges and so stained in spots that it looked black. There was no water in the thing, and if there had been and he'd slipped in, it would not even have covered his socks.

It was familiar—no question—only tiny, neglected, and worn. Like his memories.

He bent down and twisted the tap that still poked from the wall. Nothing. Next, he sat on its dirty cement ledge, like a footstool, and let his fingers brush its pocked surface. He closed his eyes, wondering if it would conjure up the sound of singing children.

Christopher gave him a moment and then sat at his side. "I am sorry, Taj. I know you were hoping to find more."

"Do you realize that I sat in this very spot as a child," Taj asked, "that I sang songs right here? I remember it! I remember it now so clearly—and look at me. I'm back at the fountain—an empty fountain. What do I make of that? What do I do with that?"

"It is interesting how life, at times, brings us back around."

"The thing is, I remember this place being more . . . I don't know . . . daunting. I remember it as a kind of friendly fortress. But really, as I look around, the walls aren't even that high. Chris, why didn't I just run away? Why couldn't I have just found my way back home?"

He was staring at Chris, but his words seemed to circle back, asking himself the questions.

"Taj, can't we all ask that about times in our lives? Besides, you were just a child. The bigger problem we have now is that there is no orphanage. No records. No clues. Where do we go from here?"

Another good question, without a good answer.

Silence spilled from the fountain until Taj disturbed it. "Did I tell you that as a kid, in America, I was a Boy Scout? Do you have Boy Scouts in India?"

"Yes, I have seen Boy Scouts. Did you enjoy it?"

"I enjoyed the challenge. I got about every merit badge known to mankind."

"Did you go camping there, in America?"

"All the time."

Was Taj leading the conversation . . . or was it leading him? A smile cracked at the edge of his face. "Which meant that I needed a lot of camping gear!" He faced Christopher. "And to buy the gear, my parents made me earn the money all by myself. I mowed lawns, cleaned yards, typical kid jobs, but then I realized if I knocked on doors wearing my scout uniform, I could sell about anything—Christmas cards, crappy chocolate, cheap popcorn—whatever."

"Why, then, did they buy it?" Christopher asked. He didn't seem to notice the spark flickering again in Taj's eyes.

"I think they were just so surprised to see a uniformed Indian standing on their porch that I could have sold them anything. Here's the funny part . . ."

"Is this story supposed to be funny?"

"We're getting there. I was a curious kid, and so one day, for fun, I knocked on doors selling only a joke and a smile."

"A joke? You sold a joke? It must have been very funny."

"Not really. 'Why did the Indian run across the road?'" Taj didn't wait for Chris to shrug. "'Because he was in a big curry.'"

"You're right. That's not funny."

"No, but I earned nearly double my usual amount."

Christopher was just noticing that the conversation had steered off track. "What does this story have to do with the orphanage being closed?"

Taj stood. He strode toward the street. "Follow me, kind sir."

"Where are you going?"

"To see if anyone in this country has a sense of humor."

Nobody answered at the first door, a home that sat across the street from the orphanage—nor the second, nor the third. Taj was ready to bang on the fourth when he glanced down the block to see an old woman sitting on her front porch eating breakfast.

"There!" he said, pointing. "We'll talk to her."

Taj acknowledged the woman, as he had all his customers, with a grin and a greeting. When she spoke back in Tamil, he let Christopher step up.

"Good morning. How are you?" Christopher asked.

She bowed a *good morning,* as if it were common for strangers to drop in, and then clutching her cup of masala tea with two hands, she huffed at the liquid, still too hot to drink, through a gap in her smile where a tooth was missing.

She blew and sipped and sipped and blew, but as best Taj could tell, very little information was being exchanged. Chatting with the old woman was fine if she could share something about the orphanage. If not, they were wasting time.

It wasn't until her cup of tea was nearly empty that Christopher posed the question.

"We are here to inquire about an orphanage that once operated down the block." He was about to tell her the name, but the old woman's eyes were already glowing.

"Yes, yes, the Lincoln Home," she said. "I know it. My husband worked there for several years."

Taj yanked his head around so quickly his neck cracked. Even he understood the words Lincoln Home.

Christopher passed Taj the news and then continued. "That's very nice. What did he do there?"

"Christopher . . . Chris," Taj interrupted, "ask her when he'll be home. When will her husband be home?"

"I will, I will. Relax. Give her time."

Before he could, the front door swung opened, and a man stepped onto the porch. He nodded graciously to both Taj and Christopher, as if their visit were expected, as if they were old friends of the family.

He sat beside the woman. He was many years younger, and she introduced him as her son. He listened politely to the timid conversation, even participated when Christopher gestured toward the sky and complained about the lack of rain, yet all the while the man kept turning back to stare at Taj, as if perhaps, he didn't trust him. It might have been because Taj was speaking English, or that he was continually nudging Christopher to move the conversation along, or because he was the only one dressed in jeans and a T-shirt.

Taj couldn't have cared less. "Ask her!" he said again to Christopher, this time poking him in the shoulder.

"Ma'am," Christopher continued, "we have several questions about the orphanage. Since your husband worked there, we'd like to speak to him. Can you tell us when he might be home?"

Even masked with a well-wrinkled face, her sadness soaked through. "I'm sorry," she said, "my husband died two years ago. He knew much about the orphanage, and I'm certain he could have helped."

Taj could read the lines in her face, could see it wasn't good news. Another literal dead end.

The son interrupted. He was pointing a finger directly at Taj, jabbing it at him. "I think we've met," he said.

When Christopher translated, Taj shook his head. "He's mistaken. Tell him it's not possible. I grew up in the United States. It's my first time visiting India."

The man listened. His shoulder lifted. His eyes shrugged their reply. "I could be wrong." He tipped his head graciously and excused himself to go back inside.

As Christopher explained to the woman that they needed to speak to her neighbors, in search for others who might have information about the orphanage, the woman's son returned.

A smile now broadened across his face. He dropped a rectangular black-and-white photo onto the tea table in front of Taj and pointed at two grinning boys.

"You. Me," he said.

Taj bent close. Unbelievable! It *was* them!

The two boys in the photo were standing in the orphanage

courtyard, scrawny brown arms draped around scrawnier bare shoulders, each boy gripping a plump balloon animal in his free hand.

The man waited for Taj's glance before he tapped himself on the chest. He spoke his best English.

"I am Vikesh Rajamani. You remember?"

Despite the hot, muggy morning, a breeze floated across the porch and kissed Taj's neck. His sweaty arms shivered. He rose to his feet. He leaned into the man's gaze.

"Vikesh? Vikesh! Yes, yes! I do remember! We played as children at the orphanage!"

Even though the man's next words were Tamil, Taj didn't need a translator.

They clasped arms, held their grip.

"Greetings, my lost friend," Vikesh exclaimed. "It's so good you came back!"

The sun had reached a peak in the sky and was already sliding downhill by the time Taj and Christopher said good-bye to Vikesh and his mother. They had reminisced about skinny clowns who conjured animals from colored balloons, pretend battles in a courtyard to save India, and a sick little girl whose name neither could recall.

One could argue that finding Vikesh was astonishing. Encountering a friend from the orphanage was so unlikely that it appeared fate had woven their paths together with delicate fingers, sending the message that greater powers had taken interest in Taj's journey.

At the same time, one could also contend that it had all been a colossal waste of time.

While the men had laughed and marveled at the memories, each taking turns murmuring *I remember when* as if it had been story night at an old folks home, nothing new had been learned. Vikesh had no suggestions as to where Taj should turn next.

Another brick wall. Another wall topped with shards of glass.

In spite of the coincidence, the memories, Taj was no closer to finding anyone. If a higher power was indeed causing people's paths to cross, it seemed to be only for taunting.

Taj and Christopher walked back toward the old orphanage grounds and sat by a wall in the shade. Christopher waited as Taj studied his hand-drawn map, as if it had suddenly changed.

"There is something else I remember," Taj finally said. "A car ride."

Christopher listened.

"Once I was taken, I remember being in some sort of bus, and then a car, maybe a Jeep, for a total of about three hours. Isn't it odd I can still remember how long?"

It took Christopher a few minutes to flag down a taxi. It took longer for the driver to understand where they wanted to go.

"Listen, sir," Christopher repeated. "I'm telling you that we don't have a specific destination. We want to you to take us to the edge of town and then start driving around in an ever widening circle. We need to visit all the cities and towns that are within three hours."

"That could take days!" the driver protested, unsure if he should be pleased or perturbed.

Taj's answer was simple. "Then we'd better get going."

Pollachi, Palakkad, and *Perinthalmanna.*

The first few cities were exciting, each bustling with possibility. The routine was the same:

1. Head to the center of town.
2. Look for locals.
3. Show them the map and ask if they know of any place in the city that might match.
4. Explain that it's not a joke, that men have never been more serious.
5. Climb back into the taxi and ask the driver to keep circling.

At every step, with every widening arc, Taj studied the streets for anything that might be familiar. When they reached the edge of town, it was time for the next step:

6. Drive like crazy to the next closest city.

Malappuram, Ponnani, and *Guruvayoor.*

The burden of work has quashed countless good intentions. Taj had vowed not to give up. Still, it was a bit confusing to know how much time he should spend circling. If he rushed things, if he dismissed a visit too quickly, he could be leaving his family behind, driving right past them. But if he stayed too long, fussing about whether the place honestly looked familiar, he'd run out of time long before he'd run out of cities.

Either way, the result would be miserable failure.

It was after dark when they finished the first night. Rather than return to Coimbatore so Taj could sleep comfortably beside his wife, he asked Christopher to locate a cheap hotel. It would save them precious time in the morning.

Taj counted out money for the room and for the taxi driver, who'd insisted he be paid that evening if they expected to wake up and find him waiting. To the natives, Taj must have seemed like a rich American. They couldn't know that his wallet cried otherwise.

Taj and Christopher awoke with the sun, ate a quick breakfast, said a short prayer, and climbed into the arms of the still sticky vinyl seats waiting for them in the cab.

Kunnamkulam, Ottapalam, and *Cherpulassery.*

Lunch was swallowed but not tasted. The sun watched from a cloudless sky.

Thrissur, Paravoor, and *Perumbavoor.*

Maybe the next city will be the one. Maybe his family will be there waiting. Maybe there is reason and purpose to all the pain and turmoil. Maybe God is finally listening.

"Drive faster."

"Just one more."

"No! Nothing looks familiar."

Christopher placed a hand on Taj's shoulder. "It's time we head back for the day."

Taj didn't answer, couldn't answer. He knew that his new friend was right, that there was no money for another hotel.

When the cab pulled up to the home in Coimbatore where he and Priya were staying, Taj was the only one to get out.

"Aren't you coming?" he said to Christopher.

"When is the wedding?" Christopher asked.

"Two days. We can still go out again tomorrow."

"Taj, listen . . ."

Taj didn't want to listen. His throat hurt. His feet were swollen. Perspiration was carving tiny rivers though the dust that had settled into his hair and was dripping dirty drops from his ears. It had been a terrible, miserable, disappointing couple of days. He would admit it. But he couldn't give up. Not yet. Not while there was still time.

"I'm not giving up, Taj," Christopher insisted, reading Taj's face. "I just have an errand for work. Take a couple of days off. Take a shower.

Use soap. Enjoy the wedding. Spend some time with your wife. You have a few days after, true?"

"A couple."

"I'll be back."

"Okay, I'll be here."

When Taj walked inside, he wasn't alone. Anguish was clinging to his shoulders. He quietly showered. It wouldn't wash off, no matter how hot the water.

Priya stirred as he slipped into bed.

"Hey, hi . . . any luck?" she softly asked.

Taj lay beside her. She couldn't see him shake his head.

Perhaps Christopher was right.

He closed his eyes and pressed his body against his sleepy wife. She snuggled. "You can tell me all about it in the morning," she declared, with words so drowsy they could barely be understood.

And then, like Taj's hope, she went quiet.

Tap-tap. Tap-tap.

Taj was still asleep when the tapping started. He peeled himself out of bed, whispered to Priya that he'd answer it, and stumbled to the door half asleep.

"Taj?" Emanuel took half a step back. "Man, you look like . . . Are you feeling well?"

"Peachy," Taj mumbled. "Got in late. Couldn't sleep. What do you need?"

"Can you tell Priya that instead of helping Auntie with the *sambar idli,* Mother would like help with the rice? They are meeting in about an hour."

"I'll let her know."

Taj was about to close the door when Emanuel interrupted.

"Taj, there's one more thing." He stepped inside. "I looked for you yesterday, but you were gone. I've been thinking about your map. May I see it again?"

Taj rubbed at his eyes. "Sure. Just a second."

When he returned from the bedroom, the now dirty map was unfolded. Emanuel took it, studied it.

"What is it?" Taj asked. A large road map of southern India was still spread out across the table.

"Can you show me where you've been?" Emanuel asked.

Taj started at Pollachi, dragging a slow, feeble line with his finger to city after city after city—all those he and Chris had visited the days prior.

"I've been thinking," Emanuel repeated, "that you should go and check out Erode. It's in the opposite direction—right here. There's a river that wraps around it, vaguely similar to your map. No guarantees, but it might be worth a look."

Taj's tired eyes stirred open.

Erode? Was this finally his answer?

"Show me again," he said, focusing on the larger map.

There it was, to the east. One of the cities still waiting, obscure enough he probably would have missed it.

Priya was standing now in the doorway, watching.

"Did you hear?" Taj called. "He thinks I should try Erode."

A familiar problem nudged him on the shoulder. "Wait . . ." Taj turned to Priya, then to Emanuel, and then back to Priya. "Christopher is gone," he said.

"Taj, I have a buddy who lives in Erode," Emanuel offered. "If you want, I can get word to him and have him meet you at the bus station.

I'm sure he can show you around, perhaps even put you up for the night. If you make the next bus, you can be there by noon. I just need you to make me one promise."

"What's that?"

"Find them or not, I expect to see you back here at my wedding."

Taj glanced to Priya. They had come as a couple to support Emanuel and her family. So far, he'd hardly seen her. He waited.

She nodded her permission.

He faced Emanuel. Gratitude edged forward in his voice. "I wouldn't miss it . . . and Emanuel?"

"Yes?"

"Thank you."

When he spoke next it was to the space between Priya and Emanuel. Was he speaking to both, or neither?

"I'm certain I'll be back for the wedding."

They responded in unison. "How do you know?"

"Because I'm running out of options."

CHAPTER 35

Hope is an avid painter. The picture that brushed into Taj's mind included a busy but picturesque bus station. A gray-haired woman would be arguing with the ticket seller about the fare to Nagpur. Children would be tugging at their fathers' lungis, begging for rupees to buy candy. Conductors would be hollering. Travelers would be scrambling and . . . there would be fruit sellers. He clearly remembered the fruit sellers.

The longer Taj painted, the more detailed the scene became. He would exit the station and recognize a path heading north—or south, or east, or west—that would beckon him to a park, a place packed with slides and swings and teeter-totters and waiting children. Eager boys might even bunch around him as he'd stroll toward a group of huts that would remarkably fit the location scribbled on his map. His mother—older now but no less anxious—would pause for an inquiring second before running toward him with gawky outstretched arms.

Music might play. Strangers might clap. The sky would certainly smile. A spontaneous party could ensue—with dancing. Lots of dancing. Norman Rockwell would be jealous.

Erode had a bus station, but there were no singing birds. It wasn't picturesque. It wasn't memorable. There was nothing at all worth painting.

Taj stepped down from the bus into a smear of oil on the cement. The acidic aroma of diesel fuel was doing its best to subdue the stench of urine. It was a battle neither could win.

This place wasn't quite as dreary as Madukkarai, that was true, but it was trying its hardest. Dust, sweat, vomit, stink. People running in countless directions. Taj could list three ways it was similar to the other cities he'd recently visited: *crowded, chaotic, unfamiliar.*

The station itself was mostly outdoors, a massive parking lot divided by long rows of T-shaped overhangs, some made with cement, others constructed of tin, each providing a place for buses to park, people to gather, and a pretend semblance of order. Around the perimeter were merchant's stalls, vendors selling liquor, others selling food, even several selling fruit, but nothing that Taj recognized as familiar from his childhood.

Emanuel's friend Isaac was waiting, as he'd promised.

"Welcome, Brother Taj. Emanuel told me you are in search of your family. I am very pleased to help."

Isaac was the shortest Indian Taj had met and perhaps the leanest. What the young man lacked in muscle, however, he made up for in mood. He was starving dog skinny but fat dog happy.

The visit started like all the others. Taj pulled the map from his pocket and held it out for Isaac to examine. "I know it's rough, but do you recognize where this might be?"

Also like the rest, Isaac shook his head—but at least he was smiling and positive. "Yes. I can tell you for certain . . . it does not look familiar."

"Then we'd better get going."

Taj flagged down an auto rickshaw, and the men climbed in.

Erode had a river, the Kaveri, that swathed it like a scarf. That much Taj knew from Emanuel. The Kaveri was large—too large. It not only wrapped the city but its tributaries feathered off in unending directions, like ants furrowing through soil. As it turned out, nearly any location in Erode was near some arm of the Kaveri.

Trying to match up the location with a park also didn't help. Isaac wasn't aware of any children's parks in town similar to the one Taj had described, and neither was anyone they stopped on the street.

"How about huts?" Taj asked. On its face, the question was ridiculous, like a desperate, drowning man grasping at foam.

In every other city, when he'd run out of options, he'd resorted to driving in a spiral, starting from the center of town, scouting for lost memories. Today, every building, every block, every never-ending street they circled seemed to turn and look away. When the sun finally dropped over the horizon, Isaac directed the driver toward home.

Isaac had already warned Taj that his home was meager. Taj hadn't realized that meant he'd be sleeping in the slums. The place was a good dozen blocks west of the bus station, though Taj quit counting as the surroundings grew increasingly . . . *humble.*

Isaac motioned left, letting Taj follow him down a dirty alley, along an open cement ditch that trickled liquid too putrid to contain much water, and up a flight of metal stairs that barely clung to a crumbling cinder block wall.

A grimy gray door greeted them.

Surely the building had to be abandoned, but once inside, Taj could hear movement coming from unseen rooms.

"I'm sorry. The electricity is out," Isaac said, though Taj found himself wondering if they had electricity at all. "I told you not to expect much," Isaac added.

"No, it's fine," Taj answered, but his words hesitated.

Isaac fumbled in a darkened corner before retrieving a well-used lamp. He struck a match and lit the wick.

"Are you hungry?" Isaac asked, pointing to a small cupboard the flickering light revealed hiding in the corner.

"No, I'm good. Thank you." Another lie.

"My father and mother both get home late. You'll be staying in Jacob's room. He's gone until the weekend, working in Coimbatore."

With the lamp in hand, Isaac led Taj to an adjacent bedroom—but there was no bed, no bathroom, no running water. Just a mat on the floor, a folded dirty blanket, and a chair waiting in the corner for company.

"Take this lamp. We have another. I'll leave the matches on the floor by the door. If you have to use the toilet, it's in the back, over there." Isaac pointed to a dark opening on the wall opposite to where they'd entered. Though he tossed back a nod, Taj didn't intend to find out if the family owned a Jacuzzi.

"Thanks, Isaac. Thanks for helping me, for letting me stay."

"Good night, Taj. I'm sure we'll have better luck in the morning before you have to go back."

Lamplight skipped across the young man's teeth as he grinned. An optimist amid squalor—how ironic.

Taj lay down on the mat, though he stayed fully dressed. There was no way he was taking anything off in this place. When he blew out the lamp, the room almost thanked him.

Taj ignored the darkness that settled in to every crack, corner, and cranny. He'd made it a habit not to stew about life in the dark. He'd found that although darkness encourages introspection, it also distorts life's problems, makes them larger and more pressing than they need to be. Worries, he'd learned, are like rabbits: they compound in the dark.

It might have been that he was dozing off, starting to dream, or still suffering from jet lag, because as he lay in the lightless room, trying hard not to consider his situation, the only thoughts lining up for answers in his head concerned *his situation.* The darkness was whispering, asking questions of its own.

What on earth are you doing here? You're alone . . . in India . . . in a slum. America has given you everything. Why are you wasting your time here?

A patter of footsteps scratched across the floor beneath—too soft and quick for a child. A rat, maybe? The noise stopped, as if it also waited for answers.

Perhaps he should have listened, should have stayed with Priya, should have been content with life and how it was unfolding. He really was so blessed after all. Why so antsy then? Why was he so drawn to connect with his past? What drives a person to seek his roots, to connect so personally with his culture, to be a part of a family?

He had posed these questions to one of his professors in school—in a philosophy class, no less. The teacher had retorted that it's an innate desire wound into our genetic makeup, a *survival-of-the-fittest* mechanism—but the answer had never made sense to Taj.

Wouldn't an instinct to survive push a person to change with their environment, to adapt, rather than press him into wasting precious time futilely glancing back? It wasn't survival Taj longed for. It was belonging. He needed to know if he was important, if he mattered, if he was loved.

The darkness continued to whisper. *If you were truly meant to find your family, why the setbacks? Why the roadblocks? Why the failures?*

The darkness had a point. Going to London, meeting the Tambolis, finding Priya, connecting with Christopher, coming to India, running so randomly into Vikesh—what were the chances? It had all felt so miraculous, so hopeful, like a sign from God that He was watching, that He was aware, that He cared, that everything would work out.

What a crock of ox!

He was alone, in the dark, in a third-world slum. It wasn't working out at all!

When Taj couldn't answer the relentless questions in his head, when he doubted, the darkness seemed to smile around him. Taj mumbled with closed eyes. "I guess either God loves a really great story or he has a seriously twisted sense of humor."

The next whispering wasn't a question.

Give up, Taj. Go home. Go home.

A knock at the front door rattled him awake. It was followed by voices speaking Tamil.

Footsteps shuffled toward him. "Taj, are you asleep?" It was Isaac.

"No."

"There is something I need to tell you."

"What is it?"

"When Emanuel said that you were looking for your family, that you had been taken as a child, possibly from Erode, I thought it might be useful to ask around to see if anyone remembered a family from years ago whose child was lost or taken, a child who would now be about your age."

"Okay."

Isaac was panting.

"There is a woman standing at our door. Taj, she says she's your mother."

CHAPTER 36

The woman was invited inside where she sat on the floor. Lamps were lit. Taj rubbed his eyes and then studied her features in the dancing light. She was a bony Indian woman with crooked teeth, leathered skin, and a tattered sari. Had he passed her on the street, he would have presumed her homeless and perhaps dropped her a little loose change.

"What is her name? Where is she from? What can she tell me about my family? Have I been missed?" So many questions.

She was stumbling through half an answer that Isaac seemed to have trouble translating when another knock shook the door.

Isaac rose and opened it. More Tamil voices spilled into the room.

When Isaac spun back around, his eyes were wide, surprised. He looked first at the old woman crouched cross-legged on the floor. Next, he glanced to Taj.

"Taj?" he said.

"Yes?"

"Another woman at the door says *she* is your mother."

By the time Taj boarded the afternoon bus, seven women had come knocking, each declaring she had lost a son, each claiming the Indian boy raised in America—a man now rich by India's standards—was absolutely, without question, her child.

Yet when asked, three could not remember their boy's name. The remaining four spoke of their lost child fondly—two of the women even shed tears—but none of their children who'd been taken had been named Chellamuthu. None of the circumstances matched.

On the bus ride home, Taj stared straight ahead. He no longer cared about watching hunched old women hobble down the street, wondering if they were his mother. He was drained. He was sick. His heart pounded beats of sorrow in his hollow, hurting chest.

It was over. He was done. He had failed.

It was time to admit that life doesn't always go as we expect, that sometimes there are no good answers, that sometimes personal pleas are uttered in vain.

It was time to let *street dogs* lie . . . it was time to go home.

The wedding was a blur. Taj sat next to Priya and nodded politely to anyone who greeted him. He didn't eat. He hardly smiled. He barely said a word.

When it was nearly over, Taj excused himself and headed to bed early, not feeling well, and was asleep before Priya slipped in.

He rose late the next morning and by lunchtime, had already started to organize his suitcase for the trip home.

Then Christopher entered the room. "How was the wedding?" he asked.

"Chris! You came back?"

"Obviously. I told you I would."

Christopher sat at the tiny table. Taj rested beside him.

"I heard you went to Erode. How did that go?"

"I was hopeful—too hopeful. I just wanted so badly to find something. But nothing clicked, nothing looked familiar. It was just so . . . disappointing. My heart actually aches—seriously, I have a physical pain in the center of my chest."

"I'm sorry, my friend," Christopher replied. "I truly am."

"The sad part is that I can't convince my heart to give it up. My brain keeps telling me to stop, but my gut won't let me."

"What do you mean?"

"I don't know if I can describe it. It's like my head knows there's nothing there. I've seen it with my own eyes. Nothing matched my childhood memories. Nothing felt familiar—but my heart doesn't care. It's like a stupid radio jingle that you can't quit thinking about, no matter how hard you try. I wonder if my mind is playing tricks. I could be conjuring up memories of places that don't really exist. I was just a kid."

Christopher tapped at the face of his watch. He held it to his ear, realized it had stopped.

"Battery," he explained, but he wasn't finished with his thought. "Maybe your memory's not the problem."

"What?"

"Have you considered that your memory might be fine," Christopher said, "but that the world simply kept on ticking?"

"I don't follow."

"When you look in the mirror, do you see a boy staring back or a man?"

"What's your point?"

"Perhaps, like the child who was taken, your city grew up also. Things have changed over the years."

Taj straightened. He pushed his chair back from the table. His eyes must have glowed, because it felt as if flash bulbs were going off in his head.

"You're right! You're a genius!" he nearly shouted, his words sizzling with realization. "I'm looking for a city that no longer exists! I don't need Isaac. I need his father! I need someone who knows what the city looked like around sixteen years ago."

Taj stood. "Christopher, what time is it?"

Christopher held up his stopped watch. He added a shrug.

"Priya!"

She stepped in from the bedroom.

"I have to go back!"

Isaac didn't actually have a phone. The number he'd left, where Emanuel had contacted him, was for a bakery where his mother worked. "Leave a message with her," he'd said, "and she'll deliver it as soon as she's able."

It was already late when Isaac finally called. Taj jumped right to his point.

"Isaac, it's not you I need."

"I beg your pardon?"

"I need your father!"

"I don't understand."

"The city's not the same! Everything has changed. It's no wonder I don't recognize anything. I'm heading to the bus station. I already have tickets for the early bus. Can you see if your father will meet us? Can he take us around? He'll know what the city would have looked like when I was little."

"Taj, he has to work. I'm not sure he . . ."

"Isaac! Please, ask him. I'm pleading. Tell him I'll pay him for the day."

Silence begged.

"I'll see what I can do."

Nothing at the bus station looked familiar, Taj already knew that. Nor was there a children's park in Erode, at least not one that anyone had been able to locate. About the only thing that seemed right, that fit Taj's hand-drawn map, was the river—but again, rivers flowed in many directions all across India.

When Taj and Christopher exited the bus, Isaac was waiting beside his father. Introductions were made. A plan was discussed. It was time to get started.

Taj beckoned an autorick, and the four men climbed snugly inside—Taj, Isaac, and his father jammed themselves into the back. Christopher wiggled in next to the driver up front. The cart's non-existent shocks bumped flat against its axle. It wasn't going to be a smooth ride.

Taj glanced up. The sky was clear. The clouds had not yet stirred. The sun was already stretching for the day's competition.

In college, Taj had focused on business. Oddly, it was a quote from an English class, a quote he had to memorize for a group project, that popped now into his head. *Who was the poet? Thompson . . . something.* The author would undoubtedly be more pleased that his written line had been remembered:

Many a man's dream has turned from triumph to tragedy on the closing hinge of time.

This was it. He was down to the wire. He had one day left. If he didn't find his family today, his gate of opportunity would be slamming permanently shut. Instead of arriving home with answers, he'd be lugging confusion, frustration, leaving India empty-handed and empty-hearted—and with a sizeable credit card bill. For the rest of his life he'd be wondering where he came from, who he was, how exactly his puzzle pieces fit together.

He glanced again in the direction of the sun.

If there was a caring God in heaven, he'd better smile down now.

Taj called to the driver. "Let's go!"

CHAPTER 37

One more time, the meandering autorick circled the city like a vulture. One more time Taj's eyes darted—back and forth, back and forth, back and forth. From the hobbling woman alongside the buildings on the right to the bearded young man selling shriveling, bruised fruit on the left. Anyone. Anything that could spark a memory.

Isaac's father could confirm a few additional details: yes, the bus station in Erode had been rebuilt—twice, if he remembered correctly. Yes, he vaguely remembered a park or two that were no longer there. Yet, when pressed on the details—where, when, how—he couldn't really say.

After circling the bus station, they crisscrossed over all the river's bridges, the great Kaveri that nearly surrounded the city. There were children playing in spots along the river, and whenever the rick slowed, Taj found himself pleading for a hint of recognition.

Nothing. Always nothing.

He'd crossed dozens of rivers in the last few days, and honestly, like the cities, all were looking alike.

"Where to now?" Isaac asked, as they arrived back near the spot where they'd started.

"One more time," Taj said to the driver. "Only take different streets this time."

Again the autorick sputtered forward.

Taj gritted his teeth, clamped his mouth shut. He had to in order to keep the echoes of disappointment caged in his head.

Why the dead ends? Why this far and still nothing? God . . . time to smile.

Yes, there had been *coincidences.* He'd already listed those. But to be fair, what about the failures? Stubborn relatives who refused to help, coming all this way only to find the orphanage closed, finding Vikesh, who knew nothing, Emanuel suggesting from his stupid map that he try this miserable city! What good purpose had any of it served?

He was dripping sweat. The men beside him were dripping sweat. Was anyone in the entire country not dripping sweat?

"Anything familiar?" Christopher asked.

Taj barely moved his head. Busy streets, bustling people, hurried Indians. Nothing he hadn't seen in droves.

"Where to now?" Isaac asked, after they'd circled back the second time.

The sun shone hot, blistering, even for India. Isaac's father squirmed in his seat to get more comfortable. "I think one last time, Mr. Taj," he said, and nobody else in the cart objected. Taj nodded. The driver started. Taj licked and then bit his lip.

By noon, the sun had won. It was barely a contest.

Taj tapped the driver's shoulder. "You can take us back now." His words bowed in defeat.

Christopher turned. "I'm sorry."

Taj couldn't reply.

A few minutes later, they stopped for traffic behind a handful of vehicles at Patel Road. As they waited for the light to change, Taj glanced to his right, down one of the city's side streets. It was one he'd passed before. This time, an old man was standing just past the corner. He held a machete in his right hand and a coconut in his left.

Whack, whack, whack . . . whack, whack, whack.

When he finished, he dropped it into a pile on the sidewalk and picked up another.

Whack, whack, whack . . . whack, whack, whack.

The light changed. The rick rolled forward.

In Taj's head, a channel switched. It had happened before: beside the fence in Upton Park, inside the London restaurant, beside a dumpster outside, the drawing of his map.

For a split second, Taj closed his eyes.

A memory had decided that now was a good time to raise its hand, to stand up and say something. Now, however, it was not only waving a hand but jumping up and down, kicking and screaming.

Whack, whack, whack . . . whack, whack, whack.

Taj glanced back.

Whack, whack, whack . . . whack, whack, whack.

And then, a name screamed in his head—*Banerjee.*

"STOP!" Taj screamed. "STOP NOW!"

The men beside him turned. The driver recoiled. Taj couldn't wait to explain. He jumped from the lurching vehicle onto the street and for a minute thought he'd fall. His moving legs, however, didn't have the time. He sprinted back to the old man who was reaching to pick up his next coconut.

"Banerjee?" Taj called, more to himself than to the old man holding the machete. He paused right in front of him.

The man mumbled, a reply Taj couldn't understand.

"Of course not," Taj answered, almost giggling. "By now, Banerjee would be dead."

He faced a woman passing on the street and confirmed to her the amazing news. "Banerjee would have to be dead!"

Christopher rushed up behind him. "Who's Banerjee?" he asked, wheezing.

"He's a three-fingered old man," Taj hollered.

Before Christopher could ask for clarification, Taj bolted further down the dirt alley. It opened at the end to a grouping of small cinder-block and tin houses, built together in a row. While it wasn't the scene that Taj expected, it was good enough. Sights, smells, sounds—all so buried—were already out, stretching to finally get warm beneath the Indian sun.

When Christopher reached him Taj's fingers were trembling. He was pointing. His voice was cracking.

"This is it, Chris! This is it!"

Christopher couldn't see anything but a row of homes. A woman in front who was beating the dust from a rug with a stick stopped to watch.

"There were huts here," Taj said, still winded, as Isaac and his father reached them. "This is where I lived!"

Taj pointed right. "The river! Isn't the river that way, half a mile, a mile maybe?"

Isaac's father was still catching his breath. "Yes," he confirmed, almost surprised. "It is."

The skin around the old man's eyes gathered. His brain seemed to just be waking up.

Taj had already twisted left. He was stretching, pointing. "Over there . . . that direction a few blocks . . . there was a children's park!" It wasn't a question. His words were certain.

The old man stood a bit straighter. "Wait! Yes, yes! You must mean the park by the water works. In the far corner, many years ago, there *was* a separate children's play area."

"Our hut would have been about there," Taj aimed toward a cinder block home. "They're gone now, but this is the spot. I lived here. I played here—all around here. This is the place . . . this is it!"

Taj headed around the cinderblock structures, past where the huts of his childhood had once stood.

"This way!" he called to the three men following him dutifully down a newly created alley. And as Taj rounded the corner, it was there—still standing, almost asking, *Where have you been? I remember you, boy.*

It was the cement home of the landowner.

A new awning stretched along the front, steel and canvas, all painted blue. It couldn't mask the memories that waited in the shade beneath.

On any other day, under any other circumstance, Taj would have admitted that the home wasn't nearly as grand as he'd remembered. The brass that framed the carved teak door wasn't as ornate or shiny. The granite steps he'd once climbed to enter the home were fewer than he'd remembered and not nearly as wide. The creamy pink plaster that dressed the building's façade was not as rich or as colorful.

But today, every inch was magnificent.

Christopher glanced toward Taj as if asking, *What do we do now?*

The answer was easy. "Knock!"

Taj waited at the bottom of the stairs, close enough to hear but still out of the way. Christopher knocked, waited. The door pulled open.

She was old to the boy of eight. She was beautiful to the man now waiting at the bottom of her stairs.

She looked surprised to see four strangers standing at her door.

"May I help you?"

"Is your husband home?" Christopher asked, wanting to be respectful.

Her head wobbled sadly. "He's passed away," she said.

"We are sorry to hear that. Sorry to bother you."

He took a step down, translated to Taj what had transpired. Isaac and his father also looked as if they were leaving. "It's not considered polite to disturb a widow," Christopher explained.

Taj was shaking his head, couldn't believe what he was hearing. He hadn't come this far—the other side of the planet—to leave questions unanswered simply for the sake of *politeness.*

"No!" he declared, leaving no room to wiggle. "Talk to her. Ask about my family." He wasn't offering Christopher an option.

Christopher turned and caught the old woman's attention before she closed the door.

"Madam, I'm sorry to bother you, but we are here to ask about a young boy who was lost many years ago . . ."

The old woman bent forward. She didn't wait for the stranger to finish.

"Chellamuthu?" she exclaimed with bright eyes, her mousy voice peaking with excitement. "Yes, I know the child. Has he been found?"

Because of the women who had come forward at Isaac's to claim Taj as their child, he had decided with Christopher that until they could be certain it was his family, they would tell anyone they encountered that they had come as emissaries for the lost boy, Chellamuthu, that he had sent them to uncover information about his childhood.

The explanation didn't slow down the animated landowner from sharing. With Taj listening, and Christopher translating, she told how she would sit with the boy and give him advice. She remembered that he would take her cattle to feed in the banana groves, that when he disappeared his mother was distraught, beside herself, as any mother would be. His father was even worse. He took to the streets drinking toddy and smoking ganja, never again able to integrate back into the family and cope with the loss.

"Ask where they are now," Taj nudged. "Where do they live? Are they still alive?" Every question nervous, every word laden with worry, every lost second waiting for translation agony.

The old woman shook her head as Christopher asked. "The family moved away about ten years ago." She scratched at her thinning hair, as if it might help her recall to where.

It didn't.

"What else?" Taj whispered to Christopher. "She must remember something!"

"Wait," she added, "the child's brother, Selvaraj . . . he'd been bleaching fabric with his uncle. About the time the family moved, he started his own bleaching company."

"Your brother," Christopher announced with a trace of satisfaction. "His name is Selvaraj."

They prodded for more, implored her to think of anything else that could help, but no other memory jarred loose. They thanked her graciously, promised to return with more information, and bowed their good-byes.

On their walk back to the street to catch another autorick, Taj laid out the facts. He was trying to stay optimistic.

"We have two more pieces of information. I know my brother's name and that he likely owns a bleaching company. We can ask around, right? How many bleaching companies can there be in Erode?"

Isaac's father, who'd been content to watch the events unfold, shuffled his feet. It was obvious he had something to say.

Taj turned, waited. “Do you know something that will help?”

“When do you have to leave?” he asked.

“I leave tomorrow. If I’m going to find my family, it will have to be today.”

The man’s words were shy, scared to come out. No one wants to be the bearer of such tragic news.

“Taj,” he muttered, “you asked how many bleaching companies there could be? Erode is the bleaching capital of India. There are hundreds!”

CHAPTER 38

After cotton is woven into cloth, before it can be dyed with vibrant colors and patterns, it's bleached a snowy white. The operation is simple. Several cement pools, each a dozen feet across and at least knee deep, are filled with bleach. Adjacent rinsing pools are filled with water. Long pieces of cloth are churned into the bleach by a worker standing knee deep in the pool. After proper bleaching and an adequate rinse, the fabric is draped on wooden poles in the sun to dry. It isn't rocket science. Short of arranging for a large enough piece of land to build the ponds and mount the drying poles, it's a relatively easy business to start.

At the first factory, when Taj, Christopher, Isaac, and Isaac's father strode in, the older man in charge seemed afraid to even glance in their direction. He claimed, with short, single-word answers, that he'd never heard of Selvaraj and offered no further direction as to where they might look.

When the scene was repeated at the second factory, it dawned on

Christopher that four strangers marching in and asking interrogating questions would be the tactic used by undercover police. So in the third factory, Christopher entered alone. When he came out, he was smiling.

"They said there is a factory six blocks from here that is owned by a man named Selvaraj."

When they arrived at the address given, Christopher suggested that Taj join him.

"Is Selvaraj in?" Christopher asked a young man folding fabric in the yard.

"Just a moment."

He disappeared into a shed where voices could be heard.

A heavy-set man in a lungi soon approached. "I'm the owner. I'm Selvaraj. What do you need?"

He might have been Selvaraj, and he might have owned the bleaching factory, but if he was Taj's brother, the years had not been kind.

Christopher asked anyway. "Did you lose a brother several years ago, a brother who was taken?"

"I don't have a brother," he grunted. "I'm an only son. What's this about?"

Wrong Selvaraj.

The scene of rejection replayed at other factories. Each visit fruitless—and at every stop, time was ticking. Not wanting to burden Isaac and his father any longer, Taj thanked them for helping. They were missing work to come along, and Taj hated for them to stay longer than necessary. He and Christopher could continue on without them.

A glance was exchanged between the man and his son, then a whisper. When the father spoke, he didn't mince words.

"Mr. Taj, we doubt that you are going to find your family." Isaac was nodding his agreement. "But if you do, we don't want to miss it. We'd like to come along."

At factory number nine, two brothers in charge said they'd been running their family's bleaching operation for nearly twenty years and claimed to know most who were in the business. The only Selvaraj they knew was at the location already visited. They offered no other suggestions.

It was not only discouraging news, but nearly two hours had passed since Taj and his friends had started visiting the factories.

On the dusty street out front, Taj was multiplying the numbers in his head. "At this rate," he complained, "it will take a month."

No one said a word. They'd also done the math.

"Wait just a minute," Christopher said, interrupting. "The men said they've been in the business for years, that their grandfather started it, that neither had heard of your brother."

"If that's you trying to be encouraging, you suck at it," Taj retorted.

"No, no, listen! We've been visiting bleaching factories that have been around for generations. We're wasting time. We need to see only those that are ten years old!"

Without waiting, he dashed back inside. When he returned, his face flashed news, though it was hard to tell what kind.

"We don't have much time, and the man wasn't sure if this would help, but he said there is a small factory on the opposite side of town, farther out into the country. He thinks it was started about ten or twelve years ago. He doesn't know who runs it. It's not close. If we go, we'll be passing up a dozen more between here and there that we could be checking. It's up to you."

They all turned to Taj and waited.

He stared back. *How would he know? How could he?*

All he knew for certain was that the pain pinching his chest was back, that he was feeling nauseated, perhaps from the heat, perhaps from nerves.

Was it another dead end? Taj glanced heavenward. He was tired of asking for help. Instead, he stated the obvious. His tone wasn't kind. "You're getting to be ridiculous!"

There was no answer. He didn't expect one. All he could do was offer his best guess. He faced the waiting men.

"Let's go!"

It took longer than expected to find the place. The sun would be down in an hour. The road was dusty and uneven, and as the autorick bounced the sweaty men in the back, Taj tried to gather the words he was going to need to explain his utter disappointment to Priya.

"I think this is it," the driver said, pointing.

It looked like the other bleaching factories they'd already visited, only this place was smaller. Fewer pools. Fewer drying racks. Smaller piles of waiting fabric.

An older turbaned man was rinsing fabric in one of the ponds, stirring it with his feet.

When the autorick stopped and the posse scrambled out, the worker quit mixing.

Christopher took the lead, stepping to the edge of the pond. "Good evening, sir. We are sorry to bother you, but we are looking for Selvaraj. Do you know where we might find him?"

The man's head shook back and forth. "No, I'm sorry. I don't know anyone named Selvaraj."

The reply was a dagger that pushed into Taj's heart. He'd made the wrong choice. Again. It would be dark by the time they returned to town. Time was up. Tomorrow he'd have to drive back to Chennai with Priya to catch their flight home.

"Do you know of a bleaching factory near here," Christopher continued, "that might be owned by a man named Selvaraj?"

The man thought. His turban wobbled in the negative. "No. I am sorry."

Isaac and his father climbed back inside the rick. Taj reached for the bar on the side. The smell of failure was overpowering the scent of bleach and making his nausea worse.

Christopher was ready to turn away when something in the man's expression caught his attention—it was a tinge of fear.

"Sir," Christopher said, "I assure you we mean no harm. We are inquiring about Selvaraj because many years ago he lost a brother, a little boy who was taken. We bring news of that boy from America."

The man didn't flinch.

It wasn't until Christopher had placed his foot on the step of the autorick that the man stepped from the pool.

"Wait!" he called out. "You are not the police?"

Christopher turned back to face him. "No. We only have news about a boy stolen many years ago."

The stately man adjusted his turban. "I remember him telling me once that he had a brother who disappeared. Selvaraj is my boss. He lives a few minutes away. I can take you."

Too many false starts. Too many dead ends. Too many disappointments. Was this another? Or could it be true? Had Taj found his brother?

"The fabric is only rinsing. It will not hurt it to stay in the water. If you have room, I will show you where he lives."

The autorick was comfortably built to hold three, two men in back plus a driver in front. Taj, Christopher, and the employee who had introduced himself as Ankur wedged into the back seat. Once the driver was in place, Isaac hung off one side of the front, while his father dangled off the other.

It was all the weight the little rick could handle.

A warming breeze stirred the aroma of bleach with the smell of goats as the cart full of men puffed over a slight ridge. In the distance, a woman carried a basket toward a hut. Behind her trailed two children, laughing at her red sari that was blowing like a scarf in the wind.

Ankur spoke to Christopher and pointed. He, in turn, translated the news for Taj. The words nearly wept as they came out. "Taj, do you see that woman in the red sari?"

"Yes."

"Her name is Usha. She is your sister-in-law, your brother's wife. Taj, those children," his voice cracked, "they are your niece and your nephew."

Taj couldn't reply, couldn't admit that it might truly be happening.

"Chris," he instructed, "remember what we talked about. We can't tell them who I am until we know for sure. I have to know before you say anything!" He couldn't repeat the fiasco from the slums of Erode, with so many women claiming to be his mother. His heart couldn't take it.

The autorick slowed and then stopped. The men climbed out. Ankur greeted the woman.

"Is Selvaraj home?" he asked. "These men are inquiring on behalf of his brother who was lost many years ago."

The news jerked her head around. Her voice quickened. "He's not here, but he'll be back shortly," she said. "Nana is down at the river bathing. Let me get her!"

The woman commanded the older child to take the younger one inside. She then hurried over the hill and down the tiny path that led to the water. As they watched, Christopher let his hand fall on Taj's shoulder.

"Welcome home."

Arayi Gounder closed her eyes as the water swirled around her and then flowed downstream. Each night she recited the same chant:

I salute the Lord of the southern direction who is the embodiment of pure knowledge and eternal peace. I invoke and invite the water of the seven sacred rivers—O Ganga, Yamuna, Godavari, Saraswati, Narmada, Sindhu, and Kaveri—to sanctify and cleanse, to be present in this place.

Bathing in the river was a daily ritual that she seldom missed. Like many good Hindus, she understood that rivers are sacred, that the individual soul must merge with Shiva as the rivers merge with the ocean.

She hoped the water would eventually wash her clean.

Arayi had become more devout as she grew older, more structured. She had no choice. The routine had spun into cords that kept her precarious life from unraveling.

When she'd moved in with Selvaraj six years earlier, she'd vowed never to complain about her life, to endure her struggles and live a life of devotion. She would help him bleach fabrics, but the real blessing had been the time she was able to spend with the grandchildren. She would make certain they learned their chants, said their prayers, understood that for Hindus, religion was in the very air they breathed, that all are connected to the entire universe.

"*Pāṭṭi!* Pāṭṭi! Quick!" her daughter-in-law, Usha, screamed as she neared the bank.

Arayi frowned. Usually it was the grandchildren who would interrupt—and why disturb her *sandhya vandanam?* Doesn't an old woman deserve a little evening peace?

"I'm coming!"

Arayi stepped carefully toward the bank. She reached for her waiting sari, making sure she was covered.

"Nana, come quick! There are men, strangers who need to speak with you." Usha was bouncing, trembling. It was difficult to tell if she was laughing or crying.

"Who is it? Who would dare to interrupt an old woman's bath?"

"I don't know, *Pāṭṭi*. But they bring news."

"News? What kind of news?"

"They bring news of Chellamuthu!"

Taj waited behind the other men, perhaps unconsciously hiding. He had looked forward to this moment so intently, for so long, that now it was unfolding, he was nervous to see what might actually be wrapped inside nearly two decades of yearning.

The cries of an old woman interrupted. She was rushing up the path, her spindly legs churning at astounding speed, as if the hillside had caught on fire. She was holding the loose fabric of her sari in one hand while desperately trying to tie it around her wet and wrinkled body with the other—but she wasn't about to let the process slow her down. Her old feet kicked at the path like a runaway mule, and if she tripped and tumbled, Taj was certain she would never get up.

It must have been a while since she'd sprinted so forcefully, because as she neared the men she seemed to have forgotten how to slow down. Christopher reached out to both stop and steady the wheezing woman.

"Chella . . . Chella . . ."

Her breath had not run as quickly, and she had to wait for it to catch up.

"Take your time," Christopher reassured.

A gasp. A sniffle. More panting.

"Please . . ." she pleaded, followed by another gulp of air. "Please . . . tell me what you know about my son . . . my lost boy, Chellamuthu."

She was pointing at Christopher with her two fingers as she spoke, and as she did, a voice of recollection did its own pointing in Taj's head. *Your mother used to point at you just like that when you were a child. Remember?*

The woman's daughter-in-law finally reached the woman's side. Taj still didn't move, didn't say a word. He had to be certain.

Christopher spoke to her first, staying true to his instructions. "I can tell you that we are here representing a friend who was taken from his family when he was just a child. He has sent us to try to contact his family, and our search has led us to you. Did you lose a child about sixteen years ago?"

The woman couldn't respond but not for lack of breath. She was sobbing now, weeping so desperately that her whole body quivered. She reached out to Usha for support.

A moment passed in silence while the men patiently waited, while the woman regained her composure. Isaac's father even reached out and touched the woman's shoulder, reassuring her that it was all right to take the needed time.

When she could finally speak, she confirmed that her child had been taken. His name was Chellamuthu.

Taj so seldom cried that he'd convinced himself he wasn't capable of tears. His blurry vision now argued otherwise.

"How can we be certain you are really his mother?" Christopher asked. "Is there anything about the child you can tell us so we can be sure you are telling the truth?"

Dread filled the woman's eyes as she thought. There must be

something? But what? Then, as if Shiva had bestowed a gift from heaven, her hands fell to her feet.

"You will know he is my child because he will have scars on the tops of his feet. Also a tooth that drops below the other, from the time he fell from the tree."

Memories were now flooding the old woman's head.

"Oh, yes, yes, and the fingers on his hand are scarred from when they were crushed in a grain mill. His uncle burned them in the fire to stop the bleeding."

"And his age?" Christopher prompted.

"Age? He . . . he would be nearly . . ."

She frantically glanced across the group of men. When she got to Taj she stopped. "My son now would be about his age," she said, pointing, pondering.

Her arms were still shaking, still pulsing with too much adrenaline for a woman of her age. It could be why at first she didn't notice Taj wiping at his eyes.

Taj's feet inched forward, unconsciously perhaps, as if they were prodding him, offering their permission.

When he took a step toward her, she studied him more closely. Her head tilted forward. Her eyes were tracking the scars on his fingers. Her gaze plunged to his feet, but he was wearing shoes. It didn't matter. By the time she looked back up, her heart was already screaming the news.

It was her turn to step forward. Her lips formed a question. Her head insisted she ask.

"Chellamuthu? Are you my . . ."

Before the final word could come out, she again began to sob. She stumbled forward, too weak to stand.

The man at whom she'd been pointing was already reaching for her arms, already assuring her that everything was going to be all right.

"Yes, Mother," he said quietly. "It's me, Chellamuthu. I'm home. I'm home . . ."

Tears chased one another down her cheeks to her wrinkled sari, still damp from the water of the seven sacred rivers.

Shiva had answered after all.

God had worked a miracle.

Chellamuthu had come home.

CHAPTER 39

On the bus ride back to Madukkarai, Taj refused to shut his eyes, certain that if he did, he would open them to find it had all been a dream.

Later, when he touched Priya as she rolled over and asked softly if he had found his family, Taj didn't need to answer. For a second time in a single day—a record for him—he embraced a loved one, and they both wept.

Even though it was late, the relatives were gathered. Priya insisted. After telling them the news, Taj turned to Maneesh.

"Sir, I told my family I would return tomorrow so they can meet Priya, so I can meet more of my relatives. Our return flight to the United States leaves early on Saturday, and while we'd planned to take the train to Chennai tomorrow, Christopher has arranged to borrow a car, which means we can leave as late as tomorrow night, drive through the night, and still make our flight. Sir, I can't speak the language. I need an interpreter. Priya will be there, but out of respect, I'd like to invite you to come with us, to be my interpreter, to help me as I explain to my family where I've been these many years."

The man stumbled as the words pushed him back. He looked to Priya and then to Taj. "I am sorry," he finally stuttered, grabbing a chair to steady himself. "I . . . I can't."

"But I'm giving you a chance to . . ."

The man's head dropped. His words were so quiet as to barely interrupt. "I simply can't."

"Why not?" Taj called out to Maneesh as the man prepared to flee the room.

Perhaps Maneesh didn't mean to answer. His reply, barely audible, was heard anyway.

"What if your father sold you?"

When Taj opened the door of the taxi, he was swarmed. Word had spread throughout the night, by phone for those who had one, by messenger for those who didn't.

"It's him!" his cousin Krishna shouted, as if doubting the rumors.

Clutching Priya's hand, Taj stepped into the throng, let them surround him. Instead of disappearing into a crowd and getting lost, as he'd feared at the airport on his arrival to India, today he was found.

He was summarily pinched, pushed, caressed, and patted, as if everyone had to touch him to be certain he was real, that he really was Chellamuthu. Arayi alone grabbed him by the cheeks with her weathered fingers at least a dozen times. Always weeping but with tears that traced paths across a wide and constant smile. Manju, his baby sister, now a woman with two small children of her own, stayed close but said little, clearly marveling at the wonder of this instant older brother.

Once the excitement had subsided, Taj stood on a small rise beside his brother's home and in what looked to be *Indian Story Hour,* he related through Priya his kidnapping, his life in America, and his return . . . all to newfound, wide-eyed relatives.

When he finished telling his story, he heard theirs, individual accounts, one after another, of endless searching, constant praying, and persistent yearning—and how their prayers had been heard.

Praise Vishnu! Thank Shiva! Chellamuthu has returned home.

Arayi was pinching his cheeks again when her eyes widened. She rushed into the house and returned with a tarnished, gold-leaf frame. It surrounded an old photo, taken at a wedding, of two proud parents behind three eager children, smiling at their futures that lay in store.

She passed it to Taj, folded his fingers around it so he'd understand. She relayed her message to Priya.

"She wants me to tell you," Priya said, "that she's looked at this picture every day since you were taken. She would now like you to keep it, so you'll never forget, so you'll always remember."

While they were visiting, an autorick pulled close. When Selvaraj exited, he was supporting an elderly man. The man's hair was freshly cut, his face shaven, and he was wearing a brand-new shirt and lungi.

"Taj, I would like you to meet Kuppuswami, your father."

The elderly man didn't move—perhaps he couldn't—and for a moment, Taj wondered if he understood what was happening.

Then, gathering the fresh fabric of his lungi with both hands, he pulled it up to reveal a nasty scar just below his left knee. He aimed his toothless grin at Taj.

Not wanting to be outdone, Taj slipped off his shoes and pointed to his feet to show the old man with fragile eyes his own memories.

"Priya, tell him that my feet have always reminded me to be a good person, to try my best, to do what's right—to not run away."

The old man listened, watched, nodded, and then, wiping at his eyes, sat down in the grass to rest.

Selvaraj pulled Taj and Priya aside.

"You should know that since you were taken, he's been living on the streets. He's been a drunk, a derelict for all these years, never a part of the family. I found him and brought him home late last night. When he heard you were back, that you were well, he sobbed. He insisted I get him a new shirt, that he have clean clothes, a shower, and a shave before he saw you—that's where we've been."

Selvaraj urged them closer to him.

"He also hasn't had a drink since I found him last night. He told me he's ready to come back, to live again with the family. Taj, this is beyond astonishing. It's a miracle."

Later, in a rare moment when Taj and Priya were standing alone, she wrapped her arms around him.

"There's something else you need to know about your dad, your family," Priya said. "It's rather ironic, and honestly, I can't quit smiling about it."

"What is it?"

"Your family's caste—*your* caste. You're a Gounder."

"I don't know what that means."

"It's hard to explain, especially considering your family is poor, and my family is . . . well, better off, but do you remember how my father was so concerned about not knowing your caste?"

"How could I forget?"

"Here's the punch line: despite their poverty, your family's caste is actually higher than mine." She squeezed his fingers, passed him a smile. "I guess our marriage might work out after all."

The car that would rush them to the airport and their waiting flight honked. Taj pulled Priya close, until their faces were just inches apart. "I don't know how or when, but we need to come back. These people need me and, well . . ."

"What is it?"

"This may sound crazy, but I need them too."

Before leaving, Taj shook hands with most of them, bowed to others, hugged the rest.

When the sun set on the village of Palayam, just outside the city of Erode, India, hearts were filled with more rejoicing than any could remember. Fires burned late into the night, well after Taj had departed, grateful flames enthusiastically dancing to heaven on the news.

The boy who was lost was now found. Chellamuthu had made his way home.

CHAPTER 40

January 2014

The plane landed on schedule. The airport in Chennai was sleek and modern—at least for India. Some things, however, would never change. When Taj, Priya, and their two daughters walked from the terminal, the eternal welcoming crowd was there waiting, waving. If anything, the horde was growing.

"Ṭāksi? Ṭāksi? Hōṭṭal? Hōṭṭal?"

"Thanks, dude, but no," Taj answered in English.

He and his family had been to India so many times the mob was no longer intimidating. On most trips, Taj hardly noticed them.

"Taj! Over here!"

As always, Christopher was there to meet them.

Taj drove. Chris sat in front. Priya climbed into the back of the Land Cruiser with Shaamilee, thirteen, and their youngest, Tayjel, who had just turned six.

"Can we stop and get *jilebis?*" Tayjel pleaded.

The girl was more adorable than a kindergarten costume party, and

Taj would certainly have stopped had Priya not stepped in. Somebody had to. "We have to eat first, babe, before we get any sweets. Read your book. We'll be there soon."

Taj honked twice out of habit, then pulled in front of a departing autorick. The man honked back, but considering the autorick's size compared to the SUV, it was a safe bet he'd yield.

Taj drove like a native—worse than a native, if one believed Chris. Taj had logged more miles driving back and forth across India than had most bus drivers.

"Did Joel deliver the renderings?" Taj wondered. Chris scrolled through the e-mails on his iPhone to check. "Yes. He did. We'll have a contract by Thursday."

Business, never-ending business—but with good reason. Taj had kept his college promise. He'd made Christopher a wealthy man. The two owned a software company in Chennai, an export company in Coimbatore, a construction company in Madurai, and an e-commerce company in the United States.

If a beach-going couple in the U.S. purchased a decorative grass mat to spread out on the sand, one could be assured that Taj and Chris were making a small profit. If a college professor ordered a whiteboard online, it was undoubtedly being shipped from one of their warehouses.

Not just hard goods. On the software side, the men had their fingers into everything: 3D rendering, e-mail marketing, custom programming, SEO.

Though their ventures in India had been profitable, it wasn't business that kept Taj coming back.

"Are we all ready for tomorrow?" Taj asked Chris.

"We're ready."

They stayed in the nicest hotel in Coimbatore, coincidentally named the Taj Resort, a company he didn't own. After letting the girls swim in the morning, they were back in the car after breakfast.

An hour later, after bouncing down a dusty potholed road, they arrived at Nampalayam, the village where Taj's father had grown up. Huts and homes dotted the corners of thirsty fields in all directions, dwellings likely inhabited by distant relatives.

Knowing that Taj would be coming, the village leaders had already set up tarps for shade. Food had been prepared and was being served. Shaamilee and Tayjel began to run about with first and second cousins, none of who seemed to mind that the girls couldn't communicate.

Once the head of the village signaled that everything was ready, neighbors and friends huddled around a recent addition—a new well and a cement cistern. It was the latest project of many carried out by the nonprofit company Taj and Christopher had set up to help people in the villages.

Prayers were offered. Hands were gratefully clasped. Smiles were passed around by all for the taking.

When Taj flipped the switch, an adjacent diesel generator rumbled to life. A PVC pipe that protruded into the cistern gurgled.

Everyone waited. The anticipation was akin to watching milk boil. When a stream of clean water spit and then spewed to begin filling the cistern, all cheered—everyone but an old man who was standing alone in the adjoining field. Christopher had pointed him out a few minutes earlier. He was one of the field workers, a furrowed and weathered villager wearing nothing but a small loincloth.

After the cement reservoir filled, it overflowed, sending water down a series of recently dug ditches to flood the adjacent fields.

The old man hadn't cheered because he was weeping. He'd lived through drought; he'd stared famine in the face; he'd surveyed starvation firsthand. There would be no more relying on rain that might never come, no more watching crops wither as children whimpered with empty stomachs.

If anyone understood what this new source of water meant for those in the village, it was the old man. It was indeed an occasion for tears.

Priya was standing beside Taj when Christopher leaned close. "You could so easily have been one of these hungry villagers, but look at you, Taj. Look at the good you're doing. Honestly, it's amazing how your life has worked out, how because of your journey, you're able to help others."

It was meant as a compliment, and Taj should have bitten his lip and thanked his friend for his kindness. He knew better. Instead, he turned.

"All we're doing here is taking one small step to help these people. That's it! Let's not make it into anything more than that."

Perhaps because Chris was his friend, Taj felt he could freely speak his mind. He didn't give his startled partner time to answer.

"The pump works great. I think we're about done here. Priya, grab the girls and let's get everything loaded up."

It was after midnight when Taj finished his work on the computer. Midnight in India meant noon in the United States. There were always decisions that needed to be made in some part of the world.

Shaamilee and Tayjel had long since fallen asleep in the adjacent room. Priya was in the bedroom waiting.

"Taj, you shouldn't have jumped all over Chris like that. He was paying you a compliment."

"I know. I didn't mean it. I've already spoken to him. I've apologized."

She wasn't about to let the conversation end there. "Do you want to talk about it?"

"Look, I just hate it when people try to tie life up with a pretty pink bow. That's all. It's usually more complicated, more messy than that."

"What do you mean?"

"I didn't tell you about church a couple of weeks ago, did I?" He already knew the answer.

"No. What happened?"

"It was the day you stayed home when Shaamilee had her cold. The lesson was on Joseph who was sold into Egypt and how it all worked out so marvelously for him, so he could help his family, and how it showed God's hand in our lives."

"So?"

"As I was sitting there listening, it made me so angry, I had to leave. I got up and walked out."

"Why?"

"I just kept thinking that these people don't have a clue. All I could think about was how disappointed and distraught Joseph must have been, staring up from that pit at his brothers. How sick to his stomach he must have felt when he was sold to strangers. How torn apart his father must have been when he was taken. How broken and hurt Joseph would have felt, all those years of hell when he was deprived of a family."

When Taj realized he was clenching his teeth, he stretched his jaw, demanded it to relax.

"That's all," he finished. "It just bothers me when everyone oohs and aahs. I get that Joseph's family survived because he ended up in Egypt. I do. But did anyone ever sit down and ask Joseph how he felt about it?"

Priya pulled Taj close, gave him a moment. "We aren't talking about Joseph here, are we?"

"I'm just giving you my insight."

"And I'm giving you mine. Taj, you've been keeping your story all bundled up and protected. Do you remember how your mother would call you a little volcano? You haven't changed. You need to let it out, address it. Maybe call someone."

"You think I need a therapist?"

"A therapist would probably help, but I don't see you going there yet. Perhaps you just need to start by talking. Tell your story. Give it a life and see what happens. See how it makes you feel. You have some friends who are writers, don't you? Start with them."

"Do you think it will help?"

"You've got nothing to lose."

CHAPTER 41

June 2014

It was the fourth meeting with the writers, or perhaps the fifth. For Taj, the discussions were all starting to blend together. Each session delved deeper into his story, peeling away its layers. After the writers had driven away, Priya entered the room and snuggled beside her husband.

"You seem more relaxed since you've been telling them your story."

"You think?"

"I'd say so. What did you talk about today?"

"They asked about Eli and the kidnapping. They wondered if I blamed him."

"What did you tell them?"

"That's just it. I was torn away from my family as a boy. But if it weren't for being kidnapped, I'd be living right now in a village in India, speaking Tamil. I wouldn't be married to you. We wouldn't have our incredible girls. How can I blame Eli, despite what he might have done? Maybe that's the problem—there's no one in my life to blame."

Priya nudged closer. "Except maybe God?"

He was married to a psychology major. He was used to her introspection.

"It's curious you say that." Taj reached toward the coffee table and picked up a letter. "I've been going through some of Mom's scrapbooks. In one of Eli's letters, those he wrote to my parents before the adoption, he thanked them for adopting a child from another country and then he wrote this: '*He who keeps the orphans keeps them from harm, watches over their lives, their comings and goings. He keeps them like a shepherd keeps his flock.'* At first it sounded like he was talking about himself, since he owned the orphanage, but each child was only with him for a short time. Because he was writing to my parents, I wondered if he was talking about them."

"You sound skeptical."

"The more I read it, the more I think Eli was implying that the keeper of all orphans is God. But the thing is . . ."

"Yes?"

"In a way, you're right. In spite of all that I have in my life, all the gratitude . . ."

"Go ahead."

" . . . I still have a hole in my heart."

Priya pulled him tight. "Taj, you were torn from your family; you've spent so much of your life in emotional survival mode. Of course you have a hole. Anyone would. We all live with holes of some kind or another, and we spend our lives trying to fill them—so quit fighting it."

"What do you mean?"

"Hasn't telling your story helped?"

Taj took his time. Honesty deserved sincerity.

"Some days . . . which is odd."

"Why odd?"

"I don't know. All I've done is share my story. You tell me."

A giant moment of silence circled the room—warm, comfortable silence.

"They say stories are redemptive, Taj," she finally declared, with a tone so full of confidence he wasn't about to argue. "Take your father, for example. Have you thought more about your kidnapping? Do you think he was involved, that he might have sold you?"

Taj shifted. "I don't know for certain, but does it matter? I'd like to think my father wasn't involved, but if I'm wrong . . . Look at us. It's like Eli. How can I do anything but thank him?"

Priya leaned in, kissed him gently. "That's what I'm suggesting. Sharing our lives with others, the aches, the joys, the struggles, the passions of our hearts—it lets us see past the shadows to discover the glimmer of possibility."

It was several moments before Taj spoke.

"While I figure out what that means, can we go back to the part where you kiss me?"

Taj was on the phone when Shaamilee entered his study. She waited for him to hang up.

"Hi, honey. What's up?"

"When do we leave for India? I have to know for school. Mom told me to come and ask."

"I'm leaving next week. The rest of you are coming mid-August. We'll be back right before school starts. Don't worry, you won't miss any classes."

"Okay." She was about to leave but turned.

"Dad, how come Grandpa and Grandma never come? Have they ever been to India?"

"No, no, they haven't."

"Why not?"

"It's far. They're getting old. I don't think they've ever wanted to come." The words were still warm, still floating in the room, still shaking their heads. If he was going to be completely honest with his daughter, and with himself, he needed to amend his reply. "Actually, it may be a little bit my fault."

Perhaps the truth was sandwiched somewhere in between. Perhaps neither he nor his parents were ready because, like characters in stories, they needed adequate time to heal, to grow, to resolve.

Stories, Taj had learned, need to simmer. Forgiveness takes time.

After Shaamilee had gone to bed, Taj picked up the phone. "Hey, Mom. It's Taj." He listened. "Good, good. Hey, I have a question. How would you and Dad like to come to India and meet my mother and my family?"

Linda was silent, no doubt stunned.

Taj nudged her. "I would really like you to come."

CHAPTER 42

June 2015

Linda was raised in a culture where you hug. Arayi was raised in a culture where you greet others by pressing your own palms together while offering a slight nod. Linda won.

After the two women pulled apart, Taj made the formal introduction.

"Mother, I'd like you to meet . . . Mother." He didn't bother to repeat it.

They had gathered in Arayi's home, the one that Taj had built for her. It wasn't luxurious by American standards, but it was ideal by Indian standards—a measure Taj had grown to appreciate.

It didn't take long for Linda to break out her scrapbook, methodically arranged and sorted, page after page of memories that she was anxious to share. The language seemed no barrier. The mothers laughed and pointed and giggled as if they were both nineteen—and for a moment, as memories erased years, perhaps they were. Linda called the boy in the photos Taj. Arayi called him Chellamuthu. The same boy smiled.

"Women love their scrapbooks," Taj commented.

"Mothers love their children," Priya clarified.

For the most part, Taj stood back and stayed out of the way. He kept laughing at Fred, who couldn't quit glancing around and repeating, "This place isn't like *National Geographic* at all!"

"What are you thinking?" Priya asked Taj as they watched.

"I'm thinking this is a pretty great day."

On every trip to India, Taj would stop to visit Mrs. Papathi Iyer, the landowner. This time was no different. She was getting older, more frail, but always welcomed him with love. While Linda and Fred were introduced and the adults got acquainted, Shaamilee and Tayjel ran to play out front. They'd visited with *Patti* plenty of times.

Adjacent to the landowner's home, she'd rented a small building to a young couple who had saved up to purchase a mechanical loom, a machine that produced beautiful Indian saris. It was a noisy contraption but a fascinating process to watch, as its bobbin kicked back and forth, back and forth in hypnotizing rhythm, dragging strands of silk across colorful taut fibers.

Once the adults finished talking out front, Taj, Priya, and Chris escorted Fred and Linda next door so they could see the loom in action. Papathi waited on her steps and watched the girls play. It didn't take long before she was corralling them with her old fingers, calling out to them in her crackly, high-pitched voice.

"Shaamilee, Tayjel. Come here, girls."

The sisters obeyed.

Papathi Iyer was a wealthy woman, by both Indian *and* American standards. She'd learned English in school decades earlier, and while seldom perfect, she spoke it well enough that the girls could understand.

"Listen," she said. "Tell me, what do you hear?"

The answer was obvious, for drowning out every ambient noise in the courtyard was the clanking of the automated loom.

Tayjel spoke first. "The weaving machine." She motioned toward the neighboring building.

"That is correct, Tayjel. What sound does it make?"

"It's loud. *Clickety-clack. Clickety-clack.*"

"Do you know why it makes this noise both day and night?"

Shaamilee answered this one. "They're making *saris* to earn money." Her dad would be proud.

"Yes," Papathi confirmed. "They *are* making money, but that is not the most important part . . ."

The woman's eyes, while aged, hadn't lost their gleam. "It's the sound of a young family making their way in the world, working together with hope of a better life."

"Does it ever stop?"

Every crease in Papathi's lips smiled.

"Life never stops, child. Even when it's noisy, unpleasant, painful, it's still the sound of duty, of love, of family, of laws older than time that help us to ultimately find contentment—to be happy. It's the sound of our universe. It's the sound of purpose."

Papathi turned her ear toward the clacking.

"What you hear, my children, is the sound of *dharma*."

AUTHOR'S NOTE

In telling a story based on true events, a fiction writer needs the freedom to compress time, rearrange dialogue, merge two characters into one, or make any number of changes to improve the story's arc, plot, pacing, and delivery. As such, this story is labeled *a novel.* That said, it's based on the life experience of Taj Rowland (Chellamuthu)—and barring a few of the above-mentioned exceptions, we attempted to follow his account as closely as possible.

In the years since Taj reconnected with his family in India, he has played an integral role in their lives. His mother there still pinches his cheeks—and always calls him Chellamuthu. His brother, Selvaraj, left his fabric-bleaching business and entered politics. For many years, Selvaraj has been the mayor of his village in India and an important and revered figure in the community. Taj's father passed away a few years after Taj returned, likely from the long-term effects of his heavy drinking during the time Taj was missing. However, from the day Taj reconnected with his family to the day his father died, the man never returned to the streets. He remained at home as a functioning member of his family.

Taj and Priya recently built a beautiful new home in India with an amazing view that ironically, to bring his story full circle, overlooks Madukkarai and the location of the orphanage where he stayed as a kidnapped child.

To this day, despite many family gatherings over the years, Taj's father-in-law has still not spoken to him in any detail about why he refused to help Taj find his family in India. When writing this story, we didn't know much about him, other than his having been associated with the orphanage and being converted to Christianity by the orphanage owner. Because of this, we have fictionalized his character and account.

As noted in the story, the owner of the Lincoln Home for Homeless Children, Eli Manickam, passed away a year or two before Taj returned to locate the orphanage. His name, along with others, has been changed. Because his true intentions and justifications for the events that occurred are not known, we've puttied the gaps with presumption.

However, writing a fictional story based on fact is more than simply filling in holes. There are also times when interesting pieces have to be painfully left out. For example, five years after Taj first arrived in the United States, Linda Rowland received a call that confirmed she was finally getting her long desired daughter—a baby named Ana, adopted from El Salvador. Linda remembers that Taj loved to carry Ana, telling his mother that he knew how to take care of his new sister because he'd helped tend other babies so often in the orphanage. The problem we faced was that Ana's addition to the Rowland family occurred right in the middle of our ten-year gap—a time in our story when the reader leaves Chellamuthu as a child and doesn't return until Taj is in high school. In truth, there simply wasn't a good way to work the addition of Ana into the narrative without disrupting the story's focus or length.

Such are the decisions a writer makes, always asking the same echoing question: Will it improve the story? The result is for the reader to judge.

Regardless, Taj hopes that sharing his experience will help others, not only adopted children from India seeking to connect with their Indian families and heritage, but also children living in remote villages in India, with little hope for a better life.

To that end, Taj supports charitable organizations that seek to change both individual lives and generations, including *Taprish*, an NGO in India that serves the underprivileged.

For added details and insights into Taj Rowland's story, please visit www.TheOrphanKeeper.com.

ACKNOWLEDGMENTS

Thank you to the many readers and editors who provided such amazing input and wisdom; Alicyn Wright and Kathy Pliler for patience and faith; and Brad Pelo, for introducing us to Taj and his remarkable story. Thank you, Anne Barker, LIMHP, LCSW, for your thoughts and wording concerning the notion of hide-and-seek and that we all want desperately to be found. Thank you, Christopher Raj, a true Christian, for your insight into India and your lifelong friendship with Taj. Lastly, thank you, Taj and Priya Rowland, for trusting your story to nervous hands and waiting patiently as it came to life.

STUDY GUIDE

The following questions are intended to stimulate personal thought and group discussion. If you are using them for a book group, we suggest that rather than trying to cover every question, you select a few that feel pertinent to your group.

1. The book's dedication reads: *To the lost child in all of us, searching for home.* Can you relate to the plight of little lost Chellamuthu? In what ways are you also an orphan? In what ways are you an *orphan keeper*? Who in the story could be called an orphan keeper? Why?
2. Eli poses the question, "If a child is kidnapped from hell and carried to heaven, should we condemn the kidnapper?" How would you answer? Was Eli *saving* children by taking them out of poverty and abuse to give them a chance at a better life, or was he *condemning* them? Is there any justification for his actions?
3. It's not unusual in India for kidnapped children to be intentionally maimed and then forced to beg on the streets in order to collect money for those *caring* for them. It has been argued that giving to

these children encourages the practice. If you walked past such a child, would you give or refrain? Why?

4. When Taj returned to India as an adult, he remembered the orphanage as being three to four hours away from his home. If you were a kidnapped child of seven, would you have been able to gauge the distance so accurately? Why would Taj (Chellamuthu) have perhaps been more mature than the average seven-year-old American?
5. The Lincoln Home for Homeless Children was established to help poor Indian orphans find new homes. Did it lose its purpose over time? Is greed always destined to push noble aspirations aside? How can the slide to greed be prevented?
6. Linda quotes *The Phoenician Women,* by Euripides: "This is slavery, not to speak one's thought." How was Chellamuthu enslaved? How do we enslave ourselves in a similar manner?
7. It was an amazing *coincidence* that Priya, when first dating Taj, discovered a letter written years earlier by her own father to Fred and Linda Rowland. Later, Taj *coincidentally* met Vikesh, a child with whom he had played at the orphanage. Later still, as Taj drove past his unrecognizable childhood home, he heard the hacking of coconuts, causing him to stop, listen, and remember. Do you believe in coincidence? Are our lives guided strictly by chance, or is there something more that might explain these situations?
8. Linda dreamed that Taj would marry an Indian girl, which he eventually did. How important are dreams in our lives? Can they predict the future? If yes, how is that possible?
9. When Taj saw Priya's picture, it was love at first sight, with his instant declaration that he was going to marry her. Do you believe in love at first sight? Is it rational? Why? Why not?
10. Many Indian parents still arrange the marriages of their children.

What might be the benefits of arranged marriage? What might be the drawbacks?

11. Taj eventually discovered that he was actually from a higher caste than Priya and her family. What do you know about the caste system in India? Why do you suppose it has endured for so many years? How would you respond if you were taught that you could never rise above the duties of your caste? Although we don't follow a caste system in the United States, do socioeconomic conditions often limit our potential? What other conditions might also be limiting?
12. When Taj was desperate for help to search for his family, he begged Christopher Raj, a man he'd just met in person the day before, to take time off work, leave his family, and return to Coimbatore to assist. Christopher, with barely a hesitation, jumped on the train for another ten-hour trip to help Taj. Would you have made a similar decision for a virtual stranger? It turned out to be a choice that dramatically changed the course of Christopher's life (and that of Taj). What lessons can be learned from Christopher's actions? How careful should we be with our own *everyday* decisions and how we interact with others?
13. In the story, Arayi visits with three astrologers. The last one tells her that her son will return, and when he does, *he will fly*. Although the timing of the visit to this astrologer was presented in the book as having occurred shortly after Chellamuthu was taken (for the sake of pacing and plot), in real life, it occurred years later, about eight months before Taj actually returned. Do you believe there is any validity to astrology? If not, how do you explain the accuracy of the astrologer's prediction?
14. What in the story points to the possibility that Chellamuthu's father sold him to the orphanage? What points to the probability that his father was not involved? Does it matter? Why? Why not?

15. Taj cherishes his wife and daughters, family he would not have if he had remained in India. That said, he still feels conflicted over having been ripped from his family in India as a child. Should Taj be grateful he was kidnapped, or should he be angry?
16. In the final pages of the book, Priya talks with Taj about his father's possible involvement in his kidnapping, as well as Taj's ongoing angst. When Taj confides that sharing his story has helped, she notes that stories are redemptive. Is she right? What parallels can be drawn between redemption and the telling of stories?

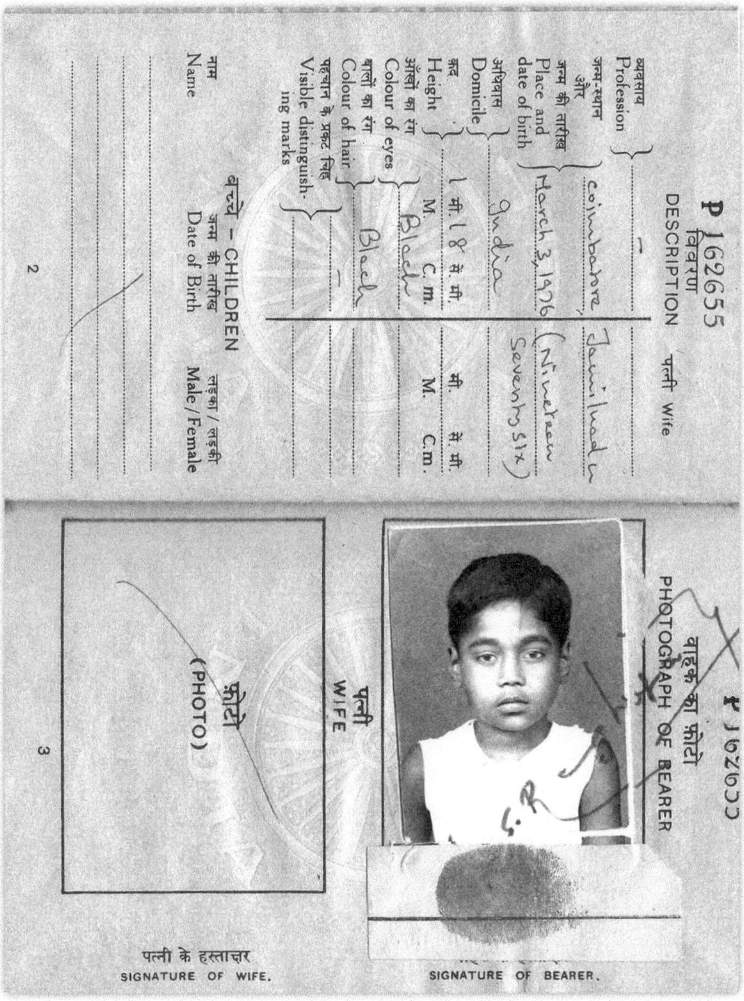

Chellamuthu's passport.

Chellamuthu arrives in the U.S. just before Christmas.

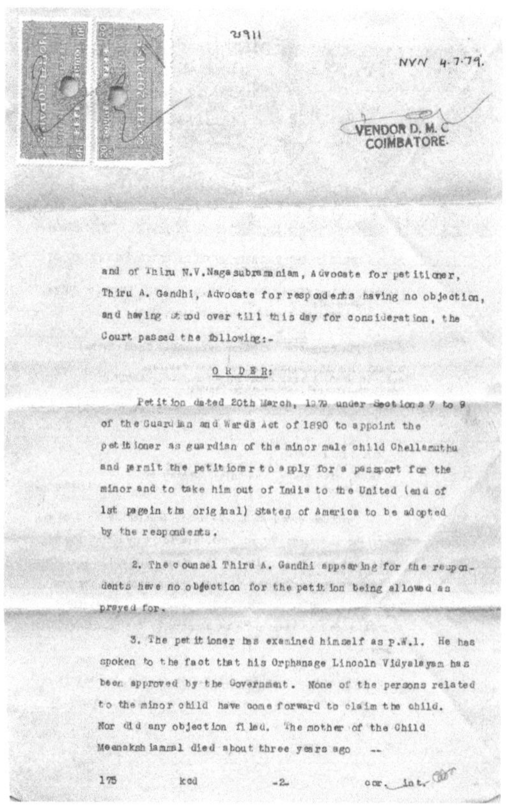

NVN 4.7.79.

VENDOR D. M. C
COIMBATORE.

and of Thiru N.V.Nagasubramaniam, Advocate for petitioner, Thiru A. Gandhi, Advocate for respondents having no objection, and having stood over till this day for consideration, the Court passed the following:-

<u>ORDER</u>:

Petition dated 20th March, 1979 under Sections 7 to 9 of the Guardian and Wards Act of 1890 to appoint the petitioner as guardian of the minor male child Chellamuthu and permit the petitioner to apply for a passport for the minor and to take him out of India to the United (end of 1st page in the original) States of America to be adopted by the respondents.

2. The counsel Thiru A. Gandhi appearing for the respondents have no objection for the petition being allowed as prayed for.

3. The petitioner has examined himself as P.W.1. He has spoken to the fact that his Orphanage Lincoln Vidyalayam has been approved by the Government. None of the persons related to the minor child have come forward to claim the child. Nor did any objection filed. The mother of the Child Meenakshiammal died about three years ago --

175 kcd -2- cor. int.

A page from the falsified court documents claiming Chellamuthu was an orphan.

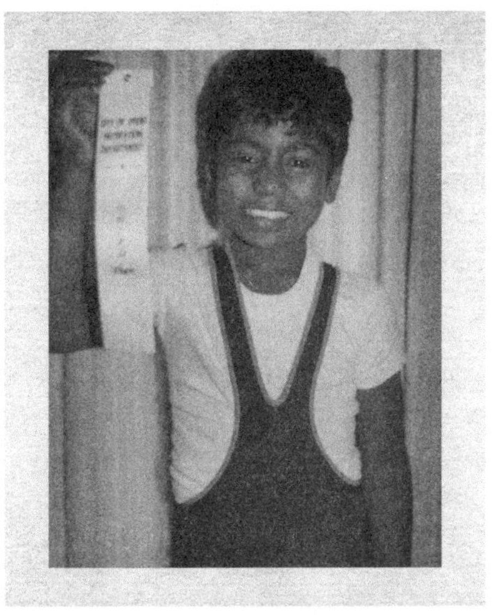

Taj wins a third place wrestling ribbon.

February 1, 1984

United States Embassy
Ambassador Harry G. Barnes Jr.
New Delhi, India

Dear Ambassador Barnes;

In December, 1979 we brought a young boy out of India for adoption purposes.

We made Chellamuthu's adoption arrangements through Mr. [redacted], of the Lincoln Home for Homeless Children, Madukkarai, P.O. 6411054, Coimbator Dt., Tamil Nadu, S. India.

We were adopting an orphan, or atleast that is what we were told by [redacted] and what was indicated on our legal papers from the Indian court. However, now we are able to communicate with the boy, he tells us this is not really so. In fact, he had a mother, a father, three sisters and two brothers.

How or why he came to the orphanage, may be an unanswered question forever but we would like to know as much about the young man as possible. He is now twelve years of age and is intent on wanting some details. Some day he wishes to return to India and at this point, we have not an accurate clue as to where to send him in search of his "roots". It may be a lost cause, but we cannot leave it without a valiant try

We have written [redacted] several times but have been unsuccessful in getting him to respond concerning the matter. I contacted Senator Hatch for help and he suggested we write to you and ask for assistance.

Can you supply us with any documented information as to birth records. (we have been told it could be traced through the passport information) Birthdate, birth place, parents name and address, date he was brought to the home, any information may be of help in the years to come.

The boy is a great joy to us. We love him dearly. He is now an American Citizen and enjoying everything that America has to offer... but as I have stated - he would like to know more. Enclosed are copies of papers I thought could be of some help in the search. Please let us know what if anything can be done.

Sincerely,

Fred Rowland
Linda Rowland

One of the letters written by the Rowlands to the embassy seeking help.

Taj and Priya's wedding.

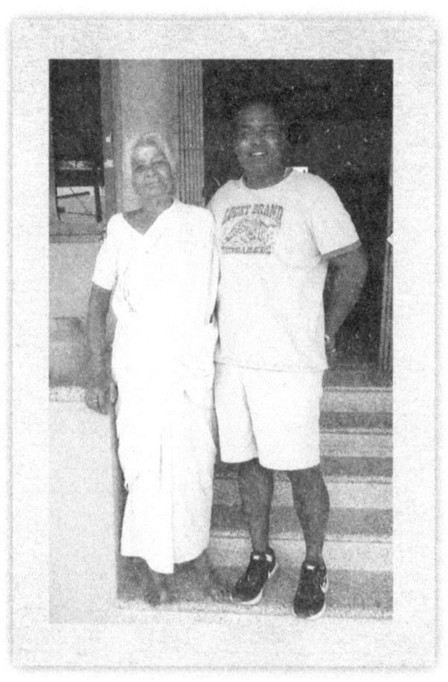

Taj stands beside Papathi, the landowner.

Taj and Christopher Raj today.

Taj with his mother, Arayi, today.

Priya in front of what remains of the old Lincoln Home orphanage.

Taj, Priya, Taj's parents, and his extended family. This photo was taken the day after Taj found his family when he returned with Priya.

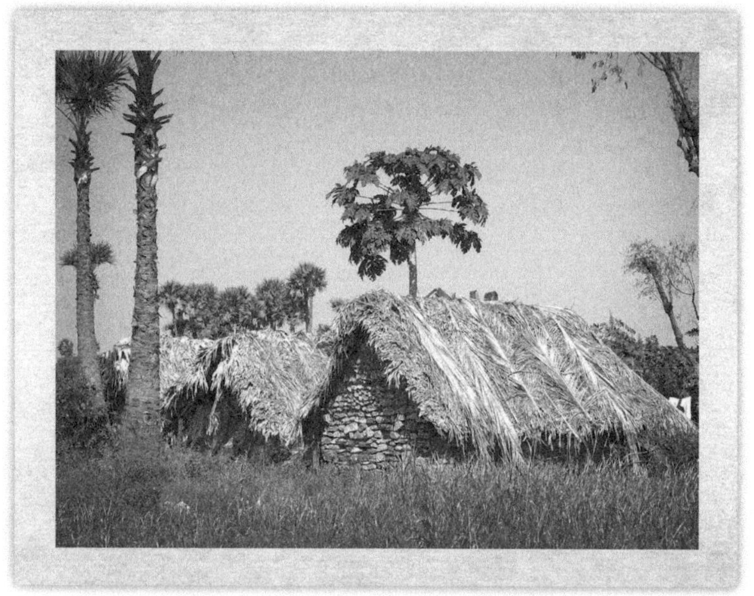

Huts in the village where Taj's father lived.
These are similar to those Taj lived in as a child.

Mothers meet for the very first time in June 2015.

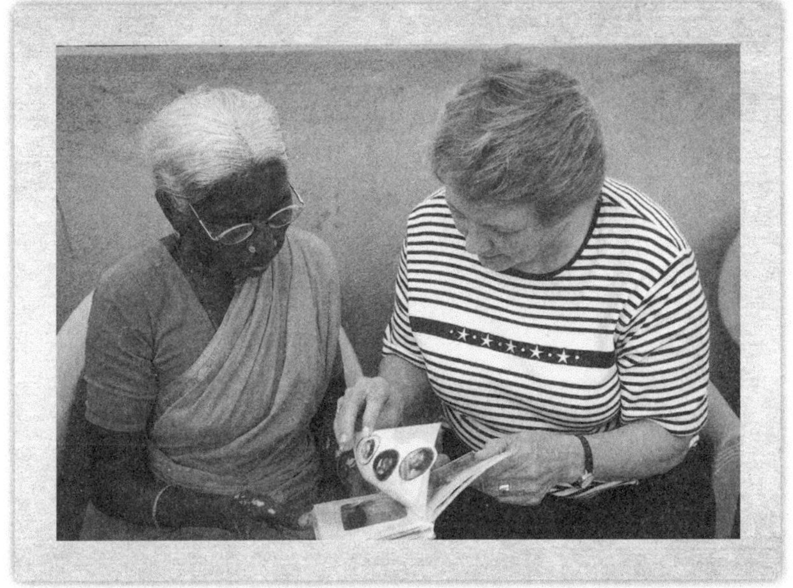

Mothers love their children.

Even today, Taj's picture hangs in a building in the village where he lived as a child, and his relatives still marvel at his return.